THE LIGHTBEARERS

WINDS

ONJEL BERCIER

ISBN 979-8-9991991-1-9 (Paperback)
ISBN 979-8-9991991-0-2 (Hardcover)

Library of Congress Control Number: 2025912209

All references to a historical period are fictional. The characters, names, and places mentioned in this book are products of the author's imagination.
First Printing Edition

Contact information: onjelbercier+books@gmail.com

ONJEL BERCIER

WINDS

THE LIGHTBEARERS

For we wrestle not against flesh and blood, but against principalities, against powers, against the rulers of the darkness of this world, against spiritual wickedness in high places.

Eph. 6:12 KJV

PART
I

PROLOGUE

Since the oldest memory of childbirth, as written in the sacred Foundum, babies were never simply born into a world but cast into a state of chaos and troubles, shrouded by a veil of sorrow, and encompassed by a long-winded war waged in the hidden realm. It was a war unannounced, yet one in which everyone was wholly entailed. A war between winds.

There were three kinds of winds that El's beloved believed in. Malellum— winds of terror, ciellum— winds of assistance. And the Elwind, the one above them all, the one that all winds and all creatures were beholden to. Still, the malellum had their own leader they preferred to El. Girgum, El's appointed host of Earth and abuser of such power. He aimed to corrupt all that was orderly, blameless, or in some sense 'good'. And it was only by the help of those less fluid beings— the ones bound to their state, living through physicality— that such a plan thrived.

It was a matter of contracts made between the hidden and physical realm (between humans and malellum) which allowed for a great deal of darkness to be freed on Earth. Come to afflict the innocent and embolden the wicked.

There had long been a need for light in a place so devoid of it. Spanning the centuries, many prayers had been made to El in good faith for His corroding world to be made whole again. And at long last, the people of the church, El's beloved, were given a prophecy...

The Elson was said to be the bringer of light. In every form of the word. Truth, enlightenment, vitality, and even sometimes a searing heat to one's conscience. But with all of that foretold glory, one would hardly expect the humble reality that manifested to them.

And his coming was just as enigmatic as his passing. Both were easily footling and yet undeniably memorable.

There were few who were fortunate enough to have encountered the Elson. One being Fredrick Truit. He wasn't much older than twenty when he met the stranger at Faulkner Station. He was waiting for the arrival of his brother's lawyer, though it was not necessary that they meet, as Fredrick had grumbled a few times in the past hour. He had already insisted to the lawyer that he decided not to testify against Felix in court. The drama of a scandal was not something he wanted to be involved in any longer. The association to Felix was enough to threaten his business. He could not afford to deal with the mess his brother made. It wasn't safe for his wife, Krishta. And it wasn't safe for Truit & Co. which served to be the only child they ever had. As he sat in the waiting area far from the ticket window— the sun raying through the station and warming his bench seat— he was interrupted from his thoughts.

"What are you waiting for?"

Fredrick turned his head, lifting his attention above his newspaper to the man sitting next to him. The question he asked was trifling and idiotic, yet Fredrick curtly answered, "The train." He flapped his paper and continued to hide himself in it.

"I didn't mean the train. Everyone has something in life they wait for, whether that's a train, a chance, a child…"

Child. That word pricked at Fredrick's heart. He'd thought about the word so much, he couldn't stomach the sound of it. Why couldn't he and Krishta have had a child? They had so much room for one in their hearts, and their empty manor. He ignored the man's comment, dipping his head further toward the paper.

The stranger sat silently for a while before saying, "The dress catalog must really be interesting to you."

Fredrick shot the man a confused look, then checked the page again. The page he was not even truly reading. Sure enough he had been staring at the dress catalog for about three minutes. He looked at the man again and said in annoyance, "Is there a reason you chose to speak to me?"

"There is a reason for everything I do. Same as you. I know you give your all to the things that matter in life. And I know you are a great husband, businessman, and father."

The stranger's presumptuous claims were odd to hear.

"Sir, I'm flattered, but you don't know me. I have no children."

With that, the stranger slapped his palms on the bench and stood up. "Not yet." He started to walk away.

Now intrigued, Fredrick had to say something to the man. "I say, sir. Who are you?"

The man stopped and turned halfway towards Fredrick. "My name is Shersul. Tell your wife that you both will have a child. By the end of your brother's trial." He left Fredrick to wonder how he even knew about the trial, or anything else he seemed to know. Fredrick could not simply stare back at his newspaper after such an enigmatic encounter. He found himself reflecting on it deeply, forgetting why he was even where he was. By the time he finally realized an hour had passed, there was a rumbling, whistling din in the station, bringing his attention to the incoming train. He exhaled, waiting for it to come to a stop, for the passengers to get off, and for the long-awaited attorney to appear...

Early Summer (1895)

Lilian's aunt and uncle were hesitant to break the news to her. But she knew as they all sat together in their warmly lit dining room by the bittersweetness of the supper as well as the dismal grins they'd all shared. The air that night spoke of silent goodbyes.

Shersul had been her mentor and friend ever since he had met the Truits. Ever since he had prophesied to her relatives that they would have a child. Who would have thought that child would be Felix's daughter— their niece?

Shersul was a usually cheery figure to Lilian. Never did she see him without a grin on his face. But now he looked into the whole family's eyes with a hollow expression. There was no hidden message behind his eyes as there usually was. They just looked on with a sense of waiting.

Lilian could not help but study him, wondering what was wrong. Her aunt tapped her arm, saying, "Stop that. It's rude to stare." Lilian glanced at her once, then back at Shersul who ate his buttered loaf slowly. It was awfully quiet tonight. She hated it.

By the time he finished wiping the crumbs off his mouth, Lilian quickly fled from the table, refusing to catch any more of the depression. She ignored the censure of the adults, leaving to find solace in the chirping lulls of the outdoors just beyond their back terrace. She was only nine and a half. She never dreamed of saying goodbye to her friend.

But Shersul, like always, found her sulking. He sat beside her. And for a while their silence was undisturbed.

"Lilian," he began. "You know I have to go."

"It's not fair!" she blurted most defiantly. "You're mine. The world can't have you."

"No, Lilian. You are *mine*. But so is everyone else."

"They don't need you like I do. They don't deserve you."

"And I suppose you think you do?"

Lilian loured at her feet, slouching with her knees up. It just wasn't fair. "You're my only friend."

"I will send you a new friend."

"And I'll refuse them! I will!" She hid her face in her arms.

Shersul patted her back. "Oh, Lilian. I have to do this. And I know why it is you do not understand. You don't hear the voice I hear. Or see the things I see. It's all fiction to you. But it is the unseen that matters most." He lifted her head, wiped her tears, and covered her eyes with his hands. "So, I am leaving you with a gift. As long as it remains with you, remember me."

A tingling sensation started to spread over her eyes, and she knew something had changed. Once he removed his hands, the world as she once saw it transitioned before her. Beams of light jutted from Shersul like cords reaching out to the world. Tucking in her chin, she watched the thin cord tethering his heart to hers. Though it felt unusual, she smiled in wonder at it.

Then something broke her smile. She heard the sound of people, young and old, bewailing whispered complaints that were beyond her understanding. But she knew that whatever their problems were, she wanted so much for them to feel better.

Then in the distance, she saw the rising of an angry smoke. It grew and grew greedily until it started progressing madly in her direction. Piles of smoke tumbled over itself, then rolled into a step, stacking tall until it took human forms. But these beings were far from human. They dragged on as they approached, chanting the name *Truit, Truit*. Lilian tensed in terror. Shersul sat by, not saying a word as the smokey beings charged for them.

Closer, they came. Collapsing and reforming with each step. Shersul put his hand over Lilian's heart. The beings halted and stared with tiger eyes. They took one more step...

"No," Shersul said plainly.

Their bodies dispersed and thinned into the air.

Lilian gasped, looking again at her friend.

"You see. They cannot hurt you. But I won't lie to you. They will come back as they always do. But they are never a threat to you, if you keep my words in here." He tapped the left side of her chest. "So, can you be brave now? For my sake?"

Lilian gave him an uncertain grin. "I think I can." Then as he moved a little from her, she recanted. "Wait. No. Who will protect me when you are gone?"

Shersul's gaze stilled as he considered her point, his interest suddenly taken to the space beside Lilian, leading her to do the same. "Show yourself," he said.

After his command, the atmosphere in that space seemed to warp and ripple. The air whooshed around, wrapping upward and downward, until the body of the ciella became more visible. Even as he stood still, the air his body consisted of continued to flow vigorously. Eternally. Lilian's mind could hardly comprehend the existence of such a wondrous creature. She noticed a sword in his transparent belt. He drew it out, revealing the blade made of flames. Its bright heat emitted toward her face, a darling and glorious weapon. By Shersul's nod, he slipped it back and bowed.

"Lilian, meet your guardian ciella. His name is Tarfwin. I am giving him charge over you. He will see that you are kept safe until your power strengthens. And besides him, you will have the Elwind to guide you towards all truth. You see, I have given you everything you need to fight Girgum and his winds."

The whole time, Lilian gaped at the wind who seemed to her as tall as a pine tree. He was without a nose, ears, hair—all those distracting things. But he had unforgettable, cat-shaped eyes, the most electrifying shade of green. She asked Shersul, "What does Girgum want?"

"Your heart, Lilian. And he wants their hearts, too." Shersul gestured outward.

She looked at Shersul once more, still wanting to cry, but kept those tears in as best as a little girl could. The world needed him just as much as she did. She could only agree with Shersul that he was doing everything he could to ensure that she would be cared for while he was gone. "Okay. I'm... I'm *sure* I can be brave now. I hope I can."

"I *know* you can." He cupped her round cheek.

Lilian threw her arms around him. And he held her for the longest time, until she finally let go.

Becoming

Late Autumn (1901)

It was inevitable what Lilian's heart had become by her sixteenth year, resembling an unblown whistle; hollow, inoffensive, and meaningless. It was the result of all the years her soul spent decomposing. She was a girl who had learned the art of liquidating all that she was into her jewelry and gestures. No longer a person, an ideal. Every member of her body now moved according to rationale. Every free thought was reared to propriety. She was dead. Dead in thought, in spirit, in will.

And what's worse was she didn't even know it. Her smile, which she currently dabbed in rouge, endeavored to deceive herself into believing that she was authentically what she had always been.

The mirror on her vanity table captured a mature beauty, dressed in white. Her shoulders, bare. Her overlong locks, romantically coiffured atop her head. She was not a child anymore. Far from it. By the end of tonight, she'd be a woman. A lady of society.

Gracie, her maid, helped button up her heels. Every time Gracie made a new adjustment to Lilian's appearance, she could not help but sigh in admiration. "One more thing to complete you." She lifted Uncle Fred's gift out of the tiny, bejeweled box on her vanity; a black diamond brooch in the shape of a butterfly. She pinned it right in the center of Lilian's décolletage just below the choker of pearls.

Holding the back of her chair, the girl rose to her feet. Her gown was embellished with floral embroidery. It was made of heavy silk, flaring down into a bell shape. The edge of her shoulders was lightly draped in lace.

"My, Miss Lilian. I don't need to see the other ladies to know you'll outshine them all."

Lilian grinned. "Thank you, Gracie." Though she was contrarily certain that Julia Louisa Dorvan would be the belle of the ball.

Upon deciding that Lilian was ready, Gracie hurried downstairs and into the sitting room where Uncle Fred and Aunt Krishta, Lilian's beloved relatives, were flipping through the family album. Reminiscing on their earlier years. Uncle Fred was only 39, not looking a day over 25, even with his red eyes and raw nose due to his ailment. Aunt Krishta, who was not much younger, still kept her youthful glow. He had married her for her prudence and robust character, but he certainly was not blind to her soft blue eyes or her rutilant cheeks. Sitting close to Krishta on the sofa, one arm resting behind her, he gazed at her while she spoke as if he was still that young man so enthralled by a brilliant young woman.

"Oh, Fred. This was us at our wedding," Krishta said. "You were so nervous. It even shows through the picture."

Krishta soon landed on a page with a tiny vignette displaying a black and white photo of two Uncle Fred look-alikes, about the age of seventeen, dressed formally in vests, ties, and top hats. The one on the right (Felix), leaning heavily on top of the other (Fred) and laughing while his brother simply looked upward into the camera and smiled a short smile that revealed just a peek of his teeth.

"You and your brother." Krishta said this with a dull voice.

"Now, Krishta," Fred said. "He gave us Lilian."

"Yes. That's just about the only good thing he's done."

Gracie had no wish to interrupt the couple, but it was time for the subject of the night to have *her* turn at making memories. With a cough, she gained their attention. "Master Truit. Mistress. Miss Lilian is ready for you."

They promptly rose to their feet and followed their maid to the foyer, waiting at the bottom of the stairs. Gracie called for Lilian. And down the walnut steps she came, the hem of her skirt gliding over each step.

Lilian's relatives gazed adoringly at their niece. Uncle Fred was the first to meet her with a hug by the time she reached the bottom.

"Thank you, Uncle."

Uncle Fred lifted his head at Krishta. "Seems our Lilabug is all grown up."

"With the same poise and womanliness as—"

"You," Lilian finished for her. Though, she knew that her aunt was going to say 'as your mother'.

Aunt Krishta grinned despite it.

Lilian was not made ignorant on how she was brought into the world. Her relatives had told her that her mother was a Russian lady of society, well-adored by men and women for her quick wit, her attractive presence, and her good heart. But her mother was a victim of her father's unfaithful behavior. Her poor mother died after giving birth to her, and her father shortly after that. This was not a past Lilian liked thinking about. She found it impossible to ever associate with two people she had never known. Two people who couldn't be more irrelevant to who Lilian was now.

Looking into Uncle Fred's caring stare, she knew that no one in the world could ever replace him.

He smiled at her, his hands resting on her shoulders. "I have tried my hardest to make you disinterested with polite society. But you are bred for it the way your father was."

"Polite society is not all bad. It can just be a little *too* polite, sometimes."

"Fake is the word," he said.

"Now, let's not have any of that." Aunt Krishta came forward and gave Lilian a kiss on the cheek. "You look beautiful, darling." Aunt Krishta's eyes narrowed on her niece. "Are you excited to see Paul again?"

Lilian looked to the side, bashfully. Paul was the gentleman who'd be escorting her this night. He used to be her closest friend. But in the recent months, he had not been acting like the Paul she knew. He often found reasons to avoid seeing Lilian. There seemed to be something troubling him. He had gotten accepted into Hiplum University, and she resolved it was probably stressing him out in some way to prepare for such a change. "I can only hope he shows up."

"He will."

"He wouldn't miss it for the world," Uncle asserted. "You only have this one night to make your debut, and I'm sure you'll do fi—" Fredrick coughed a chesty cough that was rather startling. Krishta placed a hand on his back in concern.

"Thank you," Fred said.

"Are you sure you want to go out?" she inquired, her tone a sincere appeal.

"Yes, I do." He was adamant. "I will be alright."

Krishta frowned at him for a few seconds before saying, "I suppose we should hurry up, Fred. It's nearly ten o' clock."

"Not before we've prayed." He reached for the hands of both women who were special to him. And even Gracie, being that she was part of the family, took hold of Lilian and Krishta's hands. They bowed their heads as Uncle Fred began.

"Father El, creator of life, tonight we thank you for *Lilian's* life. We thank you for all the preparation she has been through, in school, church, and home that has made her the woman she is. A heart with so much to give. As she participates in the debutante ball, may there be many fine young men who see her worth. As you do. For Shersul's sake."

"For Shersul's sake," the women repeated.

Just as they moved toward the front door, Lilian paused to ask her uncle, "Uncle Fred? Do you really think I have done everything I should?"

"Of course." Uncle Fred's eyebrows drooped exaggeratedly over his eyes as he leaned forward at her. "You have, haven't you?" he asked in a dire tone.

Lilian laughed and looked away, waving her head.

Uncle Fred put a hand on her shoulder. "Promise me something, Lilian."

"Yes, Uncle?"

Uncle Fred's face calmed into a serious stare. "You may be polite with *them*, you may even be polite with *us* someday when you live on your own. But promise me that you will never become too polite with El. Promise me that He will remain your closest friend."

Lilian could not have understood the weight of her uncle's words. But ever since Shersul's departure, she had tried to stay focused on El's voice all on her own. She had begun to learn how to balance her awareness of the hidden realm with the life she now lived. Shersul's gift still remained inside. Not often used but there. She only hoped she could keep up the balancing act. "I promise," she said.

"Then I have no doubt that you are doing *everything* you should."

The Preuve de Beauté Hotel was the grandest in Hiplum. The steps to the entrance were circularly terraced. The height of the building gave Lilian chills. Lilian and her relatives walked up the steps, locking arms. Doormen waited by the entrance. As they entered, the music that filled the atmosphere did well to ease Lilian's nerves.

They made their way to the Grand Hall where the music was coming from, which was entered from various openings. The room was white like the ladies' dresses with a floor of marble and a ceiling made of domed glass supported by bars to allow for a breathtaking view of the celestial expansion that canopied them. The white theme carried on with the filigree that adorned the walls. The insets, mounted by fresh green vines. The hall was lit by sconces at each post, and a quartet played softly in the corner of the room. It all worked in harmony to encourage the mood for refined tease and coy glances.

There were many men and women seated at their tables placed at the outskirts of the room, waiting for their daughters to be presented. Lining the center of the room, like the inner ring of a square onion, were chairs designated for the debutantes and their escorts. Lilian looked around for *her* escort as her foot began to tap nervously. Her relatives said he would arrive, but she knew the opposite was more likely. He hadn't even shown up consecutively for the rehearsal of their dance. He had told her quite often that there were some things he needed to study before he'd leave to Hiplum University. Little had he understood that he was leaving her no time to say goodbye. She had hoped that this night he'd get to see her in full glamor and grace, and that she could present herself as a woman before him.

"Oh, Paul. Where are you?" she whined under her breath.

"Right here, milady."

Lilian turned around to see her friend standing there with a warm grin on his handsome face. "Paul." She refrained from the urge to embrace him.

"Well now, there is our son," remarked Aunt Krishta.

"*Aunt Krishta,*" Lilian whispered sharply, guiltily blushing. She hoped Paul received her aunt's remark as a motherly endearing joke— the kind you chuckle lightly to and move on— and not an informal acceptance into the family. Though she wouldn't be wrong. Paul was practically family and all the man Krishta Truit could ever want around her niece. He was everything Fredrick Truit could want in a potential nephew. And to Lilian, he was a dream.

"Very good to see you too, Mrs. Truit." He kissed the madam's hand, then switched his gaze to Lilian. "And *Miss Lilian,*" he said with a cautious tease before kissing her hand all too briefly. She bowed her head acknowledgingly.

Paul then greeted Uncle, exchanging nods and shaking hands as men do.

The band stopped playing all of a sudden. They were preparing for their next piece. A pat on the back from Uncle

Fred, let Lilian know she must go. Paul took Lilian by the hand, and they made their way to the main entrance of the hall where the presentation would begin.

They met with the group of young ladies and gentlemen waiting in a line. Everyone was hushedly disclosing their excitement. As Lilian became more aware of Paul's hand clasping hers and their shoulders touching, she aimed to lift her eyes at his handsome face. Oh, if she could without being noticed by his dreamy eyes.

From behind the arched doors, the announcer could be heard, "Presenting..." and the doors opened. Each debutante walked forward when their name was called. Finally, he called out, "Presenting Miss Lilian Truit and her escort, Paul Partridge." Paul and Lilian stepped forward and stopped at a good distance to bow and curtsy.

"Miss Truit is the daughter of Felix Truit, the world-renowned physician, may he rest in peace. And she is the niece of Fredrick Truit, from whom lies her inheritance. She also attends school at Hiplum Academy."

They continued walking forward, then split up to sit in their seats parallel to each other. When the music started, the ladies and gentlemen all stood and walked over to their corresponding counterpart. Paul and Lilian met face-to-face, exchanged a bow and a curtsy, and began to perform the presentation waltz.

Holding one hand and standing side by side, they walked forward then back, forward then back. They joined hands and kicked. She turned into him, and he spun her. Now they were together. Just enough for Lilian to capture his scent. Notes of rose, vetiver, and leather were poignant; a calming scent to match his being.

"Is that Orval by Molinard?"

"Only you would know." He shook his head amusedly and spun her. "Why? Do you like it?"

"Am I supposed to?" she mused. They started walking forward, clasping one hand in a tango-like manner.

"How am I doing?" Paul said as he spun her again, then they both spun on their own.

She knelt, rose, and they joined once again.

"I know I had not been to the last two rehearsals," he continued.

They let go of one hand and continued their routine, going forward then back, forward then back. A dance that would only end once they revolved 360° around the dance floor.

Lilian waited till they were together again. "You're doing just fine. Just fine."

"Good." He smiled.

As they continued, Lilian was nearly forgetting the crowd. Until one shadowed face stuck out among the rest. A face that recurred in her worst dreams, full of threat and rancor. He stood there watching like an owl eyeing a rat. As Lilian spun once more, Paul noticed the unease on her face.

"What is it, Lil...?" With realization, Paul quickly pulled her up from her last kneel. "What is *he* doing here?"

Their dance came to a halt once the music stopped. The crowd rose with applause. There he was, still sitting in the far back, smoking a pipe. Spencer Wesman. His stare was unmoved as he was even so bold as to raise his eyebrows at her in a vexing manner.

Memories poured into Lilian's victim mind. Memories of his endless violence and harassment towards her. The lies about her he'd spread like wildfire to the whole of Hiplum Academy. It was a relief when he left, not by expulsion, but because his father wanted to start him early as a manager in their bank. Or so Lilian was told.

"Lil," Paul whispered behind her. "We have to sit back down."

She immediately came to awareness. "Oh. Right."

They were on their way to their seats when the sound of glasses smashing and table collapsing echoed across the room. Everybody turned to set their eyes upon an old man lying prostrate against the marble floor. Hovering over him— a furious Fredrick Truit, panting and clenching his fists.

"Uncle Fred!"

Uncle looked up at Lilian. His red eyes shot with confusion as if he did not realize what he had done. Lilian advanced toward him.

"Uncle, is everything alright?"

"Assailant!" shrieked the old woman who was likely the smitten man's wife. Her exclamation startled Lilian to jump. "Is this your buffoon? He has no right to wear a gentleman's suit with such ruffian ways."

"Oh, I am so sorry for the trouble, ma'am. I…. Uncle, why did you…?"

No answer was given. Krishta Truit came to her husband's side. "Come on Fredrick. I think it is time we leave."

"Leave? Already?" Lilian whispered. "But they're about to start dancing with the fathers."

Aunt Krishta gave Lilian a look that let her know this was not the time for discourse. The two, inched away, Krishta's hand on Fredrick's shoulder. Fredrick turned to place a hand on *Paul's* shoulder. "Watch her."

Paul nodded.

Then Fred looked at his niece, a weary expression on his kindred face. "I love you. I'm sorry you had to see me this way."

"I love you, too, Uncle Fre—"

Lilian was interrupted by Fredrick's harsh cough that continued as he walked away.

After Lilian watched them leave, she looked at Paul. "I don't understand. My uncle never behaves this way." She glared at the couple over her shoulder that was still riled over what happened. She knew something was not right about the situation. Perhaps it was the fever that made her uncle act so inappropriately, but she had a feeling it was not unprovoked.

Lilian had to sit out the next dance, looking upward as she felt her skin crawl under a despiser's gaze. Paul never did see all that Spencer would do to her. Sure, he was there for the slander and the lies, and some of the abuse. But not the moments when Spencer would will her hands to harm herself or bind her legs mid-walk to make her trip. That was unnatural abuse. The kind that no one could see.

She wondered if Spencer's intrigue for her still existed; wondered if him being away for two years somehow made him forget about her. This was the worst night to have to worry about Spencer. And now with her uncle's disorderly display adding to the angst, she could not find a way out of worry. She was certain he had come for some definitive reason and prayed it was not in any way related to her.

Finally, the dancing was over, and all the ladies lined up to curtsy to the ambassador, then it was time for their dinner. Everyone sat at the long table for their feast. Lilian tried to converse with the girls at her sides. Julia was looking as spectacular as Lilian had expected. She wore a carnation in her golden hair, and a ruby pendant dangling from the chain of pearls she wrapped around her long neck. "Julia? Rose? Nice to see you again."

Rose, a heavy-set ginger with a silver ribbon in her hair, turned to Lilian with only pity on her mind. "Oh, poor Lilian. How embarrassing it must have been to endure your uncle's misconduct."

"Let's hope your looks make up for it," Julia said.

"Do you think they might?" Lilian asked.

"That's up to the men to decide. I wouldn't expect too many suitors, though. Six or seven at most."

Lilian was not offended. She actually enjoyed the rare honesty from Julia. But she didn't need six or seven. Just one. Just Paul.

"You know, this wouldn't be the first time."

"The first time what?" Lilian said to Julia, who tasted her wine for a second.

"That your uncle has made some controversial gaffes. Or at least I hope that is what they are." Her narrowing amber eyes seemed to allude to something. Something that Lilian did not comprehend.

"Do explain."

"Well, I'm sure you know your uncle has taken to speaking on certain matters such as Mister Muggri's former involvement with the slave trade."

"Yes, but that was some time ago. All has since been forgiven."

"Forgiven, so you say," Julia's gaze became more intrusive, "yet he has declined all offers to join Muggri Corp."

"Indeed, however—"

"He does understand the benefit of a unified network of business?"

"Yes, he does. But—"

"My father has seen the numbers on Truit & Company. And he isn't liking it."

Lilian shut her mouth, staring at Julia warily. She hoped Julia was not saying what she assumed she was.

"He says the trajectory of things isn't promising. If your uncle does not comply soon—"

"Comply?" Lilian responded sharply. Mostly to stall whatever Julia's conclusion would be. Her father was Fredrick Truit's greatest shareholder, and one of the last.

"Yes," said Julia. "The world is moving toward efficiency. Which can be best achieved through a union of trade. If he does not meet our progress, he shall be cut off."

Lilian's eyes widened in plea.

"That's right. My father has plans to pull out. If I were you, I would make sure your uncle dearest understands that. Or your only hope of continuing in luxury will be through marriage." Julia looked over at Rose. "And being an El's beloved already limits her options."

"She won't be a problem as long as she keeps her ideals to herself," Rose stated.

Lilian was surprised to hear them mention her association with El when she hardly ever mentioned it herself. She was already very quiet about such personal matters, as was normal to do in polite society, or so she had thought.

Sitting between the two, she felt trapped in a silent bubble of despair. One she was careful not to burst, knowing that it could only induce a burping mess of a situation. Her uncle, as Lilian was aware, had many more qualms with Mr. Muggri than he ever cared to disclose to her and her aunt. She assumed it had to do with the fact that Muggri was a very powerful, influential man. Sometimes, it seemed to worry Fredrick Truit. For what? She did not know.

"A letter for Miss Truit."

Lilian brought her attention to the silver platter being lowered to her from the waiter's gloved hand. The sudden break in thought gave her a sense of relief. She lifted the letter, half-excited. Or half-anxious, depending on the sender. "Thank you." She unfolded the piece of paper and read:

I want to speak to you. You cannot escape this.

At first she thought the message was from Paul, which made her elated and a bit flustered at the scandalous tone. But then she saw the S at the bottom of the letter, and her heart dropped. She finally looked to her left and caught his dark stare from across the hall. He rose from his seat and stepped out through the grand doors. Lilian folded the paper repeatedly into a tiny square— the tiniest she could fold— and placed it back in the envelope. After three breaths of preparing her thoughts, she excused herself from the table. As she walked past the seats, a sly hand caught hers. She looked down at her escort's face. He mouthed, *Where are you going?*

I'll be back, she replied.

"Shall I go with you?" he whispered audibly this time.

She wished Paul could go with her yet knew that this was a matter she could not bring him into. She shook her head, giving him a smile.

With her head up, and her back straight, Lilian left the hall. As she went through the doors, her anticipant put himself in her way. He said nothing as he held out his hand. She stared at it in trepidation. Nonetheless, she put her hand in his. He took her outside, down the terraced steps and along the cobblestone walkway.

Lilian kept her gaze down. She knew he was trying to build her anxiety by not saying a word. He loved to play with his food. But she took advantage of the quiet moment to think of a way to evade his unpredictable wrath.

It was not until they were a few buildings away from the hotel, to Lilian's despair, that she heard him speak. "How is your night going, Miss Truit?"

She kept her calm. "Wonderful, Mister Wesman."

"Surprised at all to see me?" He regarded her out of the corner of his eye.

"A little. I admit that I did think back to your past behavior, but I see how foolish that was of me."

"Really?"

"Yes. After all, you are not a boy anymore. We are ladies and gentlemen. And I trust you know how to treat people. As they say, time changes things."

His head lifted upward as he released a pensive breath through his nose. "And how has time changed *you*?" He stepped around to face her with his hands held behind his back. Spencer had sickly eyes that were the darkest shade of black. They lacked a twinkle, having the same reflectionless effect as the eyes of an untamed beast. Only a fraction of his soul was human if he even had one.

"I..." Lilian wasn't sure what to say.

"Time is ticking, Lilian. Destiny brings us closer to battle. I am recruiting for *my* master's army. How about you?"

Lilian gawked in worry for a moment, then laughed incredulously. "I haven't a clue what you are talking about."

"Truly? Don't tell me you've forgotten the prophecy?"

"Prophecy? Amazing. Absolutely amazing how you are still repeating that same nonsense. Spencer, you just don't understand, do you? There is no prophecy. Nothing is calling you to be my enemy, nor I yours. It's all your choice. I hope one day you realize that." Lilian turned around, holding her skirt as she began to walk away. She managed a few steps before her knees locked, and she could take no more. A chill enveloped her.

"What's the matter? Can't seem to get away?"

Lilian's heart began to pound while her back still faced him. The invisible force buckling her joints would not release her. She felt him move closer behind her until his breath could graze her ear.

"You see, Lilian. No matter how hard you try to trivialize what is coming, it still comes. The war comes. And if I were you, I'd prepare." With no more than a nudge on her back, she fell to the ground with a gasp. She shuddered as he came to a kneel, leaning over her. Lowering a hand, he took hold of her chin, turning her face to his. Lilian was subject to his shadow. "I applaud your efforts to make us anything other than enemies." His face drew closer as he whispered, "But know that every minute of the day, I spend hating what you are and what you represent. Know that no matter how many steps you take toward forgetting your fate, I take more toward your destruction."

When he said 'destruction', a brief image overtook him. The image of something dead as well as deadly. Something pallid and deviant. But in a moment the image was gone. She was only staring at his wicked visage. "What is it you want from me?" she said. "Have you only come here tonight to scare me?"

He let go of her and stood. "I came to see how you've been getting on." His eyes dropped as though he was disappointed. "I must say, I thought you would have grown since the last time I saw you. But clearly, the only growth is in your bosom."

Lilian placed a conscious hand on her chest. "Why, I never..."

"It's true you're not the only one, you know. There are more lightbearers out there. Anyway, that's what Girgum says. But I can't see where their light is coming from. Tell me. For I seem to have forgotten. What *did* become of your dear Shersul?"

To Lilian, that was the cruelest thing he could have asked. She did not know what happened to Shersul. Not since he had told her he was leaving only to never return. He was not simply the Elson, he was her friend. Her brother. It hurt to even think of him now.

Spencer sighed. "Just go, Lilian. Go and dine. Dance. Drink. Have your special evening. You know we will meet again soon. Very soon."

The moment she felt his oppressive power leave her, she got up and ran as fast as she could in heels in the dark, past the few lit windows of shops. Past the old bank Spencer's father owned.

Lilian heard what she thought was a cackle. She felt something whip by. She turned her face to see nothing beside her. Nothing but the open street. Just as she thought it must have been a bird, another strange bluster hit her face. A cackle, loud to her ears now. The sounds and blows were not uncommon to her. And unlike most people, she understood what they were. The torturous winds called malellum.

But knowing them did not keep her from being startled. Lilian carried on until the hotel was in sight. As she came around the corner, her face found someone's chest. Lilian almost immediately pushed off the person, but her nose caught the comforting scent, and she looked up at his lapis blue eyes as they captured the glimmer of the moon.

"Lilian, I thought you were inside. What are you doing out here?"

Lilian held him tight. "Paul, hold me. I'm scared."

Paul's arms went around her. "What's happened?"

She remained silent, still clinging to him with a profusion of quick and heavy breaths. "They… they were after me. All of them at once."

"Lilian?" He pulled her off of him and stared in her eyes. "Do you need me to take you home now?"

Lilian frowned. "No, I— I couldn't. The night isn't over."

"*Our* night *is*." He stared with assurance.

Lilian could not disagree. "Alright. Yes, you can take me home."

Paul brought Lilian to the front of the hotel then guided her to his car. Finally, they got in, and he drove her out of the town. As they roved on, Lilian saw that they were passing 'the tracks'. A rusty, derelict sight where wild greenery had germinated around the iron bars. This railroad had ceased being in use since before Lilian was born. And she thanked El for it.

"Oh Paul, why not stop for a while? Just a while."

Paul shook his head. "Not tonight."

"Then when? Please, Paul." She bit her lip before saying, "With all the dancing, we hadn't had time to talk."

Paul looked at her, his eyes spoke of his concession. "Alright." With one hand on the lever, he slowed the car to a stop. Paul hopped out of the automobile and walked over to Lilian's side of the car. He reached out for her hand. She took it, letting him pick her up by the waist and plop her down. Then they walked onto the tracks, her hand in his.

Paul took a deep breath in through his nose. "You feel that?"

"What?"

"Nothing," he replied.

He was right, it did feel like nothing. It wasn't hot, cold, or windy out. There were only a few times in Lilian's life where she could recall the atmosphere being so nondescript.

She closed her eyes and took it in, releasing the stress bottled inside. She had no idea when she'd started feeling like her world, everything she believed in, was dependent on her resilience. Dependent on her sanity. Like the moment she broke, so would her entire reality. And Spencer would be a fundamental catalyst to her collapse. His presence had evoked an old sense of insecurity she thought she'd overcome. And his threats scared her almost back to adolescence. She knew it was ridiculous, though. There was no prophecy. No real one, anyway. And she had no idea what being a lightbearer meant. That wasn't an occupation. No, it was only a word meant to distract her from the reality she *did* live, and from the duties she *did* have.

After the long ponderance, she opened her eyes and saw her friend looking at her curiously.

"You were spectacular tonight," he said.

"Me?"

"You." He stepped closer. "You don't even understand how stuffy a room is without you in it."

"But… but my uncle—"

"Oh, your looks will make up for it." He smiled, his dark blue eyes staring into hers. "Don't worry. You'll have many suitors after your hand."

It was torture how he mentioned other men as though she was not looking straight at him, now and forever. "Paul, why have we not been as close as usual? I feel like ever since your trip with Uncle—"

"What do you want me to say, Lil?" He turned his face, stepping away. "You know I've been busy. I'll be off to HU soon. I need to concentrate." His hand was tense at his chest. "You know becoming a doctor is important to me."

"Of course. I understand that." She held herself as she said, "I just can't help but feel…"

His head tilted toward the midnight sky. "Like I'm avoiding you." He finally looked at her again and approached with intent in his eyes. He knelt before her, taking her hands and drawing them to his face.

Her hands smoothed not only the sides of his face, but just below his pillowy lips. As her eyes reviewed the sight of them, her reflex triggered the pulling in of her hands. But his hands kept hers still. And she was forced to watch as his lips parted to say, "Lilian Truit, if I were avoiding you, do you think I'd get this close?"

Her eyes widened at his own. Perhaps it was only her presumptuous mind, but she felt a forwardness in his words.

"Sometimes I wonder," he whispered, "what you see in me."

She had the feeling his question was not meant to be answered, yet she *did* answer. "I see a man who is brilliant, kind, and loyal. A man who can do anything he puts his mind to." Lilian sighed. "And I also see a hopeless… hopeless doubter."

Paul grinned as if she had gotten it right… but not completely. He stood up, walking backwards again, then he gestured all around at the tracks. "Remember how we met?"

Lilian nodded. It had been a cool day in March. Paul was a twelve-year-old newcomer to Hiplum and a student at Hiplum Academy. Lilian was a spoiled ten-year-old girl, living a peaceful, pastoral life in Corlu. Though she felt lonely sometimes without another child to play with.

Meanwhile, Paul was having a hard time making friends, being a very technical boy who had made up his mind about the world and the people in it very early on and had the habit of infuriating people with his presuppositions… that were often correct. They ran to the only place they could go where no one else made them feel bothersome. The abandoned railroad tracks. There, out of precious coincidence, they met. Lilian was intrigued by the boy and found him to be kind. And he seemed to enjoy her company as well.

Realizing how similar their lonesome circumstance was, Paul told Lilian of his plight, and she agreed to join him at school. They were friends ever since. It was Lilian who pointed out the significance of the tracks being somewhat of a border for both towns. There, they weren't subject to either side. Nothing was expected of them. They could be safe from their troubles, even making it a rule to leave worry behind the moment they step onto the tracks. This was their haven.

"It was you who told me, 'Even if both Corlu and Hiplum are blown to smithereens, we'll always have the tracks,'" said Paul.

Lilian laughed at the memory.

"Now, whether or not that remark had any logical standing," Paul continued, "I chose not to bother you about it. Because I knew you believed it. And even now, I know you still believe it— believe in our friendship. I've never had to ask you to, you just do. It's one of the things I admire about you, Lilian. And it gives me some hope in this world."

Lilian crept closer to him. "Paul. What do you see when you look at *me*?"

Paul tilted his head at the question. He remained where he stood, but his gaze fell upon her dark brown eyes. "Lilian... when I look at you, I see..."

"Yes?"

Whatever he was thinking must have been loud inside his head, but as his eyes drew down from hers, she knew it was not meant for her ears just yet. A tear fell down her cheek. Thankfully, it was too dark for him to notice.

Then the ground began to shake under them. The railroad rumbled furiously. Which could only mean one thing— a train was coming. On these nearly ancient tracks, a train was coming.

Normally the very sound of a chug and puff would have made Lilian act with immediacy, but she simply couldn't believe it. She looked down the tracks, squinting for a light. In three seconds, a light showed. It was true. And the train came closer and closer and...

"LILIAN, MOVE OUT OF THE WAY!"

Clutching onto her dress, he dragged her close to him and threw himself with her off the tracks and onto the grass of the other side. Lilian looked up at his face, which was extremely close to hers. The warmth and weight of his body against hers had her disconcerted. His breath against her forehead.

Even while she secretly indulged in this moment, a shiny distraction at the corner of her eye garnered her attention. Lilian tried standing, moving Paul off of her. She peered through to the other side as the carts of the train passed by. There it was. A bright figure, unmistakably looking her way. Lilian gasped. Her heart twinged as she became re-acquainted with the eyes that were like green galaxies swirling within. How she had missed those dazzling eyes. But how was he here now, and why? It had been so long. She moved no muscle in her face as she held his stare.… Then he began to turn away.

"No!"

Nearly becoming defaced as she jumped in the direction of the moving train, Paul pulled her back. "Stop! What are you doing?"

Lilian turned her face to Paul, then looked back, and the passer-by was gone. They stood there, confounded, until the train passed.

"What were you thinking, Lil?" Paul demanded out of care.

"You didn't see him?"

"See whom?"

Lilian bit her lip, remembering. *Of course he didn't see.*

Paul's car drove across the courtyard of the Truit manor where hedges, flowers and cobblestones resided. They owned around 7 acres of land— enough for a garden, maze, and orchard though they were humble people who never boasted of their riches.

They got out of the car. Lampposts illuminated the path to the front door. Paul and Lilian shared tired smiles at each other before he faced the door and gave it a knock.

When Gracie opened the door, they could hear a soft melody playing inside. "Miss Lilian. Hello there." Gracie turned her face to Paul and smiled in surprise. "Mister Partridge. Good to see you."

"And *you*, Gracie, dearest."

Gracie he-hed into her palm. "Do come in."

They stepped in and, turning to their left, entered into the sitting room where the fire in the hearth reflected spurts of light and shadow dancing on the walls of the room. The silhouette of a large mass turning in the room was also cast on the wall before they saw who it was.

"Uncle Fred..."

Uncle Fred was standing on the carpet. Aunt Krishta, wrapped in his arms as they swayed to the soft, distorted notes projecting from the gramophone. They had moved the coffee table to the side to allow them some room.

"Hello, ag—" Paul began when Lilian held his arm as a signal to pause.

The sight of her relatives sweeping the rug in their formal apparel was too adorable to disrupt. Fredrick Truit was keeping his cheek on his wife's as they moved in a circle. Then Lilian noticed a subdued dispiritedness in his face as he was rubbing her hair as if consoling her in some way. Then she wondered if they were dancing together or moping together.

His back faced them, Krishta's neck resting over his shoulder. Her eyes blinked open and she realized there was company. "Oh, you two are back."

Fred turned around to them. His solemn face quickly became more lively. "Back already?"

"We thought it was best considering..."

Uncle Fred frowned. "My display. Forgive me, Lilabug."

"No matter, Uncle. I had a great time, truly."

Uncle Fred's gaze switched to Paul, his eyes wide as if inquiring something.

Lilian noticed Paul's slight shake of his head. "Is something wrong?" she asked.

"No, no." Uncle Fred gave a cheery laugh, coming over to Paul and resting an arm around his shoulder. He squeezed his side in a fatherly manner. "I'm just happy to see the both of you looking the way you do tonight. Like fine adults."

"And both so handsome together. One would think them bride and groom."

"*Aunt Krishta.*"

"*Mrs. Truit.*"

They spoke chastely, the two of them. Lilian looked at Paul for a second as she pondered his reaction. When he returned the look, she turned her face away.

"Oh, dear," Aunt Krishta giggled. Her aunt did love to say things to stir up discomfiture. She turned on the lamp beside the sofa they had pushed back, adding more light to the room. Then she came up to Lilian, taking her to the sofa for a sit while Uncle Fred started to speak with Paul.

"How was your night?"

"Alright."

"You're going to have to say more than that. Did you not talk with the other debutantes?"

Lilian fiddled with her fingers. Those girls were always so indifferent to her. Lilian never understood why she felt shunned. She knew that whether she was present or not, no one would care. And if any of the ladies did have something to say to her, it was a reminder of the ties between their fathers and her uncle. A reminder that her importance hung in his reputation. "I did," was all she said.

Her aunt clicked her tongue. "Oh." She rubbed Lilian's back maternally. "If it'd been fate, they would welcome you into their hearts."

Lilian frowned. "If I am not liked, then I shall be a disgrace."

"Do not say such things," Aunt Krishta urged. "Look at me."

Lilian resentfully drew her gaze to her aunt's wisteria eyes. Eyes that called out the shame in her after realizing what her remark entailed.

"Am *I* a disgrace?"

Hearing her aunt's question, Lilian felt like she was horrid for even thinking what she'd thought. "No, of course not."

Her aunt gave a small grin, taking the hand of her noble niece. "You are special, Lilian. You have nothing to prove."

"But I do not feel—"

Krishta interjected with a calm hush, "El will prove you to them. They may never like you, but they *shall* respect you." She leaned her head forward. "But your uncle and I, no matter what, will always love you. So why would you ever think you are a disgrace?"

As Lilian's mind dwelled on that wise deliberation, she conceded her worry and embraced her darling aunt.

"Lilian?"

Lilian ended their hug, regarding Paul who was kneeling before her. "Paul? What are you doing?"

"What am I doing?" he repeated her. Then asked it genuinely, "What *am* I doing?" as he turned his face to Uncle Fred for a brief second, then quickly to Lilian again. He smiled at her nervously.

Lilian drew in her chin. "Are you alright?"

"I am." He slipped his hands around hers. Lapis eyes, taking in the sight of hers. Making her almost forget her relatives' grins. "Lilian, I know I'll have to go soon. To fulfill my..." A soft cough from Uncle Fred interrupted Paul's speech.

"Yes?" Lilian said.

Paul swallowed. "Well, what I mean to say is that I..." He trailed off again as Uncle's coughs continued.

"Go on," Lilian encouraged, leaning forward as much as propriety would allow.

"I think it would be best if we..."

Sharp coughs persisted.

"If we what?" Lilian urged.

The final startling hack of her uncle shook the atmosphere in the room. He was impossible to ignore. "Uncle Fred?"

Paul shook his head with pressed lips. "I can't do this," he said as he stood up and rushed to the French doors of the sitting room then let himself out.

"Paul, wait!" Lilian stood to her feet and followed him. She caught him at the front door. "Paul! Does his coughing really bother you that much?"

The back of Paul's tailored tuxedo faced her. His hand held the cold iron knob. Slowly, he turned and faced her, apparent worry tightened his face. "It's not just a cough."

"What?" Lilian paused warily for him to explain though he would not. "Do you know something?"

Paul's gaze lifted above her. "Just pray for him. Your prayers always seem to work."

Something about what he said inflicted fear upon her. She was still, staring at him with a question she did not want to ask. She could tell he'd be unwilling to answer. He seemed to be *frequently* hesitant to answer her tonight.

"Paul." Lilian hesitantly reached for his hand, wanting to feel the warmth of it again. Her fingers slipped between his. She whispered, "Elspeed."

Paul's expression relaxed. He turned up a grin as something like sorrow clouded his eyes. "I will see you tomorrow."

"Are you sure you won't be too busy?"

"I'm sure."

Lilian smiled sweetly. "Then I'll see you." She felt a tad dissatisfied to let go of his hand, but did. Of all the people she knew, she wondered what impression she made on Paul the most. Did he see her as a lady or the same uncultured child she used to be?

As he shut the door behind himself, she let out a solemn breath. Back to the sitting room, she walked…. But she could hardly enter when she noticed something terrible. She gasped, looking at the blood dotting her uncle's fist.

Gracie, who had been standing in the corner by the pianoforte, was the first to act. "Master Truit." She pulled out a handkerchief. "I'll get that for you."

Aunt Krishta beckoned to Lilian. "Well, don't just stand there. Come in."

Lilian knew her aunt was making an effort to dismiss the situation. But she was too distraught to enter the room. "No, I... I think I'll go upstairs. I'm... tired."

Aunt Krishta frowned but nodded. So she ran upstairs to her bedroom.

Lilian's legs gave out as she made it to her room. She fell upon her bed, clinging to the bedspread. She buried her face in it, smelling the jasmine aroma it was sprayed in. She shook her head at the unacceptable notions about her uncle whispering through her mind.

"It's alright," she asserted. "Everything is alright. I just..." she lifted her head, catching her distressed look in the gloomy sheen of the mirror, "need to get ready for bed."

She approached the vanity and sat down, taking her hair out of its coiffure. She took hold of her boar-bristle brush and brushed her raven curls in long strokes, consciously keeping them from touching the floor. For they were that long. She aimed to not only draw out oils with the brushing action but the thoughts revolving in her head. Yes... this always calmed her.

She turned her face from her miserable reflection. Away from her globular eyes carried over from her mother. For inside them was this enigmatic glint she never understood. It meant something, she knew. Like some kind of mark placed on her by El. This mark of specialness. A curse that kept her from being who she wanted to be— an accepted member of society. And that was all it seemed to do.

Paul was wrong. Her prayers of late had not worked. She had prayed many a time for her uncle to heal from his sickness, thinking it was merely a prolonged cold that carried its way from spring to winter. Yet she knew something had been amiss. However, she hadn't sensed it as anything dire. At least that was not what the doctor had imparted.

By the time she was dressed in her nightgown, she was afraid to slip into her sheets. Afraid to sleep while the image of her uncle's blood was still fresh in her mind.

Then Lilian heard a sound. The sound of footsteps. She watched the door. As expected, in came Uncle Fred. His silhouette stood there in the doorway, studying her face.

"I hope you were not taken aback by what you saw," he said.

Lilian swallowed before saying, "I know it's nothing, right? It's just blood. When have I ever been afraid of blood?"

"Lilian, it's alright. Tell me."

Uncle Fred's words freed her to let a tear loose, then another, till she could no longer see beyond her watery eyes. She covered her eyes with her hands and sobbed. Uncle walked closer and brought her into a hug. He picked her up and sat down on the bed, holding her like a baby. Her hair, dragging across the floor. He waited till she was ready to talk.

Finally, gulping, she said, "Uncle. Are you going to die?" Then she buried her face in his chest to avoid seeing his reaction. She said it. It was in the air now.

"I cannot say," she heard him say. "I will let El deal with me as he sees fit."

"But El knows I need you."

"Oh, Lilian. There is still so much I want to teach you. So much you do not know. But I cannot forget how alike we are. You have what it takes to learn what you need. You are slow to act, and you adhere to the teachings of Shersul. You are everything your aunt and I hoped you would be."

And she was not a fool either. "You're saying goodbye." She looked up at him.

"I am saying all that I'm saying."

She put her head down again and stared at the wall. She tried to change the subject. "I spoke to Julia tonight. She says Mr. Dorvan is considering—"

"Pulling out. I know."

"Why does it seem like we are being... shunned."

Uncle Fred sighed. "I told you Lilabug. Polite society may seem glamorous, but the reality is a bunch of pompous, legalistic..." He stopped himself in an effort not to— Lilian believed— spoil her fantasy. She knew that a fantasy was all it was, but it hurt to think that she could be excommunicated from what pleasures high society did have to offer.

Uncle Fred continued. "I want you to understand something, Lilian. Knowing this will help you when you are your own woman. I came from a time in which people flourished in silence. No one cared about what you agree with as much as who you are or what you have done. But I believe now there is a demand for us to wear our beliefs on our sleeves. And we must meet that demand."

"I don't understand."

"I think you do." Uncle Fred exhaled through his nose while in careful consideration for the next words he would say. "There are many things, Lilian, I regret not fighting for. People in my life I should have tried harder to reach. I was never really a zealot for anything, even those I loved. But I believe that when you were born, El intended for you to succeed where I have failed. Though not really a fighter, you have the forte of enduring quite a lot from people. It is what I admire about you the most. You can suffer long with someone. And I want you to stay that way. I do. But I know that in time, you will finally know enough about people. Your girlish dreams shall fade. And you shall tolerate less from them because you know so much."

"But Uncle Fred. Just how bad can it all be?"

"I'm afraid... I cannot say."

Lilian pondered his words even though she was still unsure why he said them. She soon gave up on thinking about it and simply let herself indulge in his embrace. She tried to remember everything about her uncle. His agreeable smell, the comfort in his voice, and his unwaning love for those that mattered to him. She keened her side to the heartbeat pulsing in his chest, praying silently that it would never stop.

After some time, Fredrick finally left. Lilian strolled to her window and gazed at the view of their garden. The blue light of the moon poured into her room. She had the feeling she should try again to make her will known to El.

She whispered, "El, you know what I need and desire. Why does it feel like nothing goes the way I need it to? Help me understand." She closed her eyes and said, "For Shersul's sake."

Vicissitude

Lilian woke to the caw of a crow. Her eyes blinded a moment by the white light through the window drenching her room. It may have been a Sunday morning, but something in the air unsettled her. A dangerous notion rested in the front of her mind, unwaning. She quickly jumped out of bed and ran downstairs to see if what she felt was true. The further she scuffed, the better she could hear what sounded like a wheezy cry. Her heart dipped a moment.

"Aunt Krishta?" Lilian called. She came around the left corner, and through the kitchen to her relatives' door. Gracie was nowhere to be found, probably hanging the laundry. The crying stopped as her footsteps were detected. Lilian knocked on the door.

"Aunt Krish—" her aunt cracked open the door, and by the expression on her face smeared with tear streaks, Lilian had an idea of what happened. The room seemed to have muddled around her, like she had been plunged underwater. She was ready to burst into tears, but that would mean admitting to a truth she wasn't ready for. The dangerous thought began to ring a little louder in her heart. It rippled through her like small, taunting waves of emotion, causing a shiver through her spine and pounding in her chest. Aunt Krishta opened the door wider, revealing the master bed. And in it, a lifeless Fredrick Truit.

Lilian's aunt tried to bring her further into the room, but Lilian shook her head and recoiled.

"Mm, mm. No." She shook her head then dropped to her knees by the doorway.

Krishta crouched beside her. "Lilabug—"

"No, get away. I'm fine," she said in a highly controlled tone. Her sight switched from her lap to the floor repeatedly as the truth settled itself in her mind. Her eyes widened with the realization. "No. It's not true. It's not true." Her breaths quickened. She lifted her gaze at her aunt.

"Lilian."

"It's not true!"

Krishta leaned in, and Lilian met her with a fast hug. Sobs of agony filled the room. Lilian couldn't— she wouldn't— accept it. How could she possibly believe that her uncle wasn't there in the room, hearing their every noise? How could she let go of the one most dear to her? She could hardly breathe.

Then she heard a sobering sound. It made a raucous in her mind, shaking the walls of the room, at least to her. She could have sworn that the picture frames on the wall by her aunt's vanity were vibrating violently, about to fall and break. In fact, the vanity, bed, everything shook with the sound. It was the sound of a train whistle. And she knew in that moment that the hidden realm's train of fire— the kindlum— had arrived for her uncle's soul to take him away to the waiting place that he may one day reach Aversum. By the second that the powerful chug of it waned, she knew there was nothing more to cry about.

Lilian carefully handled her aunt, moving her off of her. She then stood up and wiped her cheeks. She walked over to the bed. A bucket of acid vomit fumed by the bedside, testifying to how he had retched all night. The sight of a pale-faced Uncle before her. His eyes were closed. But his mouth rested open. Lilian tried to envision a colorful him. The one that smiled every morning and kissed her forehead every night.

There was no sound from her now. No emotion. For, it was all depleted at the doorway. Lilian raised a hand to his face but retracted. Would she dare to feel his cold, pale skin? No. No more proof was needed. "He's gone."

Three Days Later

The funeral was slow. It was on a rather bright day, which irked Lilian. But when she gave it a thought, Uncle Fred would have wanted it to be on a lovely day.

It was on this day, she realized who those 'other relations' were. In all truth, Lilian had never built a real rapport with her extended family. Whatever faces she might have seen in her early childhood were all forgotten. It was a lot of 'well-wishes from Cousin Who and Aunt What's-Her-Name'.

There were also reporters who came. Aunt Krishta had surprisingly not rebuked them, and Lilian knew why. Aunt Krishta wanted everyone to know just how important her husband was. She had even invited all members of the small church in Corlu. There was nothing too intimate about the occasion, and nothing too drab, either.

Lilian could not help but wonder if her uncle would make headlines or just a short appearance in the obituaries, but he had ought to be given some kind of veneration for his contribution to society. No matter what anyone said about him, Truit & Co. manufactured the best lathes of the age. It was a shame that all of his progress would be put to a halt.

During the reception, which began closer to noon, it felt strange having all of those unfamiliar faces in her home (scrutinizing her home).

"Hmm, it's not the biggest of manors, but it's charming," said one individual Lilian watched from above the banister. She knew that eventually she could not hide away from the crowd, though she wanted very much to.

"They definitely went the Spartan route, didn't they?" his friend joked.

"Yes, well, inside this plain wooden box," the first boy said, raising up his cane and waving it slowly about the area, "is gold. Gold for those fortunate enough to be a relation of Fredrick Truit."

With the mention of such motives, Lilian came plopping down the stairs. The two young men looked at her.

"Oh. Lilian, is it? We were just admiring your quarters."

"Oh, yes. That *did* look like admiring, didn't it?" she said sarcastically.

They gave each other a look. One cleared his throat. "So, how are you coping?"

"Slowly. I've managed. How about you?"

They were not sure what to say.

"I'm teasing."

They both laughed in relief. Then the one with the cane said, "So, my mother has told me about you, Miss Lilian. That you've recently debuted."

Lilian squinted. "Has she? And who exactly is your mother?"

"Why, your grandmother, Gladys."

Lilian's eyebrows shot up as she observed the young man who was a couple years younger than herself. She was moved to chuckle a little. "That would make you my uncle."

He smiled. "Yes. My father, Geoffrey De Leon, has been Mother's second husband."

"You're kidding. Did she tell you much about Uncle Fredrick?"

"Sometimes. If she was ever disappointed enough in me to spiel about him."

Lilian understood well. Her uncle's shoes were hard to fill.

"Lilian, dear," Aunt Krishta called as she approached. She had made herself well-donned in black with some choices of jewelry, yet appeared as the most modest thing among the gathering. *Plain enough to look solemn, and adorned enough to seem resilient*, her aunt had told her. "We're about to start reading the will."

Lilian wasn't sure why her aunt decided to do the reading on the day of the funeral, but alas, into the sitting room she went. Her aunt took a seat in the armchair facing every figure in the space. Only one reporter was allowed in the room. He sat on the arm of the sofa with a notepad and pencil. Beside him, sitting respectfully, was Pastor Hemmings and his family. Lilian was most glad to see them.

There were many dark heads about the room whom Lilian did not know. Though it was apparent by their features that they all had Truit blood in them. All the men, even the old ones, were nearly tall and dastardly. While the women were fairly average in height and ranged in various degrees of 'well-endowed'.

One particular maiden, well past her first bloom, was a woman in a black-veiled hat. Behind the veil, one could make out her bodacious features; her heavy-lidded eyes, sharp cupid's bow, and overall lush appearance. She was most likely tall when standing, but for now she was sitting. Like some mysterious doll surveying the room over her Roman nose. She demanded Lilian's intrigue.

And beside her, was the inarguable matron of the family, Gladys De Leon, formerly Gladys Truit. She was a mature beauty with silver streaking her hair. An air of tolerance for little more than propriety was detectable around her. Even now as her face rested, it was not hard to see her rearing and scolding her children into the successful adults they came to be.

The last person Lilian noticed stuck out to her like a rose in a briar. Standing against the floral, green curtain on the left corner of the room, near the pianoforte, was Paul. He didn't lift his head at Lilian when she came in. It seemed like he was deep in thought. Like someone ushered him into a room he was not aware to be standing in or why.

"Now, everyone," the attorney announced, "I understand this is the part of the ceremony you've all *really* been waiting for."

A light laughter was drawn.

"And, it is with great honor, that I read to you this will here," the attorney pulled a sheet of paper out of his case, "which has been verified as Fredrick Truit's own writing. His wish for how the fortune shall be distributed. While you sip your wine, I want everyone to be respectful to the family and accepting of the words penned down plain and simple."

Everyone became hushed while the attorney began to read:

I, Frederick Truit, of sound mind, without external influences or pressures, do hereby declare this to be my final will and testament. I make this disposition of my estate to ensure that my wishes are carried out upon my passing...

I bequeath my cherished lathe factory, along with all its assets and associated properties, to my beloved niece's husband. Which is a union I believe is not far from being established...

At the mention of a husband, everyone's surprised gaze fell upon Lilian. She coiled under their eyes, feeling an awkwardness after she glimpsed once at Paul's distant gaze.

Why did her uncle have to write something so presumptuous in his will?

It is my fervent hope that he will continue its operations with integrity and dedication, honoring the legacy it represents. If for any reason he declines, then it shall be my wife's responsibility to handle or defer.

The remaining estate, including investments, financial accounts, and personal property, shall be inherited by my devoted wife, Krishta Truit. It is my belief that she possesses the strength and wisdom to manage and distribute these assets in accordance with our shared values.

I hereby leave my mother, Gladys De Leon, and my sister, Barbra Truit, a generous portion of my wealth and other valuable possessions as a token of my love and gratitude. I trust that they will utilize these resources to enrich their lives and the lives of those around them.

Lilian caught a smirk coming from the lady under the veil, which gave her reason to assume that she was Barbra Truit.

It was the last paragraph that provoked a stir in the room when the attorney finally read:

Lastly, to right a wrong on behalf of the family name. I want to ensure a comfortable lifestyle for my long-denied niece... Tessaline Truit, if she may choose it.

"Sorry, could you read that last part a second time?" insisted Lilian. Surely her uncle did not misspell her name.

"Uh," said the attorney, "It says, 'Lastly, to right a wrong on behalf of the family name—'"

"No need to restate it," the matron interrupted. A scorn settled on her face. "We all heard it clear as day. I knew when I got here there would be some mess stirring up."

Krishta responded, "Is that so? It seems to me the only stirring is in your tone, ma'am."

"*You* must have put him up to this. You did befriend her mother once."

"The will says, 'without external influence'. My husband grieved *with* me when I concluded my friendship with Marian."

Gladys smirked. "Your husband." She muttered what everyone heard, "My son."

Lilian tapped her aunt's shoulder. "But who is Tessaline? I don't understand."

Aunt Krishta's adversarial stare remained on her mother-in-law, though the rest of her was relaxed in the comfy chair.

She made an exquisite effort to keep her calm even as all their eyes regarded her with contempt. "Fredrick's choice is his to make. I do hope we can all accept what is written plain and simple."

"But who is—" Lilian quickly stopped herself from prying.

"She is irrelevant," the veiled woman spoke so everyone could hear the velvety sound of her voice. "And she shall be treated as such like always." A chuckle rose from her chest. "Honestly, why are we acting like it matters? Is Tessaline Truit present in this room?" Her head moved from side to side demonstratively. "Do any of you even know where the girl is nowadays? That's what I thought. She is just as unimportant as she ever was."

As the hour of conclusion was approaching, the guests retreated outside to engage in some conversations and be up to date with each other.

Lilian continued to distance herself from the others, holding her breath for them to leave. Though, she kept an eye on the lady in the veil whom she could have sworn to have seen glancing her way a few times with something in mind to say. After making sure Aunt Krishta was not overwhelmed— which she did not seem to be as she spoke with Pastor Hemmings and his wife— Lilian escaped to their orchard.

She was happy to rest among the orange and apple trees that were in season this late November. The air had finally shown a coolness in the past few days. She breathed it in deeply, not wanting to escape this moment of silence.

Lilian came to the slope of the hill, peering down at the valley. Therein lie the narrow path to the lake where Shersul would take her to fish. He often took those moments to teach her life lessons. Of course, she was too young at the time to fully comprehend his words. But those had been the best years of her life. She never could feel that same bliss she once felt when Shersul had been around.

He had promised her that she would still have the Elwind watching over her. But the Elwind had long ago stopped speaking to her. Perhaps it had to do with her busyness after being enrolled in school. There were quite enough voices juggling in her mind to keep focus on El's. But she had hoped that the time she spent at church would make up for it. It didn't. Eventually, she just became numb to the silence, seeing as it was for the best.

However, standing on this hill, she could not help but miss the days when she knew El almost as well as He knew her. It would have been nice for the Hidden Father to show himself since her uncle, the one earthly father she knew, was dead.

She turned her gaze eastward. In her mind's eye, she caught a glimpse of some familiar set of eyes lurking in the leaves. With a returning whip of her head, she gasped. "Tarfwin?"

The mirage was gone. Again.

"Who are you shouting at?" Paul Partridge said as he moved closer behind her. She turned around to see him holding one of their apples in his palm.

She smirked, even at the sadder him, who somehow looked even more handsome this way. "I'm surprised you actually came today."

Instead of responding in kind, Paul's expression hardened. "What do you mean by that? You think I don't care about Mr. Truit, my dearest mentor?"

Lilian immediately apologized. "Oh Paul, that wasn't what I meant. I was only teasing, you know."

He still seemed offput, taking a bite of his apple. "Well, it's an odd time to tease."

"Your right. Forgive me, I..." She stared at the white rose placed in his vest pocket. A silent reminder of death. "How are you? I saw you at the open casket. You looked like you were about to erupt right there in the room."

"I was not about to erupt."

Lilian's eyes fell to the hem of her dress. "Sorry. I... I don't know what I'm saying." She scolded herself mentally for having managed a steady line of insults to his character.

Paul's gaze drifted over her. "I can't believe he's truly gone, Lil. I just can't."

"I know."

"Maybe.... If only he held on just a little longer, perhaps another year, I could've found a cure."

Lilian clasped his arm, causing him to release the apple. "No, Paul. It couldn't be helped." She knew in an instant how forward the action was when Paul looked down at her. His lovely, iridescent eyes pierced her soul. But there was something about his words that puzzled her. She released him. "Did you know?"

"Know what?"

Lilian gave him an earnest expression. "Paul, tell me the honest truth. Did you know that it was more than a cold?"

With the sight of his frown, she had her answer. And it drew a look of shock from her. The appalling awakening made her stumble back. She would have nearly tumbled down the hill had he not grabbed her.

"Careful, Lil."

She pushed him away. Stepping backward now into a tree. She leaned upon it, her eyes watching the boy she thought could never keep a secret so critical from her. "Why did you not tell me?"

"I was sworn to secrecy."

"I thought we didn't keep secrets." A slight quaver laced her words.

Paul gave her a look of utter regret. "I wanted to tell you, believe me. But when your uncle rathered you be free of that burden—"

"You really think it would have changed anything had I known? You think I cannot conceal my sorrow? You think I'd let my uncle know that I knew he was going to die?" Her composure broke with struggled words. "You think I'm weak?" Lilian hid her loose tears behind her arm.

"Weak? Oh, Lilian." He advanced over to her and forced on her his delightful embrace. Like always, she took to him without resistance. His fingers stroked the back of her neck. "I could never think that about you. You are anything but weak." He pulled her out to look at her face. "But just look at you now. You're all out of sorts. Couldn't even hide your jealousy at the reading."

"Jealousy?" Lilian whined in disagreement.

"Yes. In the will, when he mentioned another niece." Paul put his hand on the side of Lilian's face, smoothing a thumb over the tear on her bottom eyelid. He smirked. "I saw the narrowing of your eyes."

He then placed the back of his other hand on her forehead. "Your head got a little hot, didn't it?"

Lilian grinned as he ascertained her the way a doctor would. She didn't want him to stop touching her. His eyes suddenly began a pert twinkle. "And so did your chest." The last touch he made sent her blood coursing. It was the most polite rest of a hand on the black lace of her wool bodice. "All of which signals jealousy."

Lilian was taken out of her senses. She could bask there in his shadow. But the cool breeze snapped her into awareness. "I was not jealous. Just confused. If this Tessaline Truit is my cousin, and matters enough to be in his will, how had I not heard of her? And why is no one willing to talk about her?"

"Hm, that may be something to ask your aunt." Paul lifted his hand from her chest and walked in the direction of the manor. "Shall we stay out here for the rest of the evening or say goodbye to the guests?"

Lilian joined him, taking hold of his waiting arm. As they walked back toward the gathering, she continued to ponder on the name Tessaline Truit.

Tess shot her pistol for the seventh time. She aimed at the targets she had set up for herself. Whenever her gun got loud, the forest quieted, and the trees trembled. But it made no difference every powerful bang that jolted her arms, or the end release of her finger on the trigger. Nothing would release her from the memory that had chased her through the years. The day that everything in her life changed.

Nothing could make her forget the shouting behind a bedroom door the moment after her father ushered her pregnant mother in. *Tessaline remembered watching the clock silently in the main room of the apartment, singing to herself. Waiting in tearful prayer and wanting very much to see her mother. To comfort her. To know if she was alright.*

The screams and cries only prolonged for two hours. Until finally, they stopped, giving precedence to the less mature, tiny, filtered cries of an infant. Tess couldn't help but wonder why she only heard one baby crying. Then her father stepped out from behind the door. A mystery swaddled in his arms. Slowly, he crept over to Tessaline. She stood enthusiastically from her bench seat. "Papa!"

"Shh. Come see your sister."

Tessaline's mouth formed an O. She was certain it would be a boy. Her father bent slightly down, tilting his arms so Tessaline could see. A peek of dark hair became visible. With two fingers, she pulled his arms lower. In astonishment, she gasped quietly and smiled. This was the little one who'd caused her mother such pain?

The baby in her father's arms resembled nothing of her and her mother and everything of him. It was kind of funny because Tess resembled her mother in every way and not her father. And the difference was stark.

The baby gained a button nose, raven curls, and eyes so dark they were considerably black.

And from Tess's mother, she gained a slender nose, silver eyes (though her mother's were a light blue), and bone straight hair the whitest shade of blonde.

Even through their differences, Tessaline felt a strong connection to the child. For she had asked her mother before the labor if she thought she would make a great big sister. Her mother told her she had no doubt in her mind, and that the moment the baby was born Tessaline wouldn't doubt either. Now, she felt it. That sisterly urge or rather instinct to protect the little one at all cost. No longer was she alone. She had a friend.

Felix gently handed the baby over to her older sister. She flinched only a little. She was a big one, heavy too. But Tessaline was determined not to drop her, even though a feeling inside her made her want to jump in giddiness. The little one breathed slowly in and out her nose. She smelled like strawberries and chocolate. Tessaline put her nose on the baby girl's shiny hair.

"What's her name?" inquired her to her father whose gaze was ever pensive and in the doldrums.

He looked down at his daughter. Opened his mouth. And the memory ended there. Always before he could say her name.

As Tess stared into the distance, gun pointed ahead of her, a gloved hand slid over hers. She swiftly turned around and was met with a freckled face. Above his angular cheeks were eyes so gentle they seemed to be stuck in a forever squint. His lips, a modest shape, and hair such a striking shade of red. But even while knowing her target, her barrel remained directed at him. Her cold expression, unshaken.

"So what— ya gonna shoot me, now?"

"Maybe."

"But I'm too pretty to die," Jase playfully bemoaned.

"Yeah, but I think you're annoying enough to shoot."

He smirked, daring to come closer and press his pigeon chest up to the barrel. "And what would you do with me after?"

Tess looked at the ground then back at him. "Use you as fertilizer."

"Yeah right." He pushed her hand away. The pistol dropped to the leafy ground. Then he scooped an arm around her waist and pulled her close to him. He pressed his mouth on hers and moaned contently as he tasted her ruby lips. Tess couldn't fight it, taken by his charm. Detaching his lips from hers, he gave her a look that told her enough to say, "No."

"I didn't even say anything."

"You didn't have to. You're givin' me that look again."

"What look?" His hands moved around her back and he squeezed her closer, acting ignorant of what she meant.

"That 'Today, I'll ask her to marry me, and she might actually say yes' look."

"*Will* she say yes?"

"I already answered that."

His gaze grew hollow. Without anything to say about it, Jase let go of her and changed the subject. "Have you been practicing for tonight?"

"Yes. Have you?"

"Of course. I'll show you." He demonstrated by jumping up and grabbing onto a nearby branch, then swinging into flight and landing on the other side. "See? Still got it."

"Mm, it looked a little—"

"A little what?" he said, while stepping toward her with daring eyes.

"Heavy."

"I'll show you heavy." Tess did not expect his arms as they quickly scooped her up. She guffawed as he ran with her back to their little house in the clearing.

"You forgot my gun!" she squealed. But he didn't hear her.

Resolution

Lilian had been made privy to her aunt's plans for the following week which seemed to expand by the increase of minutes: She would need to meet in person with the factory executives in Brord and learn about the current economic and financial status of the company to conjecture their future profits and hopefully create a decent growth plan.

In the meantime, the most immediate anticipation would be the scheduled dinner with their shareholders and suppliers. Which was passed on to Lilian's ears as 'another grueling night in which she would be obligated to entertain a room of testy, old men'.

She understood the critical importance of it, but if they had to entertain any more people in their humble villa, she was sure she'd lose her shrewdness altogether; something she could not afford to do.

While it was still the afternoon, Lilian and her aunt sat together on their back patio. They had not gone anywhere public since the... ordeal. It took everything in Lilian just to leave the confines of her room.

Aunt Krishta drank her lemonade while re-reading the bullet-points on her to-do list. Her forehead, now showing eleven lines that were not noticeable before to Lilian. A sigh came out of her. "I shall have to go into town for the cake and restock the pantry for tonight."

Lilian laid her hand on her aunt's. "Can Gracie do it?"

Aunt Krishta frowned. "Lilian, Gracie will be busy with her own chores. She'll be needing our help to prepare."

"Well then, can I come with you?"

Krishta laughed. "You're asking to leave the house? I must be in a dream. If only I had known that mentioning errands would have you feeling venturous again."

Lilian took a second to rethink her words, then sat back in her seat, realizing she really did not want to leave. She shook her head. "Never mind."

"Well, what's gotten you all unstable?"

"Just... not quite ready. For any of it," she mumbled. Lilian could tell her aunt was frowning even more at the way her niece seemed to be in a quandary. She wondered how it wasn't the same for Aunt Krishta or Gracie. How were they so able to move forward dutifully? "Do you think you can actually do it? Run the factory?"

Her aunt slowly nodded. "I must. I understand that it is not conventional for a lady. But we are under significant circumstances. And I must." Aunt Krishta leaned forward, taking hold of Lilian's hand again. "Your uncle trusted me with this responsibility, with his home, his assets, because we were of the same mind. And until I find someone else suitable for the job—"

"Like... my husband?"

Aunt Krishta's gaze went still.

Lilian continued. "What exactly did Uncle mean when he wrote that?" Lilian could see that her aunt was guilty by the way she shifted her seat.

"Oh, you know how we feel about the idea of you and Paul. And we had expected that.... Well, that night of your debut, he was supposed to..."

Lilian finished her aunt's blatant thought. "Propose?"

Her aunt was silent.

"*That* is what he said he couldn't do. You were *forcing* him." Lilian scooted out her chair and stood up.

"Now, dear. Don't be so dramatic."

"You made him get on one knee," the niece accused. "I can't believe you would do something so..." Lilian stopped before uttering the word 'foolish'. "You made me— each of us— look desperate."

"Oh, enough of that!" Her aunt stood up as well. "I am sure I didn't raise you to be taken for granted. Just how long shall he make you wait for the inevitable, Lilian? Say what you will, but your uncle only wanted to ensure your security before he left us."

"Before he…? When did he tell you he was going to die? Because he never once told me."

Her aunt's expression went grave. "It was far too late when he told even me."

Lilian laid a hand on her chest. Her breath was gaining weight the more she dwelled on the sadness. She was angry but not sure who that anger was directed at. "I think… I need a moment alone."

"And I understand that you do. You may go." With a sigh, she added, "But hopefully, by the time you return, you will be in a disposition tolerable for dinner."

Lilian began to walk past Aunt Krishta but paused with one more question in mind. "Will I have to speak to any of them?"

Her aunt scoffed. "Of course. You wanted to be an adult."

With that, she took off across the field toward the hedge maze. A place where tall green borders dissected tiled spaces and pathways. A place— much like the tracks— where she could hide.

The path, though narrow with tightly coupled walls, wasn't too devious, and she had gone through it so often before that she knew how to get to the very center. The center was a reserved area where an ensemble of a table and garden chairs had been placed for the benefit of recuperation and reward. There was a time when the family would spend birthdays and holidays doing scavenger hunts or races to the center to then indulge in the display of sweets and refreshments Gracie snuck there. *Ah, yes*, Lilian thought gloomily. *What fun that was.*

She was amused to take a seat. Her mind was as silent as her mouth. She listened to the tintinnabulation of the wind chimes that were hung on a wooden pole's hook. She started pondering her duty as an heiress and wondered what exactly she was wasting her time for in the manor. There was nothing for her in the rural fields of Corlu nor the bustling streets of Hiplum. In both, she remained insignificant and alone.

The name her uncle had written in his will was once again spoken in her mind. Whoever this elusive Tessaline Truit was, Lilian imagined she must know a thing about loneliness considering her excommunication from the family. And as for the reason for that, Lilian wanted very much to know. Although, she was not the type of girl to confront people, much less her aunt. "I wonder if Aunt Krishta has plans to notify Tessaline of her inheritance. It isn't right not to. Even if her whereabouts are unknown, someone should try to reach her."

Lilian had no idea why she had allowed the thought of the mystery person to bend her mind. After all, her name was only mentioned within one single sentence. But she felt like it must have been important because her uncle had willingly offended all who were still living on this girl's behalf.

"'To right a wrong on behalf of the Truit family'," Lilian recited. "I wonder if she was never acknowledged by the family because of misbehavior or poverty. And whether it was *her* misbehavior and poverty or her *parents*. And who would her parents be? A *cousin* or *sibling* to my uncle? No, it couldn't have been a sibling. He only had two and one of them is dead with me as his only child while the other is a spinster. Oh, and then there's the extra one who is much younger than me, so yes it would have to be a cousin. Did my grandmother ever have siblings or would Tessaline be my cousin three times re...?" Then her thoughts seemed to run into a wall, and whatever was beyond that wall, she could not access. She started to think Paul was right about her being out of sorts.

She raised her face at the sky which was turning maroon as the sun sank. How long had she been sitting there? It did not deter her, however, from asking one more question that was frequent in her mind. And this time she did not speak to herself. "El, please speak to me. Tell me why you had to do it. Why did you have to take him from us, from me? You took my father before I could talk, Shersul before I had any friends, and now my uncle before I could learn how to live. Who next?" She immediately regretted that question as the image of Paul's beautiful face entered her mind. "I don't see how I deserve this. I *don't* deserve it."

Lilian put her forehead upon the latticed iron surface of the table. She could feel the wind that passed through the singing chimes stronger against her back. "Wind is so strange," Lilian moped as she began another line of thought. "It comes, it goes.

Without warning. Much like your Elwind." She stood up angrily from her seat, this time not looking up but forward into the atmosphere as her eyes clouded with tears. "And you wonder why we are so polite."

The guests entered the manor at around 5:40 p.m. By then all the women of the house were prepared and well-dressed, Gracie included. She was allowed to pick a nice brooch from Aunt Krishta's room to go with her uniform black shirtwaist and frilly white apron.

As for Aunt Krishta, she opted for a modest choker and black velvet gown. It did not take much for her to look radiant even in mourning.

Lilian often fancied she resembled her aunt. But while Lilian was more fleshy throughout and almost enchanting like an Aphrodite of Knidos, Krishta was better labeled as darling and matronly. The best Lilian could do was try to match her aunt's simplistic garb with her own made of heavy silk that was ruched at the hips and gathered to one hip-side.

In her mind, it was much simpler than her usual inclination. But any fit that managed to drape romantically around her figure was much too distracting. This proved to be true now as the investors, who at times would engage each other on business matters with confident ease, immediately became hostile whenever poor Lilian offered them wine or an understanding of the schedule while standing a little too close.

She, however, took it as a response to her aiding them poorly. Lilian was relieved when the food was fully prepared. It was now time for the men to enter the dining room. Gracie escorted them through the cream doors leading to an annexed space with walls clad in a chocolate-colored textile. A mirror on the wall faced the entrance so that they entered with a quick look at themselves. Nearly every head either bore silver hair or was catching.

But there was one still richly auburn in accordance with his absent daughter's. Lilian caught sight of him with a tight expression. It was Mr. Dorvan, Julia's father. His money had been a great component to Truit & Co.'s success. They couldn't afford to lose him.

Aunt Krishta was the first to take her seat at the long table. The rest followed with the hostess. As Lilian started drawing out her chair, the man beside her beat her to it. She smiled in gratitude. "Thank you, sir."

The old man returned a nod before sitting.

From the new view, the men were slightly less intimidating to Lilian. She could now be discriminatory with the impressions of each face rather than see them as a mass of figures standing tall and wide as they had in the foyer. Now the intimidation came with their non-telling stares. Though without signaling their thoughts, Lilian had an idea they were all brimming with questions and expectations. She began to look at her lap as their gazes remained on Krishta Truit, thinking, *What are we going to tell all these men?* In the best-intended way, she pitied her aunt.

Krishta Truit began, "I would like first to thank you all for coming and acknowledging us in this difficult time. My husband would be very pleased to know that all of you still care about this business."

Lilian could not help but notice the subtle tilt of Mr. Dorvan's head to her aunt's statement.

Krishta continued. "Sitting in front of you now, I wish I could tell you how grateful I am, truly. I understand that things may seem quite uncertain for us, more uncertain than they really are, in fact. However I want to assure you men— as much as a woman can—" she said this with a hand gesturing towards herself and a charming squint of the eyes that drew a light chuckle from the guests, "that the loss of Fredrick Truit does not equate to the loss of his vision, his hope, or his success."

She spoke with an unshaken elegance that half-surprised Lilian. "For the time being, I shall have paramount authority of Truit and Company. But I am not going into this with a new mind. Any of you with passively active wives may understand just how much time we women spend learning alongside our husbands. So, I know what you may be thinking is, 'can a woman run a factory?' And to that I would say…" her lavender eyes rested on Lilian's, "that whether I am of either sex, I can do very little without your help."

Lilian gazed at her aunt in wonder as she became acquainted with her confident poise. A trait that had no doubt always been there, but she seemed to have often overlooked it.

"And that is why I believe you should continue to trust in our company, and I am giving my word that you will all yield a return comparable to what our history together has already yielded."

"Ms. Truit," Mr. Dorvan said. His voice was voluminously deep. "First of all, I want to give my condolences. El's tidings on your family. And I say this with the utmost respect, knowing well that Fredrick would not have chosen a wife that could do any less than carry out his vision with excellence. However, I think I speak for many of us by asking… 'Would you be able to do what he could not?'"

Lilian was puzzled by the vague question, though she could see that it was well understood by the men amongst each other.

"What he could not?" said her aunt.

"Yes."

"Care to explain, Mr. Dorvan?"

"Yes, ma'am. You see the world is changing, and I think it would be in our best interest to follow the trend. Many businesses in the past few months have gone to *deorsum*— excuse my crassness— but we are talking about old, trusted companies that we've all worked with." Many heads either bowed or nodded solemnly to his point. "Instead of following the trend that leads to failure, I say we follow the one that leads to coming out on top. Which is why I see no further reason to continue with Truit and Company unless it associates with Muggri Corp."

An applause was given in support of the man's idea.

Lilian's gaze switched to her aunt, wondering what her response would be. The man's argument had been convincing, and Lilian saw little— or honestly, no fault in it.

Aunt Krishta's disposition did not falter. She took a bite of her turkey, chewed slowly, then swallowed before saying, "Your sentiment is valid, Mr. Dorvan. I appreciate a candid opinion. And I want you to know that I move according to my own rationale, not my husband's."

"Yes, ma'am," he answered quickly to keep a good air about.

"But on this matter, Mr. Dorvan, he and I happened to be of the same mind."

Lilian shifted in her seat, taking bites of her salad with anticipation.

Her aunt continued. "The world *is* changing and progressing, which is why it needs lathes. And Truit and Company still boasts of having the best lathes in the country. When another factory is created, they come to us. So as long as there is still a high demand, we cannot even begin to discuss binding our business to a corporation whose influence may threaten our own."

"But who's to say you'll still be the best in ten years?"

Aunt Krishta seemed almost put out. Lilian noticed her leaning slightly forward in her seat. "Truit and Company is well-equipped with engineers who are working as we speak to improve upon the original design."

"However—"

"If we ever find ourselves superseded, *then* we can consider other options."

Mr. Dorvan was unable to respond to that.

"We shall stick to what has worked as a stone in a fluid stream." There was no flinch or falter. Her conclusion left no room for discussion and no err for critique.

While all the men stared in surprise, Lilian grinned with pride. With a strong desire to show her support, she lifted her glass and said sweetly, "A toast! To the future— the bright future of Truit and Company!"

Aunt Krishta met Lilian's gaze with expressed delight.

After a few seconds of no response, the man to her side lifted his glass. Then more were raised. They repeated in agreeance, "To the bright future of Truit and Company!"

When the guests had finally left the manor to its unbothered charm, Lilian started up the stairs.

"Lilian," Aunt Krishta called before she ascended half of the way.

"Yes, ma'am?"

"I love you."

Lilian smiled, feeling less of a desire to go to bed as she gazed at her aunt. She stepped down to meet her at the bottom. "I love you, too, Aunt Krishta." She leaned against the newel post. "And I have a confession to make."

Her aunt's brows lifted though she was not surprised.

"I doubted you," Lilian said. "I seem to be doing a lot of that now, and I'm sorry." She felt a heat of shame rising up her neck. "And when you spoke the way you did at dinner, well, I *was* proud."

Her aunt nodded. "Oh, I know you were, Lilian."

"But it also made me a little... sad." Her eyes turned down to look at her hands.

Aunt Krishta moved closer, resting her hand on the one Lilian had placed on the post. "Sad? Why?"

"I don't know. It's silly."

"Lilian, what's going on with you?"

"It's just so evident that you know your own mind. You know who you are. But I'm not so sure I know who I am anymore."

"*Lilian,*" her aunt said piteously while cupping her cheek with a delicate hand. "You are the same girl, the same genuine heart, the same determined mind you have always been."

Lilian wanted to agree fully. In a way she did, for it sounded true. Just not *as* true as it once did. But she decided not to make any more of an issue about it. "Goodnight, Aunt Krishta."

"Wait." Her aunt gently tugged her arm before she could turn away. "I have a suggestion that might appeal to you. There is a friend of mine. She runs an orphanage in Brord. A lovely old woman, Dalia Cora Witherman. And she is always looking for volunteers."

Lilian squinted, trying to grasp what her aunt was suggesting. "And you think I should be a volunteer? At an orphanage? In Brord?"

"I think it would be good for you to be part of something useful. And since I have plans to meet our workers on the outskirts of the village, it might be nice to have a look around. I haven't been there in so long."

Lilian took the words into consideration. The last thing she wanted to do was leave the Truit manor. However, she hated how stagnant her life currently seemed. Perhaps going to a new place and working around children *would* be good for her. "I do like the sound of it."

Krishta smiled. "I hoped you would. Quite timely for me to think of it, yes? Although, I doubt that I'll have any time to actually escort you there."

"Hmm? Then how will I—?"

Aunt Krishta tapped her forehead then lifted the finger out, signaling that another idea just came to mind. "Of course! You can go ahead of me."

"What?" Now Lilian was beginning to think her aunt was spouting out notions rashly. Did she want her to go unaccompanied? "With whom?"

"I'd just have to notify her of your arrival in advance. Oh, she will be shocked, I am sure, to hear from me."

"Aunt Krishta," Lilian urged, suppressing her yawn and sudden feeling of fatigue. "Go with whom?"

Her aunt eyed her coyly. So, the answer was clearly implied. But Lilian presumed nothing until her aunt finally said, "Why, with your friend, Paul Partridge."

Lilian started to shrug off the entire proposal. "No. He won't do it. And it would be inconsiderate of me to ask him." Again, she went up the steps, quickly this time.

"But Lilian…" her aunt pleaded.

"Aunt Krishta, he has his priorities in place."

Her aunt gave her an incredulous stare. She uttered plainly, "Then maybe you need to be his detour."

Lilian thought her aunt incorrigible. She even said it: "You're incorrigible." But at the same time, she could not help being amused at the woman's cleverness. And watching the smirk on her aunt's face, she knew that her remark was more of a lesson that might be worthy of reconsideration.

"Incorrigible?" Krishta scoffed. "Just how do you think I got your uncle? A man cannot see a diamond from a quartz if not given the time to appreciate it."

Lilian shook her head with a smile, proceeding unhindered to her room.

Away

"Now, you will take care of my niece, correct?"

Paul tipped his hat. "Of course, ma'am."

Aunt Krishta laid a hand on his shoulder, staring him straight in the eye. "You better. Because as of now she is all I have."

He looked downward, gulping down some emotion he felt.

"Well, besides Gracie," Krishta mentioned on a lighter note. She grinned at her maid, then kissed Paul's cheek.

Paul then went outside to wait for Lilian to finish saying goodbye. Lilian gave her aunt and maid a long hug each.

"You know, I told myself I would not cry," Aunt Krishta said, holding a handkerchief up to her cheek. "But my eyes betray me."

Lilian laughed softly. "Aunt Krishta, I am only going before you. You act as though we are parting forever."

Her aunt sniffed. "No, it's just the pain of knowing that one day you will."

"Don't." Lilian shrugged off the silly idea, kissing her aunt's rosy cheek. She put on her velvet coat and hat and, without another word, left her home.

Paul watched as Lilian slowly made her way to his automotive, still deciding whether or not she was committed. "Lilian?" he whispered. He never had to say too much to get her attention.

She turned to him, her face infused with gloom. Restful, elegant gloom. "I cannot help but feel a bit... queasy."

Paul's face showed a humdrum agreeance. She inched closer, being soon comforted by a gracious hug. When she was as ready as she could be, he picked her up and put her in then went around to the other side. As he settled in, rubbing his hands together, Lilian's gaze remained on the Truit manor. Paul placed his hand on her gloved one.

"They'll be fine."

"I don't doubt that."

"*We'll* be fine."

Her ready protest dissolved as she stared into his eyes. Whenever Paul spoke to her in such a way, she could not help but forget what silly worry she felt. His sure and comforting tone won her mind over, bringing her to agree. She gave him a trusting grin. Once his eyes finally pulled from hers to the road, the car started in motion. He slowly drove in the roundabout created by the fountain centering the courtyard.

Just as they began to move away from the yard, the sight of a glossy black object emerged around the corner. Lilian sat back in befuddlement as the car approached. Her eyes went wide at the driver's features. She was looking straight at the complacent grin on the thin lips belonging to Spencer Wesman. Despite her expectations for him to at least slow down and acknowledge them, his speed only increased. His stare struck at her unapologetically.

She gasped with urgency, turning to Paul and wondering why he was being less reactive. The vehicle rushed forward, passing on the other side of theirs. Lilian's gaze continued to follow it with the craning of her neck. She tapped Paul's shoulder. "Paul, did you see him?"

Oddly, he kept his focus ahead in ignoration.

"Paul?" she repeated, shouting this time.

"I saw him." Paul's answer lacked life. It offered no opinion and made Lilian all the more concerned.

"Why would he come *here*? I think we should go back just to see what the visit is for."

"No, Lilian."

"What?"

He turned his face to her again, saying softly but firmly, "We can't go back."

Lilian didn't like the way he said it. Like there was something more to it, something he knew that she didn't. And it had to do with Mister Wesman.

Sitting beside him in his *Roi-de-Belges* was usually one of Lilian's favorite things to do. But at the moment, she felt resistant to him. Though he tried to make light of the awkwardness by commenting on the scenery, she gave him no acknowledgement. An hour of silently bouncing over bumpy road went by, and he kept making occasional glances at her.

He tried again. "You know, I had been to Brord once with my father. Long before I ever moved to Hiplum. The place was quaint then. You would have liked it. Nice community. I wonder if it's still the same since I left."

Lilian was honestly intrigued to hear something about the place he was taking her to. "Are they country people?"

"She speaks!" Paul exclaimed, a winsome smile on his face. "By El, Lilian, you've been the definition of hostility for most of your time with me."

"Only since you seem to have befriended secrecy."

"Secrecy?"

"Yes. And you can't even deny it." Lilian tried to sound less bothered by it than she actually was but failed.

Paul's face went pale as he stared ahead. "If there's anything I keep secret, it's for a good reason. After all, let's not pretend you don't keep secrets of your own."

If Lilian had taken the time to apply his words to herself, she would have found them to be true. But upon hearing anything that sounded like an accusation, she said defensively, "Me? What secrets have *I* kept?"

Paul tucked in his chin, refusing to continue such a dispute. "Would you like to know what I have been studying recently? Nothing requisite, just a separate intrigue of mine."

She loathed the change in topic but allowed it. "What?"

His voice lowered as he uttered, "Bacteriology." His expression turned grave. "I want to find a cure for the illness that took your uncle."

"Pneumonia," Lilian breathed. It hurt to even say the word.

He nodded. "I want to make sure it never happens again to anyone."

A genuine feeling of gratefulness swelled inside her, but soon abated. Lilian sighed. "That's a fine ambition. But he's gone now. You could save a million lives and nothing, nothing would ever change the fact that *his* is gone."

Paul stared at Lilian for a few seconds before turning his eyes to the road again. She knew her discouraging response affected him when he said, "All the ways I expected this to go, none were this. What happened, Lil? We used to be fun."

Lilian gazed at him somberly. She remembered what her aunt had said about his almost-proposal— how he had refused to follow through with it. It had been devastating to hear. As she looked at him now, it was that thought that caused an ache in her chest. "I don't think it's our fault, Paul. Blame it on our circumstances. Even now, we're at a loss. You're taking me to a place I know nothing about. And afterwards, I fear I'll never see you again."

She saw Paul's eyebrows pinch at the truth in her statement. She was a grieving girl with no more hope ahead of her. And no man willing to claim her. None of this was what Lilian ever dreamed of. She wondered if it was all just as disheartening in the same way for Paul. Or was his regret truly as simple as a regret for not 'being fun'?

Just as she was beginning to lose hope in him, Paul slipped his hand around hers, lifting her fingers to his lips. Her heart sang mournfully as he pressed a long kiss against her knuckles. Given her current state of depression, she was not eager for him to kiss her, unlike how she would have only dreamt but a few weeks ago. But this much was accepted without inhibition.

Stranded

One Day Later

"How did you sleep?" Tessaline slid Jase's coffee mug to his hand. It was early in the morning, but Jase had to get going soon because his new job was far away from where they lived. Or at least he had to make her *think* he had a reason to leave.

"Fine. I slept fine," he groaned. It was a trick question, he knew. But his answer was honest. Jase didn't mind having to sleep on the couch again. It was more comfortable than bed sometimes. What unsettled him was the interrogation he knew was coming the next morning. With the way he'd been behaving, showing up late every night, it was only a matter of time before Tess would start to lay those big, silver eyes of hers on him anxiously like she was doing now.

Jase didn't like hiding things from Tess, and he rarely did. But the fear of losing her meant he had to. It was but three weeks ago when Mr. Truit, the head of the factory where Jase worked, died. And for some reason after that, the supervisor at Truit & Co. went into a wild fit of firing with Jase being one of the chosen firees. He understood why. It was not like he wasn't talented when it came to manufacturing lathes, but he often had a habit for sharing his unwanted opinion of more efficient ways to get things done.

But in spite of losing *that* job, not too long ago Jase had found another job, working at a plastering agency. It was fine until someone at 'the top' expressed that they had an issue with Jase's father's reputation (even in his grave the ol' man continued to ruin his life), so again he was out of a job. Tess knew about the first time but not the last. And he had a reason for not telling her.

When she was only eighteen, the age in which they let you out of the orphanage, Jase had promised her then she'd never have to toil in a hazardous factory or work day and night sewing up dresses and hats for other women. He knew she didn't so much mind the idea of working, but as long as she could be Jase's beneficiary without any pressure of marrying him, the offer was hard to refuse. So she let him keep his promise.

Lately though, he worried that she was catching on to his lies. If Tess ever doubted his ability to take care of her, he knew she'd break his promise for him. She made it a habit to find reasons to leave him. Even if there weren't any, she would make one. Loving Tess was the most challenging thing he ever did.

"Still not gonna tell me what kept you last night?" Tessaline slumped forward over the table.

Jase remained silent, sipping the coffee a few times to stay occupied. Tess patiently waited for him to respond. He tried to wait her out. Just a few more averted glances and artless sips of his coffee should do it.

She stood up from her seat, slamming two palms on the table. "That's it!" she exclaimed, stomping toward the front door.

Jase jadedly asked, "What do you think you're doing?"

She turned to him. Her nose, blushing a salmon color. "Goin'! I'm sick o' this!"

He watched her hesitation to grab the nob. "You're not *goin'*," he stated with surety, "just goin' *out*. I know the difference." Jase stood up and went around the table slowly to her. The sight of her grimace made him feel terrible like only *her* grimace could. He lifted a hand to her chin.

"No. Don't touch me." She stepped back against the door.

He hated the way Tess would harden her heart to him in anger. No matter how loyal he had been to her for the past five years, he wasn't sure she would ever truly love him. She cared about him, but even that was a way of caring about herself.

"Tess, you just have to trust me. Look, I'm sorry for coming home late."

"You know I can be reasoned with, Jase. If it's the job that's keeping you, which I highly doubt, just tell me."

He laughed. "What's the point if you'll doubt it anyway? You don't want me to tell you that. You want me to say that I've been out acting like my father. You want me to say that I've been drunk even though in all these years you've never seen me hold a bottle. Or that some wench on the street caught my eye and is takin' up half my attention before I make it home to you."

"Jase." She turned her face from him, abashedly. He could be too harsh with his point sometimes.

He put his hands gently on her shoulders. "You know I want you, Tess. And I'm trying to show you I'm worthy. But every time I mess up once, it's like you forget all the good I've done."

This unseemly situation they were in was not the way he'd have wished to live with her. If Jase had a choice, he would have done things right and married her. Almost every month he proposed. But every time, her answer was no.

"Now, I have to go." He planted a soft kiss on her forehead. "And I hope that when I get back—"

"I'll be here," she snapped. "I'm always here."

"Alright." He took hold of the knob and she moved aside. Jase opened the kitchen door, and feeling suspicious, held out his hand. Light drops caught on his fingers. "Ah, rain."

"Take your hat, then." Tess already took the large cowboy hat off the coat hanger and was handing it to him.

"Thank you, ma'am," he said, offering her a charming smirk before he put it on. He noticed how Tess bit back her want to smile.

"Just be safe, okay," she said. "Then come back to me."

"I always come back," he remarked as he put one boot out the door.

It wasn't long before the light shower grew into drizzling heaps, the road's coating being sprayed upward as the wagon wheels drew along it.

As was the usual order of things, Jase had taken the two stronger horses, Paisley and Popcorn, because they were more capable of pulling the wagon. Thus, leaving the worn veteran, Jaundice to Tess's oversight if she ever needed to take lightweight trips to town. Jaundice was her favorite, anyway.

All three horses and the covered wagon were Jase's only real assets inherited from his deceased father. Four other things in his life he fought to keep besides Tess.

The crisp air blew around him. He was not sure where to search next for hire. At least somewhere that would pay well or allow him to use his creativity.

It took a lot to keep paying his rent on time, but he always made it happen somehow. As far as Jase knew— and he knew it for a fact— there were only two reasons Mister Thomas hadn't stopped renting the house out to Jase. One— because he paid on time every time, and two— because Tess lived there too. Mainly the second reason. Jase was just lucky the old man didn't come to the property often and bother them. But whenever he *did* come, his focus was not on Jase, the man of the house, but the beautiful young woman who, though not a lady by higher standards, could not look undesirable if she tried.

The farther his horses trotted, the better Jase could hear a distant din of popping and rumbling that was strange enough to pique his interest. He flicked the reins, inciting their whinnies. They took him around the bend to where a fine-looking 'machine' was driving in the sludge. It had a yellow ochre body with a black tarp attaching from the back and unfolding over the red seats. Jase came faster to parallel the vehicle. He didn't mind how he looked. There were newcomers in Brord. Rich newcomers.

Through the pouring rain that dripped from the brim of his hat, Jase peered over at the young gentleman and even younger lady sitting in their seats with weary faces. The boy— which he was to Jase— driving the automobile was gripping his leather wheel so determinedly it was humorous.

Jase decided to make his presence known, waving to them. The girl saw. She patted the boy's arm who gave Jase a quick glance before disregarding him. The girl waved back with a half-smile while squinting her eyes.

She was pretty, having a quintessential prettiness for the times. She matched her traveling companion in an all-black ensemble. Mourning attire.

Jase turned his gaze forward again. Then he heard the girl scream. Looking back over, the car was moving off the road. The boy was turning his wheel hard in the other direction, but none of that seemed to be working.

"Paul, just stop!" the lady cried.

He reacted swiftly, depressing the brake lever just as one side of the car, the side the girl was on, fell over the berm on the shoulder.

Jase was debating whether he should stop to see about them. He did not actually have anywhere to be, after all. Considering it, he came ahead of them, then yanked on the reins, "Whoa!" slowing the horses to stop. After hopping down, he approached the automobile. "Are y'all alright?"

"Yes," said the young man.

Jase came closer and tipped his hat at them both, exposing his fiery curls to the rain. "I'm Jase Foster." He shook hands with the driver.

"Paul Partridge." He turned to his lady friend. "And this is Miss Lilian Truit."

Had Jase heard that right? "Truit? As in related to Fredrick Truit?"

The young lady nodded with a minor grin. "He was my uncle."

The girl didn't know how fateful her sentence was. Now Jase was considering walking back to his wagon and leaving the two stranded. Of course, it was only a thought.

"I'm not sure what happened," the young man said with a look of annoyance. "The wheel stopped working."

Jase didn't hesitate to say, "Let me take a look."

Before Mister Partridge could object, Jase went on his knees, lay on his back, and slipped his head under the car. Above him was the map of mechanisms working in tandem. He saw the problem immediately. It was too blatant not to see. "Just how old is the car?" Jase shouted.

"It's relatively new and the latest model of its kind. I bought it earlier this year."

"Well, I'd tell you to come and see what I'm seein', but I don't think you'd want to."

"What is that supposed to mean?"

Jase eased himself out from under the car and stood back to his towering height by Partridge's side of the car. "I'm seein' a lot of rust traveling from the pitman arm down to the gearbox and across the linkage. Which would explain why the wheel stopped working. If the pitman is loose, the wheel has no effect."

Among the mechanical jargon, there seemed to be only one thing Mister Partridge heard. "Rust? Are you sure?"

"You can check for yourself."

Mister Partridge started switching his gaze back and forth as if wondering whether stepping out and getting as drenched as Jase was necessary. The girl looked at him and encouraged the idea. "Go on."

Before the boy decided on rushing into it, he questioned Jase. "How do you even know this much about automobiles?"

"I…" Jase looked down, laughing. "I read about it."

His answer seemed to have intrigued them both. Mister Partridge frowned at the ground below him as if not eager to soil his worsted wool suit. Nevertheless, he rose from his seat and followed Jase's direction, looking under the car.

Jase continued to stand above him with his hand on the rim of the car. The girl watched him, or perhaps he was watching her, and she found it odd. But as he stared unapologetically at her face, it was obvious to him that her heritage was in the Truit family. *She favors her father, alright.* Jase only stopped staring when she turned her face the other way.

"You have got to be kidding me!" Mister Partridge exclaimed as he scooted back out, his head coming up. Then he stood. "I cannot believe they sold me a car with old— no, *ancient* parts!"

"Believe it," was Jase's poor consolation. Though he was only joking, the statement worked in making the boy even more flustered. It was evident in the way Mister Partridge grimaced at him before looking at the girl. They shared each other's disappointment.

"What can we do, Paul?" the young lady asked.

Jase watched their expressions, feeling bad for them but not too bad. They were in a better position than him, anyway. Jase wished his cares were this trifling. *Imagine sulking over a broken car that they could have... fixed.* Then it hit him just how significant the situation was. He began to derive a brilliant idea.

"If you're interested, I am really good at fixing things. It's my job, actually."

Mister Partridge held up his hand. "I am sure you do sir, truly. But I will not be taking my chances with someone who has only ever *read* about cars."

"*Paul*," Miss Truit scolded.

"What?"

"Are you really being decisive right now when we are stranded on the side of the road, and I need to meet Ms. Witherman today?"

"Ms. Witherman? You mean Ms. Cora? Dalia Cora Witherman?" Jase said.

The girl sat forward. "You know her?"

"Yes. Why are you looking for her?"

"I'm her new volunteer."

"Well, I'll be."

She smiled as they came to an understanding, then quickly dropped it with a look of concern. "Please, I cannot stand to see you getting rained on. You can come and sit if you like."

Jase accepted her offer without hesitation, stepping through the front, swiveling seats on his way to the back. His height made it difficult to walk without his head brushing the roof. Only after he'd done it did he realize the look of appalment on Mister Partridge's face. And he understood it. Here Jase was, a stranger, plopping his muddied behind down on someone else's luxury seating.

But as mad as he was, Mister Partridge said nothing. Jase sat in the middle of the long leather seat in the back to be beside Miss Truit so she could speak to him. Paul hopped back in, sitting himself in his driver seat. His hair and back were completely soiled.

"As I was saying," Jase began, "I'm a fast learner when it comes to new territory, and I know how to fix things. In fact, my last job was working at your uncle's factory." He made sure not to mention that he was fired from the factory. He also did not mention that he was once a blacksmithing apprentice to his father. Mentioning anything related to his father could work against his chance of making a deal with these rich folks.

"Really?" Miss Truit said, sounding impressed to Jase's relief. "And do you know if there are any *actual* car mechanics in Brord Village?"

Jase smiled. "Good question. The answer— no. We aren't that advanced, you see."

Miss Truit's eyes narrowed on Mister Partridge. "Paul, I know the decision is up to you," she tipped her head in a vouching manner at Jase, "but I really think we should let him do it."

"Lil, this will require replacement parts. What does *he* have?"

"Well, you know as well as I do how scarce these parts are."

"Exactly—"

"Let me finish. Parts are scarce. And this is a German car, Paul. Do you really want to wait forever and miss the chance to go to Hiplum University?"

The man raised his eyebrows, completely silent. There, she had done it. Jase was impressed at how well her argument worked in making Mister Partridge concede. He turned to Jase, saying, "How do you plan on making up for the bad parts?"

Jase nodded at the question. "I can make them."

"How long will that take?" Mister Partridge asked.

"Perhaps a few months. Five or more."

Mister Partridge groaned.

"But if you wait for the actual company to do it, it could take a year."

"And why should I believe that? Why should I believe anything you are saying?"

Jase looked upward. These questions were getting harder to answer. Luckily, he liked a challenge. "Because it would be more foolish to trust them twice when you can look me in the eyes and know my intentions. You can make complaints directly to me. And you can sue me just as quick as you employed me. That's the beauty of local business, sir. The way I personally prefer business."

Mister Partridge frowned. "It would still be a long time. I can't stay here forever. I may have to take a train back to Hiplum." He looked at Miss Truit. "And leave it with you."

"Me?"

"Yes. I need this, Lilian. Please promise me you will take care of my car until I get back."

"Get back when? Next June? I am not even sure how long *I'll* be here."

"Don't you want to help me? I would do it for you."

Jase waited patiently for Miss Truit to make a decision. Finally, she said, "Alright. If you really need me to keep your car for you, then yes, I will."

"Thank you." Mister Partridge turned to Jase, sighing. "How much should I pay you?"

Finally, he asked the question Jase was waiting for. Although ironically, Jase was not prepared for it. He never had the option before to choose how much money his skills were worth. So he thought about all of his expenses, the money he would need for his horses and Tess, and the 13 dollar rent. Quickly, he settled on a number. "Forty-nine dollars."

Mister Partridge didn't flinch. "Forty-nine? Why not just ask for fifty?"

Jase felt slightly dumb when he put it that way. "Because I'm… humble?"

A giggle followed. From Miss Truit's lips.

Mister Partridge reached into his coat and pulled out some 5-dollar bills. "Here is twenty-five for now. That's half of fifty, you know."

"I know," Jase asserted, annoyed.

"Good. You get the other half as long as you do not break anything."

Can it really get any worse? Jase thought, though he didn't say it. He held out his hand. "Challenge accepted."

Paul shook it.

Jase stood up and stepped out of the car. He then gestured at his wagon. "In the meantime, you two will need someone to take you to Miss Cora's."

Newcomers

They watched as their suitcases slid around in the wagon bed. While they sat safe from the rain, Mister Foster was sitting front seat. They kept quiet while the clopping of hooves and screeching of the wheels became the only noise.

Paul and Lilian shared a long gaze of uncertainty. They knew they had no choice but to trust the stranger, but that didn't rid them of consternation. They looked forward, watching the view from the back of Mister Foster's seat.

After reaching the other side of a hill, they caught sight of the low buildings set together in a small valley. They crossed a short bridge resting over a still lake.

"Etowah lake," Foster was kind enough to explain. "There's lots of fish there."

"I love to fish," Lilian said.

"Really? I didn't think ladies of society cared for the smell."

Lilian knew he was only joking, but she couldn't decide whether to answer with a quip or accept that perhaps there was a bad image placed on fishing. So she chose not to further mention the idea.

The wagon rode on through the main road cutting through Brord, passing up the strangers standing on small strips of pavement in front of the uniform line of amenities. The town lacked the industrial architecture Hiplum boasted of. Existing as only small shops and department stores. A post office to the left, doctor's office to the right, and so on.

Mister Foster made a right turn past the pub, finding a building after it with the sign: *Sweetgum Cottage Inn*. The only place so far that was comprised of irregular shapes.

Adjacent to it was a pawn shop. Then they approached the end of the street where there was a large, quaint home, gated in iron and fenced in brick. Lilian had seen bigger orphanages in both Corlu and Hiplum so she knew this would likely have fewer children than usual.

Jase ranked in front of it. "Here you are, ma'am."

"Thank you so much."

"It was my pleasure. And don't worry. I'm sure Ms. Cora will forgive you for being late. Heck, she might even thank you for it, knowing how hard it must be to prepare for visitors with all those kids." Jase stepped down. She heard his boots as he came over to the back end of the wagon. "I'll help you down."

"No. *I* will," Paul insisted as he hopped out of the wagon, turning around with an outstretched hand. "Ready, Lil?"

It had always been Paul who helped her out, so of course she would not deny him his job. Down she went with a hand in his, ending up in his arms the moment her heels met the ground. She turned her eyes off his grin.

Mister Foster used his lended key to open the gate. After grabbing their suitcases, Mister Foster went ahead of them, waiting at the green door. By the time they were up the steps, the door was opened. A girl near Lilian's age with auburn hair, round eyes, and distinct jowls stood in awe. "Jase! I— I mean, Mister Foster."

Jase leaned against the side jamb, hand on hip. "Ethel, why are you saying my last name?"

Ethel's face flushed as she eyed the threshold, then him again. "Ms. Cora insists on it. She says it's how volunteers address every adult."

"Well, that rule only applies if she's listening."

"Nice try," said the woman who suddenly appeared from behind the girl. She was a pretty old lady whose age was only made apparent by her silver side-hairs. She looked at Ethel and tipped her head as a kind of dismissal. Ethel left.

The woman only noticed Jase at the door. "Hello, sir. What brings you here? How is Tess doing?"

"Oh, she's fine. I just came because I was told you had a visitor coming."

She smiled. "And who told you that?"

Jase stepped aside, gesturing to Lilian. "The visitor."

The woman finally laid eyes on Lilian. Her smile grew. "It's you! You're here! Oh, I am so glad."

Lilian came forward, grinning sweetly. "Nice to meet you, ma'am."

Ms. Cora took hold of her hands. "It has been too long to finally meet you. Look at you, you're just a lovely thing." Her compliments were very enthusiastic. "Well come on in. I'll show you around."

Stepping in, she and Paul gave everything a look around. They had nice walls halfway boarded in a reddish wood, and two hall entrances facing them.

A vase and table centered a big gallery wall that existed under the entresol— which there was somehow room for even with the third floor not being very high off the first.

"It's really lovely in here," said Lilian.

"Yes, it took some years for my Todd to finally afford this place."

"Todd?"

Ms. Cora was cut off just before explaining. The sound of the rain was still prevalent. Ms. Cora walked to the door again. "Mister Foster, you aren't coming in?"

"I have to go," he said to her.

Seeming to know what he meant, she frowned with what looked like empathy. "I'm praying things get better for you."

The man's expression went from content to sad. "Yeah, well, there's better luck when *you* do it."

"Jase," Ms. Cora said just as he started to turn his back. "Has Tess met her yet?"

Jase looked over at Lilian, shaking his head. "I'm not so sure that'd be a good idea, anyway."

Lilian wondered what he meant by that or why Ms. Cora did not seem to like his answer.

Before Mister Jase finally left, he took a moment to shake Paul's hand. "I'ma get started on the car," he said, winking in a way that was meant to garner trust, yet it only did the opposite. Then he tipped his hat at Lilian, his easy gaze cutting through Ms. Cora and Paul who stood in his way. "It was a pleasure meeting you, Miss Truit."

He had an amiable presence, gentle eyes, broad build.

Leader.

The inaudible word was whispered in her mind. A word coming out of nowhere. So being wise, she ignored it. Lilian nodded his way before turning back around to admire the gallery wall. The door was soon shut.

"Now, who are *you*?" Miss Cora's question was directed at Paul.

"A friend of the family, ma'am. Paul Partridge. Very nice to meet you." Paul held out his hand. But the lady saw how dirty he was and did not shake it.

"How about a hot bath, Mister Partridge?" she said as kindly as she could.

Paul cleared his throat. "That would be refreshing, thank you."

"Ethel!"

The girl immediately rushed down the stairs at Ms. Cora's beckon.

"Yes, ma'am?"

"Please show Mr. Partridge to my bathroom upstairs. And have his clothes cleaned as he bathes."

"Yes, ma'am."

Ethel reached for Paul's luggage, taking it from his hand. She waddled forward with the heavy suitcase, leading him upstairs.

Ms. Cora stepped toward Lilian. "How are you, dear?"

"Oh. I'm well."

"How is your aunt?"

"She is doing better than expected. She should be here tomorrow."

"Wonderful. I cannot wait to see her again after all these years."

Lilian smiled. Then she noticed just how quiet everything was. "Where are the children?"

"In the middle of a lesson. I can show you. Come."

Lilian followed her through one of the archways. They passed by the doors at their sides, coming toward the wide French doors facing them at the end of the hallway. The sound of a class shouting in one accord was clear. Through the glass of the doors, Ms. Cora and Lilian viewed the rows of children sitting at their desks and facing an old woman with a yardstick in her hand who pointed toward the sentence written on the board. Lilian could hear her saying, "And what part is the predicate?"

"The last part," the children shouted. At least the younger ones. There were some who looked older than twelve. They were quietly writing in their own books.

Lilian counted 30 children altogether. Well, 30 seats. "There is a child missing."

Ms. Cora squinted at where Lilian was pointing. "Oh, yes. My, you're observant. Hugh is his name. He is sick right now, so we let him study upstairs." She pointed at the teacher. "That is Miss Sally Wayne, the new teacher. I'm glad to have her here. She has definitely taken up half my load. It's not easy taking care of this many children, though I love 'em to death."

"Are they all orphans?"

"No. This is a haven for children who were either orphaned, homeless, or forced to work abroad to help their families. Some parents just want their sons or daughters to be given better treatment and opportunity. Both of which we provide here."

"And what made you realize you wanted to do this."

"The same reason your aunt took care of you."

Lilian caught her meaning. "You could not have children?"

"But I do now. More than most mothers could ever have." She looked through the glass one more time before saying, "Let's go before they see us."

She and Lilian turned to their right and kept walking.

"Now, you must be famished. Lemme get you something to eat." Ms. Cora took Lilian to the mahogany doors of the dining room. They could hear feet padding the carpet as two staff members came out from around the corner, in the middle of a chat. They stopped when they noticed Lilian.

The girls curtsied. "Oh, hello. You must be the new volunteer," said the taller one. "I'm Maude. And this is Patricia."

"Pleasure to meet you, Maude. Patricia."

"Could you girls get the doors and then tell the cook to fix her some eggs and toast?" Ms. Cora asked. She whispered, "And bring out a slice of pie, too."

They did as Ms. Cora said, opening the doors together. Lilian went in, sitting at one end of the long table. She waited as Ms. Cora walked away for some time until the food was brought on white plates. Some for Lilian, and some for Paul whenever he was done with his bath. Lilian could not bear to wait for him to enter the dining room before taking her first bite.

Ms. Cora's pie was certainly something to praise. The woman watched with anticipation as Lilian chewed. "Well?"

Lilian dabbed her lips with a napkin, swallowed, and smiled. "Delicious." She admitted that much but refused to discredit dear Gracie who was the plum pie maker back home.

Ms. Cora grinned contently and sighed. "It's so nice to have finally seen you. Here in the town, your uncle had helped so much. Have you ever seen the factory?"

Lilian eyed her plate in regret. "No."

Ms. Cora was understanding. "Well, you'll be able to see it from the room I'm giving you. No one's been up there since Todd's death. It used to be his reading room. I've since added a bed for guests."

"Who is Todd?"

"My late husband, Todd Witherman."

A shrill 'achoo' came from behind the cracked mahogany doors of the room along with a few shushes. Ms. Cora rolled her eyes. She pressed a finger to her lips, telling her guest to stay quiet as she stood up and crept over to the doors. She grabbed the handles and flung them open.

"Alright. That's enough eavesdropping."

Suddenly, the room erupted into chaos as a swarm of children burst in. Their voices, a cacophony of excitement, filled the air with shouts of 'Hey, there!'

Lilian recoiled slightly, overwhelmed by the sudden onslaught of energy. Ms. Cora's attempt to correct them, insisting on a more formal 'Hello, Miss Truit' was lost in the din. Lilian felt a mix of amusement and bewilderment as she watched the children, their youthful exuberance both endearing and daunting.

Lilian gripped the arms of her chair as 30 children surrounded her at once, asking, "What's your name?"

"Why are you all in black? Somebody die?"

"I *like* her dress, it's pretty."

"It's black. Black is not pretty."

"*She's* pretty."

"I think she's rich."

"She's rich?"

"Are you rich?"

"How come you don't talk?"

"Girls! Boys! Stop overwhelming the guest," Ms. Cora shouted. "Who wants pie?"

Immediately, little hands were raised. They each sat down to take an equal slice from two pies that Maude so honorably cut for them. The older kids grimaced at their small portions.

Lilian smiled as all the excitement quieted down, looking out of the mahogany doors and wondering when Paul would come down. As soon as she did, his lean self emerged from around the corner, making his way into the dining room. Feeling her smile stretch wider than before, she did her best to drop it.

Once he had entered, he came and sat next to Lilian. Lilian stared at him in his clean clothes and neat hair. She wished to go up and bathe *herself*. "How are you feeling after your bath?"

"Wonderful." He began forking his eggs. "I have decided to stay a while here. Until you are all settled in."

"You will?" Lilian quelled her excitement, answering calmly, "For how long would you say?"

"Two days. I will leave a day after your aunt arrives."

"You should stay at the inn down the street from here."

"Yes, that's what I was planning on doing."

"How often will you come to check on me?"

Paul finally looked up from his plate. Lilian could see how she amused him but didn't care. "Every morning."

"And afternoon?"

He smirked. "Yes."

"And just before dinner?"

He sat back in his seat, side-eyeing her while pretending to think deeply about it. "Yes," he whispered.

Her winsome smile returned.

The little girl sitting on the other side of Lilian tugged at her sleeve.

"Yes?"

"I have to go," the girl stated in a sharp whisper.

"Oh, um…" Lilian looked around her at the other volunteers, then realized that she was now one of them, and that this was just the start of her new job at Ms. Cora's. She turned back to Paul. "Excuse us."

He nodded, grinning.

Lilian stood up, taking the girl by the hand. "Alright. Perhaps you can show me where the water closet is."

The girl led the way, bringing her back to the foyer. She opened the door that was built into the side of the stairs, revealing a little room with a toilet and sink.

"Do you need any help inside?"

The girl shook her head, hopping from one foot to the other. "No, thank you." She quickly went in, holding the handle on the door to shut it behind her.

A weak voice from above caught Lilian off guard. "It's you."

She looked up, startled to see a boy peering from the stairs with a red blanket draped over his shoulders. His brown, fuzzy hair was disheveled, and his nose sickly rosen. He stared at her with pale, unfocused eyes. The notion settled in her mind that he was blind.

"Excuse me?"

"It's you. You're the fisher."

"Fisher?"

"Hugh! Now, I told you to stay upstairs!" The complaint came from the auburn girl, Ethel. She came up the steps, scowling. "Do it again, and I'll tell Ms. Cora you've been disobedient."

The boy didn't even acknowledge her. He had chosen to keep his focus on Lilian. It almost seemed like he could actually see her. But as soon as Ethel had made the final step towards him, he rushed back upstairs.

Ethel let out a huff, turning her attention to Miss Lilian. She leaned on the rail. "It's not easy taking care of that one. He's always on his feet."

"He must be the one Miss Cora was talking about. How old is he?"

"Nine."

Lilian leaned in. "And can he...?"

"Nope. Can't see a thing. But, oddly enough, that never stops him." Ethel came down to properly introduce herself. "I'm Ethel Milford." She extended her hand which Lilian gladly shook.

"Pleasure to meet you, Ethel. I am—"

"Lilian Truit, heiress of the Truit Estate and niece of 'my Krishta dear'," she said with the same soft voice as Ms. Cora and a hand on her heart.

Lilian laughed. "I see Ms. Cora has told you about us."

"Just the important stuff. Like who you are to Tess."

"Tess?"

Ethel's face froze the more Lilian squinted her way. She frowned. "Oh. Sorry, I... I thought you..."

"Thought what?"

She looked away from Lilian. "Sorry, ma'am. I should go." She scuffed away.

"Wait, but..."

"I'm done!" the little girl said as she opened the door behind Lilian.

Lilian turned around. "Huh?"

"I'm done."

"Oh." Lilian took her by the hand again. "Come on, then."

"Now, I understand that you are grieving, so I won't be expecting too much from you. You can sleep in late if you like." Ms. Cora said while sitting next to Lilian on the side of her new bed. The room was on the third floor, raised above the back garden Ms. Cora owned. The walls were decorated in black and eggplant harlequin stopping at the semicircular window from which the garden and beyond could be espied. An iron tub existed by the wall facing the bed across the room.

"Oh, Ms. Cora, please. The last thing I want is to be anything but useful."

"Bunk. I mean nonsense. No one is rushing you to do anything. I take care of all my girls and if they were to need a break, I'd give it to them. We are a family here. Let me treat you like such and let that be the end of it."

Lilian grinned. "Well, if it's nothing you wouldn't do for the other staff…"

"Good." Ms. Cora patted her lower back. She then stood up. "You take your time getting used to the room. I'll be downstairs in my office." She left Lilian there, inside a box dressed so properly for a person in their mourning period. The darkest room in the house.

Lilian got up and went to the window. There, beyond an open field, existed the one mark of industrialism on this town in the form of a beautiful, brick monster. Thick and wide with two chimneys protruding upward and releasing their smoke.

Lilian never believed she could be any more proud of her uncle. But seeing the factory as it was in person, her admiration was beyond great.

Lilian rested her forehead on the glass and grinned. "I made it, Uncle Fred. Auntie always said that half your heart was in Brord. So, I suppose I made it to the other half. Now I just want to see what you loved so much about this place."

Continuing to watch the smoke rise from the chimneys and swirl around in the sky, she found something satisfying about seeing it curl and wave into mere vapor, moving upward in a string of black against the gray sky. Her eyes were all too focused on it. So much so, that she caught a glimpse of something quite animated within the smoke. Something which seemed to turn and wink at her.

Lilian blinked, blinking away the silly image. She must have been very tired indeed. Respecting her sanity, she moved away from the window and toward her bed. She could do with a nap.

Drifting

Tess held herself against the breeze, watching as her redheaded friend fed the horses in turn. Jaundice always got his apple first. Jase would usually leave it on the ground for him because he was a slow eater for a horse. But this time he rubbed his hand down Jaundice's muzzle, holding the apple up for him to finally decide on taking a bite. Jase paid no attention to Popcorn who greedily nudged at his neck for that delicious looking apple.

Tess laughed. "You're actually feeding him this time?"

"Yeah."

"Why?"

Jase's honey-tinted eyes caught hers. "I just figured it was time to stop neglecting him. He's yours. And I want a strong horse carrying my bride-to-be."

Tess scoffed though she didn't find it funny. And neither did he. "I don't remember saying yes to that."

"You will."

She crossed her arms and sighed incredulously. "Jase, how long before you see that I'll always disappoint you."

"Tess," he said in a visible breath, moving closer to her. His head, just above her eyes. "Say what you will, we're meant for each other. And the day I stop believing that will be when I'm in the ground."

She gave him no acknowledgement. It scared her how honest she knew he was being. In a perfect world, she'd've loved to hear those words. But the fact was that she did not love Jase. He was her easy way to comfort and nothing else. But sometimes she hated herself for not loving him. He deserved to be loved, adored, and that other word Ms. Cora said so much— cherished.

Jase was not wrong to think they were meant for each other. It seemed like all the circumstances of her life which put her in his way were telling her that he was meant to be her husband. But the more she thought about having a husband, the more she realized she'd have to be a wife. And she knew what trouble that was.

He still stood over her, staring like a dog desiring a bone for doing a good job. Flecks of lime green, staining his eyes. "Jase, feed the others, please."

She saw his face go back to a worn expression. He pulled two more apples from the bucket and gave them to Paisley and Popcorn.

She couldn't understand why he put himself through this misery. She often thought of leaving, just to end his pain. But leaving might just cause him to 'end' *himself.*

"The rent's due Thursday."

Jase looked down at his boots. "I'll take it to him."

"If *you* take it, he won't accept it."

"I said I'll take it!" Jase snapped. He stomped away toward the house.

"Jase!" Tess ran up behind him, grabbing onto his thick arm. "Jase, that's one of the only times I ever go out. Now, you can't take that from me."

"You think I don't know what that old man wants with you?"

Tess froze, hearing the implication in his words. She had never heard him speak about Mister Scott in such a way. Even if she *felt* he had ought with the man, it was something he never actually said. And she preferred things that way.

Jase shook his head. "Sometimes I think he gets it."

Her hand met his face with a loud slap before she could stop herself. His cheek, blushing a bright red.

Tess dropped her hand to her side. "Sorry."

"It's okay. I overspoke." But it wasn't okay.

"Will you let me go on Thursday?" she insisted.

Jase's eyes lowered. "*Let* you? It's not like you needed my permission." He moved away from her, going to the house.

It was true. She didn't need his permission.

There was a young boy shouting on the street where Ethel was now directing Lilian on their short expedition for the newspaper Ms. Cora asked them to get.

So far, Lilian was enjoying her tour of Brord. Everything was so charmingly simple, the people were friendly, and Lilian could have sworn that the sky was bluer in Brord than in Hiplum even in such a dreary season. A welcoming smell of buttered biscuits currently pervaded the block where the bakery resided. She got the strangest feeling that she was at home.

Though she had waited all morning to see Paul, he did not show up. She did consider walking to the inn but thought better of it. Calling on a man was not very becoming of a lady.

Ethel's hand took her arm. "Come on. Let's be quick. I want to get back in time for lunch before they eat all the cornbread that *I* helped make." They approached the loud boy who was wearing corduroy overalls under his wool coat and a flat cap.

"Here! Get your paper here! Here! Get your paper here!" the boy continued to shout.

"We'll take one," Ethel said.

The boy turned around with wide eyes and a wider smile. "That'll be a five-cent," he said, holding out his ink-stained hand.

"Five-cent?" argued Ethel. "For smudged ink?"

To that, he looked at his stained fingers and saw that the words he touched were slightly blurred. "It's hot off the press," was his excuse. "Look, do you want it or not?"

"I'll pay you with this lucky two-cent coin I found."

"I was told 'no negotiating'. Now, if you can't pay—"

"Oh, fine. Just wanted to see if it would work." She dropped the pennies Ms. Cora lended into his palm.

With her quick eye, Lilian saw the words printed somewhere on the page mentioning Shersul's name. To see his name written down made her emotional, to see his name in a news article made her intrigued. "I'll take one as well."

Once she made her payment and the paper was in her hands, Lilian immediately shook it apart. Her eyes skimmed down the left-hand top corner of the front page.

$200 REWARD

FOR THE APPREHENSION OF SELF-CLAIMED "ELSON"

The community is alerted to the pursuit of Shersul Smithson, wanted for charges of disorderly conduct. Smithson has evaded capture since last reported sighting. Authorities have issued a warrant for his arrest.

A reward of $200 is offered to any person providing information leading to his capture. Citizens are urged to report any knowledge of his whereabouts to the local sheriff's office.

"No. No." Her face sunk closer to the page with the hopes she had read it incorrectly.

"What's the matter with you?" Ethel asked.

Lilian lifted her focus off the paper and up to her fellow staff member. "I didn't know this was going on."

Ethel, looking puzzled at Lilian's vague remark, moved closer to see what Lilian was reading. "Oh!" She started laughing.

Now *Lilian* was puzzled.

"That's just some old 'spiracy."

"It is?"

"Of course it is. No one's actually seen a werewolf."

"Werewolf?"

"Yeah. You know. Half wolf, half man."

"Yes, I know. But why are you talking about werewolves?"

"Well, it's what you're reading, isn't it?" She pointed to the article just below the one mentioning Shersul.

This one was almost as intriguing as the first, detailing claims of multiple witnesses having seen something large and hairy in the woods. Along with that, the author noted significant reports of people disappearing all over Brord. Lilian read that part aloud. "People disappearing? Is this true?"

"No one that I know personally. But there was a family working at the creamery that moved out a month ago. The widow said her husband had gone into them woods with one of their sons. Both went missing."

A pulse of worry flooded Lilian's ligaments. To think that a werewolf could be the culprit of a missing father and son was downright absurd, but she had known things more absurd. "And you wouldn't possibly believe…?"

"That it was a werewolf? Ha, like I would," Ethel scoffed. "I mean, would you?"

"Here you go, son," a familiar tenor called from behind Lilian, startling her. She spun around, her heart racing, to find him handing a few coins to the newsboy. The sudden scream that escaped her lips seemed to echo down the street.

The newsboy jerked his head towards her, his eyes wide with surprise. Ethel froze, her eyes mirroring the boy's shock. Even an elderly couple across the street paused, glancing over curiously at the sudden outburst.

He, unfazed by the commotion, calmly took the newspaper from the boy, his movements deliberate. As he stepped closer, his gaze was fixed on Lilian, a mix of amusement and something unreadable in his eyes. She felt rooted to the spot, her earlier excitement replaced by a cold wave of fear. "Why, Lilian, am I that ugly?" he asked, his voice laced with a teasing undertone.

Lilian looked down at her feet as he continued to lower his eyes on her. "Spencer."

"Wait. You two know each other?" Ethel said, slowly taking hold of Lilian's arm as if she sensed her unease.

"Of course she does," Spencer said. "We're good friends. Aren't we, Lilian?"

She curled into herself, unsure if she was permitted to leave. She likened Spencer to a snake the way he always slinked out from around some corner, ready with pure lies to loose off his black tongue.

Her eyes narrowed as she whispered. "What are you here for?"

He held up his item. "The paper."

Her lips pinched together before groaning, "You..."

"What?" he threatened.

Whatever she had thought to call him, she quickly stopped herself.

Ethel tugged on Lilian's arm. "Well, I think we should really get going. Miss Cora is waiting."

Lilian would have gone with her. But her feet had become practically glued to the pavement. Ethel tugged harder. "Lilian?"

"It's not me. He's doing it, not me," she said softly while looking up at Spencer's sickly eyes.

Ethel let go. "What?" She gave Lilian a few more seconds to follow her. When she figured Lilian had made up her mind to stay, she started to walk away. "I don't have time for this."

Lilian waited until she could no longer hear Ethel's shoes to say, "I asked what you are here for."

Spencer crossed his arms with a smirk. "Wouldn't you like to know."

"Are you two gonna move out the way? I'm workin' here," the newsboy said, making himself remembered.

Lilian raised a brow. "Are we, Spencer?" She felt a hand suddenly hold her at the torso.

"Is there a problem?"

Craning her neck to the side, she saw Paul's face. "Paul. You did not come this mo—"

He held a finger to his lips, silencing her. He looked again at Spencer.

Spencer said, "What are *you* still doing here?"

"Still?" said Lilian. "What do you mean? Did you know that Paul— that *either* of us would be in Brord?" She turned her head again to Paul who seemed just as unsurprised as Spencer. "I don't understand what is going on. Have you two been… chatting?"

"Can y'all move out of the way like I said?!" the newsboy shouted.

Paul laughed. "Don't worry. We were just leaving." He shared another steely gaze with Spencer before turning Lilian around and walking the other way.

Lilian did not feel right turning her back on such a monster as Spencer. But Paul's confidence made her not mind it. Still, she wanted to understand what exactly took place. "Why did you not call on me?"

"I was just a little delayed is all. I fell into a deep sleep last night."

"Oh." She slapped her forehead. "Of course you were tired. You drove two days in a row."

"Don't beat yourself over it."

"I really am sorry, Paul. I hope you are well rested."

"I am, thank you."

She grinned shortly then went back to frowning. "He scares me, Paul. Spencer is nothing but a snake."

"Lilian, watch the way you speak. It is not becoming of you."

"But he *is*."

"Well, you are going to have to behave around him."

Lilian came to an abrupt halt. "Paul Partridge, be serious."

"I *am* being serious. You should behave yourself in all company. Especially that of an eligible young bachelor."

Her eyes went wide at the presumption. "Eligible?" He must have known how outlandish it sounded, how averse it was to her soul. "What are you suggesting? No, don't say it."

She held up her finger. "I've already stopped listening." She started making brisk steps to get ahead of him.

As far as Lilian had been aware, both she and Paul shared a mutual disgust for Spencer. Why would he now make it seem as if he were trying to hand her off to him?

They crossed over to the next block. She ignored his presence behind her, stopping with intrigue for the green attraction they nearly passed up. It was a department store.

She peered in to see the small space decked in orange carpet and paisley walls. Its contents were arrays of organized clutter so to speak, stored in bins, and displayed on shelves. A wide table in the middle of the room, which defined the path of movement for the customers inside, carried folds of fabric. The fabric was quite outdated, but pretty nonetheless. Lilian could spot an umbrella rack, grandfather clock, and a typewriter that sat on a stand against the wall near the writing desk, telegraph, and other writing tools. Streamers were hung about the room from wall to wall for no specific reason other than to bring attention to the items.

However, none of those things impressed Lilian. It was in fact the sight of the old man standing behind the counter with his apron on. And his wife sitting by on a bench with their toddler nursing upon her lap. Then an older boy came skipping up behind the clerk to watch his father handle a client. His young eyes, so full of wonder and delight, ready to assist his father however he could.

Lilian watched with the same delight, sighing. "Isn't it wonderful?"

"What is?" said Paul.

"Family. Love." She turned to him. "Could you want for anything more?" Her eyes gleamed at his for a lengthy two seconds. It was a dangerous game to play on his timid mind. She broke her gaze, laughing a little. "I mean besides having the career of your dreams." She waited for his eyes to show agreeance, but instead, she saw in them a steady frown.

"No, I suppose not."

Lilian leaned against the brick, turning her face up at him. "If it's not too intrusive of me to ask, are there any women you have been considering?"

"For… marriage?"

"Yes. Marriage."

Paul looked again through the window, his focus drifting from her. "No."

Her heart hung on though she almost believed him. It was the involuntary twitch of his upper lip that gave him away. "You're lying, you know."

He turned his face back toward her with lifted brows.

"But I'll allow it." She moved off the wall and kept walking, making sure to brush his shoulder with her own. He turned to walk at her side now.

"Aunt Krishta should be in Brord today," she recalled. "Will you take me to Uncle's factory?"

"If you like. It will be a long walk, though."

"Yes, but I think I won't mind it. I need to move my legs after being driven so long."

"Yes, we wouldn't want you to have weak legs."

Lilian paused to give him an admonishing stare. He tried terribly to hold back a smirk.

Just as they reached the corner where the pub was, a stunting clamor of besotted men resounded out the doors, drawing their attention. Thrusted outside and into Paul and Lilian's way was the taut and tall body of a red-haired man— Mister Foster. The crowd inside roared with the man who threw him. Foster quickly jumped to his feet, charging toward the man with his fist up. But the timely slam of the door against Foster's fist caused him to yelp and swear viciously.

Lilian held Paul's hand, moving closer to his side. She didn't know what was going on.

Mister Foster swore again at the pavement this time before noticing the two standing there. Upon recognizing the young man who had employed him, his eyes filled with shock. Paul's eyes, even more so.

"Uh…" Foster straightened his back, placing his leather hat back over his unruly curls which stopped at his ears. "Hey, y'all. Please excuse my behavior. I..."

Paul just looked at him without a word to be said.

Ignoring Paul's unforgiving reaction, Mister Foster switched his attention to Lilian and tipped his hat. "Doesn't matter. I'm sorry for gettin' in your way." He turned to cross the street.

Paul looked at Lilian who shrugged in return. She was already starting to regret encouraging Paul to employ Mister Foster, but it was not like they had a choice. They kept walking around to the street where the inn was. As Paul's pace slowed while approaching the doors, Lilian asked him, "You aren't coming to say hi to Miss Cora?" She gestured toward the home at the end of the subdivision.

"Sorry. I would, except—"

"Except what?"

His gaze darted as he was unable to give an excuse. As she waited for his answer, watching him stand against the noon sky, she ignored his silence, taking a second to admire him while unconsciously inching closer. He was frozen in curiosity as she did it.

Before any question was required, she caught herself being strange and broke her stare.

Contrarily, Paul's stare intensified. "There, just now. You became so full of it," he whispered.

The comment surprised her. "Of what?"

"What I see. What I have always seen in those deep, dark eyes of yours." His hand slipped out from his pocket, and her heart stopped as he brought it to the side of her face. The feeling of his delicate fingers made her skin flush and heart skip. She delighted in how gentle they were, the hands of a young scholar. "Light," he breathed out.

Her brows joined. "Light?"

"Yes. And it deserves to be shown, Lilian. Not hidden. You have to understand just how much I mean that. Just how important it is that you stay who you have always been."

"But I'm *not* who I have always been. Can't you see that?" She wanted him to see that. As long as he saw her as her same old self, she'd still be part of his same old affection.

He frowned. "Yes. And I'm to blame for it."

"What do you mean?"

His hand dropped from her face. Again his eyes seemed to drift, concealing whatever thoughts he continued to withhold from her.

His strangely frequent withdrawal was beginning to prick at her nerves. "Should I disappear?"

"What?" Her remark caught him off guard.

"Well… you keep looking away."

"Sorry, I don't mean to…. Lil. You don't know me like you think you do."

She blinked at the statement. "Are you joking right now? If you are, you will have to tell me. You know you're terrible at jokes."

"I'm *not* joking." He was adamant enough to almost convince her.

"Alright. Then tell me what it is I don't know."

"I can't do that."

"Why?"

His body faced more toward the doors of the inn. "Because you will hate me if I do."

"Impossible." She could tell he disagreed with her but placed her hand on his shoulder. "What is troubling you? Tell me. You used to tell me everything." She brought her face just a little closer to his. "I promise I won't hate you. All I know how to do is… love you."

Finally his lapis blues lifted and focused on her eyes, becoming more trusting and giving her some assurance that he was opening up. "Lil, I…"

"Yes?"

With the shut of his eyes, he came back to his senses, moving her away. "We will continue this conversation later. Alright?"

Lilian was madly confused and slightly embarrassed but would not press him further. "Alright." Slowly, she turned around again and stepped away while breathing out, "I'll be waiting."

As an hour of corralling children, cleaning messes, and doing anything else Miss Cora asked of her passed by, Lilian had been eager to finally continue her talk with Paul. At 3:00 p.m., the children were taken out to play in the garden. So she went upstairs to freshen up. Her second change of clothes for the day would be a little more fitted, with a decorative lapel and lowly puffed sleeves. She had considered a veil. *But it's so pretentious*, she thought. So her usual hat would have to do.

Lilian was now downstairs, watching the front yard from a window. She had given him thirty minutes of her patience, but there was no sight of him. Lilian was becoming more put out with him as the time incremented. She had paced the floor about fifty paces and stood still for about fifteen minutes.

"Poor thing," Ms. Cora said after entering the foyer. She had been gardening. Lilian could tell because she was still wearing her gloves, now pulling them off finger by finger. "Is he still not here?"

Lilian looked once more out the window then shook her head. "I wish I knew what was keeping him. He knows I have to see Aunt Krishta soon. If he does not show up, I may have to go alone."

Though she had answered the question, Ms. Cora fell awfully silent for an odd moment. She started to keen her eyes on Lilian's appearance, her gaze drawing down to the young lady's shoes. It stunted Lilian as to why the old woman was being so strange. "Well, aren't *you* looking smart."

Lilian clicked her tongue. "Oh, well… I simply needed to change clothes."

Ms. Cora let a giggle loose.

"Why are you laughing?"

"Li'l lady, you won't be able to fool a formally married woman. I understand how he makes you feel."

Instant heat rushed to Lilian's cheeks.

"He's only down the street. Why not call on him?"

Lilian showed a disagreeing shock in her eyes. "Call on him? Absolutely not. That would be—"

"Practical?"

"Improper."

Miss Cora regarded her with heavy lids, not sharing her anxiety. "Li'l lady, I'm all for being proper when it's practical. And at the moment, you can't afford to miss seeing your aunt." She began to walk away. "But you can do whatever you think is best. No need to listen to me."

Lilian loathed the idea of stepping out of the security and comfort that etiquette had always provided her without fail. But Miss Cora was right. Perhaps Paul somehow forgot to come. She could at least make sure he was alright.

It did not take long for her to make the final decision of stepping out the door and leaving through the gate. Soon she was on her way towards the Sweetgum Cottage Inn. It also did not take long for her better judgement to chirp inside her ear. *But what will I say after going in? How will it sound if I ask for him?*

By the time she had arrived by the inn, all those thoughts quieted. It seemed almost like rebellion just to commit to going in. But she wanted more time with Paul. Even if he was not making it easy for her to have that with him. She stood before the doors and quickly straightened out her dress some more. In as much time as it took to inhale and exhale a readying breath, she walked inside. She looked around with appreciation as soon as she was inside. From the canary wallpaper to the homogenous use of an inoffensive wood— likely sassafras— that made the coffered ceiling, imperial staircase and everything else until at last, the floor. The head of a buck on the wall above the front desk caught the most attention, having been the first thing to greet her. Somewhere to her left, there was a sitting area where a few guests were enjoying coffee as of now. Their voices were hushed and for the most part everything was quiet in the inn.

Lilian saw no one working the front desk, but approached it anyway. There was a little bell sitting atop it, so she pressed it. Just as she had done the action, up shot a lanky man— possibly in his late twenties— with a dark unibrow and mustache. The mustache, having bits of breadcrumbs due to the sandwich he was currently indulging in. His forehead wrinkled in surprise as if he had been caught in a heinous act.

Lilian's eyes were wide due to the funny way he had appeared. "Hello," she said to start him off.

Seeming to realize she was in fact addressing him, the man gulped down the piece he was chewing, cleared his throat and leaned forward with a grin. "Uh, hello, indeed. Very nice to meet you, ma'am." He held out a hand. "Call me Pete."

Lilian gave him her hand which he kissed. "Hello, Pete."

Pete's grin was soon a smile. "And what's a pretty girl like you doing in these parts? Oh, but don't answer that. No need to tell me. I'll figure it out, anyway. All that really matters to you, I suppose, is if you can get a room. Well, you're in luck since we're not full. Was full an hour ago but not at this moment..."

He spoke so fast she was unable to interrupt him to say what she was truly there for.

"... Got one room left for you, and let me just say, it has a mighty fine view..."

"Sir? Uh, sir?" Lilian tried.

"...There's not much space, I'm afraid. But you are just one lady, anyway. Unless you aren't— that is, single, I mean. Are you single? Oh, don't answer that. I'll find out. But for a low price of seven dollars and twenty-five cents, you shouldn't mind the space. Of course, I can't tell you what you should or shouldn't mind. I'm just ramblin', you know, so please excuse it all. But what do you say? Shall I take you up there?" He spun around and marched toward the board behind him where all the keys were hung, returning thereafter with the key to the aforementioned room. "Here you are."

Lilian opened her mouth to protest, but closed it with a grin of amusement. She kindly shook her head at him.

He looked at the key in his hand then her again, blushing with embarrassment. "You didn't come for a room, did you?"

She giggled. "No. I…" Lilian looked from side to side, then leaned in to whisper, "I'm waiting on someone. One of your tenants."

He nodded, whispering back. "Oh, sure. Who?"

"Could you tell Paul Partridge that Lilian Truit is here?"

The man's smile froze a moment before the corners of it lowered into a worried clench.

Lilian was unsure if she had said something wrong. "You can, can't you?"

Pete exhaled deeply. "Ma'am. I'm afraid he left just an hour ago."

"Left? Where did he go? When will he be back?"

"Likely not ever. You see, Paul Partridge is why we have a spare room now. Took all his stuff with him and checked out of the inn."

His words fell on her tender ears like flecks of fire singeing her before cooling just as quick. "He left? But it wasn't time to leave. He would not go without telling me."

"Well, that's true in a way…" Pete reached under his desk and pulled out an unsealed envelope. "He said to give this to whoever asked for him."

Lilian hesitated for a moment, eyeing the letter. She was wondering how to feel in this moment as a tinge of sadness and misunderstanding mixed within her. She gently took the letter from Pete's hand.

"Don't worry. It's not all bad," Pete said as if to reassure her. "Not that I read it," he added with a nervous chuckle. "But forgetting to seal an envelope can lead *anyone* to spy its contents, you know…. You know?"

Lilian did not mind his remark. "Thank you anyway." She turned around and— while already unfolding the envelope— walked to one of the empty chairs to sit. A deep breath helped in slipping the card out. The card smelled like Paul. She imagined— as she read the words— that he was standing in front of her, saying them to her face.

My Dear Lilian,

I know you must be very disappointed and angry with me. I only hope you can forgive me for this haste departure. Please understand this much—— that I never meant to hurt you.

Lilian, even in the midst of such confusion, please believe me when I say that I did not leave because I found any fault in you. No, rather, it's due to the fault I keep finding in myself every time I stare into your pure, unsuspecting eyes. El knows how those eyes condemn me.

I am not the boy you thought I was, Lilian. I never have been. I have hurt you and your family in ways more indirect than this, and in doing so I have betrayed your trust. I should not tell you now what I have done. Not while you aren't yet over your grieving period. But El knows as much as I do that I am not worthy of being your friend... though I once dreamed of being more than that.

By El, I wish with all my heart that I could have stayed. At least I can be sure you are in safe care. But Lilian, if you are still reading this letter even through your tears, I need you to heed my words carefully. For, the state I have left you in is the most precarious state of your entire life.

The same beast that has broken me apart is now after good souls like you. Do not be fazed by the obscurity of my words. I am writing this as frankly as I can for your tender understanding. So entreat me with your efforts to follow what I say whether you understand it or not.

Lilian, my heart, I do not know what is coming your way. All I know is that you must never ever be *so quick to trust anything or anyone. I am afraid you will find that in this world, even El may fail you. Look out for your light, Lilian. The world is so undeserving of it. Yet, I know that it will try as it may to snuff the light right out of you. But if you succeed against it, it will give me hope for my own success.*

~ Yours Undoubtedly, Paul

When Lilian reached the end of the letter, what she had heard were many contradictory conclusions. That he did not want to leave but did so anyway, that he may or may not have loved her beyond a friend, and that all she had ever known him to be— no matter how sure she was of him— was not the real him. And so, it became incredibly clear to her that Paul Partridge was the most confusing man she had ever met.

Allies

Her chest was sore of disappointment as she took aimless steps along the pebbled road. There were still some shallow puddles in places where the road dipped. It had to be almost a ten-mile walk around the outskirts of Brord Village to the factory. She had decided that at some point she would run, but for now, would conserve her energy. On her right was the lake Mister Foster had told her about. Dry grass and bare trees surrounding it.

She almost passed up the lake in a hurry, but all of a sudden felt unable to continue. She stopped and directed her gaze upon the still water, moving closer down the littoral slant. She saw herself in the water. Her eyes were still glinting in the way she hated. So she covered them with her hands. Now she saw nothing.

These eyes somehow made Paul leave me. She lowered her hands, looked at her reflection again, and cried. When the pain became too much for her, she looked upward at the sky. "You did it again. I might as well never love another man in my life." She crouched down and picked up a rock. "I have tried to understand you. To understand your plan for me. I didn't know the plan was for me to end up alone!" Lilian threw the stone with all her strength, then watched as it hit the other side of Etowah Lake.

Hate Him, the sudden voice in her mind said, though it was not the Elwind's. Lilian's eyes shifted from left to right, confused. "Hate Him." There it was again. This time it was as if she could hear it clearly while feeling a breath hit her ear.

"No," her head shook. "I don't hate Him." With that said from a most genuine place in her heart, she felt the looming wind leave her. However, she knew it was sure to come back.

The next thing she became aware of was the trotting sound of horses and the creaky wagon they pulled. She looked above her and saw Mister Foster's wagon appear on the bridge. With the tarp down, she could see the mound of junk he carried in the bed.

Lilian tried to look away and not be noticed. His wagon approached the end of the bridge, turning onto the road. She heard him slow behind her.

"Afternoon."

Lilian closed her eyes and inhaled deeply.

"Afternoon," he repeated louder.

She turned around, looking upward at him on his high seat. Lilian pointed to herself.

"Yes, you."

"Afternoon," she replied.

"What are you doing here all alone?"

"Just enjoying some time to myself, thank you."

His eyes squinted at her. "So, I'm guessing those are tears of joy?"

Him pointing out her tears made Lilian wipe her cheek. She was silent, hoping he would not ask her what she was crying about.

"Need a ride?" he said.

Relieved, she answered, "Yes. I do, actually." She watched him hop down, coming around to her. He held out his hand. "I'll help you in."

She gave him her hand and he guided her to the wagon, hoisting her up to the seat. Soon, he was also in. "Where to?"

"My uncle's factory. I assume you know the way."

"Of course." He kissed the air twice, and the horses started to canter.

For some time, they rode without talking to each other. But every so often Lilian could see from the corner of her eye that he opened his mouth with something in mind to say. "Is something the matter?"

Mister Foster acted at first as if he had not heard her. But he soon looked her way. "Oh, it's just.... About my behavior this morning, I just got into it with my landlord over his last minute decision to raise the rent." A grimace shown on his face. "That man thinks he can play me. But I know all he wants is to.... Sorry, it don't matter to you. But you ain't holdin' it against me, are you?" His question was earnest to the point it moved her. Perhaps it had something to do with the newly apparent hue of his eyes which resembled the dewy ochre of honey. She hadn't seen them up close before. Despite his gaffes, she saw a sweeter soul.

"*I* wouldn't. But I am not sure whether *Paul* would." She frowned, looking the other way and murmuring, "And besides, he may just forget to pay you."

"What?"

"No worries. If he does, I will pay you instead."

"You didn't hire me. You're saying he'd forget to pay me, but why would he forget?"

"Because he's gone." Just as she said it, she was swallowing down a lump of pain. "He left in a rush because.... I don't know." She watched as Jase's expression dimmed while facing the road again. "I apologize on his behalf, Mister Foster."

"Jase." He looked at her with a passive demeanor showing that his frustration was not for her. "It's Jase."

"I apologize on his behalf, Jase."

"No need." He turned his attention back to the road. "I'll fix his El-forsaken car. And I'll do it for free."

"Are you sure?"

Jase did not respond, so she believed his mind was made no matter how unfruitful the effort of fixing the car would be. However, a new thought entered her mind. A rather intrusive thought. "Jase, if you don't mind me asking, why are you not still working at Truit and Company?"

Jase's shoulders tensed a moment before shrugging. "'Cause Truit and Company is managed by men who hate progress. And anyone who suggests better ways to get things done is apparently a liability."

"Really?"

"Yep."

If what he said was true, it was a very serious issue. Lilian never knew a man more in favor of progress than her uncle. To hinder such a thing by firing employees would go against his vision for the company. Now Lilian was too interested in the details of this story. "And what ways did you have in mind?"

There was an ounce of surprise in Jase's eyes when he looked at her again. But noticing that she was fully listening, he proceeded to tell her his ideas.

By the time the wagon came upon the square of land the factory occupied, Lilian was rendered speechless by Jase's flawless solutions for optimizing the workflow.

In fact, she became so enveloped in his long explanation that she hardly noticed where she was and that the ride had stopped, until Jase said, "Here we are, Miss Truit."

"Oh," she said, looking across the field. Before she could say another word, he had gotten off his seat to help her down. Lilian placed her hand in his as she hopped to the ground.

He grinned. "Alright. Be safe."

Would it be right to let him simply leave? After all that he has said? There was so much potential there, and Lilian knew how rare natural intellect was to come by. She wanted to know why anyone would overlook him, understanding well what it was like to be overlooked. As she watched his eyes, it became harder to dismiss the problem. She put aside her pain temporarily, now feeling a yeuk of necessity to help the man. She smiled in return, her hand gently tugging his. "Come with me."

"What?"

"I could show you to my aunt. Once she hears your ideas—"

"Uh-uh. Sorry, I can't just walk on up there where I'm not wanted."

"But this is your chance to explain yourself. And they won't say anything if you are with me."

"Miss Truit—"

"Lilian."

He sighed. "Lilian, this is not what I came here for."

She squinted with interrogation. "Did you have somewhere better to be?" In a second, she heard herself. "Sorry, that sounded rude."

Jase's eyes lowered. "It did," then lifted to her with a following smirk, "but it's true."

Lilian, for some reason, kept note of his forgiving answer. "All I am saying is that you helped me, so now I want to help you."

She could see that he was considering her point. "Like allies?"

"Yes. Like allies. You deserve to have your job back. Won't you fight for it?"

His golden eyes flickered as he looked ahead at the building. His gaze went back to her. He shrugged. "Guess we goin' in."

Lilian was happy with herself for persuading him. Before he changed his mind, she started across the sparse grass. He followed behind and they came through one of the three open entrances that were like great gaps on the building's side. The scent of iron preceded the sight of men in aprons and welder's gloves. They moved out of the way with suspicious glances as Jase and Lilian entered. All the workers operated among chains dangling from above them that were part of some pulley system attaching to the ceiling and walls. The room was toasty thanks to the furnace set against one wall. Lilian sauntered through the rows of long tables at which metal parts were being assembled. There were wooden barrels in almost every corner holding metal parts and components already assembled and organized accordingly.

They must have been short on tools considering how frequently they were passing them amongst each other. A worker's hip bumped her out of his way as he passed. Lilian was the one to apologize.

"Do you know where you're going?" Jase asked over her shoulder a little closer than she expected him to be.

Lilian craned her neck, regarding him. "Not really. I'm looking for my aunt. She is having a meeting with the executives."

"Well then she wouldn't be down here in *this* mess. I know where to go. Follow me."

She said nothing as he took hold of her hand, walking her back outside. He brought her over to the short side of the building where an iron rail led up to either the second floor or the rooftop. Jase turned to her, pointing upward.

"Up there?" she said.

"Yes. The director's office is on the second floor."

"Oh, okay." Lilian held onto the cold rail and stepped onto the first step. As she continued up, she felt him move away more and more. Lilian whipped her head around. "Jase?"

His shoulders tensed as his back faced her. He was caught tiptoeing away. Jase finally turned around. "Yeah?"

Something about the action penetrated a soft spot in Lilian's heart. "You're not leaving me, are you?"

"Well, I...I..."

"I'm doing this for *you*." Lilian's face hardened from disappointment to frustration.

And so his gaze endured as if he had suddenly become aware of something. He moved toward her. "No. I'm not leaving you." Jase tipped his head up, telling her to keep going.

They went up the steep stairs. At the second level there was a skinny door in chipped red paint. Jase went ahead and opened it. They entered a dim hall. The floor on this level was varnished and rich in color. They followed the curve of a wall around to an open space lit by a row of windows.

The natural light highlighted the portraits on the adjacent wall. Pictures of the factory as it was being built, then of the many certifications, and mentions in the paper of Fredrick Truit's remarkable work. Pictures of the town— of Fredrick shaking hands with some smart man standing on a podium, a crowd watching behind them.

"Who is that man? Do you know?" Lilian inquired, not realizing how she was wasting time by standing in front of a wall.

"That's Hank Barrymore. Our former mayor."

"My uncle was friends with the mayor?"

"It was just a photography opportunity. It's not like they had any real rapport."

Lilian turned to him, frowning. "How would *you* know?"

Jase was silent for some time before admitting, "I wouldn't."

She stepped forward a little to stand in front of the large portrait of her uncle. The sepia photograph displayed a very stately, younger Fredrick Truit.

Lilian was unable to rip her eyes off the image of her favorite person in the entire world. It was a struggle to keep her eyes dry. Somehow, a tear still slipped its way onto her bottom lid.

"Are you alright?"

Lilian swiped a finger over the tear. "Sorry. I am wasting time."

He gestured ahead. "When you're ready."

The lenience in his words gave her time to come back to her senses. On her move, they continued through the hall. Coming near a door with the words 'Director's Office' pasted in gold letters on the opaque glass.

Lilian listened by the door until she heard the voice of her aunt saying, "And that would be the cost of distribution?" To which a man answered, "Yes, ma'am. We've been trying to find ways to cut the cost, however…"

Both Jase and Lilian were surprised by the following voice calling from behind them. "Hey! What are the two of you do…?" The man paused with a shocked expression, his eyes dimming on Jase. "You." His forward step was full of threat. "So, we're trespassing now, are we?"

Lilian positioned her short self in front of Jase. "We are not trespassing. He's with me."

"And just who are you, li'l lady?"

She stepped forward, extending her hand. "Lilian Truit."

The man took a moment to study her face before realizing she was telling the truth. He bent down, now obligated to kiss her hand. "Sorry, missy. I don't know how I didn't recognize the owner's niece. I heard you recently debuted, is that right?"

"It is."

"And you are even lovelier than your picture in the papers."

"Oh, thank you."

"Now that I think of it, I did see your picture myself," Jase added for some reason. "He's right. You *do* look better than it."

Lilian was less interested in talking about herself. "Well, my aunt is expecting me. She did tell you I was coming, right?"

"Yes. And when I was alerted that there was a girl lurking around here, I should have immediately known it was you. Forgive me, ma'am."

"All is well."

The door was then opened behind them. Lilian turned around and saw another man, old and fat, standing between the doorway. "What is all this noise I'm hearing? Oh, hello, youngun." His censure was abandoned when he saw the young heiress standing there.

"Hello, sir," she said. "I'm here to see my Aunt Krishta."

"Lilian?" her aunt called for her. So, the man moved aside so Lilian could enter.

"Aunt Krishta," she said excitedly, running to her dear aunt with her arms open and ready to embrace. But just as she started towards her, thinking better of her behavior, Lilian slowed her pace and lowered her arms to her sides. She came over to her aunt with sudden, remarkable poise. Lilian proceeded behind the leather chair her aunt was sitting in, resting her palm on Aunt Krishta's shoulder.

Aunt Krishta raised her hand up behind her, taking Lilian's face and moving it down over her shoulder to kiss her cheek. With a grin she said, "Oh, my darling. Are you well? Did you make it here safely?"

"Yes, ma'am."

"Is Paul here with you?"

Lilian tried not to frown too much while shaking her head.

"He's not? Well, how did you get to the factory on your own?"

"I didn't. *He* brought me." Lilian whirled her head to Jase who stood between two men's stern gazes.

"What are you doing here again?" said the older man. "I thought we got rid of you."

"Leave him alone," said Lilian. "He is with me." She pleaded with her aunt. "Aunt Krishta, this is Jase Foster. He used to work here."

"I know. I remember him," her aunt stated with an expressionless demeanor that confused her. She beckoned him with her hand. "Come here young man."

Jase seemed suspicious of Krishta's stale welcome as he stepped forward into the room. He stood with a straight back and unapologetic height that diminished the other men in the room to rats. He took his hat off, baring his messy mop of fluffy, red curls to everyone.

"It's a pleasure to see you again, Mister Foster. Have you been taking good care of my niece?" Krishta's question was simple but the tilt of her head gave some impression of encoding within her words. Encoding that Jase understood.

"Ma'am, she is as well as when you left her."

Dismissing the awkwardness in the air, Lilian continued to explain him to her aunt. "He was fired unfairly for having ideas— remarkable ideas for helping the company and its workers."

Aunt Krishta listened to Lilian with a lifted brow of intrigue. Her attention soon rested on the old man by the door. "Is this true? Have you been firing my husband's employees for having ideas?"

"Of course, not. It's just that the boy would rather share his ideas than do the task at hand."

"That's a dang lie!" Jase spoke out, producing a startled reaction out of the women in the room. "'Scuse my outburst ma'ams. I hate to be the one sayin' it, but I know I was considered a great help around here, taking on other men's tasks and helping them out when a part wasn't working right. You could ask any of the men here who know me, assuming he hasn't fired them all."

The old man scoffed. "This is utterly ridiculous. Don't listen to a thing he says."

"Hold on, sir," Aunt Krishta raised a hand. "Every man here is allowed to explain himself. And I intend to hear him out." Addressing Jase, she said, "My time here is running short. So go ahead and tell me your ideas, Mister Foster."

"Uh..." Jase seemed confounded that he was given a chance to speak, as if his mind had not fully prepared for this moment. Lilian stared and smiled as a cue for him to start. "Right. My ideas." Jase cleared his throat and began.

"The first problem I had noticed after working here so long was the lack of order when every worker moved around to weld or sand his piece. So I had proposed we make positions for certain men to do these small, repetitive tasks."

"Fair idea," said a man sitting opposite Aunt Krishta as he cleaned his spectacle with his sweater. "I see no fault in that."

"Who's to say that would've saved us any significant time." the old man argued.

"We could have done a study like I asked of you." Jase said. "But you said it was inconvenient."

"Is that what you said, Hardy?" said the man who had met Lilian at the door. His head was tilted sideways with a half-judging stare directed at his co-manager.

Hardy's eyes darted from one confused expression to the next. "I can't remember what I said. But I know that we employ engineers to be useful and do hard work, not small tasks."

As Jase shifted his weight and bent over slightly with his hands on his hips, Lilian saw that he was ready with an answer. "A man my age would do it. Granted, a man with less experience than I have, bringing me to my next point," he looked over to the man with the spectacles, "which is that you, sir, should open up a program to train men on the job. Right now, most of the workers are over fifty. I mean, I have nothin' against it, but where is the future of Truit and Company in that?"

"That's debatable. However, so far, I am hearing you advocate for things that benefit the *workers*. What about the company?"

Jase gave a nod of recognition. "To that I'd say, 'what is the company if not the workers in it?' If you help them, you *are* benefiting the company. If you want Truit and Co. to stand out, allow your workers a chance to give input, design tools to fit their needs, or anything else to help the factory's production."

Hardy spoke up. "Oh, this is just rich! Demanding things of the director? You should be ashamed of yourself."

"It's not like I work here anymore, remember?"

"Then why are you here?"

"To get his job back," Lilian said, interrupting a discussion between men. Jase shook his head slightly at her.

"Sorry."

"Well, he is not getting it back," said Lilian's aunt.

"What? But Aunt Krishta—"

"Because he will not be a worker. I want him here as a manager, instead. Clearly the young man has all the ideas. Let's see if he can make them happen."

Hardy stepped forward. "Ma'am, with all due respect, there are already enough of us overseeing production, operations, *and* quality control."

"I thought *he* decides that." Krishta pointed to the man across from her.

Who then said to her point, "I do. And I think if there is room for anyone else it's him." He pointed fondly at Jase. "I like your directness, boy."

"Thank you, sir." A grin emerged on Jase's face. His eyes suddenly cut to Lilian's, and she found herself grinning, too.

"Now the only question is, 'do you want the job?'" The director asked, pulling at Jase's attention.

"Depends, sir."

"On what?"

"I'll just say this. I've got a woman at home, three horses, and a new rent price of twenty dollars."

"Ah, if you're worried about payment, don't be. You'll get a stipend of a dollar-fifty a day. Now, how does that sound."

Lilian noticed how Jase's eyebrows shot up. And for good reason. Who would say no to a dollar-fifty a day? "Make it two and we have a deal."

Now it was Lilian's brows which shot up. She watched for the director's reaction.

To her surprise he was grinning like a bobcat. "Mister Foster," he said with an amused scoff, "where did you learn to negotiate like that?"

Just as he said it, Lilian knew exactly where; Paul.

"Alright. Two it is."

"What? Are you kidding me?" the other managers complained. "He gets fifty cent more than us and he hasn't even started?"

The director seemed nonplussed as he stood up. "Yes. Because he *asked* for two. You got a problem with that, Hardy and Willis?"

In fear of losing their jobs, the two remained silent. *A smart decision*, Lilian thought.

After all was said and done, Jase and Lilian were told to stand outside the room while Krishta Truit resumed her meeting. Just before it, Jase had had a short conversation with the director who had further introduced himself as Mr. O'Reilly. By the way the man had pulled Jase aside for a word, Lilian assumed he was affording Jase a spot under his wing. And by the way Jase gratefully received his advice, she assumed such care was not something Jase often experienced.

Now waiting just by the door, she could not stop grinning for how everything turned out.

"I oughta thank you," Jase said beside her.

Happy as she looked his way, she said, "Oh, I did nothing at all. You should be proud of yourself."

"Yeah, but you coaxed me into going."

"Coaxed? That's a very devious word. I prefer 'persuaded'."

He laughed. "Alright. You *persuaded* me into going. If not for you I'd still be hunting for a job." He moved closer, looking solemn as if there was a sudden need for him to share something with her. "I'm really sorry about your uncle."

"Oh." Her gaze dropped briefly. "Thank you."

"I'm sure it hasn't been easy for you dealing with his death."

"No, it hasn't." Lilian wasn't sure whether she wanted to say much more about it. "Sorry, I am not really in the mood to…"

"No, I understand." His focused gaze beckoned hers. For a strange two seconds, they seemed to share an understanding. "I think about my father all the time. Even if I hate to admit it. But every time I use this skill he gave me, I imagine him standing next to me and saying, 'That'll do, son.'"

"That'll do?"

Jase laughed. "A 'that'll do' from my father was like a standing ovation."

"Oh." She returned the laugh.

Finally, the door swung in as Aunt Krishta stepped out. "Alright, Lilian, are you ready?" she said while pulling down the veil on her hat.

"Just allow me a second to say goodbye to Jase." Lilian turned back to him and smiled.

Before she could speak, he did. "Would you like me to take the two of you back?"

"No, thank you," Ms. Truit answered for them. "I have someone waiting outside." Her assertion was followed by a curious wink at Lilian.

"Well then, it was another pleasure, Lilian," Jase ended. They took a moment to shake hands, his somehow warming through her glove.

With careful haste, Lilian soon joined her aunt. As they left the factory, she said, "I don't know why, but I am surprised there is a charter service out here."

"Yes, I know. And here is another surprise. Our car comes with a traveling companion."

Lilian stopped and eyed her aunt. "Gracie?"

Krishta shook her head. "No, someone of the opposite sex. And rather avid about you."

Lilian returned a confused look. It wouldn't make sense. She hadn't made many acquaintances with men. After her failure of a debut, she was certain that no suitor would come for her hand. She was not sure she even wanted that. Paul was the only man she ever wanted. Her face stung with anticipation, or perhaps it was due to the chilling air. "Who is he?"

Aunt Krishta said nothing as they finally approached the car. And when they did, Lilian wanted to run in the other direction. He sat in the backseat of the small vehicle, smoking his pipe. A puffy, stinky cloud obscured his face, until finally settling in the frigid wind. He seemed very satisfied with the sight of Lilian coming closer for some odd reason. Whatever it was for, she did not want to learn.

And she could not believe that at this moment her aunt was guiding her towards a car with him in it. But could she complain? Paul did say she should behave herself in Spencer's presence. Oh, how she wanted to scream right now in Paul's ear. And oh, how she loathed Spencer.

Suffocating

According to Aunt Krishta, she came to know Mister Wesman soon after the funeral when making a trip to the bank for a new checkbook. Spencer had assisted her while also mentioning that he recognized her name, saying he was friends with Lilian Truit back at Hiplum Academy. Aunt Krishta spoke with such gullible fondness for the encounter that it made Lilian want to leap out the car.

"And from there, he offered to be my new accountant. Wasn't that nice?"

"He did? An—And you said yes?"

"You bet she did," Spencer said from the front seat next to the driver where he had put himself so Lilian and Krishta could sit together. It did not make much of a difference when the seats were so tightly spaced that she could easily slap the back of his head without reaching too far. Well, perhaps she could if he wasn't halfway turned with one arm over the back of his seat just so he could watch her seethe at his uncanny smile.

"I am surprised you never told her about me, Lilian."

You are lucky I never told her about you. "Must have slipped my mind."

"You never slipped *my* mind."

What was he doing? Lilian could not work out what he was up to but noticed how his every comment made her aunt look at her with a suspicious glee in her eyes.

"So, does anything look as it used to, Aunt Krishta?" Lilian said as a clever attempt to switch off whatever thoughts her aunt was having.

"Yes. Everything." While Aunt Krishta's tone was appreciative, her eyes showed a little of something like disappointment. Then she seemed to look around for something.

"Is everything alright?"

"Oh, I am just tired, dear. I am sure you are, too."

Lilian let out a sigh of agreement. "Yes. It *has* been a long day for us. I wish we could have spent more of it together."

"Maybe tomorrow. It will be my last day here."

"Yes, I'd like that."

"Would Mister Wesman be willing to join us?"

Spencer was about to answer when Lilian strongly interrupted. "No!" Her aunt eyed her with shock. Lilian wrapped her hands around Aunt Krishta's arm in the most daughterly way to escape her censure. "I simply thought… it would be the two of us."

Aunt Krishta looked puzzled, giving Lilian a curious tilt of her head.

Lilian needed a better excuse. "I would love to go window shopping with you. It will be such a feminine expedition, I doubt Mister Wesman will be interested."

"Well, it depends on the store," Spencer said with a minor wave of his head, mouth drooping consideringly.

"Anywhere, you wouldn't dare step foot in." That came out with more aggravation than Lilian meant to show. But now that she said it, she could not stop herself from staring him down with a feral gaze.

She felt Aunt Krishta's hand on her shoulder. "It's alright, dear. It can be about the two of us. I only thought you wanted to catch up on things with your friend. But I see that's not what you want."

Lilian knew by the way her aunt looked at her that there was nothing more she needed to say. So, she closed her mouth, sat back in her seat, and did her best to ignore the way Spencer kept his eye on her. Before she knew it, the car came to a stop. Lilian looked up at the hanging sign of the inn with relief.

Her aunt stepped out and stood aside, waiting as the driver took out her bags.

Spencer was still turned against his seat, smiling at the girl before saying, "At ease, Miss Lilian." He sucked through his pipe once more then sighed, letting the smelly gas fill her face and not caring how she coughed in response.

The smoke was everywhere. It was so stifling that it woke Lilian out of her sleep. She rose with palms clawing at the air, jumped from her bed, and barged out of the attic. She found herself surrounded in the choking thickness that must have risen from the lowest floor. Coming down the first set of stairs leading to the second floor, she stumbled upon the rail and looked below her while coughing violently. Thinking that there was no way to wake up the others in time, she shouted as loudly as she could. "FIRE! FIRE!"

She plopped down on the step, nearly giving up as the gas seemed to cloud her head. Again she shrieked the word with all the air in her body. No one seemed to respond. Still repeating it, her fatigue was getting to her. And the word was said with less and less effort as she rested her head between the wooden bars of the rail. Now it was only a whisper escaping her lips. Lilian focused her mind on that whisper. So much so that she did not notice the confused group surrounding her.

The children watched in distress. "Fire where?" they asked.

It was Maude's hands which jostled her back to consciousness. "C'mon, sweetie. Wake up."

Lilian let go of the bars, realizing how tightly she had been gripping them when her palms ached. Someone had turned on the lights. Lilian opened her eyes and saw the many little eyes staring back at her.

"What's wrong with her?" some asked. "Why was she screaming?"

Lilian blushed with embarrassment as she understood what an uproar she caused.

Maude, who was holding her at the shoulders, kindly asked, "Are you good, Miss Lilian?"

"Uh... yes, I— I am so sorry, everyone. I really did smell smoke."

"It's alright," Ms. Cora reassured. "You just were having a little nightmare is all. Do you need help going back to your room."

"No, thank you. I've been too much trouble already."

"Are you sure?" Ms. Cora asked again, but Lilian was already on her feet, padding up the steps. She left the startled-awake bevy of children on her way back to her room while feeling the prickly awkwardness in the air.

Finally, she slipped into the attic and gently closed the door. The following sound of a little boy coughing beside her made her almost jump. He was silent and without surprise. She recognized him as the blind boy she had seen on her first day at Ms. Cora's— Hugh. He hadn't been downstairs at all since then.

Yet here he was, staring at the general area she stood in. His brows expressed urgency. "I need to talk to you."

"Me? What about?"

"'bout the dream you had."

"Oh, I am fine. Really."

"No. You won't be soon. *We* won't be."

"Pardon?"

He must have sensed the discomfort in her tone that leaned toward withdrawal. It must have been the reason he was silent for a few seconds. "I have to tell you this..." his palm relaxed open at his hip as he spoke with caution and some measure of impatience. "I think you should have a sit."

"Uh..." Lilian turned around, looking towards her bed, or at least the shape of it. No light had been turned on in the room, not that it made any difference to a boy who could not see. It was too late in the night to entertain this boy, but his behavior had her both bemused and amused. And it felt wrong to turn him away without hearing his concerns. Rarely (if ever) did anyone come to her for concerns.

"Let me just turn on the light first." Lilian sucked down a yawn as she came to the side of her bed. She felt for the lamp chain. Finally grasping it, she pulled. "Ah, now I see you clearly."

He made his way to the edge of the bed without any trouble and sat right down. She stepped around to join him. "What were you saying?" She said with a sigh and a smile.

"You saw the smoke. I know you did. I've seen it, too. It's coming to Brord."

"What are you talking about?"

"The Elwind said we had to be ready... he said..." The boy started to shiver at whatever words were churning his mind. He was gulping frequently, looking increasingly more ill.

Lilian did not know what to do other than bring her arm around him. "Hey, it's alright." She patted his side. "No need to worry."

"But there *is*. You aren't ready. Now *no one* is."

"Ready for what?"

"War."

She had nothing to say to that, turning still by the word.

"Lilian?"

"I heard you. Look, I am sorry but.... I think it is time you go to your room."

"But... I can't do that. Not now. I waited like Shersul said for the Fisher to show up."

"Shersul? You spoke to Shersul?"

"Mm, hm. He told me all about you once. Said you used to be his friend."

"*Used* to be?" It was a lash to her soul. How could Shersul speak like that? Like he had decided to discard her from his heart?

"He said you lost your way."

"*Me*?! *I* lost my way?! He left!" Lilian pushed off her bed to stand. She started pacing around the room. "What else did he say?"

"You're not mad, are you?"

"Just tell me what he said."

"He said you were special to him. *Still* special," Hugh said. Quite adamantly, too, as if to gain back her interest. "And he wants to make you a Fisher."

Lilian stopped pacing with her hands holding her back. "I have not gone fishing since I was a little girl."

"Not like that." Hugh stood, himself. And slowly stepped in as straight a line as he could, meeting her across the room. Then his eyes drew up until they rested on her. Somehow.

"I thought you couldn't see."

He shrugged. "I use a different kind of sight. The one Shersul gave me. The one he gave you. 'Cept you won't use it."

Lilian's gaze fell regretfully. "I forgot how." Her voice cracked as the woeful realization caught in her throat.

"That's okay. He's not done with you. He wants to help you remember. El has chosen you to bring him an army. To catch men the way you caught fish."

"But why has he chosen *me*?"

"I don't know. He never told me why."

This was too much for Lilian to process. From the boy's mouth she was hearing hope, purpose, and change. Three daunting concepts she had left behind her. It was frivolous to hope, purpose was a lie, and it would kill her to ever be expected to throw away the image she had so finely curated for herself and change. "Well, I am sorry to have disappointed you," Lilian said, "but I have to be up early tomorrow to catch up with my aunt, so..." Lilian did not necessarily need to meet her aunt at an early time. For, Krishta would be in Brord for the whole day. Lilian simply needed a fair enough excuse for the boy to leave.

His eyelids lowered. "Won't you think about it, at least?"

Her sigh was the only answer she gave.

His shoulders fell, as did his concern. "Forget it. You're not listening." His socks padded the ground as he walked to the door then felt for the knob. "Nobody listens."

"Should I help you downsta—" her sentence was cut off by his unapologetic slam of the door. The clammer worried her that the others would wake again, though after a long silence, it seemed no one heard it.

The way he left filled her with a sense of shame. But she had no reason to be ashamed of offending the wild thoughts of a nine-year-old boy.

Evocative

Today was the day for Tess to leave... for a while. But a while was all she needed to spend without being stressed about housework and horses or being disappointed by Jase's many excuses for why he'd come home late, or missing a good chat with Ms. Cora and playing with the children. A Jase-free day was like a sweet taste of peace.

After her quick dressing, she practically skipped to the kitchen, made a plate of eggs for Jase along with his coffee on the table, and took her reticule as she stepped toward the door. Upon pulling the knob, there was an equal force pushing the door open from the outside. Tess frowned at the man standing in the threshold. "I thought you were asleep."

"I was only mucking out the stalls. What, did you expect to walk out without giving me a kiss first?"

"Yeah, that was pretty much the plan."

He didn't have to ask as his fingers slid down the small of her back. "Come here." He drew her in for a quick kiss.

Tess then held up the purse in her hand. "I sure hope Mr. Thomas accepts it."

"He'll accept *anything* from *you*. Only I did see him yesterday at the pub, and—"

"What were you doing at the pub?" Her question came out as accusatory as it truly was, though she meant to sound insincere.

Jase's eyes flickered due to the sudden interruption of his sentence. "I wasn't drinking, if that's what you think."

"Sorry. What were you saying?"

He rubbed between his eyes for moment, as if becoming frustrated by the fact that she still expected the worst of him. "I was trying to say that he told me he was raising the rent."

Tess shook her head at him. "Tell me you're lying." But she knew he was telling the truth. "By how much?"

"He's asking for twenty dollars a month now."

Her eyes skimmed the sight of her kitchen, now feeling confused at what she was even doing trying to leave the house with a dollar less than the original price. "And you only thought to tell me this now?"

"It's alright, Tess."

"Alright?" The way he spoke so calmly annoyed her.

"Yes," he said with a curious smile. "I have something for you. Wait here." Jase moved past her to get to the cupboard. From the jar they usually kept their funds in (the jar she hadn't cared to inspect this morning, thinking it would be near empty) he pulled out an amount of four five-dollar bills, leaving one in the jar.

Tess was so surprised, she half-shrieked, quickly covering her mouth with her hands. "Jase, you must be trying to kill me!"

He let out a strong laugh. "Why do you say that?"

Tess started to hold her chest, breathing heavily. "Where in El's name did you acquire that much money?"

"Some boy from Hiplum asked me to fix his car. So he paid me twenty-five upfront. You should see the thing. She's a beauty, Tess, I've been keeping her by the shed and thought you would've noticed by now."

Her mind recalled that she had seen something glint from behind the shed when she was outside pumping water.

"Take it," he said, holding out the money.

Tess took it, rubbing her fingers over the handful of paper and feeling, to some degree, wealthy. But it would only be for a moment because she'd have to hand it over to Scott soon. "Anything else you should tell me before I leave?"

He held up a finger. "Actually, I was gettin' to it. I got a new job."

"New job? By El, Jase, what happened to the old one? At the plastering agency?"

"That one fell through. See, I was waiting to tell you—."

"You always wait to tell me everything!" She slapped the table next to her.

"I just knew it would stress you out to tell you that. So I searched for a job all that time, Tess. I searched hard."

"Stop. Just stop." She turned to hunch over with her palms on the table. "I don't ever feel like I know what's goin' on."

Jase came and held her at the shoulders. "I'm sorry. I really am. Hey, it's not just any job, Tess. I'll be a manager at the factory."

Tess winced. "The factory? You mean the same factory that fired you?"

"We had a talk about that, and they apologized."

She turned around, placing her hands on his forearms. "Why would you ever go back to *those* people. You're too good to let them use you."

"Well, I can tell you one thing, it wasn't my idea. I met someone. She helped me plead my case."

By the way Jase smirked with lowered eyes as he mentioned a 'she', Tess tried not to curl her lip. There was a certain way a man could say 'she' that would hint to the lady's age. "Who?" she asked in a flat tone.

"Tess…" He stared silently into her eyes as if the lady's name was too terrifying to pronounce.

"C'mon, Jase, spit it out. Who is she?"

"She's… your sister."

Tess's hands drew into her chest. She watched his eyes, seeking out a sign that he was lying. But she knew he would never lie about something like that.

"You spoke to her?"

"Yes, and she was actually nice."

"Nice?" Tess rolled her eyes. "Oh, yeah, I'm sure she is."

"It's true, Tess. I think you should meet her."

"Now, you're losing me." Tess stepped around him, moving toward the door.

"Krishta said 'hello'."

Tess stopped right in front of it. "Why are you telling me that? I don't care what that woman said. She was nice too. Then she left."

"You know, that was sixteen years ago."

"So?"

Jase hesitated to give a rebuttal. "Nothing."

"That's what I thought." Her opening and shutting of the door was so quick, it was practically one motion. She walked around to the stables and opened one of the stalls, snapping her fingers at Jaundice. "Come on now."

He leaned his head forward toward her with a horsely grunt. She put her delicate hand on his shiny muzzle lined with short hairs. She rubbed the side of his warm belly. "There is no one I can trust better than you, you hear me? No one." She placed her forehead on his. The horse's darling black eye regarded her for a moment before closing, enjoying being petted.

Tess couldn't stop the old memories from flooding in. She wiped her eyes as they dripped the smallest tears. "Alright. Time to go."

Winter (1892)

A rumble and roar of a crowd, a swinging of shops' doors, and a medley of crying babies in carriages. These were the many noises of the younger Brord Village. The way it was when Tess was a youth. She could hear the sounds perfectly. And she could smell the familiar aroma of Mr. Hankinson's cornbread.

Tess opened her eyes. Her body was bent over the booth display. It was an early winter morning, and if you were lucky, the freshest bread would be there waiting for you. Tess must have been lucky. She slipped her hand out of her coat pocket, inspecting her funds for such an option. Not enough. She knew better than to pout. Instead, she gave the baker a small smile. He returned his own with understanding.

I didn't want it that bad anyway, thought Tess. But just as she decided she would go home to her sick mother, someone's shoulder brushed against hers. He leaned over the display, switching his gaze between her and the bread. Tess took in a breath and sighed, shaking her head. She waited for the tall boy to say something. He always had something to say.

"It's the cornbread you want, isn't it?"

Tess ignored him, looking the other way.

But persistent Jase would not be ignored. He brought his head closer to the side of her face. "*Isn't it?*" he repeated.

"Yes!" she said, annoyed. She would not look to see the smirk on his face.

"You know, I made ten cents yesterday."

"Did you?"

Jase held his coins up to her. "And the first thing I want to spend it on is a warm, buttery, sweet, delicious—"

"Oh, stop torturing me already."

Jase laughed. "Of course, I may be feeling generous enough to share. For your mother's sake. Consider it a gift, Tess." Jase paid for the cornbread. It was then wrapped inside brown parchment paper. Before giving it to Tess, he said, "I don't get a thank you?"

Tess grinned, taking it from his hand. "Thank you, Jase." A genuine glimmer of appreciation in her eyes.

That simple act alone made the boy giddy inside. His eyes beheld her in a starstruck gaze. Tess regretted it immediately.

Turning away from him, she suddenly stopped when he asked to walk her home. She wanted to refuse but knew that he was just going to do it anyway. They walked around, leaving the busy square.

"How has everything been for you?" Jase initiated.

"Fine."

"Tess. I'm tryna make small talk here." How inconvenient that the boy actually cared to know how she was. For most people, a 'fine' was sufficient.

Unremorseful, she granted him a response. "Ma still sees Papa's ghost. Dr. Mazel still demands his stipend for 'treating her'."

All Dr. Mazel did was delude her mother with that awful poison, opium. At first, it had her mother slow and relaxed. Queer to how Tess was used to seeing her, but it relieved her ma's depression which was all that mattered to Tess at the time. Now her poor mother couldn't distinguish up from down. Tess was so angry at the results, she told the doctor never to come near her ma again. But he never let up on the price. And so the girl was forced to work for the local seamstress until she could pay him back.

"What happened to your aunt? I don't see her anymore when I visit," Jase thoughtfully noted.

"I don't really know. S'far as I know, she just stopped seeing us. No letter to explain. No nothing."

"Really? She just up and forgot you?"

"Something tells me Fredrick Truit had something to do with it." She spoke her uncle's name with such disdain. Unwilling to talk about it anymore, she diverted the subject. "How long was your pa at the bar this time?"

Jase gave a wry laugh. "What do you know, he's still there. I was up this mornin' filling in for him. Cleaning, and kilning, and quenching 'til my arms went tired." Jase brought his forearms up to his eyes. Tess knew it was only a device to bring her attention to the muscle building on this young man.

By the time they reached the apartment Tess shared with her mother, Tess told Jase goodbye. They were comrades in their sad reality. It was one of the things that made them good friends. The world would never understand the trials of them two as much as they. "Tell your pa when he comes to that I said hi," she said as she went inside.

Tess only took an hour to prepare the morning meal: eggs, bacon, and cornbread. The last one was the surprise. She brought the tray into the room where her pale mother sat up in the small bed. The bed she hadn't left in weeks since her broken heart caught up to her.

"Ma," Tess called softly as she inched to her side. "I got a surprise for you. Cornbread, warm and fresh from the square."

Her ma slowly lifted her eyes to her daughter. "Felix?"

Tess felt disgust tight in her throat. "No, Ma. It's me, Tess. Your daughter." She watched as all the faint hope and excitement in her mother's face left in a flash.

"I brought your breakfast, Ma. With cornbread this time. Try it."

Her ma didn't say anything. Her lips didn't move. There was no change in her face, no promise of recognition or acknowledgment. As if Felix Truit was the only person who existed in her world, and Tessaline Truit was the ghost.

"Ma?"

"I should have come back to you, Felix. I should have made amends somehow."

Tess's frowning eyes started to show anger. Her mother was rambling again in that same remorseful jargon. "Stop it, Ma. Please, stop. He's gone. He left us like this and he's not coming back."

Marian Truit didn't hear her daughter's voice. "Oh, Felix, I made a mess of everything on my own. Didn't know what I was doin'. I was just so angry at you. But I still wanted you. I always wanted you. Just look at the way I've raised our daughter. She ain't no woman no how."

Tess was on the verge of tears. In belligerence she uttered, "That's not true! You taught me everything I know. Everything I am is because of you."

Suddenly, it was like Marian's head was clear enough to snap at her daughter directly. "I failed you!" Her shout came out feeble and yet powerful as though it took all the energy from her. Her eyes stared at Tess. And she knew that at that moment, her mother really saw her. "I taught you how to assert yourself, how to care for yourself, and how to fight off waywards. But I never taught you how to suffer someone, how to receive, how to agree. And most of all, I never taught you how to forgive. And if I ain't taught you none o' those things, then I ain't taught you womanhood. And I done failed you!"

Tess's eyes were beading with tears. She was choked to silence. Marian slowly realized the words she uttered. "Oh, Tess. My Tess." She drew the girl into her arms. The frail woman still had a tight embrace. With a raised head, she said, "Thank you, El. Thank you for a moment's clarity. Thank you for truth. And thank you for my Tess. Be with her if I can't."

Tess was crying in her mother's arms. She soon realized she was the only one crying. Her mother had stopped speaking, and her embrace was loose. Tess picked up her head. "Ma? *Ma?*" A traumatic feeling reached her as she stared at her silent mother. Eyes still wide open. Tess's heart dropped. Slowly and steadily did she shake her mother off of her, without a loose tear or following whimper. She just sat there in her silence, immobile.

Present Day

Brord had not changed much to Krishta, but there was less racket in the streets than she remembered. She supposed there was less need for it since the town had settled nicely to its current state. In the earlier days, nearly everyone was a stranger. Now just about the only stranger walking the streets was her. She took her time soaking in the comfortable sight of each shop sitting as one of its kind. Then it occurred to her, there was no competition in Brord. There was only *the* post office, *the* department store, *the* eating house. And no one seemed to care just how stunting the situation was.

As she had been learning in her chats with Mister Wesman, neighboring cities hardly noticed Brord's existence. *"It's practically not on the map,"* he'd said. And what a shame it was. Brord Village deserved some recognition. So far, all that made it famous— and not by much— was the factory thriving on its outskirts.

"Aunt Krishta, are you getting tired, already?" The voice of her niece walking four paces ahead of her interrupted her thoughts.

"No, dear. I'm simply reminiscing."

"Oh." Lilian stomped her heel against the ground, stopping dramatically to allow Krishta a chance to catch up.

Krishta eyed her, smiling. Lilian replied with laughter.

"You want to go to the bakery next? I've heard their brownies are delightful."

"Wherever you decide to go is fine by me. Just as long as we stay in the square. I have not been here in a while and I hate being lost." Krishta would not have been lost at all. The true reason she wanted to remain in the square was to avoid seeing someone she couldn't bear to see again. Make no mistake, if she ever did cross paths with Tessaline Truit, she would embrace her firmly with a humble apology and tell her of her inheritance. Or at least she would in a dream. But it had been too long now. She couldn't claim to really know the girl who would now be a woman. Who was to say that Tessaline would even accept her apology, or her inheritance? Judging by Mister Foster's words, she would not find any forgiveness from Tessaline.

The best she could hope for was to have this walk with the niece she raised, and then leave Brord as soon as she could. After so many brief halts in Lilian's step, it became clear just how slow Krishta was moving. "Excuse me, I know I'm moving slow."

"You're alright. I can dawdle, too."

Krishta smirked. "I don't know why you declined Mister Wesman. He would have been a much better candidate for this."

Her niece let out a contemptuous sigh. "No, Aunt Krishta. He would have been much, much worse."

Lilian's behavior made no sense to her. There must have been something she knew which Krishta did not. "So, what bothers you about him?"

Lilian's face turned pale while regarding her aunt again. "Nothing. I am not bothered at all by Spencer."

Krishta stomped *her* heel against the ground.

"Aunt Krishta."

"What has he done to you?"

"Nothing."

"Then why can't you stand to be within five feet of him? I saw the way you cringed. If he makes you uncomfortable, I want to know why. I wouldn't mind firing the man for you." She would do anything for her niece. She could always find another accountant.

She saw the sadness overtake Lilian. Watched as her bottom lip quivered with eyes blinking upward. "He said things about us. About me."

Krishta's motherly concern made her catechize. "What things? When? To whom?"

Lilian breathed deeply before speaking. "Well, for example…. Once at H.A., I found Paul's hat where he had left it in the yard of the school after falling from his bicycle. I decided to hold on to it for him. Then Spencer found it in my satchel, and for the whole semester, he would tell everyone that I liked to cross-dress."

Krishta frowned, slowly ingesting her words. "Lilian, dear, those are just the antics of a boy."

"It's not all. He would even say things about Uncle Fred. That he was uneducated and a shame to the Truit name."

Krishta remained silent, hesitant to have her mind swayed.

Lilian gulped as she continued. "And the worst thing he ever said, which greatly tainted my reputation since my first year there, was that my father was a… a *bigamist*." she whispered the word.

Krishta had nothing to say against that. Just deeply concerned. *How did he know?* She placed a hand on her shivering niece, sensing that there was even more troubling her beyond what she admitted. "Lilian, I am so sorry, but if that had been your experience at Hiplum Academy, why had you never told us?"

"Because I... I did not want to be away from Paul. And I thought that if I told you, you would have pulled me out."

"Lilian, listen to yourself. You kept this a secret from us, making it seem like everything was perfect. And the reason was so you could be with Paul? That's your excuse?"

The more she spoke, the more Lilian's eyes filled with tears. "Well, now it sounds foolish."

"Because it was."

"You don't understand. The rest of it was good. I enjoyed my time at H.A., I did. Spencer was just a nuisance to me."

"If he was only that— a nuisance— why do you still have so much anger in your heart for him?"

Lilian stepped back with widened eyes. "Anger in *my* heart? I am the one who gave him the benefit of the doubt. I truly thought he changed, but—"

Krishta held up her hand to interrupt. "So, it seems you have been solving your own problems for a very long time without telling your uncle and I."

Lilian's mouth shut tight. Her eyes looked forward, showing a want to escape the conversation.

But it was Krishta's turn to speak. And she would hear her. "Well, *I'm* making a decision now. If you could endure the boy all those years ago, there is no reason you cannot endure him now. In fact, you are going to get to know him well. Because he has told me his plans to court you."

"*Court?* Aunt Krishta—"

"Hush. Now, I don't know about the ruthless boy you met in school, but the man I have come to know is very intelligent, well-bred, and has an affluent heritage. So I think it is time to leave school behind you and realize that you are a woman in waiting."

Lilian's eyebrows squeezed together, looking as though she was being volunteered for torture against her will.

Still feeling righteous in the matter, Krishta at least wanted to make her niece feel more at ease about it. She took hold of Lilian's gloved hand. "I am doing my best to help you secure a future for yourself. Ms. Cora told me how much you enjoyed working around the children. And that is all very nice for now. But it is not what I see for your future." Krishta never realized just how many issues her husband left her to deal with since her husband's death. There was the responsibility of the factory, the weight of being in the city of her lost niece, and the struggle to find Lilian a man suitable for her. As Lilian continued to stare mournfully, Krishta rubbed her aching forehead. "I don't know what I am doing, after all," her words heavy with fatigue. "What kind of future do you see for *yourself*, Lilian?"

"There was only one I ever saw. One with Paul. Now he's gone."

Krishta drew her into her arms. "I know you loved him. And I am so sorry he couldn't stick around. Perhaps it was not meant to be." She pulled Lilian off her to look into her eyes. "And perhaps El has opened another door for you."

Lilian winced.

"I am not saying he is the one for you. All I am saying is to give him a chance, alright?"

Before she could get a definitive answer from Lilian, her eye caught sight of someone ahead. A small-framed young woman stepped across the street from their side to the other. She wore a short-brimmed hat of straw, not ideal for such a climate, over her silky white coiffure. It was her side-profile that garnered Krishta's attention. The way that the white winter sun's light dotted the fleshy tip of the lady's slender nose.

"Aunt Krishta?"

"Huh?" The lady became a blur as her focus drew back to Lilian. "Suddenly, I do think I am tired. I want to go back to my room if you do not mind."

Lilian's expression said she did mind, but her mouth said, "No, you can go. It's fine."

As they turned around, Krishta began to feel an onset of more than a headache. Possibly a migraine.

Rescued

Tess stopped by the red door of Mister Scott Thomas's apartment. A place that resided in the quietest part of the town where only the richest, oldest, most recluse of the townspeople lived. The perfect place for someone like Scott, which is what she called him whenever Jase was not around. Scott insisted she did.

Before she could knock, she heard him slide the metal lock. The door drew in. She stared up at the gritty smile of the man as he took a moment to look her up and down over his spectacles. "My, you look marvelous."

"You say the same thing every time."

"'Cause it's true every time."

"Stop. How ya doin', Scott?"

"Better now that you're here."

Tess rolled her eyes. "Figured you would say that." She did not mind the old man's advances as long as he kept to himself. The last thing she wanted to do was make him think she didn't appreciate him for letting her and Jase live in his house on the field.

"Come on in." He moved aside for her.

"Actually, I have to be somewhere else." She searched her pocket. "So I'll leave you the money, and—"

"Where?"

"'Scuse me?"

"Where do you have to be?" Scott patted the top of his head where his grey hairs were thinning the most.

"Ms. Cora's." That was always the easiest answer to throw at him. She gave him a smile, pretending not to hear the interrogation in his tone. "I always see her on Thursdays to give some money to the home as charity."

Scott replied with a chuckle resounding from deep in his chest. "You can skip the visit today. I think you'll want to hold onto your money what with the new price I've put on the house."

With him mentioning the house, she had to say, "Yes, Jase told me about that. May I ask why exactly you are doing this?"

Scott almost spoke, then shut his mouth, gesturing again into his home. "Sorry, but I don't accept business inquiries made at my front door. Now, if you want answers, you should step inside."

It was clear that she had to follow his rules. She wanted to know why he raised the price. Perhaps she could persuade him to lower it back to normal. "I'll spare fifteen minutes," Tess said, setting her own rules. "No more than that."

He said nothing, waiting as she stepped over the threshold and into his apartment.

Tess had never been inside the place, and she never wondered how it looked. But she could not have expected the splendor and finesse that existed on the other side of the red door. Mister Thomas had let his eclectic taste run wild.

The immediate burst of vibrance that greeted her was the wallpaper displaying different species of monkeys running, creeping, and hanging by the loops of their tails from the tails of other monkeys. These walls were donned in an array of ornate mirrors as if he needed to see himself through over fifteen glass shapes. A pendant light fixture made of stained glass with an ombre of green to orange hung from the ceiling. It cast an ochreous glow on the mosaic floor. There was a musky presence in the space that made the apartment feel smaller than it was.

Tess flinched as she felt his hand on the small of her back, urging her forward. "This way to my office." He took her down a skinny hallway clad in dark green stripes and lined in colorful rugs past a wrought iron bench. Tess's interest slowly drifted over the scary wooden masks on the walls, one of them covered in a coarse fur and shaped to look like a wolf. Its shadow bounced under the flickering light of a broken lamp.

"Sorry about the light," Scott said. "I'll have to get it fixed."

Tess ignored the flickering while also ignoring her growing want to leave. Something about it all made Tess wonder exactly what strange fantasies Scott obsessed himself over. The air grew camphoraceous around them, causing Tess to feel as though she were closed in. To keep going was like entrapping herself among a weird and eerie world, but she said nothing. It would be unwise to show any apprehension now. Continuing forward, they approached a black door. He turned the knob and opened the door to a room swimming in the richest, deepest shade of green.

In this room were leather chairs seated beside a limestone hearth. Scott had utilized the right side of the room for shelving and displaying more of his strange sculptures in the glass of his ornate *étagère*. In the leftmost corner was an executive desk sitting by a window with an imperfect view of the street outside. The only reason a window was there was for light. And in spite of it, a golden chandelier was poled to the ceiling.

"Do make yourself comfortable," he said, gesturing toward the chairs.

Tess stepped over to the fireplace and sat down. She felt him move toward the other side of the room and watched as he poured glasses of gin from the buffet of the *étagère*. Before he could come very close to her she held up her hand. "Uh, no, thank you."

Scott frowned. "Why?"

"We don't drink."

"We?" Scott looked around the room teasingly even though he must have known what she meant.

"Jase and I. I try not to encourage it, knowing how it affected his father."

Scott's mouth pulled into an amused grin. "So what your saying is you'll deny yourself a bit of fun because of Jase even when Jase isn't around."

She opened her mouth to argue but was cut off by his sigh.

"We all know what a tragedy the boy's father was. It's a real pity." His eyes drew down as if he truly felt sorry for Jase. Then he bent forward, holding the glass out to her. "But your purity cannot undo his breeding."

His words were likely duplicitous... yet sensible. The piney aroma omitting from the glass whet her senses. It had been a while since she enjoyed a strong beverage. Usually, women in Brord didn't drink so early and only in the presence of men would they drink at all. But she *was* in the presence of a man. And she knew that it would probably be rude to not accept the glass, so just to keep the peace, she took it in hand.

"Now, Scott—"

"Sip first."

Tess took a sip. Feeling the gin burn down her throat, she winced and handed it back to him. "That'll be enough for me."

Scott took it away for her and came back to sit in the chair across from her. "You were saying?"

"Just that I wanted to know why—"

"Why I raised the rent. Right." He started to look around his room as if it was new to him.

"Mister Thomas?" The name rolled out slowly before Tess realized she had said it.

His head snapped back in her direction. "Tessaline, Tessaline, Tessaline." He tsked. "We talked about this. You should call me Scott."

"Sorry." A cold sweat came on to her. "It slipped out."

"What do you think about this place?" he asked her.

Tess kept from frowning, noticing how he was wasting her time. "It's nice. I guess."

"You guess?" His eyebrows drew up and his head tilted, a flab of fat appearing out the side his chin.

"I don't live here," she said softly.

He rubbed a finger against his lips in thought. "Well, I am not going to tell you what you should or should not like. I understand that it's an acquired taste."

Tess was trying to see where he was going with this conversation. In order to get back on track, she at least needed to make sure she was still in his good graces. "Scott, I… I really do appreciate everything you've done for us."

Scott shifted in his seat. "Yes, well, I'm glad you do."

"Really? Then could you tell me why you—"

"You know, with a voice like yours, Tessaline," he ignored her as she huffed, "you could make a beautiful siren."

The comment threw her off. "A what?"

His eyes narrowed. "Yes, yes, I think you could. You do know what that is, right? A mythical creature with the power to lure men to their deaths with no more than a song."

Tess leaned forward with tense fingers. "Mist— Scott..."

"Oh, come on, Tess. Won't you amuse me? Don't you have an imagination? If you could be anything other than what you are now, what would it be?"

Tess stifled her frustration, taking in a deep breath. "The one thing I'd like to be right now is heard."

"Exactly. I'm glad we agree." He ended with a smile.

"But you *ain't* hearin' me. You still haven't answered my question."

"I believe your fifteen minutes are up."

Tess stammered, soon realizing he was right. He had cleverly waited her out. But she did not know why he asked her to come inside if he was not going to talk business. She jumped from her seat, saying discordantly, "Thanks for your time." She stepped out, entering the hallway.

"It won't last."

His breath hit the back of her neck. Tess turned around, seeing Scott had caught up to her. It startled her how quickly he had done so. "What did you say?"

"You'll never be happy living with him. He's holding you back. But I can help you, Tessaline." He took a step closer.

And she started backwards to the front of the apartment. "Stay away from me. Don't come any closer to me."

"Tessaline. You are so special."

"I said stay back!" She pulled the door open. And Mister Thomas *did* come to a halt as the nose of a musket slipped through from somewhere on the other side of the threshold. Tess's jaw unhinged in shock. Until she recognized the weapon. There was only one man she knew who still carried around an old musket given to him by his father and his father's father and so on. Her eyes trailed the side of it to the man handling it as he stepped in.

His gentle eyes, now harshly narrowed on Mister Thomas in spite of the curls falling over his face. He badly needed a haircut. His thick arms were tensed as he kept the butt of the musket level against his shoulder.

"Jase! What are you doing in here with that thing?"

"Savin' your behind, woman. Now get behind me." He cocked his head to the side as a gesture. And cocked his musket as a threat to Mister Thomas.

Mister Thomas yielded up his hands. "You aren't gonna shoot a man in his own home, are you? Besides, I just remembered she still has to pay me."

Jase kept his focus on him but asked, "Tess, you paid him?"

Tess took the dollar bills from her reticule and cast them over the floor. "There. Paid in full."

"That's right." Mister Thomas nodded. "That's all I needed."

Jase took a second to close the distance between his gun and Mister Thomas's chest. "You bet it is."

The old man's body went rigid with cautious eyes staring down at the gun, then into Jase's eyes again.

"Jase, he understands," Tess said, almost deciding to pull his arm.

"No, I don't think you do," Jase insisted, speaking to Mister Thomas. "Try somethin' again and see what I'll do. Ya got that?"

"Yes, yes." Mister Thomas nodded rapidly.

Finally, the barrel was lowered, pointing downward by Jase's hip side. "Let's go, Tess." He walked out. And Tess quickly followed behind.

"I will go over to Ms. Cora's and ask if I can bring some tea here for you," Lilian suggested while helping her aunt take a seat in an armchair. They were in the room she'd booked at the inn.

"No, don't bother yourself," Aunt Krishta said as she pinched the bridge of her nose.

"Are you sure? It will be a quick run." Lilian placed a hand on her aunt's.

Krishta patted it with her other hand. "No, really, dear. I'm sure I'll get over it. Just leave me here."

Lilian's heart ached at the sight of her aunt's sudden weariness. It underscored the heavy toll of her burdens, burdens not meant for one person. A thought struck her with unsettling clarity; her marriage could be the key to easing her aunt's load. As Krishta massaged her temples, Lilian quietly resolved there was no other way.

But what were the chances of finding anyone suitable for her in a place like Brord? She might have left all the eligible men in Hiplum. Lilian would be surprised if this humble town hid a princely young gentleman with a prestigious name and the needed gumption to take on a factory.

However, the warmth and simplicity of Brord, as per Aunt Krishta's suggestion, had quickly endeared itself to Lilian. In just three days, it felt like a second home, a sanctuary where her status mattered less than her deeds. As she watched her aunt drift into sleep, Lilian's moment of peace was interrupted by a familiar cough. She turned to find Spencer emerging from the shadows (his room on the left). "What do you want?" she whispered, careful not to wake Krishta.

"I just wondered if you would like me to escort you back."

"Why?" A sternness met her words. "Why did you come he—?" His fingertip pressed her lips shut. He beckoned for her to follow him out of the room.

Lilian eyed him suspiciously. Regardless, she followed Spencer out, her wariness translating into physical distance. As he closed the door behind them, she couldn't help but notice his all-black attire, seemingly a somber nod to mourning. Was it for Uncle Fred, or just a hollow gesture to appease Aunt Krishta? Amongst the dark fabric, a single gold pin caught her eye, a morning star with an M in its center. Some strange affiliation she did not care to ask about.

With her initial question still hanging unanswered, Lilian watched Spencer stride towards the elevator. Driven by a mix of curiosity and apprehension, she trailed him, their footsteps echoing in the otherwise silent hall. He pressed the elevator bell, and soon its gears whirred and clicked, signaling its arrival.

The ride down was a brief, tense affair. Lilian stayed vigilant, aware of the operator's presence yet conscious of Spencer's ability to inflict subtler forms of cruelty. When they reached the lobby, she exited first, Spencer close behind.

The lobby was its usual quiet self, with Pete absentmindedly nibbling on a roll of bread at the reception. Lilian turned to face Spencer, arms crossed in a defensive posture. "Alright. Now will you tell me what you are doing here?" she demanded, ready to confront whatever truth lay behind his actions.

His gaze evaded hers as he shrugged. "For your aunt, obviously. She needed me here to learn about the current financial state of your family's business."

"So, that's it? You *care* about my family's business?"

"Indeed."

Lilian pushed her neck forward, not believing a word. He was giving her nothing. "Then I suppose it is just a *coincidence* that you volunteered to be her accountant?"

Spencer responded with a squint of the eyes. "I don't see what answer you are seeking out of me, Lilian." He stood closer, lofty compared to her. He crossed his arms as well. "Unless you are suspecting I did this just to see you again."

Lilian's face pinked. "I would never presume…"

"Save it. You would not be wrong."

Her heart constricted. She stepped away from him. "Spencer, if you say anything about a war…"

"A war? No, not anymore."

"What?"

Spencer's head swiveled left to right. "Would you not rather have this talk outside?"

"I couldn't possibly." She wasn't about to go anywhere with him.

"I've given up talking about a hidden war, Lilian. After our encounter in Hiplum, I reflected on the real reason I came that night." His stare fell momentarily. Lilian was unsure if she truly saw what looked like a deep, berryish red spreading over his face. His eyes drew back to hers. They were still bereft of any remnant of a soul. "And I resolved it was all for the need to be close to the very girl I vowed to hate. You."

Even as his gaze became somewhat pining, she continued to withhold a reaction. Lilian was not going to take this from Spencer. She knew more than anyone that the only truth Spencer could tell was his first name. He had always been a liar. And she knew he was lying now. The memory of all the sinister tricks he pulled on her, making her into a laughingstock. The ill words he would say about her family. All of that— and only because he wanted to be close to her?

"You think I would believe that?" she scoffed. "You tormented me for years."

Spencer's response was less a word than a sigh. "Let's just say, people do foolish things when they feel... overlooked." He paused, his glance flickering away momentarily. "You were never one to notice the undercurrents, were you? Paul had your heart. I never stood a chance against him. So, I did everything in my power..." he discontinued.

"To... make him not want to be around me?" The information made anger heat her throat. But instead of shouting, her words came out sound. "You're evil, Spencer." Tears sprang in her eyes.

Spencer's next expression surprised her. It seemed like what she said affected him. "At least I didn't leave you like Paul did."

"What?" Lilian said, becoming more inflamed. But she heard him perfectly.

"Lilian." Spencer dared to almost take another step toward her. Lilian readied her foot to step back. He noticed and remained where he was.

"Lil..."

"Don't ever call me that. No one calls me 'Lil' but Paul." Her hand closed at her side.

His lips were tight around his clenched teeth. "Regardless, if I am to stop thinking I'm your enemy, then you can end your infatuation with a man who never wanted you."

"Infatuation? Never... never wanted?"

"Admit it, Lilian. That's all it was."

Her blurred eyes lifted to his. The audacity in his words was it for Lilian. How dare he minify her love for Paul to infatuation? And then insult her by saying that Paul never loved her? If it *was* true, it was Spencer's fault.

"You know nothing about Paul."

A sinister smirk creeped on his cheek. "No. It's you who doesn't know."

She would hear no more of this. Spencer hated to see her happy. He was the reason for all this pain she felt. For just a moment, she would love to see him feel the same pain. Taking a step toward him, she slapped his high, entitled cheek... gasping shortly after.

Realizing what she had done, it was too late to take back. He turned a contemptuous gaze on her, and she saw his true self again. She started regretting her action profusely. Then she felt someone come to stand beside her.

"Woah, what is going on here?"

Lilian turned her attention to Pete.

"Miss Truit, is this man bothering you?"

Relief washed over her. What could she say to assure him that Spencer was not a problem? She wanted to safely get out of this predicament, not make things worse. "I... I need to leave." She did her best to ignore Spencer's menacing gaze. "I mean, I was already leaving."

One side of Pete's unibrow lifted. His stare switched from her to Spencer and back to her. She used her eyes, pleading he would not do anything to make Spencer angry.

"Let me escort you, then." Pete offered his arm.

Lilian stifled a deep sigh. "Why, thank you for offering, sir." Taking his arm tensely, they shuffled toward the doors of the inn.

It wasn't until they were out that he asked, "Has that man done something to you?"

"No. Nothing more than be a menace. Please don't say anything to him after this."

"Why?"

She let go of his slim arm. "Because it would not be good for me."

His unibrow lowered over his eyes. "That sounds like more than a menace. You know, I don't have to have him in my inn."

"No, do not kick him out. Besides, he will be leaving with my aunt this evening."

Pete held her hand between two of his. "If you say so." He then kissed it. "Remember, if there is anything you need, Pete Daniels is right across the street."

Lilian smiled with a nod. "I'll be sure to remember that. Goodbye, Pete."

Pete walked back inside. And Lilian quickly clopped along the pavement, almost running back to Ms. Cora's home. She dashed towards the iron gate, getting out her key. Even as she was determined to unlock the gate, her hands were trembling. Lilian could not help but look around in a timid manner, hoping that she was a safe enough distance from Spencer's curses.

Finally, she opened the gate. She rushed into the yard, quickly shutting and locking the gate before proceeding to the front door of the orphanage. Her entire body was shivering in a way she hated, and it was not only due to the cold weather.

Standing in front of the door, Lilian knocked on its green wood. No one answered. She could not hear anyone inside. As the shiver traveled more fiercely up her spine, she had an inkling she should look behind herself.

Lilian froze, her eyes fixed on a swirling mass of bats descending from the sky. Their frantic shrieks filled the air as they swooped closer, their grotesque faces and jagged teeth becoming horrifyingly clear. Heart pounding, she frantically knocked on the door, desperation mounting with each thud of her fist against the wood— until suddenly, it gave way to the softer resistance of a person.

"Ow!" a shrill voice shouted.

Lilian whipped her head around to the beautiful young woman standing in the doorway. The woman rubbed her chest with a grimace. Lilian had no time to apologize, stepping in while brushing past the woman. "Quickly! Close the door or the bats will come in!"

"Bats?" The woman made a dubious expression, poking her head out of the doorway. "I don't see no bats."

"They were there," Lilian insisted as she panted, trying to calm her palpitating heart. "They were after me."

The woman slowly turned around, side-eyeing Lilian with cool, pale eyes. "Are you okay?"

Lilian could not handle how the woman was looking at her as if she was insane. She almost wanted to go back outside to make sure she was right but the idea was not as appealing as staying safely inside.

The woman's ruby lips cracked an amused grin while closing the door with her back. "What's up with you?"

Then another voice spoke from behind Lilian. "Hey, ally!"

Turning again, Lilian saw Jase, her new friend and ally. But she flinched, noticing the long gun he held behind his neck, using it as a place to rest his arms.

"Hello, Jase."

Jase looked between her and the one by the door. "Have the two of you been acquainted already?"

"No," the woman said, seeming to say a lot more with her eyes. Something along the lines of *"Nor do I want to be"*. Then her focus landed on the gun behind his neck. "Jase, can you put that El-forsaken thing away, please?"

Jase's blooming excitement halted as he listened to the woman, dropping the weapon from his shoulders to place it against the gallery wall. He then proceeded to introduce them. "Lilian, meet Tess. Tess, meet Lilian."

Lilian brought her stare back to Tess. "Nice to meet you, Tess. You are Jase's wife, then?"

Tess looked over at Jase. "Is that what you've been telling her?"

Jase's head shook. "I haven't told her much of anything."

Lilian was not understanding them. "So you two are *not* married?"

With a roll of the eyes, Tess responded. "We live together. That's about it. If you got a problem with that—"

"Now, did she say she had a problem with it?" Jase cut in.

"Well, you both know how *I* feel about it," Ms. Cora said as she approached the three of them. "It *is* unseemly. Do not make Lilian feel unwelcome if she does not agree with you." Ms. Cora grinned at Lilian. "How was your walk with your aunt?"

"It was fine until Aunt Krishta caught a headache. I offered to bring her some tea from here but she refused it."

"Why would she refuse it?'

"She wouldn't tell me. But I think she'll be fine after a good rest."

"Bunk. I mean nonsense. She's getting her tea if I have anything to do with it. Oh, Patricia!" Ms. Cora called as the volunteer passed by. She stopped with a slight fatigue in her expression. But it quickly fell away as she feigned interest.

"Yes, Ms. Cora?"

"My Krishta dear is suffering from a headache. Could you brew some tea and take it to her room at the inn? I believe the number is two-o-sev—"

"I'll take it to her."

Everyone faced Tess as she stepped forward. "I'll do it."

Lilian was relieved no one asked herself to do it. However, she couldn't understand why this strange woman decided it was her responsibility. And by the short silence amongst them all coupled with the glances everyone shared, they didn't seem to understand it either.

"Well, don't look all surprised," Tess said. "I won't be long." She left them, stepping boyishly on her way to the kitchen.

Ms. Cora then remembered she'd been looking for a doll to appease a temperamental child who was throwing a tantrum in the garden. She resumed the search, abandoning the foyer swiftly.

And lastly, seeing no point in staying, Patricia awkwardly removed herself from Jase and Lilian's presence, going upstairs to likely rest in her room.

All that remained was the usually soundless foyer and the young man standing with Lilian.

Jase crossed his arms, regarding her. "Hey." He put his large hand on her shoulder. "You seem shaky."

"Just a little winded."

He laughed. "I bet. You were bangin' on that door like a hound outside a henhouse."

Lilian half-frowned. A shameful shade of pink cast over her face when she thought of how unduly she had behaved, having alarmed everyone for the second time. "You believe I saw them, don't you? The bats?"

His teasing was done away with as a faint line of concern suddenly etched his brow. "Well, let's see." He slowly guided her toward the staircase, suggesting with his hands to sit on the lower steps. Jase sat and leaned back, his boots thudding softly against the wooden step as he stretched out. Lilian noticed the dirt smudges on his jeans. He was still dressed like a worker though he was to begin management in two days. It was impractical to envision him in a suit, but she knew he could look exceedingly smart in one.

"One thing is for sure," he said, "you ain't crazy. And I don't see why you would lie about it. Now, I've seen many bats in Brord, however, the odds of a whole colony after you this early in the day is kind of hard to imagine. But lucky for you," his face leaned close to hers, something naturally winsome about the assuring grin he lended her, "I have a pretty wild imagination."

A curious feeling slipped in and out of Lilian as she watched his smile. Then her gaze fell to her lap. "Thank you, Jase. It hasn't been easy for me in the passing weeks. I don't feel the way I used to. It's like I'm all alone."

"Is it because your friend left you?"

"You mean Paul? No, I don't think it is that. Though, I do wish he would have stayed as long as he promised."

Jase spoke low. "I never was much a fan of him, you know."

Lilian, holding one bar of the rail, pressed the side of her face against it, releasing a sigh from her nose. "Paul was right, though. I'm all... out of sorts."

His warm palm rested on her back. "You know, Lilian, you're not the only one. Heck, I don't even have it all together. Sometimes, it's gonna feel like you took the wrong train and the whole world is leaving you behind. But you're not left behind. You're right where you need to be."

His words swathed her anxious heart in a sash of wisdom. It surprised her, issuing a new mystery for her to uncover. The mystery of Jase Foster's mind. Jase seemed to ponder for a moment before a spark of an idea appeared in his eyes. Lilian caught the change and asked, "What are you thinking about?"

"I was just thinking about Saturday night. There is something going on then, and I thought it might be a fine distraction. Something to properly welcome you to Brord."

Lilian raised her eyebrows, a gentle nudge to her curiosity. "Oh? What's that?"

"The Masked Maiden's performance," Jase said with a casual enthusiasm. "It's a show that goes on every Saturday at the inn. There's dinner by candlelight, you could get lost in the music, and you'd get to meet the town members."

A small, intrigued smile played on Lilian's lips. "Sounds intriguing. I haven't been to anything like that in a while."

"Yeah, it's a nice change of pace from the usual," Jase agreed, shifting slightly. "Although, it's probably nothing as fancy as what you're used to."

"Oh, I wouldn't mind at all. Only, does it mean I should not dress up? I mean, I am perfectly fine with that."

"No, definitely dress up. Just pick something simple, alright?" He ended with a playful laugh.

She grinned with an understanding nod. "Simple it is." The idea of a night filled with music and mystery, a temporary departure from her current troubles, was undeniably appealing. "Thank you, Jase. I'd really like that. It sounds like just what I need."

"Anything for an ally."

Transient

Through the consistent throbbing in her brow bone, a light yet repetitive knock on her door interrupted Krishta's focus. "Who is there?" she moaned.

A voice similar to Lilian's but higher in octave with a more whistly tone spoke behind the wood. "Came to give you the tea," she said.

Krishta detected a mild accent from her. She rubbed her eyes, thinking how she had already told Lilian it wasn't necessary. Krishta's pain made it hard to watch the door, so she kept her eyes shut. "Come in, I suppose."

She heard the light crack of the door. The person approached softly but the cups on her tray made subtle tinks.

Feeling the person's closeness, Krishta attempted to lift her eyes to see her. And the moment she did, she wanted to shut them again. Not because of the delicate features she recognized, but the cold stare the woman directed through her pale eyes.

Krishta's chin tucked in disbelief. "I must be dreaming."

The young woman set her tray on the stand next to Krishta's armchair. Straightening up thereafter with a condescending look. "Then go back to sleep." She pivoted around on her heel, proceeding away.

Krishta's eyes shot awake. She stood, following quickly after her. "Tessaline, wait!"

Tess was already about to pull the door shut behind herself if not for Krishta's timely grasp of the handle. She managed to keep the door cracked. "Tessaline, please. Let's talk."

"There's nothing for us to talk about."

"Perhaps, but we must try."

"Why?" the girl demanded.

Krishta's lips pressed together as she thought of what to say next. An ache of guilt growing in her chest. "I don't want you to go on in life thinking that I abandoned you."

"You *did* abandon me. And you abandoned *her*."

"It wasn't our choice, Tessaline. Your mother, Marian, never liked or trusted Fred. It was by his looks alone that he reminded her of Felix. And nothing could change that. You know I am right. You heard her slander him on many occasions. I could not handle seeing him disrespected after all he would do for her."

"So? She was unwell. It was the delirium like you said. You could have stayed."

"And we would have. But one day she made her last request to us. She *wanted* us gone.... So we left." Krishta pressed her palm to her side of the door, sliding it around to touch her niece's hand which was clutching the handle on the other side. Tessaline flinched slightly, then relaxed her hand. "I cried shortly after it, Tessaline. I cried especially when I received news of her passing." A mucous lump reached the core of Krishta's throat as she felt her eyes drip. "I am so sorry for all the turmoil that our decision has put you through."

Krishta wondered if it would be a good time to mention her inheritance. She first wanted to see how Tessaline would react to everything she just said.

A mousley sigh followed on the other side of the door. "Come downstairs tomorrow. There's gonna be a show. We can talk then."

Krishta shook her head, glad that Tess could not see it. "Tessaline, I would love to. But I'll be gone before tomorrow."

"Then goodbye, then." Her hand released the knob as she left swiftly down the hallway.

Krishta glanced regretfully at her palm. She was glad to have had even a transient moment with Tessaline. But one moment, she feared, could not make up for all the time she missed. Sniffing back her sorrow, Krishta remembered she could not blame herself for this. So much of it had little to do with her. Her and Tessaline's lives were the way they were because of one man's fateful decision. And his name was Felix Truit.

Late Winter (1885)

Felix's eyes wandered over the grandeur of the estate, taking in the opulence that surrounded him. The luxurious drapes, the glistening chandeliers, and the polished marble floors were all reminders of the life he was expected to lead. He couldn't help but feel like an actor on a stage, playing a role that was thrust upon him.

A distracting glare caught his attention from outside. Felix fixed his eyes on the balcony. Fireworks blazed in the midnight sky and everyone marveled at the colorful show as the sparks mixed together then dispersed into the night. The medley of the harpist was muted by the thrilling screams and pops. Lovers embraced on the edge of the Brier Hill Estate's balcony. The colors illuminated on their skin, painting the people blue, purple, red, and green.

Those without a romantic counterpart were inside the ballroom, enjoying their wine and discussing business. Felix lingered by the buffet, a corner he usually occupied as he waited for the night to end, taking samples of the punch while keening his ears to the music. He couldn't escape the world in which he was bred. Not even for his wife, Marian.

Attending such events, though frivolous to him, thwarted any suspicions of his marital status. Indeed, only a single man could cancel plans at the drop of any whim-ful invitation his mother sent him. It was exactly what he wanted them all to think.

He told himself that keeping Marian a secret was for her protection. She wouldn't ever have to listen to his mother accuse her of ruining him and encouraging him to reside in a city unbecoming of a gentleman with his standing. She wouldn't have to hear them make ruthless claims against their daughter, Tessaline for having both an appearance and breeding so far removed from anyone of the Truit name. Felix would not let his people have the pleasure...

He told himself all these things to mask the truth. That nothing satisfied him. Not his rural-born wife, nor his silver-spoon relatives. And yet, he could not abandon either. While a life with Marian offered him freedom and social comfort, life as a man of status and praise fueled his pride.

But all in all, there was a price to behaving like a single man. It meant he had to leave his family on special nights such as this.

Before his mind had drifted completely from the festivities, he spotted Fredrick and his wife coming in from the balcony. Fredrick's head turned immediately toward the buffet. He needn't look far to know where he'd find his brother. With a hand resting on Krishta's waist, he approached. "Happy New Year, brother."

"Happy New Year," Felix returned. "And to you too, Krishta."

Krishta diverted her stare. He could tell it was all she could do to keep from grimacing. "I think I'll go over there," she said, pointing vaguely toward the gathering.

Felix eyed his brother as she walked away. "She still hates me, huh?"

"Yes, as is her right. For a doctor, you showed nil compassion or tactfulness explaining to the woman her inability to give birth."

"I did apologize ample times."

Freddy patted his shoulder with a wry chuckle. "Yes, well, now you'll have to wait ample times before either of us hear the end of it." Though he laughed, there was a gloom in his eyes that told Felix Freddy was not over it either.

Freddy filled a glass with punch. He glanced peripherally up at Felix as he poured. With a cough he said, "Why isn't Marian here?"

"Don't expect me to answer that." Felix responded coldly, his eyes still on the gathering. "You know my singleness is my image. And anyway, I don't want *myself* here, why would I want my *wife* here."

"Why are you here at all? You should be home on this night— morning, sorry— celebrating with your wife and child."

"My wife doesn't want me home. She made that clear five times before I left out the door."

Freddy gave his brother a dry look. "Come on, Felix. Do you actually believe that?"

Felix frowned, considering his brother's point. "No. I don't. But I think it's best. You know, it does not help that she is so naïve. She has no idea all I do for her, yet she complains and complains..." He shook his head, fighting the growth of anger in him. "Every time I am around her we can't seem to have peace."

"That's called a marital problem, Felix. And you definitely don't fix those by going to parties."

"I do this for *her*."

Fred laughed with closed lips. "I'm sure you have convinced yourself of that."

Felix waved a dismissive hand. He didn't need the lecture of his younger twin.

"You know, you are so lucky to have a child to keep you occupied," Freddy continued after taking a sip. "I'd love nothing more than an excuse to stay home with Krishta."

"Except I *don't* have an excuse." Felix tipped his glass toward the gathering. "At least *they* don't think I do."

Freddy sighed, "Right." His face showed full displeasure as he also directed his gaze at them. Their break in conversation was drowned by the melody that filled the atmosphere. It lasted a while before Freddy murmured, "I do wish you would have less secrets, Felix. Then I wouldn't have to keep so many."

Felix ignored his brother's complaint, his eyes now focused on their mother who was now approaching. Her shoes clacking on the marble floor. She used to be a porcelain doll with a harmless disposition, or so they said. But Felix and Fred had only ever seen her grow into the scary old femme she was now. The bane of his existence. Her hair, peeking grey, pulled back, and braided over and over in the back of her head. She stared at her sons over round, silver spectacles. "Felix, my boy. I believe you are idle."

"I'm afraid so, Mother."

"Well, *I* am afraid there is another here who is quite idle."

Fred turned to his brother. "Felix?"

She pursed her lips discordantly, raising a brow. "Lady Agapov."

"Mother—"

"She is a very well-bred young lady. She'd suit your intelligence, too. I have enjoyed our many discussions. You know she speaks—"

"Seven languages. Yes. You've told me."

Ms. Truit pursed her lips again. "Do you know how embarrassed you've made me each time I have to tell her father that my son, her suitor, is somehow never available to court her?"

"Mother—"

"Shut it. I will not hear another excuse. You have avoided me for four years now. Well this is a new year, and you have no excuse."

Freddy cut into the conversation. "Um, actually mother, about that. Felix has something to tell you."

The old woman glanced at Freddy, then her eyes zeroed in on her oldest son. "Well?"

Felix shot his brother a deadly stare. "I… just…" Regarding their mother again, he relaxed his shoulders. "I think I am a little rusty on my charms, Mother."

Ms. Truit laughed, holding her chest. "Not my Felix, the infamous charmer, saying such things. I'm sure whatever charms you've lost will soon find you. Now, stop wasting my precious time and get over there and talk to Miss Agapov."

"Where is she?"

"The balcony. She has decided not to come inside like everyone else. Likely, out of dread that she'd have to see you standing there like a piece of furniture."

Felix eyed his brother. His secret floating in both their eyes. Freddy looked away, suddenly. Pretending not to care. So Felix resolved that the least he could do to appease his mother would be to greet this Lady Agapov. Without any more hesitation, he started across the hall. "I'll be right back."

When he found Lady Agapov, her back facing him, all knowledge of how to greet a lady fled him. He fell silent, noticing the way her person fit the regal scene like the star of a painting. Rose vines hung from the roof and curled against the stone walls, framing her body. The north star blessed her plump skin with its light.

The back of her silky black hair was looped around itself to make a set of bows going down her head and ending in curls. The dress she wore was a mix of luxury and simplicity, made of red velvet with a giant bow sewn directly over her bustle area. Gilded fabric lined the bottom of the skirt. Short sleeves ruffled along the edge of her shoulders.

She was too darling even for him. *If the back of her is this beautiful, then I wouldn't mind viewing the front.* He stepped closer behind her.

"Dant! comeny closer."

"Lady Agapov."

"Do not speak to me."

This wasn't going well. Felix bowed his head, knowing she didn't see it. "I understand. I wouldn't speak to me either," he murmured to himself. "Look, I will be honest with you. I have to talk to you to appease my mother. So if you would let me have five minutes at least..."

She said nothing to him, continuing to stare beyond the balcony at the dark hills. Now that the fireworks were over with, it was peaceful out here. Felix wondered what the lady could possibly be ruminating when so much was happening inside. Then it occurred to him that she may find it frivolous as well. Of course, he had no right to assume her reasoning, neither did he wish to. How nice it would be if he could find a common ground with her.

Then he had an idea. "Krasavitsa, dusha-devitsa," he said lowly, "Polyubi zhe ty menya."

Lady Agapov raised her head to the familiar song. Her body seemed to still in response and he fancied himself safe to approach. "Ay-lyuli, lyuli, ay-lyuli, lyuli." Felix stopped by her ear and whispered, "Polyubi zhe ty menya."

Lady Agapov spun around with a scorn, gripping the balustrade behind her. Her round eyes stared up into his. "What do you want from me?"

Felix smirked at her reaction to him. But his heart flitted in his chest as he beheld her luscious appearance. Now as her question hung in his mind, his charm instinctively kicked in. "More time."

"Ha! More time? Wis me?"

He quickly thought about the words which slipped out of himself, ready to recant. Then the air around him grew heavy. Heavy, spicy, and dry. It almost felt like he was surrounded in... smoke. Something in him detested it, yet something else endeared him to it. A string of words began in his mind, repeating over and over again: *Win her, want her. Charm her, taunt her.* Felix mentally questioned the words. But then he noticed how Lady Agapov was starting to be impatient of his answer, looking at him curiously. He inhaled the air, shutting his eyes.... He felt himself leaning into her. "With you."

Her eyes widened. She turned away from him. "I can't imagine what changed your mind."

"Well," he sighed. "Now that I am not as busy as I normally would be, I have given it some thought and... I believe I should have given you a chance. So this is me trying."

"Singing Kalinka to me is your idea of trying?"

"It's a start." His eyes lowered upon her. Feeling amused to play with the makings of her frock, he reached for her shoulder and gently picked at her sleeve. "I can try harder."

Lady Agapov flinched, turning to him again. "You are a different breed, Mister Truit."

Oh, how lovely and crisp her voice was, falling upon his ears. "Thank you."

Her lip curled. "I dant trust you." She brought her face closer to his. "I've heard rrrumors," her r rolling tight for emphasis.

Felix put his face even closer. "What rrrumors have you heard?"

"I heard dat you are possibly married by now. Is dat true?"

Felix's gaze dropped to the ground, feeling ashamed that he was even playing with the lady's heart. He knew his answer to that would decide his nobility. As difficult as it was to do, he loved Marian. But what was his wife giving him, now? She would always plead that he stay home while knowing what obligations called him away. And when he returned, not so much as a hand kiss was allowed. Felix could not deny the fact that the love he started with Marian was a young and foolish love, budded from rebellion. It was her free, southern ways that intrigued him. She had represented all that he wanted, or what he *thought* he wanted.

He started to wonder if a marriage behind a barn without any witnesses counted as a marriage. What if it hadn't? What if...? "You're right. I *was* married. But not anymore. She was not all that I expected she'd be."

"And what if I am not what you expect *me* to be."

"I suppose it is fortunate for you that I have not set any expectations yet. However, I doubt you can be any less of who you are right now."

"Mm, true. Because I am not a fool. And if dat's what you expect of me, you will be disappointed."

"Of course, milady." He bowed, teasingly.

She squinted long and hard before saying, "I'll give you a chance. One chance." She held up her pinky.

"You won't regret it." He took her wrist and planted a slow kiss on her hand. A pinkish hue, rising to the surface of her skin.

She pulled it away, her breath catching in her throat. "But no more unpermitted caress. Understood?" And taking up her skirt, she walked inside the ballroom.

Garnering so much emotion from her was too easy. He feared he started something he could not very well stop. Nevertheless, as a husband and father, his duties remained. Still, there could be no harm in leaving open the door of opportunity. A roguish grin cracked on his face. "We'll see about that."

Thrills

Lilian couldn't help but pout at the mirror, running her fingertips along the fabric of her dress. It was made of a dark espresso silk and wrapped at the waist in wine-colored ribbon. The dress fit her hips and trained in the back, fanning out in layers of lace. An ermine shawl covered her shoulders. Her hair was banded with a red velvet ribbon, and she let a thick, curly tress from the back fall over her shoulder. Though she looked rather elegant to herself, she wasn't sure whether this *robe de diner* would do for the show at the inn. It seemed she was only a silk glove away from being fit for a gala.

"Look what you did now," she scolded herself. "Said you wouldn't get carried away."

Just as she contemplated taking it off and rummaging through her dresser for something simpler, she heard someone knocking outside of the room.

"Miss Lilian? Are you decent?" It was Maude's voice.

"Just a moment." Lilian kicked up her hem as she shuffled to the door. She opened it to Maude's frustrated visage.

"Sorry to bother you but…" she paused for a moment as her eyes began to take in Lilian's finished work. "Oh, don't you look darling?"

Lilian looked down bashfully. "Thank you. But what did you need?"

"I'm afraid Ethel's decided she isn't going with you."

"Not going? Why?"

Maude shrugged. "Wish I could tell you. She just said she won't go and told me not to ask why."

Lilian gathered the side of her gown, moving past Maude determinedly. "Excuse me." She would have to investigate this promptly, seeing as they were running out of time. Lilian did not intend to leave the house unaccompanied.

She rushed down the stairs with Maude tailing closely behind. They came to the second floor, approaching Ethel's bedroom door. Lilian gave it a light tap. "Ethel?"

Maude shook her head, leaning her hip against the door side. "That's not gone get her attention." She then gave her heavy fist one startling beat on the wood that managed to shake the wall. "Ethel, you better open this door!" Children could be heard giggling in their rooms. "Go to sleep, y'all!" she smacked. The giggles continued shortly before dying down.

Maude's beating proved effective as the door finally swung in. Ethel held it, staring at them both with a grimace. "Are you crazy?"

Crossing her arms, Maude cocked her head at Lilian. "Go on and talk to her."

Lilian addressed Ethel with a waiting expression. Ethel huffed, moving aside for her to enter. As Lilian did so, Maude continued to show Ethel an unapologetic smirk. Ethel shut the door in her face, then turned to Lilian. "Come to persuade me?"

"First, I want to know what changed your mind."

A worrisome crease appeared between her eyes, as her gaze sunk. "I don't know why you chose *me* to go. Why not Maude or Patricia?"

"Because you are my friend, Ethel." Lilian stepped closer to her, resting her hand on Ethel's shoulder. She realized it was her first time declaring their friendship out loud. Ethel returned a brief grin.

"You shouldn't have. I'm not like you, Lilian. I haven't been around adults often. I hardly see myself as one of them."

Lilian understood the sentiment. "Well, neither do I, not really. I suppose I have just gotten good at pretending."

Ethel's eyes widened. "No. Really?"

"Really. In fact..." Lilian's words were a gasp as an idea came to her, "at Hiplum Academy, I had learned some common phrases to help me in every situation. We called them breast-pocket phrases. Because you could always reach for them. I can teach them to you." Noticing the faintest intrigue in Ethel's eyes, Lilian guided her toward one of the chairs in her room to sit. Lilian took the edge of the bed, rolling back her shoulders as if assuming a tutorial role. "Now, let's say you are among a group of people having a conversation on a topic you know very little or nothing about, and they ask your opinion. What do you do?"

"I say 'I don't know'."

"No. Never ever say that," Lilian stated so passionately it forced Ethel to blush. "You say 'It's very interesting.' Or 'It depends.' And in most cases, that will be sufficient."

Ethel sat forward, tapping her chin. "Hm, very interesting."

"Exactly." Lilian hopped to her feet. "I will teach you more later. But you will have to get dressed if we are to leave in time."

"But I don't have anything to wear 'cept my—"

"No worries. I will lend you one of my gowns."

Ethel shot up from her seat. "No, I couldn't, I... I'd look silly."

"You will look wonderful."

"No. I won't." A deep frown overtook Ethel. "How could I ever be wonderful with *this* face?"

"Ethel, there is nothing wrong with your face." Lilian gently held Ethel's cheek. She felt for her. Somehow, she would have to condense an entire semester at H.A. into one hour of preparation for Ethel. Lilian reassured her, "Confidence is the key to elegance, Ethel. First and foremost. And I will help you unlock it." Lilian took hold of both her hands. "Do not despair. When I am done with you, you will see how beautiful you are. Now let's find the perfect gown for you."

As Lilian and Ethel stepped into the inn, the lively hum of conversation and clinking glasses echoed from the tavern side of the inn beyond the concierge desk. Lilian led Ethel whose face wore a mixture of nervousness and anticipation. The warm glow of the inn's lanterns reflected in Ethel's eyes as they scanned the crowd, and Lilian whispered encouragingly, "Remember, just smile and enjoy the evening."

"So many people," Ethel noted with locked knees.

"Mm, perhaps a little over a hundred. Recognize any of them?" Lilian figured it would help for Ethel to spot some familiarity.

"Mostly. Although, *he's* new." Ethel pointed toward a table where three men sat. Their ages ranged from 40 to 55 perhaps, at least for two of them. The tallest one was broad and stately. His age indecipherable from having the prestige of an older man deserving of respect, but simultaneously, a timeless youth in his body. Ethel may not have recognized him, but Lilian did. A series of articles in the newspaper featuring his image flashed in the back of her mind. Yet she could not remember who he was. The only sign of importance placed upon him was a familiar-looking gold pin on his vest. *No, still not sure.*

As Lilian's interest shifted from that table to the rest of the crowd, she spotted another familiar face. "Aunt Krishta? What is she doing here?"

"Why can't she be here?"

"She is supposed to be on a train halfway to Brord by now. If *she* is still here, then..."

"The longer you wait to take a seat," Spencer's cocksure voice spoke as the girls turned to see him, "the greater your chances of missing the show."

Just in seeing his face, Lilian had a feeling this would be a bad night. "We were only standing here to help Ethel get acclimated to the atmosphere."

"Why?" His cruel eyes pinned to Ethel, looking her up and down with scrutiny. "It's not as if anyone came to look at *her*."

"Spencer, how dare you!" Lilian chided.

But Ethel's eyes already began to show the sudden hurt he struck in her, slowly brimming with tears as she stared blankly.

"Ethel, don't listen to him," Lilian commanded earnestly.

Frozen, Ethel's eyes flickered around, a breath of appalment leaving her chest.

She turned to Lilian and bit her lip as a futile attempt to steady her quivering voice. "What was I thinking letting you bring me here?" With a shaky breath, she whirled around and darted away.

"Ethel!" Lilian called, starting after her, but was halted by Spencer's slender hand on her arm. She pulled her arm back. "Let go of me. Look what you did."

He smirked annoyingly. "I am well aware of what I did."

Lilian moderately threw up a hand. "Should not have expected *you* to show any remorse."

"Of course not. It isn't *my* fault she got offended. Neither is it yours."

"Why are you here? Why is Aunt Krishta here?"

"She said she had to come upon request."

"Request? Who requested it?"

"Oh, I'm less interested in talking about that." He bent toward her. "And far more interested in us."

She moved him back a bit with a hand to his shoulder. "Us? There is no *us*, Spencer."

"There could be."

"No, there couldn't." She tried to step closer to him as menacingly as she could manage. "And you know why?"

He drew in his chin, raising a brow of interest.

"Because I can see through your façade, Spencer. You hate me. I don't know why you're pretending you don't. But if you think I have stopped loving Paul, you're wrong. And if you somehow believe you of all people could replace him, you are doubly insane."

"Are you done?"

"Not yet. I really hope that after this conversation you will not send something else my way like you did with the bats."

He squinted. "Bats? What bats?"

"You know what bats."

He laughed, lowering a patronizing hand at her. "I am quite sure I never sent you bats. I'm partial to croquette."

"Not that kind of—"

"Now, come on, Lilian. Let's not cause a scene. I'll direct you to our table so you and your aunt can sit together."

Spencer's hand found its way to her waist, an unwelcome weight that made her skin crawl. Lilian stiffened, a surge of revulsion tightening her muscles. She fought the urge to recoil. With a subtle, yet firm movement, she eased his hand off, maintaining a composed façade. "I can walk by myself, thank you," she said, her voice laced with a frosty politeness.

Lilian followed Spencer's path past the tables and murmuring patrons. The subtle tension in her shoulders relaxed only slightly as they approached the designated table. Aunt Krishta noticed them, her eyebrows arching in surprise at their arrival.

"Lilian, dear, I didn't expect to see you here."

"I believe I could say the same. Spencer here told me you stayed upon request."

"Yes, I did," her aunt replied, looking ahead toward the empty stage across the room to dismiss any further conversation.

Who requested you? Lilian wanted to ask, though she knew she couldn't respectfully do so. If there was one thing she loathed more than Spencer, it was not knowing why people change their minds.

Spencer, with a fluid and practiced charm, pulled out a chair for Lilian. "Your seat, madam," he said, the corners of his mouth tilting in a smile that didn't quite reach his eyes.

Lilian paused for a fraction of a second, her gaze flickering between the chair and Spencer. She avoided direct eye contact with him, turning instead to Aunt Krishta. All in all, she was glad to see her.

Spencer, meanwhile, took the seat opposite Lilian, his eyes lingering on her for a moment too long before he leaned back, casually surveying the room. Lilian unfolded her napkin and placed it on her lap, waiting stiffly for the show to start.

A server arrived, placing menus before them and offering a brief respite from all the discomfort. As the server recited the evening's specials, Lilian glanced around the room, her thoughts momentarily drifting to Ethel. She hoped her friend was alright, regretting how she must have failed her. Aside from thinking of Ethel, her eyes searched the room for either Jase or Tess among the crowd. She couldn't see them so perhaps they were running late.

Just as the server left, a clear voice sounded over the crowd. The people addressed the man on stage. It turned out to be Pete. "Alright, everyone. Settle down. Thank you all for coming as usual. I see a lot of loyal faces in this crowd. Hey, Jeff! I see you made it! How's your new diet going? Lost ten pounds? Great! Only thirty more to go!"

Laughter emerged from the crowd.

Pete waved at them to settle again. "But all jokes aside, it really is great that we as a town can share in some shallow amusement together. It's just one of the ways we get along. And if you *can't* get along you can save your fists for tomorrow 'cause we're havin' none of that here, okay?"

Some whistled and clapped in response.

"Now, I know y'all have been waiting to see the performers." They all cheered. "Yes, yes, I know. However, before they can appear, we have to welcome a new visitor to our town. A very important man I'm sure you all know. He's been known to work miracles wherever he goes."

Lilian sat forward in her seat, listening carefully.

"It's said that everything he touches turns to gold. A pretty astonishing reputation if you ask me. Which is why we, as the humble town we are, are fortunate for him to take an interest in the way we run things. Without further ado, give it up for the famous and highly esteemed Mr. Jussit Muggri!"

Upon the following applause, the man Lilian had been watching earlier stood from his seat and walked up to the platform. She couldn't believe Mr. Muggri was only a few yards away from her table. Even with the distance, his presence cast a commanding shadow across the room. Standing with his fingers fit together, he seemed invincible. Lilian glanced at her aunt to see her reaction. Krishta was clapping, but her face did not reflect any amazement.

Spencer, on the other hand, let his hands fly up, clapping at the top of his head promotionally.

Mr. Muggri's lips parted and the sound came out strong and smooth. He wasn't yelling, though his voice had a natural amplification to it. "Thank you all. Seeing as my introduction was well-explained and that I myself am anxious to hear this Masked Maiden's voice rather than my own, I'll be brief in saying this." He pointed at the crowd. And like a Mona Lisa, his eyes appeared to be looking directly at anyone who met his gaze. "You know what I'm about, and you know what I can do for you. And if any of you are interested in joining the corporation, admissions will be accepted in the town square tomorrow at noon. Again, thank you."

Lilian could not help but wonder why Mr. Muggri would set his sights on this little town. Was it purely out of benevolence? It seemed so. Her uncle's many warnings about him wrapped around her thoughts. It was hard to mesh the malicious being he spoke of with this heroic figure of a man.

Muggri soon returned to his seat. Pete came up for the last time. "And now the moment you have all been waiting for… The talented, the beautiful, the beloved. Ladies and gentleman, the Masked Maiden!"

A final applause welcomed an enchanting lilt that resounded from somewhere in the room. Following the sound, everyone turned to see behind their seats as an ethereal beauty in an ivory feathered gown stepped through the aisle between the tables. Over her eyes, she wore a black linen mask. Her sharp voice floated into the air, keeping the crowd's undivided attention. Their silence allowed the unearthly sound to lift and fall around them as she moved through pitch and octave like water.

While she made light steps toward the wooden platform, her lilting broke into words. "I must explain. The reason for my pain. The bane of my whole life." Up the steps she went and finally arrived on the stage. She faced the crowd. "Some say my Papa's STILL... looking for... his wife."

A chilling sensation spread over Lilian. The woman's voice enthralled her, yet something about her presence felt familiar.

The Masked Maiden raised her head with a hand near her face as she yodeled a loud call. Then a more masculine voice echoed in reply from a place no one could spot. As a rope had been tethered to one of the beams of the ceiling, down from the mezzanine swung a well-dressed man who too wore a mask and a recognizable hat over his hair. He probably thought it would be a clever way to hide his red roots. However, if not for the hat, Lilian would never have recognized him, or consequently, the Maiden. Lilian could easily strip the masks off them now with her imagination. The truth, revealed.

He dropped onto the stage with impressive control. A fiddle, underneath his armpit. He drew it out along with the bow and began to work the fiddle, producing an upbeat rhythm.

Lilian gasped. She hadn't known his hands were so talented. Jase continued to play with one foot tapping on the wood beneath him. And Tess started tapping her own feet, then her taps became some sort of jig. She lifted her skirt and danced in a circle.

Tess caught up with the rhythm and started to sing:

"Papa was an old man with too many problems.
Too many problems that no one could solve.
O' Papa was an old man with too many problems.
Just couldn't choose, so he lost us all."

She lowered two fingers at the audience.

"Two wives, two houses, one road to connect them.
Two wives, two houses were one man's life.
From one of the houses, he gained a child.
From the other house, he lost a wife.
Papa was an old man with too many problems.
Too many problems that no one could solve.
O' Papa was an old man with too many problems.
Just couldn't choose, so he lost us all."

Lilian's shoulders bounced with the tune, her shawl slipping to her forearms. She noticed the lack of enjoyment in her aunt's eyes as she seemed to stare blankly at the performers. Though not expecting a much better attitude from Spencer, she glanced at him, finding his body turned against his seat. His eyes completely locked on the Masked Maiden. It was nice to see someone else holding his intrigue for a change.

The tempo quickened as Jase fiddled vigorously. His adept fingers pressed effortlessly on the cords. Jase made his way through the aisles, his sound following him. She wasn't sure where he attained the suit. It fit him dashingly. The liveliness in his movements and the smile he flashed made him distinct from any man she had ever known. Allowing herself to see it— he was extremely handsome, in a slightly rugged way.

As Lilian watched him dance, she was momentarily interrupted by the returning server. The server poured each of their glasses, with another placing their dinner before them. Lilian twisted her lips at the plate. She was not as hungry as her portion of steak demanded she be.

The music grew louder. She could hear it as if it were playing directly in her ear. *Wait a second.* Lilian lifted her head. Jase was beside her chair, his bow sliding just above her head. His eyes widened intensely at hers, unveiling a playful fire behind them. To which Lilian raised a brow. He raised his own and bounced his shoulders as he played to tease her. Her cheeks buzzed as others stared. Especially her aunt. Lilian burst with laughter, forgetting her previous angst.

Jase played a little riff and nodded as if for her approval. She nodded back. It seemed like he was playing solely for her. Something akin to pine, possibly juniper, emitted off his clothes. She recalled that Uncle Fred also smelled like juniper.

His arm suddenly lowered in front of her, the crowd's claps keeping the beat. He snatched a peony from the table centerpiece, bit off the stem with his teeth, and placed it in her hair. A slew of whistles and shouts began. As his finger brushed her ear and cheek, Lilian's mind disarranged with all sorts of confusion. One unruly curl ringed his eye and the side of his mouth twitched a grin. Then he eased back and danced away, his music trailing behind him. Lilian regarded her plate again, trying to ignore both Krishta and Spencer's prying gaze.

Ahead of them, Tess spun faster and faster, then leapt forward onto a nearby table, startling its occupants. All the people clapped with her at the rising tempo. With a quicker pace, again she sang the chorus in repetition, speeding up every time. The tune built up tremendously, ending with a sopranic crescendo at the very last sentence: "So he lost us all!"

Applause filled the air. The crowd's applause soon fell distant to Lilian as she caught the way Tess's gaze locked onto someone in the audience— Aunt Krishta. But why?

"Thank you! Thank you all!" she shouted in gratitude. "Before we move on to the next song, I have an announcement to make." Lilian noticed Jase's shrugging reaction to Tess's words, as if an announcement was not part of the performance.

"I'd like to acknowledge a guest here." Tess moved down the aisle in the direction of their table. "Someone I'm surprised to see show up tonight. She's had a long history of not doing that." Tess's smile turned surly, her gait nice and steady. She stopped at their table, her eyes still pinned on Aunt Krishta.

"Isn't that right, Krishta? How long would you say it's been? Three— four years?" The room fell into an uneasy hush.

Lilian's forehead knitted, gazing up at the woman. She felt a thick tension in the air by the accusation against her aunt and the attention it brought.

Aunt Krishta stared warily at Tess, showing no breakage in her composure. "Stop this," she murmured. "What are you doing?"

"'What am I doing?' she says! Oh, honey, I'm just sett'n' the record straight." She gestured at Lilian's aunt in a presentational manner. "Look everyone! The great Krishta Truit! Too high and mighty to acknowledge her own blood!"

Jase, quick to sense a problem, approached Tess. "Tess, let's not do this here," he pleaded, his voice low but urgent.

Tess ignored his warning. "You should have never come here. And I don't mean the inn. I mean the town. I'll tell you what, we don't need your stupid factory here." Tess addressed the spectators. "Some o' y'all were let go by Truit and Company, were you not?"

A plethora of agreements translated through different manners among the men. Some were nodding, while others rahed in anger. Hatred kindled in all their eyes. As Jase tugged Tess's arm, she refused to let him take her.

"Leave me alone, Jase Foster!" Tess snapped, her eyes blazing.

"Cut it out, Tessaline Truit!" Jase barked back. With an instant awareness of the name he spoke, his face turned to Lilian, bearing shock in his small eyes.

Lilian's heart skipped a beat. Her world collapsing slowly. "Tessaline?... It's *you*. You are my cousin." Her words trembled into the charged silence. This was the girl her uncle advocated for?

The reaction from Tess was cold, her head tilting in offense at Aunt Krishta. "Cousin? Oh, that's rich," she sneered. "You never did tell her the truth. Well, here's your chance. Tell her, Krishta. Tell her who I really am!"

Lilian shook her head, mouth agape as everything made less and less sense. Krishta, looking cornered and defeated, stayed silent, her eyes wide with conflict.

"Tell her!" Tess demanded, her voice echoing in the still room.

Krishta's voice, frail as a leaf in the wind, carried a truth that shattered the silence. "She's... she's not your cousin, Lilian. She's your sister."

"Correction. *Half*-sister."

"What?" Lilian's eyes darted between Tess and Krishta.

A hush fell over the crowd, their eyes wide, whispers beginning to bubble up. Lilian felt every gaze on her, piercing through her like needles. The revelation hit her like a physical blow, the room spinning around her. *My sister.*

Overwhelmed, Lilian felt a deep embarrassment flush her cheeks. How could a fun night turn so sour? Gripping the back of her chair, she moved up and fled. She had to get out, away from the suffocating atmosphere, away from the judgment and curiosity that surrounded her.

Jase's voice calling after her was just another distant sound in the chaos of her mind.

Chills

Jase made a move to follow, but Tess's voice stopped him. "Don't you dare, or I swear, Jase, I will never marry you."

Jase paused, torn as his heart pounded from all the excitement. "If I recall correctly..." Whipping back toward her, his gaze grew cold. "You never once said you *would*." He untied his mask from behind his head and threw it down. There were many moments when Jase would take rudeness from Tess, yet this was not one of them. He could not even be sure who he was looking at. Though he knew it was not the woman he had fallen in love with. "If you care about me at all, you'll wait for me." And with that, he cut through the aisles...

Outside, he found Lilian lumbering through the cool air, her furry shawl wrapped around herself. A solitary figure under the moonlit sky.

"Lilian," Jase called out gently, approaching her with caution.

She flinched, shoulders tense. "Leave me be," she demanded.

"Look, I know you're mad at Tess—"

"I'm angry at *you*!" She spun around, her eyes brimming with hurt and accusation.

Jase's brows lifted. "Me?"

"Was this some kind of trap? Did you invite me here just for this?"

His heart sank. "No, Lilian, I swear. I had no idea Tess would..." His lips pressed together. "I would never set you up like that."

His earnestness seemed to reach her, easing the tension in her shoulders slightly, though her expression remained defensive.

"How... how are you feeling?" Jase asked, his voice tinged with concern.

"I'm cold. I'm tired. And I wish I'd never come here." Lilian's gaze drifted off into the distance. "I miss my uncle. And I miss Paul," she confessed, her tone softer now. "I don't think I could deal with him going off to H.U. for more than a month." She held herself tighter. "I've just loved him for so long, you understand?"

Jase nodded. Indeed, he did understand. "How long?"

"Almost as long as we've been friends. He cared for me once when I was younger. I had fallen from an apple tree in our orchard, and he carried me inside. He bandaged my leg and sat with me until Uncle and Auntie returned from their stroll." The corner of her lips quirked upward, fondly. "It was the day he decided he wanted to be a doctor. And the day *I* decided I loved him."

Jase listened, his heart aching for her pain.

"He was rumored to propose to me, but he never did." A tear escaped down her cheek, glistening in the moonlight. "I don't know what I did to change his mind."

"Don't blame yourself, Lilian," Jase whispered softly. "There's only so much you can do," he said to both her and himself.

Just then, a gust of wind swept through, whisking Lilian's shawl off her shoulders. Jase reacted quickly, catching the delicate fabric before it could drift away. He stepped closer to redon her. She lowered her chin in allowance.

Jase took his time, delicately placing the shawl back over Lilian's shoulders. Their eyes met, and he couldn't help being struck anew by her appearance. When he had invited her, he hadn't anticipated how she'd show up.

He recalled seeing her earlier in the evening, the soft glow of the inn's lanterns catching in her hair, her elegant dress accentuating her shape— shapely as it was. The bright laughter she exuded when he serenaded her. Something about her tonight moved him deeply. Maybe it was the depth of emotion in her eyes. Or maybe it was the way she carried her pain with a quiet dignity his soul could only praise which brought him to stare.

Jase lingered in the moment, his gaze still locked with Lilian's. He noticed something unusual in her eyes, dancing within their depths.

"What in the—"

"What is it?"

"There's a light in your eyes," he murmured, his voice a blend of wonder and curiosity.

Lilian held his gaze. "Does it scare you?"

Oddly enough, some part of him felt to be in agreement with what he saw. "No," he barely whispered. "No, it's... it's beautiful." He cleared his throat, patting her shawl. "Anyways, I only wanted to make sure you're alright."

Her eyes lowered, and he knew why. How could she possibly be alright? This night was meant to clear up the mess in her mind, not add to it. He was responsible for not telling Lilian who she was to Tess. She probably would not have believed him, but it would have been better than watching Tess do it in the middle of an audience. "I really wish tonight could have gone differently."

Lilian frowned. "I'll be fine. You should go."

When Jase left, Lilian was still for a while, not eager to go anywhere. Her mind was too busy unfurling the lies she had believed all her life due to this one truth Tess brought to her attention. A truth her aunt confirmed.

Tess was Lilian's half-sister. How could that be? Did they share a father or a mother? The recollection of each lyric in

Tess's song came to mind. She couldn't have been singing about something real, could she?

"Two wives. Two houses." Lilian whispered the verse. She recalled what she knew about the scandal her father was involved in. She was never told just how heinous it was. But if that scandal had anything to do with the words in the song, then…. *Spencer. Spencer knew all along. He* had *told the truth at school about my father. Father really was a… a…* she couldn't dare say nor think it. But she knew. It was all becoming clear.

"This town is more than some place my uncle put his factory. It's history. *My* history. And it seems so many others know it except me."

Lilian felt partly betrayed. By her aunt, by her uncle, by anyone who had kept secrets from her until this point. But she also felt the refreshing air of enlightenment take her. If the key to who she was was in this town or rather the whole city of Brord, it could be the start of understanding El's purpose.

With her heart still heavy, her mind at least sobered. She breathed in the chilling air. "Alright, El. I see now. I see that you brought me here for a reason." She sucked down all complaints in her heart, knowing they would get her nowhere. "If there is anything you want to show me, anything at all. Please do."

A drawn-out period of silence ensued. She leaned against a wall as her hand gripped the ends of her shawl, her knuckles growing numb. She was going to wait for her answer. Nothing could distract her. Nothing except for the sudden whisper in her head.

He won't help you. He has never helped you.

"Please, El. Please show me."

You are wasting your time. He does not hear you. He does not love you.

"No."

Hate him.

"No."

"Hate him!"

The voice was breaking her concentration. After huffing decidedly through her nose, Lilian swerved around, swinging a focused arm. Her open palm gripped her phantom's neck and forced him backward into the brick. She was never so brutal. "Stay out of my ear!"

The clearest blue eyes stared at her frightfully from their smokey host. Its body was perpetually flowing in a motional vigor, emitting a dark gas. Lilian realized the scary thing she was gripping and released it in disgust.

The malella moved its head in the manner of a cobra while rubbing its neck. "You can see me?"

"I... can." Lilian's voice lifted more ecstatically as she restated, "I *can*. I can see you."

Before the reality of it could truly sink in, the malella dispersed into mist. Lilian tensed in vigilance. She knew winds had ways of moving swift and brisk to a sharpness that resembled a bullet. They could take on a mystical motion. Could float and fade as slowly or suddenly as they wished.

The smokey residue of the malella made a trail all around the buildings and over the street. She followed the trail with her eyes as best as she could on this dark evening. The smoke was easier to spot wherever it passed by a streetlamp, though still a challenge to follow.

She stepped forward carefully, clutching her shawl. Now there was nothing in sight. Just then, she felt a slow billow creep up her sides. Her muscles stilled as the free hands of the wind loomed up her spine, her neck, then over her mouth.

Lilian gripped its enormous fingers. She struggled to breathe. In her writhing, she managed to pull the hand off her mouth. But the wind still had her, unwilling to let go. There was a free feeling in her legs as though they dangled below her. Lilian glanced down and found herself hovering above the street. She belted a scream. However, in seconds she was much higher than before, flying over the low buildings of Brord Village. She felt her shawl slip down, the frigid air surrounding her body. As it blew around her, her ears compressed. Lilian shut her eyes, gasping in shock and screaming more.

Her screams dissipated over the clouds. In some time, her voice grew tired and eventually ceased. She viewed the land below her, being carried over a dark mass of trees. A dense forest on the outskirts of the village. Just as she began to hope against it, they were descending toward it.

It was a quick descent as they broke through the treetops. The malella carelessly released Lilian from a few feet above the ground. She tumbled over sticks and pinecones. Her hair unwound in the process with the pins that secured it becoming lost in the dead leaves. Finally stopping herself by setting down her palms, Lilian could feel the malella linger before dispersing completely. Lilian steadied herself, glancing around at the towering trees and the darkness that enveloped her.

It was eerily silent, except for the distant rustle of leaves and the soft hum of the wind. She attempted to take in her surroundings, finding only the tall shadows of the trees. It made no sense to her why the malella had brought her here. She took a cautious step forward, her senses heightened.

The area was mostly quiet due to the nature of a forest during the winter season. She held her cold arms with her hair dragging along the ground at her heels, passing under low branches, some ending up in her face. She waved them away, continuing through pure darkness.

At the sound of a howl, she halted. Bones shuttering as her mind recalled the story Ethel told her of people going missing in this forest. But Ethel herself hadn't believed in it. So, there should be nothing for Lilian to worry about. Most animals were hibernating anyway. The odds of meeting any wolves were slim, weren't they? Even werewolves? She heard a light crunch close by. Someone's feet padded the ground, their noise drawing closer. Lilian's heart raced as she turned. She saw nothing.

Whoever was there sounded as if they were approaching from her left. Lilian turned her body toward it yet took cautious steps backward. As it made more steps, she made her own, bundling her hair in one arm and keeping steady in her stride. She feared that one misstep would be her final step. As her mind panicked, a slow exhale escaped her parted lips. She kept quiet.

Her backward stride was stunted when her back hit the rough trunk of a tree. Her breath quickened. She could hear the approacher's pace speed up. This couldn't be the end of her. Not like this. Not alone in a trap of blackness, the cold eating through her dress. Lilian's eyes were wide in fear, she noticed something poking at her side. Before flinching in terror, she dared to graze her fingers over it. She exhaled a hopeful breath, pulling out the long stick, and extending it. *I am not going down without a fight.* In a weak command, she shouted, "Whoever's there, stay back! I'm warning you! I am armed!"

The sounds stopped. Lilian kept her stick poled out, firmly. The stick budged toward herself, met by the pressure of someone much closer than she expected. His narial breath shot against her face. A low chuckle moved his chest and quivered her stick.

"Armed?" His beastly hand gripped hers so tight that she released the stick. Claws dug into her wrist. He threw her down with unbelievable force. Lilian yelped as she heard a resounding pop. A slow heat swelled up her shoulder blade. She sniffed, feeling him bend over her. There was something inhuman about his silhouette, as much as she could make out. From his shoulders to his arms, she saw a line of thick hair. He made strange grunting and panting noises. As his face lowered to her, she was puzzled by the smell of him. He smelled like a hound.

"Is it you?" Lilian spoke, wasting one of her last questions. "Did you take the others?"

"Stop talking. Food should be silent." He raised his arm.

Lilian squinted her eyes in pain, waiting for the blow.... A beam of light slashed across her sight, relieving her attacker of its arm. He growled and squealed simultaneously, throwing himself back from her.

Lilian panted, confused. She raised her head at the being that stood above her on long, sturdy legs. She gazed at the face that was once familiar, now nostalgic. His body shined among the night. His flaming sword at his side.

"Tarfwin."

His green eyes regarded her for a second before he was knocked down by her attacker's pounce. Tarfwin's light made it easy to see the beast now. His giant, furry body, pointy ears and dog-shaped head. The werewolf opened his jaw, baring his teeth. One of his arms was severed, blood dripping from the wound.

Tarfwin immediately shifted to his windy form. He now made circles around the werewolf as he whipped his head from side to side, trying to follow Tarfwin. He growled again, head raised to the sky. Tarfwin's wind blew faster. Soon, a ring of his light was all Lilian could see, the werewolf hidden within it. When the wind finally settled, taking original form again, Lilian, still in pain, was amazed to see the beast lying faint on the ground. Tarfwin stood over him, drawing out his sword. The beast's eyes drew up as he heaved. Whatever darkness had clouded them now receded, leaving very human eyes, no longer the eyes of a predator but prey.

Even though Tarfwin had no lips, he spoke through the whirring sound of his body-wind lifting in tendrils off his back. "Do you know the wages of your wrongs?"

The beast's eyes rolled back and shut as he nodded his head, his hairy chest rising and falling measuredly.

Tarfwin lifted his sword. Without any sign of rage or personal ought, only duty, he pushed it down, burning through the heart of the beast. When he pulled it out and slid it back into his belt, the werewolf was dead. Lilian struggled a relieved sigh. Just as she thought that was the end of it, a steamy cloud released from the werewolf's body. Tarfwin stood back, letting the steam rise into the dark night. The long nails of the beast drew in, the hair on his skin shortened back to normal. His limbs shrunk in size and his snout drew in, becoming a nose. When the reversion was complete, his entire body was that of a bare and naked old man. The little hair he did have on his head was now thin and grey.

Lilian was dumbfounded. Tarfwin walked so swiftly to her, it looked as though he floated. "Are you hurt?"

"My... My shoulder."

He bent down, lifting her up in his arms. It felt like she was floating, except for her head due to the heaviness of her overlong hair. Though the pain in her shoulder was searing, she found it easy not to focus on it as another kind of pain rested in her heart. Tarfwin, her guardian ciella, was finally here with her. Where had he been all this time?

Carrying Lilian in his arms, Tarfwin moved with a grace that belied his powerful form. The forest, with its tangled branches and whispering leaves, seemed to part ways for them as if respecting Tarfwin's presence.

They emerged from the dense foliage into a clearing bathed in moonlight. Ahead of them lay a quaint horse stable, its wooden structure casting long shadows on the ground. The horses inside, sensing their approach, began to neigh softly.

This stable most definitely belonged to someone. But her body ached too much with exhaustion and pain to really consider that.

They entered a seemingly vacant stall quietly, finding it occupied by a rather willowy old horse breathing and shifting on its side. Tarfwin moved with Lilian to the corner of the stable where the hay was piled. He helped her sit down, arranging the hay to cushion her back.

She winced as he did. She did not need to say a word before he started gently probing her shoulder in assessment. He raised his head, looking upward for a while. Lilian assumed he was listening to El's voice. A voice that had long been muted to her. When his eyes lowered, he said, "It is not broken. Only dislocated."

Lilian didn't like what it implied as he held her shoulder firmly.

"This will hurt."

"Wait, don't—"

With a swift, yet careful movement, Tarfwin manipulated her shoulder. There was a sharp pain, a sensation of pressure, and then a sudden release as the joint popped back into place. Lilian couldn't hold back a cry of pain, but it was quickly followed by a wave of relief as the intense discomfort she had been feeling began to fade.

As he removed his hands, she stared at him, not sure yet whether she was happy to see him or not. "Why?" she said lowly.

"Pardon?" he said.

She restated, "Why now have you come to my aid?"

"You seem to believe I had left my post."

"If you had not, then why did I never see you? Why has El stopped speaking to me?"

There was a moment of no answer, then Tarfwin spoke with a rather unaffected kilter. "You've seen Ms. Cora and Miss Wayne work with the children, correct?"

"What does that have to do with—?"

"Haven't you?" he reinforced.

"Yes."

"And when the children fill a room with noise and there is no way of hearing Miss Wayne's instruction, what does she do? Does she raise her voice?"

Lilian pondered it. "No. No, she usually doesn't waste a breath. Instead, she stands amidst them and," her eyebrow twitched as she recalled the strange tactic, "she lowers her voice to a whisper. And suddenly, one by one, they quiet down to hear what she's saying."

"Because in order to hear someone, you must be interested in what that person has to say. All this is to say, Lilian, that El *was* speaking. You stopped listening."

"When? When had I stopped?" she asked in disbelief.

"Whenever you decided it no longer mattered what El had to say."

"So he is punishing me?"

"He is protecting you."

"Protecting me?"

"Yes. Though protection and comfort are not always the same. There is much else in this world that can break you, Lilian. El knows that."

Lilian sat forward. "Then why am I broken?"

"Lilian," he said cautiously, "no one promised you a life of unshattered bliss."

That was not what she wanted to hear. "Then what life *am* I promised?"

Tarfwin's dazzling eyes focused on hers. "You fail to see beyond yourself. You are not the first to deal with pain nor will you be the last."

Lilian frowned, conflicted. She sat back. "Perhaps... but it... still hurts."

"El knows your pain, Lilian. But sometimes it is pain that pulls you out of ignorance. And you need to be awake to see what is really at stake here."

Lilian was hardly listening as she rubbed her sore shoulder. She muttered, "Why have dreams if only for them to die."

"Lilian. Lilian, look up."

Reluctantly, her gaze slowly drew back to his. "Yes?"

"You want good things, Lilian. Know that there is a time for everything. But right now, you have a lesson to learn."

She huffed hopelessly. "I feel as if I have learned my lesson."

"The lesson isn't learned when *you* say it is. You are being called toward something greater than you understand. A battle is brewing in many regions. El has appointed in each one a Fisher. *You* have been appointed Fisher here in Brord. It is your duty to find lightbearers for El."

Lilian shrugged, ceding to finally listen. "What then?"

"Then you must endeavor from this day on to thwart Girgum's attempts to spawn in the hearts of the people."

"Spawn? What do you mean?"

"What he wants is to reshape this world however he can."

"He couldn't, could he? The Foundum holds all the rules, I thought."

"Precisely," Tarfwin bent his long torso, his bodywind nearly snuffing out gravely. "And just what do you think he is after?"

Her mouth hung, herself now engrossed. "That cannot happen. Someone has to stop him."

"Yes, someone is." His back moved up again.

"Right," she said, thinking further. "I suppose that would be Shersul's charge."

"That is correct."

A glow of love emerged from her eyes. "Tarfwin. How is he?"

"Alive and well."

Her chest dropped as she pushed out a sigh.

"And what's more," Tarfwin continued, "is that he still thinks of you."

Lilian should have felt comforted, only it depressed her more. "The younger me, I suspect. The one he could have looked upon without shame."

"He understands the evolution of one's thoughts, Lilian. With age comes uncertainty. But no matter how scarred or weak your spirit has become, he is waiting to strengthen it. To show you the Lilian that is truer than even what her past remembers."

Her face rested. "I would love to be that Lilian."

"Then do what is asked of you. Girgum may not possess the Foundum, but he has other ways of producing a world that conforms to his vision. He is raising an army of his own. And his work had begun long before you were born. His roots in this world run deeper than any man can fathom."

"But why am I chosen to be a Fisher? No one listens to me. Who is going to believe in a war or a realm they have not seen?"

Tarfwin's head gave a considerate tilt. "Don't you know the abilities El bore you with? The reason for that glint in your eyes?"

Lilian shook her head. "I have always wondered." Her eyes watched his, yearning for the answer.

"You see people. You see their gifts even before they do. And you can speak to people's hearts like few can."

As if a bucket of water had been dumped over her head, her mind was refreshed by Tarfwin's words. Finally, something about herself that she could accept. "I see people," she repeated. "And… I see winds."

"And soon enough you will begin to see so much more. However, in lieu of the time that has been wasted in your preparation, drastic measures must be taken to accelerate your growth. Therefore, the first lightbearer for you to find is the Zealot."

"Who is that?"

"The Zealot will be the catalyst of your army. Someone who commits their life to fighting for truth. With them, you are sure to catch a passion for your purpose."

"And how am I supposed to find this person?"

"It's not a matter of *finding* them. By El's will, you should find anyone he wants you to. It's a matter of being accessible."

"Accessible? Like being in the right place…"

"At the right time. Correct again."

"But how will I know if I am in the right place?"

"Trust, Lilian. You'll know."

In the dimly lit stable, Lilian absorbed Tarfwin's words. She could hear the other horses begin to lie down. As for the one she was sharing quarters with, his thick and heavy tail found itself in her lap. She chuckled, deciding to pet the horse's backside. The fact of her surroundings finally dawned on her, causing another laugh. She was sitting on a stiff and scratchy bed of hay in an evening gown with a bruised shoulder and loose hair. It was quite embarrassing, but there was worse. She could have been eaten alive.

Lilian supposed she would never consummately understand El. It tended to frustrate her. She hoped still that she was more to El than a pawn to be played. There wasn't much she could do about it if that were the case. But surely He, however inexplicable, possessed a merciful heart? Surely when He had allowed Uncle and Auntie to take her as their own, that was done out of consideration for their prayers? And even as her uncle grew sick, surely his passing was a merciful leave rather than a thoughtless disposal?

"Surely…" the word became a yawn drawn from her mouth. Her eyelids felt heavy.

"Do not overthink it," Tarfwin said, noticing the cogs turning in her head. "Just rest. Just… re…" His voice faded from her as a dark cape of coziness blanketed her. She lost sense of herself, giving in to the beckon of sleep.

When the bright chirps of the morning finally fell upon her waiting ears, she breathed a gracious breath. Her eyes remained shut as she sat quietly. It wasn't until she heard the sound of someone stepping over grass outside the stable that they opened without a need to blink.

The old horse she lay by last night was now standing above her. She heard two sets of footsteps coming near the stable. Lilian drew in her knees, trying her best to shrink behind the horse. A man's unforgettable timbre spoke earnestly before the boarded wood of the stall's door. "I told you she's not here. Nobody is. Now, if you'll excuse me, I have some things to take care—"

The door swung open with a creak, frigid air blowing in. Lilian tensed as her frightened gaze met his. He lingered by the door in surprise, lips parted. Jase wasn't wearing his hat, nor was he dressed beyond a set of cotton pajamas. The wind blew through his ear-length curls. A vibrant red swaying against the winter sky.

As both goosebumps and a flush of pink developed over her skin, she heard yet another voice behind him. "What in there is so shocking?" Spencer asked, poking his head. His previous grimace now softening as he stared down at Lilian. "Lilian," he said as he placed a hand over his heart endearingly. "Sweetheart, *there* you are."

Sweetheart? Lilian failed to mask her discomfort for how he addressed her, saddened to see that he still had not left Brord.

"What are you doing here?" Jase asked with a slight disappointment, as if he was too drained to deal with her. There seemed to be something else weighing on his mind. The bright countenance she saw last night was now stolen from him, replaced with something akin to misery.

Spencer turned his gaze to Jase, his scorn returning. "As if you don't know. Oho," he chuckled, "you will answer to her aunt for this."

Jase eyed him, indignant. "You think I *put* her in my horses' stable?"

"I believe I watched you run after her last night. And no one had seen her since." Spencer lifted his arm, showcasing Lilian's dark shawl between his clutch. Lilian gaped and Jase squinted as Spencer brought it to his nose, then lowered it, saying, "Tell me why it has your smell all over it."

"What are you tryna say?"

"All I am saying is the lady looks as though she's been maimed…" he looked him up and down, "by a beast."

The muscles in Jase's neck tensed as he faced Spencer completely. They were nearly the same height, Jase winning by an inch. "Now look here…"

"Gentlemen, please!" Lilian cried. Their heads whipped to her. "Jase is right. He did not bring me here. I didn't know this was your stable, and I am sorry for trespassing."

"How did you end up here?"

"It's a long story."

"Of course it is." Spencer rolled his eyes. "Sweetheart, you don't have to cover for him."

"I am not your sweetheart, Spencer. Now, can someone help me up from here?"

Jase took a step forward until Spencer pushed him back at his chest, coming for Lilian instead. He knelt down and let her wrap her good arm around his neck. Together they stood.

She hardly caught the swift movement of his hand behind her back. She stared into his pert eye as he drew it outward to let her hair slip along his arm. "I've never seen you with your hair down," he remarked through his teeth.

She suppressed her disdain, returning a yielding grin. "Since it intrigues you so much, be of some use and hold it for me."

"Indeed."

His response not only felt too eager, it stirred a discomfort in Lilian, making her second-guess her own words. Could her quip be mistaken for playing along with his ulterior tone? Or as a layman would say, had she *flirted* with him? Lilian briskly discarded the thought, moving out of the stall.

PART
II

Undertaking

Winter (1885)

His means were high.
His profit, low.
He sought himself with the world in tow.
A swindler of fate, he was by rote.
His half, he gave.
Himself, he'd dote.

That anonygraph, a word Fredrick fabricated to mean a work written anonymously, was too apropos, reciting in the back of Fredrick's mind as he became convinced nothing described his brother better. Seeking himself, swindling his own fate. And a master he was at it. Fredrick surely could never pull off the tricks his brother did. Such as the one he was fulfilling at the moment.

A disgusting, shameful trick. Fred didn't want to sit there in a cold, echoing tomb of a church and watch a marital crime be committed. But he knew he had to be there. And not because Mother urged him; he didn't need her to. Fredrick had one plan in mind. To shout his disapproval of the marriage.

He couldn't let such a thing come to pass. No matter Fredrick and Marian's distaste for each other, Fredrick knew she did not deserve to be a victim of his brother's infidelity, nor did Lady Agapov.

Poor Lady Agapov. Fredrick could not help but sigh endearingly at the blushing bride standing there at the pulpit. She was breathtaking in her pearly basque bodice lined in lace just over her deep and tantalizing v, keeping her stuffed and packaged like a doll. Like a wedding gift in itself, waiting to be opened; to be used. Everything from her snow-imitating veil, starting at her crown in fake white roses and draping behind, to the delicate frill just at the end of her gown. It was all meticulously done in tune with the entire cathedral's new makeover. All just so, for this day. A day she had long awaited. All a waste.

As deeply as Fredrick respected his brother, he knew Felix knew nothing of love. Whether it was for his wife and child or himself. As his hands sweetly held Lady Agapov's, and his eyes emitted a convincing adoration, it made Fredrick curdle inside.

And that ignorant pastor, an unknowing accomplice to a crime, grinned excitedly in his pastorly attire. Thinking, perhaps, *"Another blessed work I've done in El's name, bringing together more youth in Holy Matrimony."*

As he began his greeting speech, Fredrick found himself on the edge of his seat. The young lady next to him, his sister, Barbra, eyed him leerily. "Fredrick?"

Fred ignored her, knowing if he even told her his plans, she'd tell Mother beside her. Though he was considered rather unspokenly Mother's favorite, Barbra was quite blatantly Mother's pet. She glowered at him with her droopy eyes for just a moment, never quite breaking that aloof demeanor which was part of her allure. She was new to the market, but already gaining the attention of so many perfervid boys and men. Blooming so drastically from the little girl she once was that Fredrick felt the need to guard her from schemers much like their brother. *I'd do it for you, Barbra*, he thought, now readier than ever for his cue.

"If anyone objects to the binding of these two, speak now or forever hold your peace!"

As Fred determinedly rose from his seat, her hand gripped his upper arm. He looked at his sister anxiously, and she returned an indignant scowl. It didn't matter. He was going to complete his rise. Eagerly, she wrapped her arms around his waist and pulled him down, pinning his lower half to the seat with surprising tenacity. Their mother looked over at them with inquiring shock.

He still tried to stand, but it was too late. The wedding had moved on with the pastor's nod. Nevertheless, it was not enough to deter him. He would wait. And wait, he did. Until the lush reception hosted at the Preuve de Beauté Hotel. The sun that day beamed directly over the dome, brightening and warming the room, and giving all the guests halos. They used roses and baby's breath in the posies of the banquet table. The entire venue was out of a fairytale.

Remembering his mission, Fredrick made his way over to his brother. He was in the middle of laughing with his colleagues. Using that charisma as usual. "Alright, men," Fred interrupted. "May I steal the groom for a private word?"

Felix lowered his eyes to the floor momentarily. It was clear that he had been avoiding his twin. "Do excuse us, gentlemen, for I am my brother's keeper," he sighed. They listened and left with short accolades.

When Felix finally met Fred's gaze, he insisted they talk somewhere private. The men walked to the water closet outside the hall. Not the most appropriate space, but private no doubt. Felix turned to Fred as Fred shut the door. "Before you say anything, Freddy, I know you're angry with me."

"I'm more than angry." The grim, uncanny way Fredrick spoke surprised them both.

Felix allowed a silence to brew as Fredrick kept his gaze, clearly trying to collect his thoughts. Fred then spoke. "You must swear not to touch her tonight. Nor *any* night, until we've annulled this sham marriage."

Felix brushed past to open the door. Fred leaned back, slamming it shut as he still blocked him. His eyes grew wide with appalment. "You can't mean to go through with it. Bigamy, Felix? Have you lost your senses?"

"It's what Mother wanted."

"Don't hide behind Mother's skirts now. Since when did her whims dictate your actions?"

The following silence proved Felix was out of quips and excuses.

Fredrick, however, wasn't done interrogating. He watched his brother's eyes, finding no glimmer of regret or remorse. "I see. You *want* this. And you don't care."

All Felix had to give him was a shrug. A shrug!

Fred could not even set his eyes upon his twin. A man who looked exactly like him, but instead of mirroring him, soul and all, his eyes encased sheer evil. He wondered if this indignance was the result of his enablement. It was hitting him like a brick. All the secrets he had kept for Felix. All the moments of silently glaring, as if glaring was some soft form of prevention. Felix was not a good man, but Fred allowed him not to be. Refraining from the want to wrang his brother's neck, he said, "Felix. I'm begging you. Do not. Touch. Her. Lady Agapov does not deserve this. Swear it to me!"

"Brother. Firstly, it's Lady *Truit* now. And secondly, I, Felix Truit, do as I please. Now, move out of my way! I'll be dancing with my wife."

Fred moved out of his way. His brother left the room. Fredrick stood silently— somberly— before walking out himself. Just outside was an old lady, who stared at him as though she had seen the most egregious thing. Fred, now embarrassed and without a good explanation, simply nodded the old woman's way. She quickly averted his gaze. He stepped on and out the hotel doors. His mission, failed.

After all that formal and celebratory atmosphere, the day had finally quieted down. The happy couple found their room on the upper floor. Felix had had his eye on his lovely bride throughout the entire afternoon. She was spectacular just as the days prior. It had been only a month of him courting her, and the more he learned about Lady Agapov, the more he found himself unable to leave her presence. Dare say, he began to love her.

Everything his mother ever wanted for him, that's what she was. He saw that now. She was to him what Marian could never be. Of course, there was no denying the usefulness of his first wife—first, that sure sounded strange to say— but this one had a low romance about her. She brought him down to earth with her deep, intrusive eyes. Eyes that made the earth quake beneath him.

Now she stood in front of the full-length mirror, unpinning her silky locks. They fell loosely to their popliteal length. He brought himself to stand behind her, together staring at their reflection and seeing each other's gaze. He put his wanting hands on her shoulders, lowering his nose to the crown of her head.

Taking in the smell of her, his hands fled to her waist. He then spun her around and drew her close, grinning at her pinking face. He could feel her shivering. Understanding well his effect on his new wife, he held her arms still. "I can't believe I have you now."

She giggled breathily. "Took you long enough. But I was counting on it."

"What? But I don't understand. Why? There were so many fine suitors after your hand."

She lowered her head bashfully. "I know. But I refused dem all. And I waited."

"For what?"

"For you." She took his hand, raised it to her lips, and kissed each finger, her face turning shy. "I wanted you. Always."

With such an affectionate advancement from her, such a passionate confession, Felix found himself feeling— not flattered— unnerved.

"All dose other ladies dot I didn't have a chance wit you. But now you are mine," she smiled. "And I knew you would come around eventually. I still did not trust you, dough."

"Do you trust me now?" His eyes narrowed on hers.

"I dant know. Can I trust you, Felix?"

He froze a moment, then lowered his nose to hers. "Well, it's too late now to wonder."

She smiled, taking to his alluring shadow. "Yes," she said sleepily. "Much too late."

Felix pulled her closer in and landed his lips on hers. The room was awfully silent now. But while he should have been focused on the woman in his arms, his thoughts were fleeing out the window of the room, across the old railroad, over the hills to the familiar blue eyes he knew so well. And in them, such a pained look of condemnation. *NO.* He pulled *this one* closer, kissed her harder, till he could not hear his own thoughts. Till he was back in *this* room. In *this* moment. With *her.*

"Oh, Felix!" she gasped.

He released her. "Sit," he said. She sat on the edge of the prepped and duveted bed. She sat and watched as he slowly, painstakingly, suspensefully undid his tie, his vest, down to now his blouse.

She watched with those same ravenous eyes he'd seen before on so many other eager women. But he had never been beheld in such a way by her. Or maybe she had done so well in hiding it. That unforthcoming passion.

As he slowly, tauntingly unbuttoned, he bit back as best as he could the strangest feeling he thought could never reach him; guilt. But she was waiting, and he had no desire to disappoint.

The quaint, yellow house Jase shared with Tessaline was modest in size, boasting just one floor. Upon entering, a cozy kitchen greeted them, leading directly to a short hallway where two small bedrooms faced each other, while to the left, a dainty living area unfolded. A lone couch sat invitingly next to a table and bench before an ashen hearth, crowned by a neatly arranged stack of books on mechanics.

Jase led Lilian and Spencer to the table nestled between the kitchen and living area. "Please, take a seat. Anyone for coffee?"

"Lots of cream and sugar, please," Lilian said.

"Black," said Spencer, keening his eyes on Lilian's and winking. "Like my heart."

She looked away from him, refusing to acknowledge it.

With her eyes on Jase, she saw how slowly he came to the cupboard, opening up the icebox for the cream. Lilian sensed the tension in his body. Something was amiss.

"On second thought, Jase..." her words made him pause, "I'll do without."

Jase's eyes lifted and locked on hers, failing to conceal his heartache. "Why?"

He squinted in a way she didn't like, as if it was all he could do to not cry. Lilian took to a stand, much to Spencer's dismay. As her hair smoothed over the seat and down to the floor, she met Jase across the kitchen. "What happened?"

His hand tightened around the glass bottle of cream, his honey eyes skipping over hers.

"Jase." Lilian looked around, starting to understand. "Where is Tessaline?"

He finally met her gaze. "Gone. She's gone."

"Gone where?"

Jase shook his head, slightly lost in thought. "Last night... she packed everything 'cept her mother's wedding dress she wore onstage. She said she never loved me— that it was better for me if she left. And she left the dress, saying it could never be used for anything else." His gaze descended. "Just a way of answering my question. She'll never marry me."

"Ah, that's nice." Spencer remarked, rubbing his eyes. "Hey, I wonder when that coffee is going to be made."

Jase grimaced, turning his body in Spencer's direction.

Lilian patted his thick arm. "Don't mind him."

Spencer smirked while absent-mindedly pinching the tablecloth.

"I'm sorry," Lilian continued, regaining Jase's attention. "And I understand."

"I know you do." His brows knit considerately. "But you realize you... you just lost a sister?"

Lilian frowned, shrugging. "How can I lose what I never had?"

"Hm." He nodded respectfully. "I guess you can't."

"We can't stay long," Spencer spoke up. "I know the woman you've been staying with will be anxious for your return, Lilian. Also the longer you stay, the easier for presumptions to be made about the two of you."

Lilian pulled away, her frustration with Spencer growing. She leaned over the table, fixing him a pointed look. "Why are you still here? Where is my aunt?"

"Your aunt is on a train back to Corlu. But I fail to see what that has to do with me."

"Aren't you also meant to be on that train?"

He raised an eyebrow, his laughter declaring her foolish. "You thought I was leaving? I'm more useful here, keeping an eye on the factory accounts."

Lilian straightened, her frown deepening. Despite her urge to argue, she knew it was futile.

Spencer stood, moving closer. "Lilian, we've always been at odds. And I accept the blame for most of it. Or... all of it. But as you said, things change. And I've changed."

Her skepticism was clear. "You? Changed?"

He placed his hand gently on her shoulder. She stiffened, discomfort and confusion mingling within her. "I care about you," he said earnestly, though his sincerity was hard to gauge.

Lilian searched his face, disbelieving him yet reluctantly curious.

"I've looked for you all morning," he continued. "Doesn't that mean something?"

"I..." she began, but words failed her.

"Ahem," Jase's cough diverted their gazes. He raised up an empty bag. "Turns out we're out of coffee."

Their return to the village was made in Jase's wagon. A silent street awaited them, cool gusts sweeping through the wide alleys. The day opened up tranquilly as if the uproar of the night was merely a dream.

More gusts blew toward the wagon which Jase did not bother to cover this time. It swayed loose strands against Lilian's face though she had done her best to roll up her hair without the help of pins. Lilian pulled more at the opening of Spencer's coat to keep the cold out. He had draped it over her before their ride began. She found it strangely chivalrous of him and was not sure whether she liked it or not.

He sat closely beside her as the wagon bed rocked. Spencer's hand dangled loosely over the side of his knee with fingers grazing the side of *hers*. "Comfortable?" he asked.

"Compared to a leather seat under a car roof..." she responded, "it suffices."

Spencer's chuckle vibrated in her ear. He was far too close for comfort. "Are you considering what I said to you before?"

"What is there to consider?"

"Right, perhaps I should be more direct. I want to court you, Lilian."

She responded with a shake of her head. "I have already told you, Spencer. My heart is for Paul."

"Oh, come on, Lilian. Paul and I are not that different. I'm just as handsome, and just as smart if not smarter."

"Spencer, you cannot make me want you by pointing out your similarities to Paul. I don't even know why you want to court me. People court to know each other's minds, and you could never be *that* interested in me, nor I you. And then, if I may be direct, why would you want to *marry* me?" She turned to meet his gaze.

Spencer's expression hardened slightly, a shadow of frustration flickering across his features before he masked it with a practiced smile. "Marry you?" he echoed, leaning back against the wagon's side. "You intrigue me, Lilian. You make good arguments against me, you're quite smart in your own way, and very, very pretty. And aside from all that, I'm certain I will have more reasons once we are official."

There was a brief silence, the only sound being the rhythmic creak of the wagon wheels and the distant chirping of birds. Lilian had not wanted to even discuss this, yet she tried at the moment to weigh his words. Finally, she said, "You are quite a case, Spencer Wesman."

Spencer let out a sigh, his gaze drifting off to the passing scenery. "I know," he admitted softly. "I confess I am a wayward, a cad. But Lilian, can't I at least *try* to be better?"

"Oh," she tsked, looking away again. "I am going to have to see a lot of change in you."

"And you will. I promise I can change for you." His adamance was apparent.

As they neared the village, the wagon slowed to a stop. Jase hopped down, his face still carrying the weight of his earlier conversation with Lilian. He offered his hand to help her down, but before she could take it, Spencer interjected. "Allow me."

He extended his hand to Lilian, and after a moment's hesitation, she accepted it. As she stepped down, their eyes met, and for a brief moment, there was a sense of déjà vu. She thought of her first day in Brord, when Paul was still with her. Still loyal to her. But then the day came when he wasn't loyal. The day he left her. Contrarily, Spencer always seemed to be just around the corner. It was something she mentally noted as they walked on.

The trio continued in silence towards the heart of the village. Lilian's thoughts were a conundrum of emotions, remembering her chat with Tarfwin. Today was a day like any other, only now she had a mission to fulfill. Somewhere in this town were other lightbearers like her. And somehow, she would have to find them.

As they reached the central square, Jase stopped. "I should head back," he said, his voice heavy. "I've got things to sort out."

Lilian nodded. "Take care of yourself."

"You too, Lilian. You too." He offered a weak smile in gratitude and turned back towards his wagon. Lilian watched him go, feeling a pang of sympathy.

Turning to Spencer, she found him watching her with an unreadable expression. "What?"

"Who is he to you?"

"An acquaintance. Jase has been friendly to me ever since I first arrived." She brought her hands to her sides, trying to move from the question. "He is to begin management in my aunt's factory, tomorrow."

"Mm, how nice." His 'how nice' didn't sound very enthusiastic.

Lilian wasn't sure why he seemed bothered by Jase but concluded that it never took much for Spencer to be bothered by anyone. "Spencer, Jase is my ally. I want you to treat him well when he starts working. Alright?"

He concededly nodded.

When they reached Ms. Cora's, Lilian slipped his coat off her shoulders and handed it back to him. An immediate chill enveloped her. "Well, I must go in now. I hope Ms. Cora isn't too mad at me."

"Why would she be? It wasn't your fault. Right?" He spoke tauntingly, almost as if he understood her situation though Lilian had never clearly explained it.

"Right."

"I'll bring you in." He said, drawing out the key to the gate.

"Where did you get that from?"

"Ms. Witherman gave it to me in case I found you."

Lilian stared in awe and mild disbelief. "She gave you her key?"

Spencer began to insert the key into the iron lock. "I have a way of persuading people. Women especially." As he turned it, the light of the sun glinted off the gold pin on his vest's left breast. She had seen it before on him, but this time it seemed more intriguing, more significant for a reason she couldn't say.

A satisfying click preceded Spencer's push of the gate. Lilian was still worried about going up to the front door dressed as she was in broad daylight, yet one whip of the frigid air was enough to impel her forward.

After reaching the front door and knocking, the woman who answered held a perplexed gaze as she stood still in the middle of the doorway.

"Ms. Cora, I—" Lilian began just as the old woman stepped out and pulled her in for a tight hug.

"Oh dear, I was so worried. Where on earth have you been?"

"I'm sorry, Ms. Cora. I was kidnapped."

"Kidnapped?" the old woman exclaimed as she moved Lilian off her to stare in her eyes. "By who? What happened?"

"Uh... by someone... I couldn't see their face. They took me into the forest and thankfully Jase was there to save me."

A sneer came from Spencer who stood behind her. Lilian ignored it, not wanting to make it any more obvious that she lied. "And Mister Wesman here found me this morning."

Ms. Cora turned her eyes to him. "Mister Wesman. Thank you so much for bringing her home. I don't know what I would have done if my Krishta dear's niece was harmed or worse."

"Why, it was only right to look for her, no need to thank me."

"Oh yes, there is a need. And I would thank Mister Foster, too if he was here."

Just then, they were interrupted by the whiny blurt of a child. "Does this mean we don't get to party?"

Ms. Cora turned around to address the group of children standing together in the foyer. All of them, carrying rolls of paper in their hands. Ms. Cora shook her head with a short, regretful laugh. "I'm afraid not, Gale. There will be no need for a search party since our friend is now home."

All the little ones cried an exasperated "*Awwww!*"

"Alright, quit the theatrics and let Miss Lilian come inside."

The children stepped away from the door as Lilian stepped in. Ms. Cora invited Spencer, but he denied her, saying there was some work he had to return to. He handed Ms. Cora her key, but she told him to keep it in case of another emergency. He agreed with a bow of his head and left. As Lilian addressed the children and their disappointed faces, as well as the relieved faces of the older boys and girls, it amazed her how Ms. Cora had cared enough to prepare a search party.

A girl about 5 ran up to Lilian. "Well, I want her to see my picture of her first!" She shouted while waving her paper in the air that showed a stick-figure drawing of Lilian with her hair down rather than up. Quite an uncanny resemblance, too. Lilian took it gently from her hands. "Wow! Is this for me? It's wonderful."

The girl nodded. Then the rest of them scampered close to bombard her with their drawings. Lilian met each with grateful remarks. Ms. Cora, Miss Wayne, and the volunteers stood aside, watching the excitement. Ethel was among them, staring in silence with a frown that deepened her already prominent jowls.

Poor Ethel, Lilian thought. But she smiled at the children and said conclusively, "These are all so nice. Much better than having my portrait shown in a newspaper, I'll say."

Ms. Cora stepped forward, clapping her hands at the children. "Okay, y'all heard her. They're all very nice. Now it's time for breakfast, so go line up at the dining room. We'll have church here as well."

Lilian's smile waned as they all formed a line from shortest to tallest. Due to what she had said before, she was suddenly thinking about newspapers. Specifically, one she had read not long ago. The one that featured an article about werewolves. Just as the volunteers escorted the line of youngsters down the hall, Lilian moved toward Ms. Cora, giving her a pat on the shoulder. "Er, Ms. Cora?"

"Yes, sweetie?"

"Who writes all the articles in the paper?"

"Why do you want to know?"

"Just curious."

"Well, it's not exactly a fixed number of people, not like an agency or anything. Anyone with a penchant for writing can add their article to the paper. You might have found some silly things in there. It's just this town's way of giving ourselves a good laugh sometimes."

This answer half-discouraged the conclusion Lilan was about to make. "So, none of it is true."

"Well, some of it, yes. Good luck finding out what exactly. But Lilian," Ms. Cora's warm hands felt her face, "shouldn't you be resting? You've been through a lot. Let's get you upstairs for a bath, and I'll have Ethel bring you something to eat a bit later."

Delving

Of one thing, Lilian could be sure. The article *was* legitimate. Whether the author intended to lie or not, they were right about the werewolf. After all, she could not doubt her encounter with it.

Lilian was unable to rest as Ms. Cora suggested. She turned on her side in the bed and reached for the breakfast tray on her nightstand. Lifting it to take the newspaper it sat on, she felt an invigorating sense of duty swell within her. "Alright. Who are you?" She uttered while skimming the front page. Just under the article, she found a name. "Flora Barrymore. Hm, Flora..." Lilian repeated with a short smile. "Are you my Zealot?"

As much as she was enjoying her warm sheets, she felt the possibility had to be explored. This was Lilian's chance to take her first step into her role as Fisher. It was time to fish. She eased out of bed, dressed in one of her black suits, and headed downstairs. At the base of the steps, she saw Maude and Patricia engaging in a whispered conversation by the door. The two of them rested on each wall as they faced the other.

"So, did you hear about the feud last night?" Patricia asked with a solemn look.

"Yeah." Maude sighed. "Poor Lilian. I can't imagine sitting through that."

"We should have told her ourselves."

"Patricia," Maude said dismissively. "Don't start blaming yourself. She heard it from all who were relevant. Besides, if Ethel hadn't run out like a chicken, Lilian wouldn't've sat through it alone. Or had to walk home alone. Can you believe she was kidnapped?"

Patricia chuckled. "Crazy. But I sort of envy her. I mean, she said Jase saved her."

"Right. I wonder what that was like."

"Oh, my. Should we ask?"

"No, we shouldn't make her recount such an experience."

"Agreed." Patricia nodded, then looked back up with another topic of interest. "You heard how Jase ran after her from the inn?"

Maude paused, looking smugly at her fellow volunteer. "You don't say."

Lilian didn't understand the rise in her tone.

Patricia smirked. Her eyebrows rose as she said, "I heard Tess was livid."

Maude laughed. "I bet she was. It's a shame the way she behaved. I mean I love Tess and all, but she has been given a lot of love and yet she acts like she can't be happy."

"I hear you. I am so done pretending to care every time she brings up what happened to her mother. That girl holds grudges like I never seen."

"Absolutely. I really don't like to compare, but her sister is much more agreeable."

Maude gasped and covered her mouth in shock. "I was thinking the same."

Their fondness for Lilian half-surprised her. She had not thought of herself as likable. In Hiplum, she was always treated like a nuisance. Hearing them speak in her defense made Lilian feel warm inside. They continued to laugh, moving away from the entrance.

"Come on. Let's go bring in the laundry."

Finally, Lilian could make her move. Watching for anyone else, she crept up to the door, took a key, and let herself out. A brisk stride led her to the same corner the newsboy always stood by. Finding him there now, she was quick to approach, saying, "You there. I need you to help me. I'm looking for someone."

The boy broke his promotional chant to address her with a squint. "Listen, lady. You're wasting my valuable time. If you want information, you'll have to buy the paper."

Pouting as she felt both surprised and amused by his attitude, she reached in her purse and pulled out fifty cents, letting the coins slide around in her palm.

With wide, ravenous eyes, he reached for it. She recoiled swiftly. "Not until you help me."

He groaned. "Whatever."

Lilian's eyes narrowed on him with a look he seemed to understand well as she spoke with the authority of a mother. "And mind your manners."

"Sorry," he conceded. "What did you need help with?"

"I'm looking for a Flora Barrymore. Would you happen to know her?"

"Sure," he said, pointing across the street. "She's Hank Barrymore's wife. He keeps the shop right over there."

Lilian's gaze followed where he was pointing. She recognized the green building she and Paul had passed by the same day he'd left her. She also recognized the shopkeeper's name. Hank Barrymore, the former mayor as Jase had said.

"Uh, ma'am?" The boy said to interrupt her stare. "Your paper."

Lilian took the newspaper he handed her. "Thank you." She proceeded to cross the street. Once again, she peered through the window of the shop, her hand on the glass. The lights weren't on yet. She noticed the sign that said they were closed. It was probably too early to go inside. But Lilian was not about to return to the orphanage. She would wait.

As a warm breath blew against her ear, she jumped and pasted backwards against the building. "Spencer? What are you doing?"

"You smell like oranges again." He smiled. "Like the ones in your orchard."

"You should know not to greet a lady from behind."

"But your back was turned to me."

Lilian gave a hard stare.

"Sorry," he said. "What brings you outside this shop?"

"Nothing much. I'm only waiting to speak with someone."

He nodded. "Well, while you wait, I have someone I would like you to meet."

"Oh. Well you see, I am actually not supposed to be outside and—"

"It won't take long," he said as he came closer and took hold of her arm, guiding her forward. They came to the town's square where a group of men were setting up some kind of booth. A few people stood around, watching them work.

"What's happening?"

"Their getting ready for the applications at noon."

Applications. Lilian recalled that Mr. Muggri announced that he would be accepting applications from Brord's businesses to join Muggri Corp. "We will see how many apply," she said, feigning uncertainty. Yet she knew it was likely that a good chunk of the town would be interested in having associations with Mr. Muggri.

Spencer scoffed. "Yes, we will. And there's the man of the hour now."

Lilian's muscles tightened as Spencer brought her closer to the formidable icon. A man whose very back which faced her seemed as sturdy as the trunk of a tree. Her lips twitched as his guttural laugh hit her ears while he was engaged in a conversation with one of the old men Lilian had seen last night. He also was quite stately and smartly dressed.

Spencer stepped forward enough for Mr. Muggri to notice him. "I'm here with Fredrick's niece, sir."

Muggri turned his head, looking pleased as his eyes beheld the girl. "Miss Truit. I was just speaking about you with the mayor."

Lilian tilted her face with a squint. "You… were?"

"It is an honor to meet my rival's niece." He took her hand for a kiss.

"The honor is all mine, sir. Afterall, you are the very important person on the street today."

"Oh, nothing as impressionable as your presence last night." His remark was quick, leaving Lilian a mild sense of embarrassment as she remembered the fallout. "I must say, you should be proud to have such a resilient aunt. I have heard from Spencer here that she has been diligent with the responsibilities placed on her since Fredrick's passing."

"Really?" Lilian regarded Spencer with a cautious look. "I had no idea you two were so well-acquainted with each other."

Sensing Lilian's forbearance, Spencer replied, "Of course we are. My father holds his accounts at our bank."

"It must be a fitful change for all of you, not having your uncle around to take care of things," Muggri continued. His gaze was still and direct, almost captivating. And his voice held a sincere concern. "Just know this. If ever your aunt takes interest in my corporation, you best believe whatever issues have risen between your family and I, I would gladly put aside. If she's willing to have a talk, I'm sure I could make her a considerable offer."

Lilian was not sure what to say. She did not see a fault in his words yet the situation itself— the way this large man was speaking directly to her as Spencer watched from the side— felt subtly hostile. A distracting glint made her glance at the familiar gold pin on his vest. The same one Spencer was wearing; a morning star. "That is very kind of you, sir. I will be sure to let my aunt know of this encounter."

The man nodded. "By all means, do." He gave Spencer a look of something tacit, then turned to follow up with the mayor.

Spencer met eyes with Lilian's. But her eyes did not convey delight. "You seem displeased."

"I only wonder what just happened."

"You spoke with one of the most influential men of this age."

"But why? You know what my aunt thinks of him."

"Your aunt, yes. *You*, however…"

"Spencer, if you think I have any doubts for the future of Truit and Company—"

"No, I'm sure you don't. You haven't assessed its financial state. I have."

Something about his statement struck her with unease. "What do you mean? What is the financial state?"

Spencer eyed her, expressionless. "Your aunt hired me to keep her from making bad decisions. I am trying to do that. But the issue is, Lilian, she only trusts you."

"But I can't vouch for Mr. Muggri based on a short conversation."

"I am not asking you to vouch for him. I am asking you to watch what he does for this town and decide for yourself his intentions. I think you'll see that Muggri is a generous man. He wants to help people less successful than himself."

"You sound too certain that anyone will apply for his corporation."

Spencer's mouth set into a mild smirk. "As if you doubt it. You and I both know no less than half the town will apply."

Lilian wouldn't dare agree, but her silence was not a denial. Gazing around at the windswept streets, she imagined a long line of eager shop owners looking to make a deal with Mr. Muggri. A thought emerged that the Barrymores might also show up for it. Perhaps it would be wise to wait until then to introduce herself. Her gaze wandered its way back to Spencer's diverted eyes. "Well, I should probably return to the orphanage before my absence is noticed. Would you like this morning's paper? I have no need of it."

"Of course, sweetheart." A wink concluded his remark as he took the newspaper from her hand.

Lilian pretended she didn't hear his new nickname for her, returning around the corner where she had been. Just as she passed by the department store, from her eye's edge, she noticed someone turning the sign from 'Closed' to 'Open'. A nagging curiosity urged her to consider a detour. She looked upward at the slowly brightening sky, acknowledging her master. "Well, if you insist..." She lifted her hand to the handle, making her decision as she opened the door. A jingle from the bell above alerted the clerk as she stepped in.

The sweet-looking man she'd seen through the window before, and in the picture on the factory's wall. His eyes lifted from the counter to her with a mere glimpse of surprise and no welcoming grin. "What are you doing here?"

"Hello," Lilian waved. "My name is Lilian."

"I know," he stated bitterly. "I'm going to ask you again. What are you doing here?"

His hostile tone made her hesitate, inducing a cold sweat. She couldn't understand what caused the lack of kindness, but she refused to let it faze her. Looking around at the wooden shelves and vibrant streamers, she invited the cozy mood of her surroundings. Soberly, she answered, "If you please, I am looking for Flora Barrymore."

"What for?"

"I assume she's your wife?"

"She is. Why?"

Lilian stepped up to the counter. "I wanted to ask her some questions about her article last week."

The man's face toughened. "You must be mistaken. My wife hasn't written anything."

"But I read her article. It was her name I found at the bottom of it, and—"

His disapproving grunt cut her off. With the turn of his head, he yelled, "Flora! Someone here to see you."

Lilian's gaze switched from the man to the curtain behind him once she heard the muffled response of a woman calling, "Alright. Hang on."

The sound of her footsteps preceded the lift of the curtain. A beautiful woman emerged with warm, olive skin and black, silky tresses let down behind her shoulders with just the front of her head styled. Over her shoulder, she burped an infant bearing similar hair and skin as his mother. Then, appearing at her side was the young boy Lilian had already seen. Contrary to the man standing between them, Flora greeted Lilian with a smile. "Hi there."

"Hi," Lilian said with a hesitant grin. "I'm Lilian. Lilian Truit."

"Oh," The woman seemed confused. "Is it just you here?"

Lilian looked around curiously. "Yes."

The woman's smile faded. "Sorry, but it's just that I've never seen you before."

"Yes, I know. However, I came to inquire… about…" It suddenly hit Lilian as she felt the unease in the room and saw the curious expressions of both the clerk's wife and son that it was not a good time to speak about the article. "Never mind."

"No," Mr. Barrymore said before addressing his wife. "This young lady says she's read your article."

Flora met her husband's gaze with wide eyes. "Hank…" It seemed she could only sigh his name.

"So you *have* been writing for the paper. Behind my back."

"Oh, Hank. No one takes our news seriously, anyway."

Hank gestured harshly at Lilian. "Does that look like no one?"

Flora turned her attention to Lilian, stepping forward. "What is it you want, dear?"

"I…" Lilian straightened her posture. "I want to know how you knew about the… the werewolf."

Flora's neck tensed as she inhaled, blinking slowly. "Werewolf? Child, you must be mistaken. Nothing in that article was real."

It was an awkward while of silence before Lilian realized how long she was staring into the woman's eyes. "But it *was*. I saw…"

"You saw a werewolf?" The doubt in her voice made Lilian blush.

Seeing that there was no way to look any less absurd, she took a deep breath and pivoted toward the shop's door.

Wait.

There it was. The strangely timed voice of El with an equally strange instruction. Whether Lilian intended to or not, her steps ceased as soon as she heard it.

"Is there something else you need?"

With a reverse pivot, she replied, "Yes. I came for the Zealot."

"The Zealot?" Flora's question sounded to be asked out of understanding rather than confusion.

Lilian came forward slowly. "Yes. You know what I am talking about. Don't you?"

Hank spoke. "Look, that is enough questions. You can buy something, or you can get out."

Flora moved her baby higher up then patted Hank's shoulder. "Hank, please. Let her speak."

"Flora, we've been through enough."

Lilian wondered what such a statement implied. Each exchange with the Barrymores seemed imbued with an untold angst from a past she knew nothing about. Perhaps a past involving the Truits? It wouldn't have been the first time Lilian found her lineage linked to a phenomenon. "You knew my uncle." Her words garnered the clerk's silent stare.

She continued. "I saw a picture of you in his factory. Back when you were the mayor. I thought you might have been friends and would want to help me." Lilian turned to Flora. "I do not know why I am here. All I know is that if I find a Zealot, I will find a passion for what I am called to do."

"You think it's me?" Flora said.

"I do. I mean, I hope so."

"I am not." Flora turned into her husband, laying a hand on his chest. "He is."

"*Was*," Mr. Barrymore corrected. Desisting any further question of Lilian's, he said, "I know what it is you are trying to do, but it won't work." His voice lowered to a whisper. "You can't bring us together."

"The lightbearers?" Lilian presumed.

"Shhh!" The boy shushed with a gasp. Clearly, he knew something about his parents' secret, too.

She spoke on. "This is not about what I want but what *El* wants. He sent me here to find you."

"I don't care who sent you. My days of zealousy are over. Find someone else."

Lilian frowned, hope fading. She backed away from the counter. "Then my apologies, sir. Good day to you and your family." She turned away from their bewildering gazes and left out the door. The cheery bell sounding.

Confluence

Lilian's exit marked the arrival of noon and the bustle to follow. Already as she stepped closer toward a square, she began to see groupings of pedestrians walking the same direction to assemble in the growing line behind Mr. Muggri's booth. Lilian had little wish to spectate, so she retreated back around the corner. It felt too soon to return to the orphanage and she could not accept defeat. Having an unresolved mind, her steps ceased on the sidewalk. "I don't understand it," she said to the only one who could possibly hear her. "How am I supposed to find inspiration or zeal from a man who lacks both? And, mind you, he was very rude." She crossed her arms, responding to the silence. "I suppose I should take that as a 'wait', then?"

A louder reply startled her. It was the roused whinnies of horses. Lilian saw the familiar horse wagon ahead. While approaching it, the wagon swayed as they pawed the ground. Lilian's eyebrows stitched together as she pondered Jase's whereabouts and the cause of the horses' behavior.

"I thought Jase would have left town by now," she said while gently petting each huffing snout. "You must each be hungry. I wonder where he is."

As the horses settled down, Lilian's eyes found the building they sided. The sign above displaying the words: *Jacob's Spirits*. Lilian should not have been concerned. And she wouldn't have been. Jase was, after all, an adult man. But he was also a man with a broken heart, and a broken heart met with a brew was not a reliable pair.

It only felt right to go inside. Just in case that was where he'd be. With a curious worry, Lilian approached the entrance, a passing hesitation as she opened the door. The scent of hops and sounds of laughter greeted her as she pushed it further. She had never been inside a pub in all her life, not sure what she had expected. Whatever she had, the place was far from her fearsome imaginations. It was a well-kept environment and the people, fairly sober. Scanning the dimly lit interior for any sign of Jase, her eyes adjusted to the low light. She spotted him at the far end of the bar, slouched over a pint with a distant look in his eyes. His leather hat was in the seat beside him as he let his fierce, vermillion curls flop carelessly.

Lilian hesitated for a moment, her emotions urging her to approach Jase with caution. With a gentle resolve, she made her way through the crowd. As she reached his side, she heard him whispering a melancholic tune under his breath.

"The death of life is why I live;
To smell the whitest rose.
And what a wryest joy it gives
To be so lachrymose."

She smiled softly, lowering her hand on the counter before him to get his attention. His gaze trailed up her arm to her face. When she saw the tears coating his eyes, she could hardly look away. "Jase—"

"I went by his place today."

She paused. "Who?"

"Mister Thomas. I went to see if Tess was there. She wasn't. And he wasn't either."

A frown graced her face before her gaze drifted along the bar. "Jase... You shouldn't—"

"You don't have to worry. I could only manage one sip, you see. Stuff tastes terrible."

Passing quickly through her sudden relief, she moved closer. "Why are you here?"

He gave her a minor shrug. Then a minor shake of his head as he rubbed his sleeve against his eyes roughly. He gazed at the foaming cup again. "I wish I knew enough about myself to say. I thought I would try and see what about it was so good that my father needed one every day." She watched his small lips pinch against his teeth, holding in his anguish. "It's what he did when my mama died. It's what everyone expects *me* to do at some point."

"Oh... Jase..." Lilian lifted his hat from the seat and sat down. She placed the accessory in her lap then regarded him sincerely. "You.... You are a good man, Jase Foster. For, I never knew your father, but I know you aren't him. This... This isn't you."

Jase's face turned to her. His sullen, amber eyes began to glint with hope.

She trained her eyes on his. Having his attention, she continued to speak. "I know what it's like to be rejected, Jase. And if I could find a way to rid us both of that pain, I would. But the pain is going to be there and time is the only remedy." Her hand, seeming to move by its own volition, found its way on top of his. As it was done, Lilian hardly felt proper, but disregarded this one propriety to speak truth into him. "You are more than what your father, Tess, or the town thinks of you. You are..."

Tell him what I have told you.

"Leader. You are going to be a leader."

By the lift of his brows, his focus intensified. He opened his mouth to say... "What?" His lack of understanding was evident.

Lilian became increasingly sanguine at his reaction. Catching herself in the midst of such confusion, she pulled back her hand and said, "I mean, you are going to be a manager, right? You start work tomorrow." She stood, placing the hat on her head. "So, it would be wise not to get drunk in case any of the other managers were to see you. You know they would use it against you."

Jase blinked, considering her statement. "Yes. Yes, you're right."

"Well, I'll be heading back to Ms. Cora's now," Lilian said in a backwards step.

"Lilian."

"Yes?"

He reached out his hand. "My hat."

"Your hat?" Then she realized what she put on her head. "Oh, your hat. Sorry." Just as she started to remove it, he stood, stepping around to her. The motion caught her off guard.

"You know what," he said, his fingers sliding across the rim above her eyes. "It suits you. Keep it."

After a speechless few seconds, she chuckled. "No, I couldn't."

Jase was already moving past her, not minding her protest. "Thanks, Lilian. I know what I have to do."

Autumn (1885)

Marian's current respite took place on their kitchen bench seating as she gazed through the bay window for the umpteenth time. The painfully frequent spasms happening inside her were a cuckoo clock about to strike noon. She hoped Felix would be hasty. It was time, after all. Hadn't he realized that? Felix had told her it would be late October when she'd give birth for the second time. It was months ago when he announced it, and he had not mentioned it since.

He couldn't have forgotten this detail, although Marian knew how busy he was of late. Around the same time she became certain of her pregnancy, Felix had taken up the task of tending to a very needy patient, leaving every so often to prescribe them something or perform a treatment. He would never be specific about this patient's medical dilemma, hiding behind doctor-patient confidentiality and all that nonsense Marian could care less about. She was his wife and she deserved to know. Especially if this patient's needs were interfering with her own.

Wincing as another wave of contractions disturbed her, she rubbed her rotund womb in slow, easy circles. "Shh... Don't worry, baby. Papa's coming home soon."

"Ma?" the shrill and vibrant call of her five-year-old daughter peering in earned a head tilt from her.

"Yes, Tessaline?"

"Is he kickin' you again?"

"He is." Marian held out her arm, still holding herself with the other. "Come see."

Marian almost cracked a smile at the sound of Tess's hurried feet on the wooden slabs of their kitchen floor. She came to her mother's side and placed her cold palm on Marian's belly. Marian slid her hand down to the area of commotion. As a steady episode of kicks occurred, Tessaline gave out the sweetest giggle.

Marian continued to stare out the window. This house was just one of her and Felix's compromises. She had agreed to him buying her a house as long as it wasn't too wealthy for her comfort and too poor for his. And of all the happy mediums to exist, there was none happier. A plantation-style home close enough to noble civilization yet too humble a place for nobility to recognize. Yet still, even while matching her wish, Marian always felt it was more so Felix's answered prayer than hers. The house gave him further leeway to do what he had been doing; hiding her in plain sight.

A distant clopping preceded the horses' emergence over the hill. The window graced her with a view of her husband's coach pulling up.

"Yay!" Tess exclaimed, "Papa's home!"

Marian slid off the bench seat and stood, holding onto the high table beside her. She prepared her heart before the doorknob turned. And there he was.

"Felix. Am I glad to see you."

"Have you seen my case?"

Marian dropped her smile. "Your case? What for? You aren't leaving just yet, are you?" She said this with a heavy breath and a hand under her mound of a belly.

"I have to, Marian. I have a patient in town who's in labor."

Marian side-stepped around their table. "Felix. I wanted to talk to you about… the contractions."

"Yes, yes. They're not far apart. We have to hurry."

"Felix!" A startling burst within her was followed by a trickle down her skirt and splash upon their floor. Felix saw the puddle that appeared under her skirt and reacted with the most inappropriate expression for a doctor and a husband; disgust.

"By El," he grunted.

Marian's gaze fell upon the floor as she pretended not to see the look he gave her. "I tried to tell you."

"This is really not the day for me, Marian," he said with a tone of judgment.

"Right, 'cause I *decided* for my water to break for *your* inconvenience!" she snapped back.

"Well, I guess you are coming with me. I'll get Tess ready. Just sit down for now."

Agony

After all the fuss Felix made while getting ready. They all got into the coach and rode into the city side of Hiplum. The Truits came by an apartment building. The kind where mainly the rich lived.

Felix remained peculiarly upset. Marian sensed his irritation in how he bounced his knee and held his case against his chest while viewing the building. She told herself the anxiety was natural, considering her husband's line of work. In Marian's mind, he was fortunate to have such an excuse. If not for the urgency at hand, she would not have tolerated his behavior.

"You can stop here!" he yelled at the coachman. Before the coach could come to a complete stop, Felix pushed out the door, stepping down. Though he turned to help his wife and child out, his demeanor encouraged Marian to hurry herself. She made sure to hurry Tess as well. "Come on, baby. Let's not keep Papa waiting."

After they made it inside, Marian silently appreciated the fine interior. Tess was not so silent about it. And Felix seemed unimpressed at the moment, his mind focused on the task at hand. Felix sat his daughter on the bench seat by the door. "Now be a good girl for your mother. Sing a song. That always makes you feel brave."

"Yes, Papa."

The doctor regarded his wife. It was the most acknowledgement he afforded her since he'd been in her presence. His dark eyes were swimming in secrets. And knowing this added discomfort upon her contractions. "Come with me," he said, ushering her towards a powdered blue door. He knocked on the door.

"Dant play, Felix! Open the door and come in!" A voice yelled in a foreign accent.

"*Felix*?" Marian winced.

214

"Marian—"

"She called you 'Felix'. Not 'doctor'."

Felix ignored the heated complaint as he pushed open the door.

In the room containing two small beds, a woman lay on top of one with squeezed eyes and hyper breaths. Her belly was as big as Marian's. Finally, she peeled her eyes open. The sight of the unexpected visitor made her scoot a bit. "Felix? Who is dis?"

Felix, to Marian's surprise, seemed to have an issue working up an answer. "Allow me to introduce the other patient, Marian."

Marian bemusedly remarked, "*Other patient*?"

Felix pressed his lips together, a manner that let her know he was in some kind of deep trouble. And like always, he was making an effort to hide her, his own wife. Why— she couldn't be sure. But Marian was through with letting him be ashamed of her. She turned to the mid-labor woman. "I am Marian Truit. Dr. Truit's wife."

For some reason, the room fell into silence. The foreign lady's eyes cut to Felix, a mix of shock and disbelief. "Felix? I ask you again—"

"And I won't state myself again." Marian stepped forward, setting down her carpet bag. "I am Mrs. Felix Truit and he is Dr. Truit to you."

The other woman shook her perspiring head. "What is dis madness?! *I* am Mrs. Truit! Tell her, Felix. Tell her!"

Marian whirled on her husband who she knew for a fact was *her* husband.

Felix's gaze switched between theirs. When one set of eyes showed more rage, he switched to the other. Eventually his eyes rested on the wife next to him. "Neither of you are wrong."

Marian's crystal eyes chewed him up. "What?! What's that supposed to mean?!"

"It means you're *both* my—"

Before Felix could end his sentence, Marian slapped him as hard as a pregnant woman could. Everything— every lie he had told her, every moment when he was away, it all made sense now. Amidst the physical pain she was feeling, her spine shivered with disgust, and her mind scolded her for being so stupid. For having let him fool her. Without words in mind that she could possibly articulate, she merely screamed at him. Then, she wanted to make him feel all the pain he gave her. All reason left her as her arms moved violently, fists beating whatever they could.

Meanwhile, the other wife's wails projected off the walls around them. Both women, deep under all forms of agony.

Felix grabbed her arms and held them back from their swinging action. Stepping forward, he lowered her onto the second bed beside the other woman. "Calm yourself!"

"No!" She kicked at him. "I am done listening to you."

Felix's eyes widened at her defiance. "Fine! Fine!" He repeated much louder than she had been. He let go of her and smoothed a hand through his voluminous, dark hair. Breathing out, he spoke calmly. "But if you want our baby out of you, then you will have to listen to me one last time. Both of you."

The one closer to birth sank her head further into her pillow. "I'd rather die! I'd rather die!"

"Nonsense! You are speaking feverishly."

Felix got up from Marian's bedside and went over to the other. He checked her up. "You're getting there. Just a few more inches and we will begin."

"Dant talk to me. Dant say a word to me."

Felix gave her that. He remained mute for the next hour. By that time, she had fallen into rest, finding some miraculous calm among the tense air. For a while, they all respected each other's silence.

Marian peeked over at him. "I just want to know. Was I too demanding?"

Felix looked at her, silent as he thought about it. "No, I don't think you were."

"Hm…" As she stared blankly at the wall, it was clear his answer did not satisfy her. "So I got too *old* for you."

"Marian…"

"Too out of shape? Is that it?"

"Stop it."

"What was it?" her words quivered earnestly. "Why'd you do this to me, Felix?"

"Because I…" Felix shook his head. "I wasn't satisfied." He let out a regretful chuckle. "You are the greatest wife a man could hope for, and I wasn't satisfied. I know I should never have brought you into this, Marian. This mess that I am. I should never have married you to begin with."

Finally, as his gaze deepened with sorrow, Marian realized she never knew Felix Truit.

"I-I don't know what is wrong with me, Marian," he whispered hopelessly. "I guess… El made me this way."

"No." She shook her head, her lips tightening around her teeth. "Don't you blame El for this."

The room was suddenly shaken by another wail. Felix got up and checked his other wife again. "We're ready!" Without a moment to waste, he gripped her knees. "Now, on my count, you push, right?"

She nodded.

Felix counted, "One… two… three!" She pushed with all her strength. "Again. One… two… three!" Another push, coupled with a scream, but she was growing exhausted.

"Come on now!" Marian encouraged. "You can't give up. You can't hold on to what's ready to go. He wants to get out, and you want him out."

Felix heard the underlying message in her words.

"Here's what you're going to do," Nurse Marian directed. "Take all that anger, all that rage, and use it. Use it, you hear me?"

The woman nodded, accepting Marian's support. With a fierce scream, she gave three more powerful pushes. The baby's head appeared, then the shoulders, and finally the rest of the tiny body emerged.

Felix quickly wrapped the baby in a blanket. "A girl! You did it!"

"A girl," the woman repeated, her voice weak but filled with joy. Felix placed the baby in her arms. She smiled, her eyes heavy with exhaustion, and nuzzled the baby's head. "So precious. Like a lily. That's what I'll call you."

"Lily?" Felix grinned.

"No," she corrected. "Lilian."

"That's perfect," Marian agreed.

"Moya malen'kaya Lilian," the woman whispered, holding her baby close. She began to sing softly, "Bayu-bayushki-bayu, ne lozhisya na krayu.... Um, Felix? Do you know any English lullabies? Mine are too scary."

Felix chuckled and began to sing "Rock-a-bye Baby". As he sang, he didn't notice the blood pooling under her skirt or the dazed look in her eyes. Not until her arm went limp and the baby slipped from her grasp.

Felix caught the baby just in time. He saw the lifeless expression on his wife's face. Her eyes— closed. "No. No, no, no, no." He pressed his head to her chest, desperate. "No!"

"Know what that is?" Marian whispered. "A consequence of your lies."

"You hold that thought," Felix snapped. He set the baby in a nearby bassinet and returned to Marian, roughly positioning her knees. He inspected her cervix with a cold, clinical detachment. "Because now it's your turn."

Why did it have to be her son? Not her. Marian wondered this as she held his breathless little body in her arms. She never got to sing him a lullaby. And now the only tune to escape her mouth was that of sorrow. With clouded eyes, she watched his pale restful face. A face that favored his father's likeness. His first son, dead just as he entered the world.

Felix had cursed his own son's life. There was no other way to explain it. Marian knew she'd felt kicks inside her. She knew life was in her baby for all those months. How then could he have been stillborn?

Whether or not Felix would admit it, Marian needed no convincing that El took back a life nearly given.

After two hours, her tired arms were locked around the newborn before Felix pried them open and took him away. Marian saw the other men in the room, mute as they discussed certificates and burials and planning to haul a dead woman's body out.

Marian's mind wiped blank while they carried out their plans. All the while, a very much alive baby whined a frail whine that she tried to ignore. Felix would not let her ignore it.

With his always effective persuasion, he made her nurse the other. The one that was not hers. And she loathed every moment of it.

Time passed on like another wife. Marian slept in that room, having no choice but to be confined there until she healed. Felix showed Tessaline the baby girl as if she was the sibling Tess had waited for. But Tess had guessed right. *She would have had a brother.*

The thought sickened her. Sitting in the silent room alone, a sudden consciousness found her, bringing with it another wave of rage. Marian realized she was missing her baby, she didn't know why she let Felix take him away. She wasn't ready to let him go. To pretend as though he was never there. Just like how Felix pretended *she* was never his wife. And that other woman? Swiftly disposed of as well. Was there any value to life in Felix's eyes?

These thoughts flowed through her mind and down her face as she sobbed. But rather than simply getting angry, all Marian wanted was to get *out*. By the rooster's crow the next morning, Marian was up on her feet. Her stitches were fresh, but she just had to leave this place, or else she felt the walls would bury her.

After dressing in her fine, expensive tweed— such clothes he dressed her in— she stepped out toward the bedroom door with the strange baby.

As if Felix had had a thought to check on them, in he came through the door. He was wearing the very pajamas she hadn't seen in a while. He must have kept them here in this apartment. *His* apartment.

Felix's eyebrows rose and plummeted shortly as he realized Marian was standing. "What are you doing standing up? And dressed?"

Marian only stared at him coldly, flatly telling him, "Take your baby."

"What?"

"I said TAKE HER!"

"Ma?" Tess peeked in. "What's the matter?"

Marian said nothing to her daughter, still urging Felix to hold *his*.

With a bitter expression, he finally lifted her out of Marian's arms. Gently, he handled baby Lilian. His gaze locked on Marian's.

Marian let her quiet gaze speak before finally saying, "You promised me it wouldn't end this way."

All he could give her was a nod. She wanted to slap him silly!

"Just tell me. Who'd you love more? Don't say it's me just because I'm the last ear to hear it."

"I loved you both the same."

Marian dropped her gaze with a smirk. "Not once in your life can you tell the truth." Her eyes fell on Tessaline. "Tess. C'mon, baby, we have to go."

Tess hesitated. "Papa's coming too, right Ma? We have to take my sister home."

"That's not your sister, Tess." Marian waltzed her way around to place a hand on Tess's shoulder from behind. Looking up at Tess's father, she said, "He chose her over you."

"What?"

"It's true, Tess."

The little girl's face became a frown. "No. No, Papa loves me. Right, Papa?"

Felix may have wanted to say yes. Perhaps he would even have meant it. But Marian was asking with her eyes, *Let us go. Just end it. Please.*

He turned his face. "I'm sorry."

Marian began to pull her daughter away, but Tess fought back.

"No! Let me go! Papa! Don't let her take me away. Please don't let her!"

Marian kept pulling, seeing Felix's body tense as he pretended not to hear Tessaline's pleas until she was dragged out the door. Out of his life.

Hope

Knowing that it was still some time past noon, Lilian hadn't expected anyone to be out of the classroom, which was a fair assumption. But she hadn't accounted for one absent student.

"Welcome back." The sound of Hugh's voice made her turn suddenly.

"Hi, Hugh." Despite the fact that he couldn't see her, she didn't feel comfortable wearing Jase's hat in front of him, so she quickly doffed it.

Hugh's head perked up as if he was keening his ears on something. "Hm... Leather. That's new."

Lilian smiled shyly. Hugh must have heard her fingertips glide against the material of the hat as she held it.

She stepped forward. "I hope you have been doing your work, sick or not."

"And *I* hope you've been doing *yours*," he said, eyebrow quirking upward.

"Actually, yes. I have."

Hugh's aimless eyes squinted happily, followed by a smile. He held out his hand. "Come. We can talk upstairs."

Lilian took Hugh's hand and together they went upstairs to her room. The conversation began with Hugh asking Lilian why she left the house.

"Well, it started with a special encounter I had last night. I spoke to my ciella."

"Really?" Hughs eyebrows rose above his still eyes.

"Yes. He found me in the forest after..." Lilian wasn't sure if mentioning the werewolf was necessary. "Well, I'll just say this. He gave me a good eye-opener. One I very much needed. I've accepted my purpose, Hugh. Which is why today, I went looking for some lightbearers."

Hugh reacted to the news with a grin. "And who did you find?"

Lilian thought it amusingly presumptuous of the boy to assume she had found any lightbearers. With a smile she said, "I think I found both our Leader and our Zealot. But neither, I fear, are ready."

Hugh huffed briefly but didn't frown. "It's okay. They have to come around to it. Like you did."

Lilian squinted, surprised at his wise resolve. "A few days ago, you were trembling with worry."

"I know," he said. "But you *are* a Fisher now. It's your job to find them, and you're doing it. There was no hope in El's army, before. Now there is."

Lilian let his words settle in her soul. She was Hugh's hope. Somehow, the fact of her responsibility was growing more concrete. She held his hunched little shoulder, staring at him with surety. "I'm going to find more, Hugh. I will find them all. That is my promise to you. And to the rest of Brord."

Hugh's lips drew into a smile again. "If you say so, Fisher."

Many hours later, as night fell and everyone was sent to bed, Lilian, feeling exhausted from her busy day, knew she needed plenty of rest. Despite the excitement bubbling in her heart for tomorrow, she quickly drifted off to sleep.

Often when it came to her thoughts, Lilian didn't allow herself a single one that didn't suit her. She upheld this standard even in her dreams. Normally, every image rendered in her mind was a product of her own mental institutionalization, never allowed to be a free musing, surprise, or enigma. And it was quite a task, controlling her dreams. It blurred the line between wakefulness and sleep, leaving her unsure if she was ever truly dreaming.

But if this had always been so, nothing instituted what she was about to experience.

In this dream, Lilian's hands worked tediously as she kneaded dough, feeling her body overheat. She couldn't understand why *she* was doing it and not Gracie. Gaining some sense of self, she stopped kneading. Her eyes lifted, taking in her surroundings. This was not her home.

She had never been here, but it was a cozy place filled with fine fretwork and furniture. And not only this. There was a warm familiarity about the place that she could not rationalize, like a message intertwined in the sight of it all, claiming this house was hers. It did not make sense to her. In Hiplum Academy, she was taught that dreams consisted of one's casual experiences. But Lilian had never known this house.

After futilely calling for her maid and receiving no response, Lilian continued to knead the dough. At some point, she figured the only other reasonable thing to do was to put her lump in the oven, so she did.

With a clap of the hands to dust off the flour coating her palms, she sighed. "I did it!" Lilian sang proudly. Her lips, stuck in a content smile. A smile that was soon to fall when she smelled the unwelcome aroma of smoke. "No." Lilian searched frantically for a rag then crouched to the oven, lowering the iron latch. She removed the pan, placing it on the table with a deep frown.

Lilian watched the fuming ball of charred bread with heavy disappointment. How had she failed? What went wrong? What if this was a sign? What if she wasn't meant to bake? Or be a Fisher? Or do anything useful at all?!

A tarp of emotions blanketed her, bringing her to weep over the burnt mess. As her body remained bent, a gentle caress of someone's hands smoothed down her arms. Her eyes opened as she gasped, unable to tell who was holding her from behind.

The hands belonged to a man, young but toughened as if from hard labor. Yet they handled her in such a gentle way as though they were used to minding delicate things. Lilian's body went deathly still as his nasal breath warmed the crown of her head.

"Well, go on and tell me what's the matter," he said, his voice oddly familiar. Not like the kitchen, more like something or someone she knew she'd met before. A voice embellished with the inviting accent of the south.

Lilian feared she knew exactly who it was. "Jase?" She stopped feeling his breath above, suddenly feeling it at her ear.

His nose grazed the side of her face as he said, "Who else were you expecting, ma'am?" And with all casualness, he planted a soft kiss on her cheek.

Lilian gasped sharply, moving out of his touch as she turned to face him. "Jase Foster!" Lilian could feel her face heat. With either rage or... something else entirely. She wished she could be sure.

Jase's eyes were lit with amusement. He chuckled. "Is that any way to treat your husband?"

Lilian's breath got caught in her throat. "My... my what?"

The want for an escape drew her up from her pillow and out of the dream. Lilian looked around wide-eyed, the reality of her room concreting. Flashes of the dream still played in her head. Lilian could still feel his hands holding her in a way they'd never done. And she couldn't understand why she would ever dream such a thing.

It wasn't as if she cared for him the way she did for Paul. Confusion compounded within her, and she became furious with herself. "How could you?" she scolded. She had no right to be so reckless and inconsiderate toward an unsuspecting friend.

Poor Jase was already afflicted with a broken heart. And here she was, imagining him in such a position that she hadn't ever bothered to before.

Unable to shut her eyes again, she swung out of bed, her feet hitting the cool floor. "I don't know what's wrong with me," she grunted tiresomely. She turned on her lamp and knelt by the bedside, ready to beg. "Father El, help! I don't understand the meaning of this. But if you could rid me of such confusion, I'd be grateful." Waiting until her heart could beat at a normal rate, she managed to gain a clear mind. "I have to focus on the task at hand. If I must find you an army, then I cannot simply wonder about the street. There must be some special way to identify a lightbearer. Something we all respond to. Whether it's positive or..." her sentence trailed off with the turn of her head. She was facing the window. Though there was hardly a view with the pitch-ness of the night, she was thinking of the factory. Or, more truthfully, smoke.

Riddle

Lilian would not be leaving the home for some time. Due to the children's requests, Ms. Cora agreed to take them out for the day. She planned for a picnic at Etowah Lake. Only one volunteer was chosen to accompany them, that one being Maude. Meaning the other three were to stay and keep house.

Without Maude, the trio had little to laugh about as they performed chores. It felt like the mother of the group had gone. But they still managed fine by themselves. Lilian and Patricia, at least. Ethel made a point to be fairly distant. It was too obvious for Lilian not to notice. As they went around, gathering laundry from every child's room, Lilian decided to confront her about it.

The winter sun streamed through the tall windows, casting a cool glow onto the hardwood floors. Dust particles floated lazily in the air, undisturbed by the children's absence. Just as Ethel passed her in the hallway, Lilian dropped her pile of boys' uniform and underwear right before her feet. Ethel tried to shuffle by, groaning. "Ugh, watch what you're doing!"

"Are we going to continue like this, Ethel?"

Though continuing in step for a bit, Ethel came to a halt. Lilian watched the back of her with a craned neck, waiting. Ethel avoided her gaze with tense shoulders. The silence between them was thick with unspoken words.

Finally, Ethel turned with a look of solemnity. "Look, Lilian. I'm truly not mad at you. I just don't think I fit with your level, alright?"

"Why do you say that? Is it because of that pompous Spencer Wesman?" Lilian stepped forward earnestly. "Ethel, nothing he said was true."

"Except it is. I'm homely, Lilian. I've always known it."

"No, you are not," Lilian asserted at her highest pitch.

Ethel's eyebrows sank. "I really do believe you believe that. If only others saw what you see, Lilian. But there's not much that can be done about it. No fancy dress can make me live the life you do."

Lilian blinked, confused. "The life *I* live?"

"Don't you know?" Ethel said this with a mix of disbelief and frustration. "Men like Spencer, or Paul, or Jase. They actually *see* you."

Lilian didn't know how to answer. Ethel most likely didn't want her denial, nor her acceptance of Ethel's words. There could be no appropriate reaction that would move her past such an assessment and towards her want to console Ethel. She was simply stuck, forced to realize the validity of Ethel's point as she gazed at the floor. Ethel came forward, crouching to pick up the pile Lilian had dropped and adding it to her own.

"Can't we be friends, Ethel?"

"You *are* my friend, Lilian. But I can't let my envy ruin that." Ethel grinned softly, her adorable jowls tightening. Then she turned around and left with the laundry.

More days passed with their own inconveniences that worked in keeping her inside. Since the children had indulged themselves in the frigid weather, an overwhelming amount of them were bound to return sniffling and coughing. Soon, most of them were as absent from Ms. Cora's classroom as Hugh had been. However, Hugh, now recovering from his cold and moving about more than ever, was put to use immediately. Ms. Cora had him distribute and retrieve homework for each bedridden child. He took on the task with pride.

For Lilian, all of this meant more time away from her mission. As much as she did not mind heating water bottles over a fire, cleaning dirtied handkerchiefs, and giving out cough syrup to tiny mouths, she'd done all this before. With Uncle Fred. It brought her nothing but misery to do it all again.

What Lilian wanted was to meet with Pete. She had a request for him in mind. One she believed would help her in finding the rest of the lightbearers. If only she could find a reason to leave.

By the near end of the week, a reason came. Ms. Cora ran out of cough syrup. Lilian begged her fellow volunteers to let her go out this time. And being so well-adored by them each, no one fought her on it.

Lilian rushed upstairs to get dressed and was down within fifteen minutes. She left the orphanage, making her way to the inn. Finally, she entered. Pete was at his desk as always. He waved as soon as he saw her. "Miss Truit! I figured you wouldn't come back after that night Tess... well, we don't have to talk about it. But I never thought I'd see you again. I heard you were kidnapped, and I've been feeling down with guilt all this time."

"It's alright, Pete."

Pete disagreed with a telling finger. "Nothing is alright with kidnapping a lady. Especially if that lady happens to be a good soul like you."

Lilian blushed. "Oh, Pete. You are too kind to me." She leaned forward over his desk. "Pete, I could use a favor."

"Of course."

She loved how willing he was. "You are having your show tomorrow night, I believe?"

"Yes."

"I'd like to be in it."

"You would? Why?"

"Well, as I'm aware, you no longer have a Masked Maiden. And I believe you might need another act."

"I suppose I do. But what is it you want to do? Can you sing? Dance? Play?"

"No, nothing like that. I was thinking more like telling riddles."

"Riddles?" Pete scratched his chin, considering it. "It *would* engage the crowd." As he crossed his arms, his stare became more interrogative as if he was suddenly interviewing her. "Let me hear one."

A stammer left Lilian's lips. *El, help me.* "Now?"

"Yes, now."

Looking away from him, Lilian thought hard, certain she was about to fail this audition. She should have gone directly to the department store for cough syrup. Then as she considered that, an idea found her. The words and rhythm settled in her mind. "I provoke your mouth to open yet keep you from speaking. Sometimes I can be rather harsh on days your nose is leaking. What am I?"

He shrugged. "A kiss?"

"What?"

Pete scratched his head. "Hey, it's one of the only things that keep *me* from speaking. And it can be very unpleasant with a runny nose, I'm sure."

Lilian shook her head. "A cough, Pete. It's a cough."

"That was my next guess," he chuckled. "Alright, I might have some room for you on the itinerary. But you'll have to promise you'll be here tomorrow night."

"I will."

"And Lilian..." his voice felt less than cheery, unlike how he would usually sound.

"What?"

Pete looked concerned. "It's brave of you to do this. But are you sure you want to? A lot of the town's people know who you are now."

Lilian saw his point and nodded. "I have to, Pete."

Pete's unibrow lifted to one side. "You *have* to tell riddles?"

Lilian just smiled. "Yes, Pete. I very much have to tell riddles." Then she left him, moving quickly on her way to the department store.

The night of the show, Lilian was prepared with a list of riddles she'd spent hours thinking up. The rest of her worries would be choosing a gown. She did not intend to be at the inn long after her segment, so she chose to wear her tea gown. It was nice enough as well as practical.

But for the dash of character she could not bereave herself, she placed on a velvet toque at a tilt, white ostrich feathers falling in soft ruffles over the back of her head. Something about those feathers heightened her confidence as she swayed in front of the mirror. Lifting the list off the edge of her bed, she folded it and stuffed it in her rack. She then put on her coat.

Finally, she came downstairs. Taking the last step down, a hand caught her at the elbow. Lilian flinched before seeing it was only Ms. Cora. She said the woman's name, curious.

"Sorry, Lilian. I just wondered if you would like someone to accompany you again."

"Oh, thank you, Ms. Cora. But I have already asked Maude and Patricia. They said they'd promised to help Miss Wayne grade papers tonight. And before you mention Ethel…"

"I wasn't going to," the woman stated calmly. She grinned a grin similar to Aunt Krishta's whenever Lilian's aunt was up to something. "However, I went ahead and invited that young man, Mister Wesman, to escort you."

Lilian stared silently at Ms. Cora, then gave a soft laugh. "That's very kind of you. But I don't think I'll be needing an escort to walk a few short blocks." Lilian gestured with a flick of her wrist toward the door.

"Lilian, my dear, I promised Krishta your safety. And I won't stand to overestimate that again. A lady should always be escorted during evening hours. Now, I'm certain they taught you that at the academy."

Lilian conceded with a nod. "They did."

"Then for my sake, won't you wait for him? He should arrive any moment now." At the end of Ms. Cora's sentence, a knock was heard at the door. "And there he is now."

Lilian stood awkwardly as Ms. Cora strolled to the door. Upon hearing the door open to the windy street, she looked away with fidgeting hands.

"Thank you for coming," she heard Miss Cora say. "She's right inside."

Lilian took a deep breath as she heard the familiar sound of polished shoes crossing the threshold. She turned, offering a polite smile as Spencer approached, his hat held respectfully in his hands.

He stepped as close as he could before leaning over and saying, "It seems we're doing this again."

"It seems so, only you hadn't taken me that last time."

"Well, Lilian's act will begin in thirty minutes," Ms. Cora reminded, "so you best be going."

"Yes, ma'am," said Spencer. "But I have something for Miss Lilian first."

Lilian regarded him with flickering eyes.

From inside his hat, he slipped out a crisp white envelope with a wax emblem. He handed it to Lilian with his body turned away from her. "I think you'll appreciate what's inside," he said with a smirk.

Lilian doubted that somewhat. What did Spencer know of her to give her something? "Thank you." She softly slipped the envelope into her coat pocket.

Spencer extended his arm, and Lilian hooked elbows with him. They moved toward the doorway, saying a final goodbye to Ms. Cora, and on they went.

Lilian focused ahead of her, stepping purposefully. Spencer's tug at her arm reminded her to slow down. "Thirty minutes, Lilian. There is no rush."

She laughed. "Sorry, I am so nervous I want to move *faster*."

Spencer patted her shoulder with a consoling gaze. "No need to be nervous."

His gentleness was nearly unsettling. "You're learning, Mister Wesman. I didn't think you knew how to be courteous."

"I'm human, Lilian. And I want you to see that."

She grinned at him, still unsure of that. "How has everything been at the factory? Are you still concerned for its financial state?" Her pace slowed. "You never explained what you meant by that?"

Spencer gave a slight nod, his expression turning more serious. "Things have been difficult, yes. We've been facing some significant budget issues, and the rising cost of resources hasn't helped."

Lilian's eyes deepened with concern. "And what solutions have you come up with?"

He sighed, looking down at the ground for a moment before meeting her gaze again. "For the moment, we are working on cutting costs where we can and negotiating better deals with our suppliers. But because we are not part of a union, the charge is extra."

"That's ridiculous. Truit and Company has been trusted for decades."

"It doesn't matter, Lilian. This is what I have tried to tell you."

Not wanting to acknowledge his point, Lilian frowned and continued walking. It was clear what Spencer was doing. He wanted her to side with him on joining Muggri Corp. As much as she resented the idea, she knew Spencer was only doing his job as an accountant and financial advisor. What if he was right about this?

The inn was in view. Approaching it, Lilian found another curiosity to mention. "Have you seen or... heard how *Jase* is doing in his position?" She tried her best not to sound as though she cared all that much. "I just haven't been able to see about him since the children fell sick."

Spencer was unexpressive but answered. "I have seen him a few times when he comes to the upper level. I don't observe his work—"

"But you've heard good things said about him?"

Her interruption made Spencer squint momentarily. "Yes," he said. "Only good things."

"Good," she replied with a short sigh. "I wanted him to do well."

As they walked the final few steps toward the inn, Spencer looked at her and grinned. "Let's hope *you* do well tonight." He squeezed her arm gently as they entered the inn, the warm light spilling out to greet them.

Passing through the lobby, they entered the tavern space. Already, there was an audience of great number on each floor. Pete was currently on the stage, doing his comedic monologuing. "And then Mr. Benson tells me his son's got selective hearin'. I told him I understand completely. 'You got babies?' he asked. I told him no, but I got guests…"

A light chuckle of anticipation hummed among the crowd.

"And by the way they act when I mention the bar tab, you'd think I have a full quiver."

A few laughs were raised around the room.

"But I'm not mad, I'm not," he said with hands raised in his defense. "I understand some of y'all drink to forget, you know? Many things, for instance the past, the pain… and somehow always the price, too. I'm just saying!"

The punchlines kept coming, met with appreciative laughter and applause. It was a good show, but nothing like when Tess was there. Something about the way Lilian's half-sister could captivate a room was undeniable. Suddenly, she began to wonder where Tess had gone after she left Brord. Had she taken her musical ability and brought it to some other town to bless some other crowd with?

It felt strange to even think of her or care what she was doing. But Lilian didn't hate Tess, no matter what the girl's feelings were toward her. And a girl, she was. Lilian felt she could decide that, considering Tessaline's handling of her grievances with their aunt. But girl or woman, she had the voice of a lark.

After a while, Pete's act started to drag on. Lilian wondered if he had forgotten their agreement. He certainly loved to talk and she became convinced he was no longer following a script. Spencer, sitting in the chair beside her, tapped his fingers on the table, impatiently. He then slapped his palm on its surface as he looked up, turning to her. He leaned close to her ear and whispered, "This man could go on for hours. Come on. I want to take you somewhere."

"But, what about my act?"

"You think that after hearing an hour-long monologue anyone will be interested in riddles?"

Lilian, sadly, had to agree. "Where is it you want to go?"

"Just up to the balcony."

Hesitating, she glanced back at Pete.

"Speaking of fixing things, have you tried mending a roof in the summer? The sun's beating down, sweat's pouring off you, and then..."

"Alright, we can go," she decided, still regretful that she couldn't be about her mission tonight.

Spencer couldn't have taken her up from the table any faster than he did. Lilian followed him as he led her up to the mezzanine, and then, through one of the glass doors hidden behind a curtain which led to the balcony. Outside, it was more cool than frigid, unlike the past few days. Wooden pillars encased them as they stepped up to the railing.

Below them was a quiet street, softly glowing in its corners from streetlamps. Above them was a mass of stars.

Lilian leaned over, watching the sky in awe. She took a deep breath. "I used to watch the stars more often."

"Why did you stop?"

"I don't know. I suppose I realized how far they were."

He stared at her as if he understood. "You still think of Paul?"

At the sound of his name, Lilian frowned. "I don't... I *can't* anymore. There is so much more on my mind as of late."

"There always seems to be something on your mind. That's your problem Lilian."

She found his advice annoyingly friendly. Lilian turned to him, indignant. "You like to speak as if you know me. But all throughout my childhood, you told lies about me. What makes you think you know the truth?"

"Well, you sometimes have to know the truth to tell a lie."

Lilian couldn't help but twitch her nose in disgust.

"I know, I know. 'How sick of you, Spencer. How *evil*, Spencer. What is wrong with you, Spencer?'" He dipped his head in shame, gripping the wooden balcony railing.

Lilian sighed, not sure whether she was sighing out of annoyance or sympathy. She gently placed her hand over his. Spencer turned to her again. "I think you should look inside the envelope."

"Now?"

"If you don't mind."

Seeing no point in refusing, she felt inside her coat pocket and lifted out the envelope. Lilian carefully tore through the seal before taking out a tiny card of photograph paper. She flipped it over but couldn't see it until Spencer sparked his lighter above her.

"Thank you," she said, followed by a gasp when she realized what it was. The photograph featured a beautiful young woman with dark, voluminous hair and expressive eyes, holding a parasol in one hand. Her other hand, being taken in a young man's. A man with a face seen recurringly in the family album as well as in the face of his twin brother.

Spencer smiled at her reaction. "It's your mother and father when they were courting each other."

"Where did you get this?"

"My father kept a copy in his desk. You see, our families weren't always estranged, and we *don't* have to be enemies. You were right."

Lilian looked up, stunned to hear Spencer Wesman say she was right about something. As she glanced between him and the photograph, tears coated her eyes. No words could describe how this simple act strummed chords of joy within her heart. "Thank you, Spencer. I haven't had any picture like this of them. They looked so handsome together. And happy. It's too bad I know how it ended for them."

"I am glad you can appreciate something I've done." He closed his lighter.

Lilian thanked him again as she placed the photograph in her pocket. "I will cherish this forever. Truly."

Spencer said nothing else. His gaze did all the talking, the way he watched her face with intrigue. Lilian couldn't be sure what he was thinking of but had an idea. She stood still as he inched closer, leaving no space between them. His hand lifted to her face, fingers gently gripping her jaw.

For some reason, Lilian's inclination to pull away quieted within her. If it wasn't such a chilly night, perhaps his hands would not have felt so warm. And if the stars were not out, perhaps his eyes would still cast no reflection. Could it be that the glint she saw was simply a false glimmer of human emotion? And did she even care at this moment?

His shadow overwhelmed her, a spicy aroma snaking off his clothes and past her nostrils. He moved her head further toward his, pressing his lips against hers. His kisses were tight and born from a passion she couldn't name. Was it love? It could have been that or any other strong emotion. Or none at all. Either the case was that she excited him in some way or Spencer was merely a passionate person.

Whatever the case may have been, Lilian knew she liked being kissed. It was her first ever, and Spencer was rather apt at it.

Then the sound of Pete's announcement echoed from inside the inn. "Well, that's all for now, folks! Thank you!"

With a gasp, Lilian pulled away from Spencer.

"What is it?"

"He's done." Lilian went and opened the door, rushing back inside and down the steps of the mezzanine. Spencer followed her as she stepped through the aisles over to Pete who had already come down from the platform. Pete spotted her, shaking his head regretfully as she approached.

"Sorry, Lilian. You're too late."

"I *wasn't* late," she protested. "I have been waiting for you to be done."

"Oh." His unibrow lifted with realization. "I suppose I did exceed my time, didn't I? But I'm afraid the show is over."

Lilian stared at the stage. "No."

Spencer took hold of her shoulder. "Lilian?"

She stepped forward to Pete. "I only need time for one riddle. Just one. Please."

She could tell that his eyes considered her.

He cocked his head at the stage. "Go on."

Up she went, hastily, the wooden floorboards creaking under her weight. The people carried on with their conversation and dinner, not noticing her presence. She knew she had to get their attention but felt uncomfortable with shouting. "Um... everyone?"

Pete looked down, impatiently.

Lilian took a moment to breathe. *Calm my nerves, El.* "Everyone!" she projected.

The room piped down as they faced her. At least a hundred eyes, watching.

"I— I have a question for all of you."

"For *us!*" someone shouted with a feigned appalment, causing everyone to laugh.

Lilian felt her face heat. "Yes! A riddle. Only some of you will understand it. Only some will know the answer." She realized no one was interrupting now. They were waiting. Lilian stepped forward, her eyes surveying the array of tables as well as those seated above. It was a new, unnerving perspective. She had her question ready, the only one she had been wanting to ask tonight. "Have you seen the smoke?" Taking a few seconds to let the silence last, Lilian observed the people's reactions. A disappointment landed on her heart as she saw only confusion in the eyes of the crowd. Lilian curtsied. "Thank you," she said softly before stepping down.

Spencer looked just as puzzled as everyone else. "Let's go."

She nodded, feeling extremely foolish. After the spectacle that was already made of her the other night, this 'act' made Lilian wish *she* had worn a mask. The entire town must have thought she was a stupid, spoiled girl of a prejudiced household who could not even tell a good riddle.

Escaping through the lobby, she heard someone call out, "Hey!"

Lilian's head snapped up at the call, and she turned to see a man hurrying awkwardly toward her. Over his willowy frame, he wore a long, brown coat and a hat tipped low over his eyes. As he approached, he pushed back the hat, revealing the dry, tired face of a younger man. "I mean to talk to you!"

Spencer's grip tightened around her hand. But she let go, stepping to him. "Sir?"

The man came closer, stopping directly before her, his gaze observant. He spoke under his breath so only she could hear. "You're awfully young for a Fisher."

Lilian lifted her chin, refusing to take his hit. "I'm old enough, sir."

"Where have you been all this time, anyway?"

"Chasing the wind," Lilian replied with a knowing smile.

Slowly he too smiled, his expression softening. "So, what are you gonna do now?"

"Excuse me?" Spencer cut in. "What is this all about?"

Lilian scowled at him briefly. "Give us a moment, please." Turning back to the man she said, "Do you know any more like us?"

The man glanced at Spencer warily, then said, "Oh yeah."

Lilian's heartbeat quickened. "Is there a place I can meet them?"

"My pops and I run a mill outside of town. We can meet up there."

"That's too far."

"I'll bring you. Tomorrow, I'll come by. Where is it you're staying?"

"The orphanage."

"Then let's make it a date," he held out his hand, and Lilian shook it proudly.

"Goodbye."

Assembly

The morning after, Lilian awoke with a heart fluttering, remembering that the man she had met last night would be arriving today. He hadn't said exactly when, she realized in retrospect. However, just knowing she made plans to meet with other lightbearers was a sign that the murky rivers of confusion were parting before her. She felt she had waited long for this, yet also that it was happening so fast.

Even as her heart was brimming with excitement, Lilian knew she had to quell it in the sight of everyone else. That morning, she came down for breakfast and met the children where they lined up as usual behind the dining room's mahogany doors. Hugh was the last in line, likely for his safety. Maude and Patricia, who appeared less than well-rested from their night of grading papers, were at each door, waiting for Ms. Cora and Miss Wayne to show up.

Soon, the matrons did show up and the two volunteers let them all proceed to the room. As Lilian ate beside Ms. Cora, the woman watched her with fierce delight. Noticing this, Lilian lowered her spoon. "What is it?"

"You have yet to tell me how your night went."

Lilian took a deep breath, casting a glance around the room to ensure no curious ears were listening. She looked at Ms. Cora, lowering her voice. "It was... eventful. The riddles didn't go as planned, but I enjoyed myself."

"I'm glad," Ms. Cora replied. "I am so glad you could have that time away, considering how hard you have been working here."

"Oh, please, Ms. Cora. I am the least deserving of leniency."

"Oh don't start, lest you be accusing me of doting on you."

Lilian shook her head. "No, of course not."

Ms. Cora grinned softly, though her eyes lowered in thought. "I agree that Maude, Patricia, and Ethel have all been here longer than you, but they have families. Fathers and mothers. After the loss you've experienced, it brings me joy to see you having the will to go out and much more entertain a crowd."

Lilian adored Ms. Cora's care over her. Her words brought revelation to Lilian's heart. She had not realized just how resilient she had been.

Ms. Cora spoke further. "I told you I treat all my girls like family. And for the other three, I see a bright future, but for you, Lilian.... There may be a transition nearer than you think."

Lilian returned a confused expression. "What do you mean?"

Ms. Cora patted Lilian's hand. "I saw the excitement brightening your skin last night when you returned with Mister Wesman. The young man certainly has eyes for you. And my Krishta dear spoke fondly of him in her recent letter. I have to say, the two of you make a pretty pair."

Lilian's mouth hung open as she stammered. "Ms. Cora, whatever you are presuming— whatever my *aunt* is presuming—"

"Is entirely your business, I know." Ms. Cora took a bite of the oatmeal on her spoon, a faint smirk playing on her old lips.

Lilian ate, irritation fueling her thoughts. Why were they so avid about this? Of all the men to match-make her with, he was at the very least not her match. What Lilian wanted to know was how Spencer managed to make older women adore him so much. The most Lilian could do was tolerate him, which should have been understandable. For, she had known Spencer from a very different angle.

However, to his credit, he was displaying a new wont unlike himself. A sudden change in behavior that nearly threatened her view of him. Did it make sense to consider a man of such an undecided character for herself on account of his recent politeness?

And could she even criticize him as much as she'd like to after what she'd done the night before? After the kiss? His nimble fingers keeping her head engaged with his.... Lilian wanted to erase it from her mind. She knew she should not have let him make the advance. Even if the kiss was pleasant, the man who gave it should have to be equally as nice. The brief humanity she'd seen in his eyes must have been some trick of the stars.

Thinking of the strange moment seemed a waste of mental capacity. It bothered her how apparently she was expected to make a decision about him when all she had wanted in the beginning was to avoid Spencer Wesman.

Clearing her throat, she averted her focus to the more important anticipation of the day. She needed to ask Ms. Cora if she would let her go out again. But Lilian feared it would seem as though she were taking advantage of Ms. Cora's generosity.

Ms. Cora looked up from her bowl. "Have something on your mind, dear?"

"I... well, yes. See, there is an important person arriving here soon. I planned to meet with him."

Ms. Cora nodded with serious understanding. She leaned in. "Is this business-related?"

Lilian smiled, accepting the excuse. "Yes. Only business."

Sitting back, the woman grinned. "Then of course you can go."

Lilian brought her eyes to her bowl, relieved.

Over the next hour, Lilian completed her chores, frequently glancing out the front window. The eleventh time, she was on her way to check again. Patricia, who had already been there, informed her there was someone outside in a two-horse buggy. Lilian straightened, fixing her gown. "Thank you. Let Ms. Cora know I've left."

On her way out, Lilian felt the anticipation in her chest intensify. She had no idea what to expect, but the mere thought of the meeting set her heart racing. She stepped outside, the morning sun casting a pale glow over the yard. The buggy was indeed there, and as she approached, the man from the previous night descended and tipped his hat.

"Good morning, Ma'am. I hope I'm not too early."

Lilian shook her head, her own smile growing. "Not at all, Mister...?"

"Reicher. Ethan Reicher." He extended a hand, which she took. "Shall we?" he asked, motioning to the buggy.

As they rode away from the orphanage, Lilian couldn't help but feel a tad anxious inside. Ethan had said he knew other lightbearers, but not the number of them. If she was to meet only a few, she could possibly handle that. But Lilian hadn't planned for introducing herself to more than a handful of lightbearers. As excited as she was, the thought of failing to earn their trust sat heavy upon her shoulders. She wondered if she believed in her own aptitude. She reminded herself that El appointed her. She had to see this through.

"Had a good start to your day?" Ethan said, breaking through her thoughts.

"A good start, yes. But the rest is to be determined."

"If it helps at all, I gave them no misleading expectations of you."

Lilian wasn't too sure that it did help. "What expectation *did* you give?"

"No worries. I only told them you were young and quick-witted. I didn't say *how* young or that you are a girl."

"*Lady*," Lilian corrected him. "And not much younger than you, I suspect."

Ethan shrugged. "My reputation is on the line, so you know. I don't want to pressure you, but you *will* have to give them a reason to believe you are a Fisher."

"What about you? Do *you* believe I am a Fisher?"

He shrugged again. "That's also to be determined."

Suddenly Lilian felt she should not have accepted the strange man's offer of going. "By me and you both," she quietly added.

After passing up Etowah lake and the factory, they continued on. Dry fields were the only attraction for some time, then shrubs and trees as they came up a hill. As they rode over it, the number of trees dwindled, revealing a river. Looking over Ethan's horrendous posture, she saw the grist mill turning in the water, a house risen above it on the land.

The scene looked perfectly unassuming. Ethan guided the buggy towards the house, and Lilian could make out several figures moving about near the mill. As they came closer, she could see a small gathering of people, their gazes curious yet wary.

Ethan halted the buggy and dismounted, offering his hand to help Lilian down. She accepted, her nerves tingling as she tried to maintain her composure. Steadying herself, they turned and faced the assembly. Already, they seemed less than welcoming as they viewed her.

"Everyone, this is Lilian. Our Fisher," Ethan announced.

Lilian offered a tentative smile. She had expected to stand before a mix of ages, but all she saw were matured faces holding blank, bitter expressions. Something was certainly amiss here. *Where are the children? Or at least the young men and women?*

One old man stood forward. Lilian fixed her attention on him eagerly. He walked over to her slowly. The closer he approached, the grimmer his face became. Stopping at her side, he sneered, then continued to walk past her.

Ethan turned back to the rest of them. "Well, there's that. It seems some of us can't wait to hear a dog bark before deciding it's bad at it. Anyone else who can't abide her?"

As a response, more of them walked to catch up with the last man. An old woman shook her head while passing them. "Seriously, Reicher?"

"Hey wait a minute!" he called out. "Y'all asked for a Fisher." He pointed at Lilian, still watching the deserters. "Here she is!"

"It's alright," Lilian said, her eyes on the dirt beneath her. Then a hand rested on her shoulder. Lilian lifted her eyes to see Mrs. Barrymore with her son on her hip. "Flora?"

The woman's full lips turned up a gentle grin. "I heard Ethan was bringing you from a friend. I told Hank that Cain here was having stomach problems so he'd think I was taking him to be checked by the doctor." She rubbed her son's arm as he slept with his cheek nestled against her chest.

"But why? Why would you come see me?"

"I had to. I felt terrible for how we treated you and knew I needed to explain. There are things…" Flora's words cut off as she looked around vigilantly. Despite their secluded spot, it was clear they could not assume complete privacy. She turned to Ethan who nodded, then cocked his head toward the mill house. They came around to the porch and went inside.

Inside, the cool air fought against the warmth of the hearth fire and carried the faint scent of freshly ground rye. The interior was simple but well-kept, with sturdy wooden furniture and a large table in the center. Ethan introduced the visitors to his father, Mister Reicher, a man with the same gaunt frame his son took after. He was quiet but amiable with few questions other than, "No men could come?"

"No, Pa. They couldn't handle reality." As Ethan brought the women further into the room, his father went over to the fireplace to sit and read his paper. Ethan pulled out a chair for Flora to sit with her son. Then they all were seated.

"As I meant to say, Lilian," Flora began, "there are things you deserve to know about my husband's history with your uncle."

Lilian leaned forward, her interest piqued. *Finally.* Flora's demeanor suggested that the story she was about to tell would take a gloomy turn.

"We were a wealthier couple before all of it happened. We'd met both your father and uncle at our wedding back in '79 before Hank was mayor. At the time, all I had known about Fredrick was that he was a brilliant young man of seventeen with a passion for innovation. And due to my husband's equal want for the development of this city, he and Hank bonded well. It wasn't until a few years later that I would learn the depth of their bonds. They had become interdependent in a secret coalition."

Lilian took a moment to be sure she'd heard Mrs. Barrymore correctly. "A coalition?" Her uncle? Sharing secret alliances? Fredrick Truit wasn't the type to go around organizing furtive unions. "For what purpose?"

"To expose Muggri."

Lilian stared at all their faces, confused. Her uncle certainly had his qualms with Mister Muggri. Some of which she knew he never spoke of. Always had she wondered what about the man was so sinister.

"You are just as surprised as I was, Lilian. But let me tell the story. Please."

Lilian nodded, the sound of the fire crackling from across the room filled their silence.

Flora slowly rubbed her son's back as he snored. "It all started when Hank was riding towards town when he'd heard Felix and Fredrick had come with their father to Brord again. I stayed home, thinking little could happen on his way there, but little had I known…"

As Hank sat in the rocking carriage on this crisp spring morning, the scent of blooming lilacs filled the air, and the cheerful chirping of birds echoed around him. He was eager to see Mr. Truit and his sons. The Truits were adored by nearly everyone in town, standing for all that Hank cherished: progress and preservation. Gaining their endorsement for mayor would be an immense honor.

Coming around a bend on their usual route, the carriage came to a sudden stop, jolting Hank from his thoughts. He snapped up from his seat and stepped outside, compelled to see what the matter was. Before he could speak to the driver, his eyes had already found the cause for their cessation. A large hole in the road. Standing alongside it, a company of what Hank assumed were miners. But Hank hadn't heard of any miners in this side of Brord. He also didn't recognize any of the men there.

As Hank stood there, trying to comprehend the scene before him, one of the men approached, his face set in a hard, expressionless mask.

Hank was quick to begin with a greeting, his tone polite. "Morning, sir."

"Morning," the worker replied, his body holding a tense stance. "Road's closed," he said flatly.

Hank looked past him at the hole. "So, what's this about?"

"Private business, sir."

"It's public property. And y'all should have a sign up. Mining in the middle of the road? This doesn't look right to me at all."

The man regarded him with a cold, calculating gaze. "And who are you exactly?"

"Hank Barrymore, trustee," Hank answered with a tilt of his chin. "And I'd be delighted to check with the recorder's

office about this operation you got going on. If they did in fact register your claim to mine here, then..."

The man stepped forward. "You might not wanna do that."

Hank's suspicion grew. "Is that a threat?"

The miner's lips twitched in cruel amusement. "I'm just warning you not to get to involved in matters beyond your jurisdiction. Our group is only working as we were commissioned."

Hank's eyes narrowed. "Who commissioned you?"

"Muggri Corp."

At the mention of Muggri, Hank felt less surprised as he was curious. He had known the corporation to continually call for obscure operations, and something about them always bewildered Hank. "I see. Well, thank you for informing me. I'll be on my merry way."

"You do that, Mr. Barrymore."

Lilian listened intently, her curiosity and apprehension growing with every word. Ethan was also on the edge of his seat.

"After that encounter," Flora continued, "Hank went on to meet the Truits. And after explaining why it had taken him so long to show up, the only one who seemed the most intrigued was Fredrick. Hank had much respect for the boy, having taken him under his wing before he and I were ever married. And I think when he saw that Fredrick shared similar suspicions with him about Muggri, that was all it took to ignite his zeal. He and Fredrick started investigating the hole without my knowledge, finding a system of tunnels down there. Some going outside of Brord. He realized this wasn't the first mining project Muggri had commissioned."

"What were they looking for?"

"Hank and Fredrick believed it was the Foundum."

Lilian's mind raced. "The Foundum? As in, the *original* Foundum?"

Flora nodded. "Complete with all the natural rules El breathed into this world. They believed Muggri was trying to rewrite truth."

"But that's just a belief," Ethan spoke. "How do we know that's truly the reason for the tunnels?"

"I thought you might ask." Flora twisted a little in her seat, trying to reach into her pocket while the baby still rested on her chest. With short grunts, she managed to pull out a collection of photographs. She placed them on the table. Then Ethan spread them out. The pictures were dark but seemed to depict cave walls.

"They had taken a box camera into the tunnels. As you can see, there were markings on the walls."

Ethan moved the clearest picture to the center of the table. Lilian leaned over to see it better. The camera was positioned farther away from the wall which presented a chalked depiction of the sacred tome.

Lilian's eyes widened with disturbance. Could all this be true? "So what happened after?"

Flora's expression dimmed. "A number of things. A number of mistakes. They spent years, apparently, having dangerous investigations in those tunnels. It was 1885, the fourth year of Hank's term as mayor, when he and your uncle showed these pictures in secret to some people in our village. A few believed them and wanted to help expose Muggri's plans. But things got out of hand. My husband understands the law better than the rest of us. He wanted to first have all his evidence together. But some amateurs were losing patience. So they acted on their own terms and set some workers on fire."

Lilian failed to hold in a gasp, causing the baby to flinch with agitation. Everyone tensed as he waved his arm around aimlessly, then slowly fell back to sleep.

Flora sighed.

Lilian mouthed, *Sorry.*

Continuing the story, Flora said, "An investigation was done, concluding Hank to be at the head of it all. They said he incited the boys to set those men on fire. And because no one came forth to dispel the claim, Hank lost his seat as mayor and was thrown in jail for a season. It was the hardest time for me, being without him. But in the following year, he was free. Around that time, I became pregnant with our oldest son. So, he and I decided to live a slower life, opening up the shop. And we've been that way ever since."

"But your oldest son is not yet ten."

"My oldest son would be fourteen today."

It took Lilian a moment to fully understand what Flora indicated. The boy she had seen at his father's hip was not their oldest son. Their oldest son *would be* fourteen, as in he must have died. "Oh," she said, not asking much more.

"My own wife."

Flora looked up in awe, turning everyone's attention to Mr. Barrymore. His very presence heated the room with guilt and suspense. "Hank... how did you—?"

"How do you think? Quite enough people saw you leave Brord Village with our son. I knew there was only one place you would have gone to." His boots thumped hard against the floorboards as he came forward to lean over the table. He directed a skeptical gaze at Lilian. "So, you heard the story."

Lilian nodded, not breaking eye-contact.

"How do you think you'll stop it from happening again?"

"I don't know, sir. I can't pretend to."

"Then why should we help you? First, it was our lifestyle. Next, it could be our lives."

Lilian looked between Hank, his wife, and his son. The reality of what this family had to lose made her confidence shrink like wet wool. "I wish I knew what to tell you. But El hasn't assured me of anything either. All I know is what I must do now. There is only one order I must follow." Lilian's voice cracked with sincerity. Mr. Barrymore was scattering her hopes.

"Perhaps," Hank nodded stiffly, his imperative voice softening only slightly with understanding. "I don't doubt that. But you should leave my family out of it."

"Sir, with all due respect, your wife came to see *me*—"

"And what did she find? By the looks of it, you aren't doing your job well. You are supposed to inspire an assembly, but look..." He gestured around them. "Where is the assembly?"

Heat rose to Lilian's cheeks as she lowered her gaze to her lap. "They never gave me a chance, sir."

Mr. Barrymore placed his palms back on the table. The air quieted as he watched her. "I hope you understand what this means."

Lilian looked up, uncertain.

"It's a sign, Miss Truit. The people are not ready to war. Not in flesh nor spirit."

Lilian looked over at Flora, who seemed to side with her husband, her stare a message. *Don't protest. Let him speak.*

"I, like you, Miss Truit, didn't want to believe what was plain before my eyes. It made no sense to me. I thought, 'What is wrong with us? We aren't united, we're hardly a body.'" Hank swayed back, looking at the ceiling as if he was having the revelation all over again. "And then I realized... I could start a fire, but I had no way to contain it. Neither did your uncle."

Lilian began to deeply appreciate Flora's warning, thinking silently of the solution Hank had missed. *You had no Leader.*

Hank, not knowing how he had just given Lilian hope again, said, "So you see, Miss Truit. I know there is light in you, compelling you to do what is right. But we can't win a war just because we want to."

Pretending to accept defeat, Lilian nodded. "Your absolutely right, sir. Excuse me." She rose from her chair. "Ready, Mister Reicher?"

Eithan stood with haste.

"What are you doing?" Hank asked.

"Going back to Ms. Cora's," Lilian stated curtly. "Unless there is something else you wanted to tell me."

"Oh. No."

"Alright, well," Lilian faced Mrs. Barrymore, "thank you so much, ma'am, for telling me the truth." Then she turned to Hank. "And thank you, Mr. Barrymore."

On the way back, Ethan Reicher's countenance was severe. Though, Lilian did not share his dismay.

"You seem perturbed," she said.

"Huh?" Ethan looked at her, not understanding. "Oh, no, I'm just upset."

Lilian didn't bother explaining that they meant the same thing. "Why?"

"Why?" he echoed with agitation. "Why do you think? Everyone is completely losing sight of El's plan. I have been waiting years for some sign of purpose in my life, all for the rest of us so-called lightbearers to be selfish when it matters most." Ethan waved at the scenery around them. "Girgum is here."

"Girgum is...?"

"Here," he repeated with a vehemence that left no room for misunderstanding.

Lilian studied his eyes, wishing he was lying. Her heart began to thrum a beat that reverberated down to her gut, sounding in her ears. "How do you know?"

"I saw him."

Lilian was silent as the buggy rocked, keeping her eyes on Reicher. "What do you mean, you saw him?"

Ethan watched the road, his lips firming. "It doesn't matter now. Like Mr. Barrymore said, we aren't ready."

He sounded sure of this, almost convincing her to believe the same. But after all that Lilian had endured, she refused to let those words eat at her soul. "Who says we have to be?"

Surprised, Ethan glanced at her, then upward in thought as if he could see her point.

Lilian had more to say. "You say that we are not ready, but neither was I when I first came to Brord. It is not news to me, nor to El."

"So, you're saying El *wants* us unprepared."

"Perhaps we *are* prepared. Perhaps we have as much as we need."

"How?" Ethan's voice rose in volume though he seemed not to notice. "You just heard our Zealot say we're cooked."

"What I heard was a man whose mind battles his heart, a man who sees nothing worth his zeal because he forgot how to hope. But I *have* to hope." Lilian's voice grew with passion as she laid a hand on her chest. "I have to believe that El has shown me all these things for a reason. I have to believe that even while I feel all alone, I'm on the right path." She pointed to her eyes. "Look. Look at them. Do you see what I have been forced to see in them all my life? It is these eyes that remind me whose light I bear. But it's as if we've all forgotten the reason we are called lightbearers. He's out there somewhere— Shersul, and he is still fighting for our souls. And I would do him the greatest disservice to stop now."

With all of it said, Lilian sat back, watching the road again.

Ethan fell awfully silent. She caught him blinking dumbly. She turned back to him, quirking a brow.

Ethan dropped his reins for a few seconds and clapped. "Where was all that back at the mill?"

Lilian lowered her gaze bashfully. She could hardly believe herself. "I don't know."

"Well, you could work on your timing."

Lilian laughed briefly. "Mister Reicher?"

"Yes?"

Lilian lowered her voice as they entered the town. "Back at the mill, for a moment, I saw the Zealot come out of Mr. Barrymore."

Ethan nodded. "Your right. I think I saw it too."

"His story made me realize what I have to do next if we want to finally unite the lightbearers."

"And that is?"

"Recruit our Leader. I believe I know who he is. The only issue is *he* may not know it yet."

"Really? Who?"

She leaned toward Ethan's ear. Though nervous to say it, the words fell proudly from her lips. "Jase Foster."

Ethan gave her a look of mild disbelief. "No way. The drunk's son?"

"*Ethan*," Lilian chided. "He is not his father."

Ethan matched her whisper. "But how can he be a lightbearer? He barely strikes me as an El's beloved."

Lilian frowned. It's true, she didn't know much about his feelings towards El either. And even his actions spoke against him. Like how he had been living with Tess without marrying her. "All I know is what El told me. I know Jase to be a man of good character despite his actions. I think he just needs guidance."

"*Your* guidance?"

She felt the mild accusation in his tone. "No. No, I meant—"

"No worries, Miss Truit. I understand," he chuckled, his ragged face suddenly sharing delight. "Who am I to judge his life? I'm just a miller's son. You are the Fisher, and if you say it's him, I trust you."

"So you *do* believe I'm—?"

"I can't afford not to."

Lilian nodded, their agreement solidifying that despite their earlier trouble, she accomplished at least one thing today. This new alliance with Mister Reicher was only an overture to what she believed would soon be an army.

Remembered

6 Months Later

"I found it!" Ethel shouted as she stepped downstairs with a large box in her hands. Her shout barely carried over the sound of rain pelting the rooftop and echoing through the house.

This nightly storm had come without warning, giving Ms. Cora the idea to have the children gather in the classroom and set up a cozy camp. Pillows and blankets lay scattered around the iron fireplace, while desks and chairs were stacked in a corner, forgotten. The room, dim-lit and warm, became a sanctuary.

Ethel, meanwhile, had been tasked with retrieving Ms. Cora's old sewing stash. She was happy to do so, understanding why she was asked to. Even though she hadn't been the best of friends to Lilian, Lilian had *made* her her best friend. She didn't know the reason and doubted Lilian knew it either, but she was glad the girl cared about her in a way that most wouldn't. So, out of appreciation, she would retrieve the box, knowing no one else could feel the same excitement as her in doing so.

Lilian waited at the bottom of the stairs. "What's that for?"

Ethel smiled, keeping the surprise to herself. "Come." She led the way into the classroom. They stepped over the boys and girls with many pardons but were hardly noticed as the boys were too busy dodging each other's socks as they threw them across the room while the girls ducked and squealed.

"Ms. Cora, tell them to stop, please!"

"If you boys don't cut it out, you'll be sleeping in the basement, all of you!"

Continuing across the space, Ethel came near the large window, where a final pour-in of light— soft and gray— mixed with flashes of lightning. She set the box on a lone desk below it. Lilian stood by, curious.

Ms. Cora approached. "So you've found it! Thank you, Ethel."

"You're welcome, ma'am."

Ms. Cora turned to Lilian, eyes softening. "Lilian, this box holds something very special." The woman bent over to remove the cardboard lid, revealing a neatly folded quilt of various, colorful patterns. She lifted it out carefully, holding it up for Lilian to see.

Ethel smirked at Lilian's awe-filled expression.

"It's beautiful."

Ms. Cora smiled. "I'm glad you think so. Each of us has contributed to its design. Every girl here will eventually once they learn to sew." Ms. Cora flapped it loose, holding it higher. She pointed to the patch on the top corner. "This patch was mine. I started it off."

Ethel pointed eagerly to a green patch somewhere in the middle, a pattern of purple dragonflies inserted there.

Lilian smiled. "Pretty." Her gaze drifted over the quilt, her smile slowly fading. "Which one is Tessaline's."

Ethel felt the weight of her question. In all the time she had come to know Lilian, the girl often spoke simply, yet her words were grounded in emotions that were anything but simple.

Ms. Cora's expression grew tender. She laid the quilt gently over a chair, smoothing out the fabric. Lilian's gaze lingered on the quilt, her fingers twitching slightly as if she longed to reach out and touch it.

Ms. Cora reached down to the quilt's lower left corner. "Here," she said, pointing to a patch of deep blue fabric, embroidered with tiny silver stars. The stitches were precise, declaring Tess's finesse.

Ethel watched Lilian closely, noting the way her friend's face softened when she saw the patch and, with an unreadable expression, traced the stars with her fingertip. Ethel imagined Lilian must have felt a conundrum of confusion and admiration, possibly wondering how many layers of Tessaline she could have peeled if given the chance.

"Tessaline loved that silver thread," Ms. Cora said quietly. "Her favorite color. Her mother once made up a rhyme about her, saying she got her pale eyes from staring at the winter sky."

"Ooh, can we sing it?" a little girl asked from under her blanket, her pigtails bobbing as she sat up.

"Later, Abigail," Ethel replied, glancing at Lilian.

Ms. Cora smiled at the group of children but turned back to Lilian. "Would you like to add your own patch to the quilt?"

Lilian met her gaze. With a warm grin, she replied, "I'd be delighted."

"Good. Pick a scrap from the box and work on it when you're ready."

Lilian sifted through the colorful scraps. Ethel watched, eager to see what she would choose. Lilian finally pulled out a soft lavender piece.

"This one," Lilian said, holding it up.

Ms. Cora nodded approvingly. "A lovely choice, Lilian. You can hold onto it for later."

Ethel bit her lip, fighting the urge to say something trivial. She thought she understood why Lilian had chosen lavender. Maybe it was more than a color; maybe it was Lilian's quiet way of moving out of mourning.

The little girl piped up again. "Now can we sing it?" Abigail bounced on her blanket.

"Sing what?" another child asked.

"Tess's song!" Abigail beamed.

Ethel smiled, stepping into the circle of children. "Why not? I'm sure Lilian would love to hear it."

Lilian's gaze drifted to them with silent interest.

Ethel began clapping her hands in a simple rhythm. The children joined in, ready for her to start the song.

"Pink cheeks, fair head.
Ate so many strawberries, her lips turned red.
Stared at the sky 'til her eyes turned blue.

By the end of winter, they were silver, too.
Big eyes, pale skin.
Never was a girl like that again.
She had Mama's hands and Mama's chin.
Mama's everythin'."

The children's clapping faded as an ungracious foot-tap echoed from the doorway. All eyes turned to the scrupulous figure who watched the gathering with arms folded in distinct disapproval.

Mr. Henley was the unwelcome supervisor from Muggri Corp, sent to ensure Ms. Cora adhered to the new curriculum. They were to entertain his presence for a week. His role, other than disturbing a tender moment, was to inspect, correct—and if need be—control all proceedings under the Withermans' roof.

Ethel grimaced unapologetically his way, hoping he noticed, but knowing he didn't. *What is it now?*

"Mr. Henley?" Ms. Cora greeted him, her voice calm.

Before answering her, he took off his spectacles, cleaning them with the lapel of his robe with deliberate slowness. Just his way of displaying a lack of respect for the woman of the house. Placing them on his face, he looked up, his mouth opening with a pause. "It's nearly eight-o-clock, Ms. Witherman."

"It is, sir."

"I was… writing reports in the office."

"I understand that, sir."

"Well, I *don't* quite understand. See, I thought the children were meant to be in their beds at this time, yet here they are sprawled about the classroom floor."

Ethel switched her gaze to Ms. Cora, hopeful she'd address the patronage in his tone.

To her astonishment, Ms. Cora did not show any sign of offense. Instead, she held out her hand. "You are welcome to join us, Mr. Henley." A grateful smile was directed at him.

The children stared, wide-eyed. Ethel prayed he wouldn't accept.

Mr. Henley, however, chose not to seem the slightest taken aback, as if generosity had no effect on him.

"No, ma'am, I won't be doing that."

Ms. Cora didn't miss a beat. "Well then we will try to no longer disturb you, sir. I understand you have been working very hard, and I appreciate your efforts greatly. But I want the children to be together because I actually *like* being with them."

Ethel smirked as Ms. Cora's gentle words delivered a small, sweet reproach.

Mr. Henley withdrew his ready dispute, conceding with a nod. Saying nothing, he stepped backwards and retreated out of the room.

As the door clicked shut, Ms. Cora turned back to the children. "Remember children, it is always better to be kind."

"Yes, ma'am," they all said.

Ethel was not convinced. One quick rebuke may not have been ideal but would have at least assured everyone whom still had the authority in the orphanage. So far everything, from here to the church was under the advisory of agents working under Muggri Corp. Ethel wasn't sure how or when this began. She felt as though all winter she'd been asleep while something had been cooking up, now making its presence known this spring. She knew she couldn't say much about it, but something inside her could sense this being the start of a great change in Brord. Perhaps one that could not be stopped.

The Next Morning

Lilian took a deep breath, hesitant to draw the curtain and step outside. Spencer was out there waiting to inspect her appearance. She didn't mind him, just wanted to be sure she would still feel like herself the moment she stepped out.

For the past few months, nothing had changed. No new acquaintances, meaning no recruitments. Lilian wasn't sure why El seemed to be closing doors around her. She assumed that perhaps He was changing His mind about her being a Fisher. However, despite there being no proof of it, she knew that wasn't the case. She knew El would keep His promise somehow. She just had to wait for it.

A new wardrobe would hardly count as a change, but she had gotten so used to wearing mournful black suits that a gentle lilac frock felt like new skin. Either way, she was ready for this change and more. Even with all the uncertainty she'd had to face, an unrelenting peace in her heart kept her from going mad.

"Any day now, Lilian," Spencer called.

"Alright, here I come," she softly announced.

Lilian stepped out from behind the curtain, the sitting area brightly lit from the sunlight raying through the window of the shop. Spencer sat a few paces from her in the brocade armchair, his legs crossed as he held a newspaper up to his face. He lowered it, beginning with a tired expression before it softened with the widening of his eyes.

Lilian twisted, letting her skirt sway. "Well, what do you think?"

He stared speechlessly as his gaze traveled from her puffed sleeves to her broom skirt. "It's very…" his head tilted as he twitched his nose, "pure."

"Pure?"

"Yes."

Lilian wasn't sure what to make of that. "Is that a *good* pure or…?"

Spencer chuckled, shrugging. "Pure is always good."

"Yes, of course. But with the way you said it—"

"Lilian." Spencer hopped to his feet, meeting her in seconds while bringing his hands to her face. "There is nothing wrong with the dress. And besides," he dropped his gaze to her lacy, high collar, "no matter what you wear, I still find you tauntingly beautiful."

She innocently observed his eyes before grinning. "I suppose one can be both taunting *and* pure."

"See," he tapped her chin. "That's the idea."

As his finger dropped, her grin settled. "I agree the shape of it is quite chaste. My aunt wrote that she's sending a new wardrobe of lilac dresses for me to have. I just thought I'd try on the color first."

"Ah," Spencer nodded. "Well, anyone could have guessed it would suit you so well."

For six months, she had allowed him to court her. They seemed to be dealing well with each other. Any time she felt like changing her mind, Spencer would prove himself capable of putting her at ease. He was trying and, as far as she could tell, succeeding.

After he paid for the dress, Lilian decided to keep it on as they exited the shop. She held her breath, slowly taking in the dense outside air. She could see the heavy cloud of smoke resting upon every building, keeping the sky tinted by a thin sheath of gray. Lilian was never quite certain if she was the only one who noticed it. But since no one else mentioned the strange weather or even felt compelled to cough as she so often did, it didn't appear likely. She had feared this change for the longest time yet came to accept it.

There was a subtle weight to the smoke. And that weight, she was certain, could be felt by everyone in Brord Village. She felt it even now as they approached their chartered cabriolet.

The driver tipped his hat and smiled. Spencer helped Lilian inside and she waited for him to take his seat beside her. Once he did, she asked, "Must you take me with you to the factory? I'd rather stay at Ms. Cora's."

"Nonsense. As the woman I intend to marry one day, I'd like you to see me at work."

"But I'd rather not be seen by those same managers who I seemed to have annoyed after helping Jase get a job."

Lilian was sure she heard him reply under his breath with, *"They aren't the only ones."*

"What?"

"Nothing. Just let me take you. You won't have to worry about any rude manager, I promise."

Lilian sighed. "If you say so." In truth, she was more worried about seeing Jase. After all this time, he hadn't so much as come by the orphanage to say hello to Ms. Cora. She heard of his accomplishments through Spencer, and only when she asked. Which was not often, considering his overt agitation whenever she would mention Jase's name. It escaped her why.

Lilian didn't think of Jase too often, just during times when she felt her mind was tying itself into knots, times she wished someone was interested enough in her thoughts to help her make sense of them. Eventually, if she tried hard enough, she could find peace on her own, but Lilian could not deny the easy peace that came with talking to Jase.

It was no use missing him. It had been so long and so many things had changed. Perhaps he did too. She doubted that amid all his responsibilities, he would find any value in sharing sentiments with her as he once did.

With another sigh, she let the sight of Brord's attractions consume her mind as the cab took them all the way to her uncle's factory.

When they arrived and entered the factory, Lilian immediately noticed a difference in the atmosphere. Spencer guided her through the aisles of men at work, and there was no crowded arrangement of long tables, no bickering over a tool shortage, and not a frown inhabiting the men's faces.

It felt as though whatever tension filled the brick walls before had since fled. Strange, considering how the world outside felt more unsettling to her than the inside of the factory.

Lilian followed Spencer past the workers. They each noticed her and, to her surprise, gave genteel nods and grins her way. She nodded back, smiling elatedly.

Lilian stepped closer behind Spencer to say, "The workers seem to be in better moods. I haven't seen them operate so efficiently."

Spencer halted, glancing around as if he had not noticed. "Yes, they are, aren't they?"

Lilian giggled. "I suppose Jase's ideas have left positive results."

Spencer's eyes met her fond remark with disdain.

"Did I say something wrong?"

"No. But I hope you do not think it is that simple."

Lilian pursed her lips, patting his shoulder and hoping he would respond in kind. "Of course not, Spencer. I know you've done your job as well."

"Yes, and if not for my financial supervision, Jase's ideas would have run us into bankruptcy."

Despite— or perhaps due to— his grave tone, Lilian let out a laugh, causing a curious look from Spencer. "Sorry," she quickly pleaded. She couldn't help but feel he was being a tad melodramatic.

"This is no laughing matter."

"Oh, Spencer, don't be so difficult. Why are we down here in the first place? Wouldn't your office be on the second level?"

Spencer kept walking. "It is."

Lilian became aware of the metal door across the room that they were approaching. Spencer pulled the handle, revealing a freshly built stairway leading to the upper floor.

"And for your information," Spencer said, "this was *my* idea."

Lilian raised her eyebrows to seem impressed. "Shall we go up then."

Spencer waited as she took the steps up to the varnished floor above, ivory handrails at their sides. Facing them was the framed wall Lilian had seen her last time there. Her uncle's portrait hanging proudly within the light of the glass view across from it.

Coming up, they continued on their right toward the different office rooms. He stopped in front of a door with the suite number on a gold plaque against the wall. He turned the brass handle with a quiet click. The office inside was surprisingly more spacious than the director's. Large windows framed the room, casting a golden light over the polished wooden desk in the center. A bookshelf lined the wall, filled with ledgers, papers, and other documents— evidence of the meticulous work Spencer handled daily.

"Here is where I spend most of my time."

Lilian gasped as her eyes arrayed the area. "This is *your* office? You are lucky indeed."

"Yes, I am." Spencer moved further into the room, his finger grazing the surface of his desk. "Up here is where the real work gets done. Your uncle was a responsible man, but I must say, he lacked the know-how that would have saved him considerate amounts of money."

"My uncle was half-dreamer, half-doer. He had quite a lot on his mind." Lilian lowered her gaze in ponderance, understanding well what all was on her uncle's mind. "But I thank you, Spencer, for taking up the load."

Spencer cocked his head in her direction, speaking eagerly. "I can take on much more than this, Lilian." He came closer, his steps quick but restrained as if there was something he desperately wanted from her.

"As I have been trying to show you, this factory has been a second home to me."

Out of habit, Lilian trained her eyes on his, trying like so many times before to find a reflection. Trying to believe him. "Really?"

"Yes." He took her hands in his, standing far enough for their arms to remain outstretched. Spencer tucked in his chin, a coy smile playing on his lips, making her wonder the true reason he brought her here. "My sweet, sweet Lilian."

"Spencer?"

"After all you have seen of me, has any of it assured you of us? And if not, what must I do?" He pulled her in holding her by the arms, his black eyes studying her just as much as she did him. "Tell me, Lilian. I could drop on one knee this moment for you. My intentions have been the same since I first made them known to you." His fingers tightened around her arms as he rubbed them gently. "Don't you love me, Lilian?"

Lilian tensed, feeling somewhat stifled in his arms. Her heart leaped timidly. She had expected this would come up eventually, though she imagined herself being better prepared for it. As much as she wanted to honor his question with an equally direct answer, she found herself struggling with words. "Spencer... I..." She tried to feel comfortable in his arms but the closer he pulled her to him, the more she wished he wouldn't. His eyes waited with a strong anticipation.

"I..." The only distance she could maintain was an inch between her chest and his. She briefly glanced at the window behind him, shocked as she caught sight of a deviant reflection of Spencer's back. It looked like some creature— tall, dark, and winged.

Her breath caught in her throat.

"Lilian?"

Lilian could feel the fearful expression on her face as she looked back at Spencer. Her face calmed, unsure of what she had seen.

A sudden knock at the door cut her off. Spencer looked up, annoyed while dropping his hands from her. "Come in."

The person behind the door revealed himself to be Mr. O'Reilly, the director. He came in with a steadiness that spoke bad news. "Mister Wesman."

"Yes, sir?"

"I was told you had something you would like to show for these claims you've been making."

Spencer straightened with confidence. "Yes, I have."

Lilian switched her gaze between the men. "What claims?"

Carefully turning to her, Spencer spoke. "Um, Lilian, if you could step outside while I speak with Mr. O'Reilly…"

"Of course," she said while moving hastily toward the door.

"Thank you. We will continue our talk later."

Lilian quickly shut the door behind her, somewhat relieved. Despite his promise to resume their discussion, she was not sure she'd know what to say if they did.

She lingered for some time near Spencer's office before slowly finding herself further down the hall. Feeling an increase of boredom, she decided to go back downstairs to watch the workers. Even with their kinder demeanors, she was careful not to get in their way, spectating in awe as they pounded, welded, and assembled their pieces. The air carried odors of woodchips, burnt iron, and leather aprons.

Lilian grew more and more intrigued by the beauty of men at work, letting the clamorous sounds fill her ears. And just as well, the sound of a man giving gentle commands across from her.

"No, hold on there, son."

Recognizing the voice, she whipped her head in its direction, her heart withholding a beat. A young man, practically a boy, was over at the furnace, heating a piece of steel in the fire. He was leaning a little too far toward it before his supervisor stepped in and took the tongs from him. A man who looked like someone she knew.

"You shouldn't be so close to the fire. Just stand like this. Now, watch me as I turn it smoothly… but rapidly. See? We don't want it in the heat too long on one side or the other. Here's your tongs back. Now, try again." He moved with an easy confidence, his tone both caring and assertive.

Lilian placed her hands over her waist as she watched the back of his head. Each curl, a vibrant shade of red. No, she wouldn't jump to conclusions. His hair was more groomed than Jase's and cut shorter behind the ears. And his clothes were nice, despite having rolled back the sleeves and forsaken his blazer to the chair beside him. *Turn around, turn around,* her mind guiltily repeated.

As if the man had heard her mind, just after patting his apprentice's back, his head turned ever so slightly in her direction... before looking back at the fire. With a sudden flinch, he turned fully, bearing his freckled face for her to behold. Well-combed hair, framing it.

The sight of him felt more welcome to her heart than she had expected. A consuming warmth fell from his eyes as they locked with hers across the room. Lilian was still, forgetting everything around her. Nothing seemed so important, at the moment, as their striking honey hue.

Oddly feeling herself sway, she dug her heel into the floor for balance and broke her gaze, turning away.

"Ma'am!"

She paused, limbs numbing as his echo alerted others. His footsteps approached quickly behind her, and when he finally reached her, she looked up, meeting his eyes. She swallowed hard, stunned at how different he looked. Like he was surer of himself; a man fully.

"Hi," he said, his voice low.

"Hello, Jase." She bit her words. "Or is it Mister Foster now?"

His grin widened. "No. No, it's still Jase," he insisted without any evidence of estrangement. "But if that should change, let me know."

Lilian gave a short laugh, glad to hear it.

"So, what are you doing here?"

"I came with Spencer. He wanted to show me his office."

Jase arrayed the space with his eyes. "Where is he?"

"In his office. I'm waiting for him to finish talking to Mr. O'Reilly."

"Must be something serious, then."

Lilian dropped her gaze for a sober moment and sighed. "Yes, it must be."

"If it is, he may be in there for some time."

"Perhaps," she said, her gaze drawing up again. "But I'm a very patient woman."

Jase nodded, his golden eyes lingering on her face in a way she took note of. "Then may I be able to pull you away for a moment?"

Quite direct, he was. Lilian blinked in befuddlement. "Well, I... I mean, I can see you must be busy." She tipped her head at the boy he was teaching.

Jaze swiveled himself, waving at the boy. "Oh, not at all. He's a fast learner." Looking again at Lilian, his eyes became a roguish squint. "I fixed it."

"Fixed what?"

"Your automobile."

"My automobile? Oh, you mean *Paul's*—"

Jase shook his head. "He forfeited it. It's yours. For free."

Lilian was frankly too stunned for words. The fact that Jase had kept his promise endeared her to him with much respect. "Jase..."

He held out his hand. "Just come take a look. She's right outside."

Lilian hesitated, glancing back toward the metal door to the stairway as if she needed a few more seconds to confirm Spencer wasn't coming down for her. Jase drew nearer beside her, and she could feel herself nodding. "I suppose it wouldn't hurt to take a quick look," she said, a lightness in her voice that surprised even herself.

Jase's grin widened, and without another word, he led her outside and around the building. Ranked along its side was the bright red beauty, her *Roi-de-Belges*. Lilian ran her fingers over the polished surface. "You kept her up."

"I did more than that." Jase leaned against the side of it. "Now, I wouldn't ask you to look underneath and ruin your dress, but I can tell you that underneath this beauty is no inch of rust. Every part I manufactured has worked without fail."

Lilian delighted in hearing him speak so fondly of his hard work. She was even proud. "So, it's safe to ride?"

Jase's eyes lit up as he proclaimed, "After eight weeks of testing, I'd say so." He then slid closer, not so subtly. "You trust me?"

Lilian eyed him with a tilt of her head, grinning. "Why do you ask?"

He patted the side of the vehicle. "On my word, she's safe enough for a pretty lady in a purple dress to take a ride by the lake."

Lilian could feel herself glow pink at his complement. Looking downward to forget the sudden pounding in her chest, she said, "Jase, I may trust you, but I cannot simply leave."

"It won't take long," he replied, his voice low and insistent. "And Spencer can wait. *I* would."

For a moment Lilian thought she detected a slight edge to his statement but quickly forsook the idea.

"I just want to make your welcome here complete."

"My welcome?" Lilian laughed. "I do believe I am far past my welcome, Jase."

"Ah, so you *think*. But in my book, you haven't experienced Brord 'til you've rested by the lake. And anyway…" He slipped his hand around hers. "I think we have much to talk about."

Lilian's hand fell limp as he held it firmly. She couldn't resist finding his eyes and seeing their assuring glimmer. For a moment, the world around them seemed to still. The distant sounds of the factory faded into the background. *I must be out of my mind.* "Just to the lake, and no further?"

Jase smiled. "To the lake, and no further."

Yoked

Lilian leaned her head back against the seat, letting the hum of the car's engine and the faint lapping of the lake's water ease her mind. Here Jase was beside her after all this time. It looked like the perfect opportunity to tell him about his destiny. And yet, she was not so anxious to. How could she speak to him as a Fisher now when there was more which pressed upon her heart?

She realized how she failed to count the cost of a cordial ride with her long-disaffiliated ally. All it took was a true, unadulterated moment in his presence, sharing his smile and hearing his laugh, to make her feel a thousand times worse than before he had asked to drive her.

Taking advantage of their silence, she turned to watch him as he drove. It was a new angle, the sun tingeing his lengthy lashes a bright orange. His jaw, once lined in delicate hairs, now cleanly shaven. His lips, resting in a content smile.

She couldn't help but wonder the depth of his enjoyment, and quite surreptitiously, whether she was any factor in it. Lilian thought it was strange how having him near for this long seemed to imbue her body with a harmony of emotions, good and pure... and devastating.

The car ran smoothly over the bridge of Etowah Lake to the other side. Jase took a left and brought them far enough to a nice spot where an oak leaned over the lakeshore. A tranquil place buzzing with dragonflies and rippling with fish. The air by the lake was so fresh, she wanted to savor it.

Jase turned to her, his eyes dazzling with flecks of lime. "Wanna step out?"

"No, not yet," she said, waving away the hand he offered. Diverting her gaze, she closed her eyes and breathed deeply.

"Lilian? Is something wrong?"

Lilian opened her eyes, her emotions surfacing through a scorn. "Yes. Something is."

Jase's expression grew solemn as he nodded. "You're angry."

"Yes."

"At me."

"Yes."

With a sigh, he glided his hand through his hair. "I understand we haven't spoken since that time in the pub."

"No, we haven't." Her eyes observed him, anticipating the truth.

"I did think about checking on you and the others many times, but I couldn't."

"Why?"

"Because…" his mouth hung as he looked up. "I don't know how to explain it."

Despite her anger, Lilian's gaze softened. Between his eyes, she could tell he was trying. "Take your time."

He looked ahead, lost in the dense foliage surrounding the river. "Do you ever feel like something or someone is trying to get your attention? Like you are being called to become more than you are?"

Lilian remained silent, now intrigued.

"Well, that someone or something seemed to speak to me again. Through your eyes." He turned to her. "There is something about you that I just find so earnest, so… pure."

Surprised, Lilian glanced at her lap as the corner of her mouth curved upward. Jase's use of the word landed differently upon her ears.

"It's captivating and… scary. I couldn't bear another second of you seeing the most embarrassing side of me." His voice wavered just enough for Lilian to notice. "I avoided you… because I needed to hide. I needed to hide and work on myself."

As a friend, this information satisfied her. But as a Fisher, there was more to ask. "Did you only feel that call, as you said, when I came?"

Jase's eyes drew up, thinking. "No. I felt it a few times before. Sometimes I'd just ignore it, but it was like I knew I wasn't meant to turn out like my father. Like someone's been watching over me, keeping me from breaking."

"What someone?"

Jase eyed her disappointedly. "Look, I know it all sounds crazy."

"Not at all," she insisted, her hand landing on his forearm. "Jase, there is something I must tell you."

Immediately, his hand found a place atop hers, the slide of his fingers sent a warm sensation through her that she tried her best to ignore. "What?"

"I..." As she watched his eyes, her words came light as air. "I am so glad you told me this. And I understand completely. I've had to reconcile with the one who calls *me*. And if we may be frank with each other, that person is—"

"El," he said with her. Together, they shared an ecstatic laugh.

"So, you understand me," Jase asserted, his hand gripping hers more.

She smiled, relieved enough to say more. "It has not been easy, but I have accepted who I am."

"And what is that?"

"I am a Fisher."

The confused look Jase afforded was hardly surprising. He briefly turned his face to the lake. "A Fisher?"

Lilian laughed. "Not like that. You may not understand this yet. But I am charged with finding others who bear the Elson's light and helping them know their purpose. And when I say the Elson... I mean Shersul. Shersul Smithson."

Jase only listened, not contending with her claim.

Lilian's heart raced as she spoke, her voice trembling under the weight of her words. "I was given a message regarding you, too. You, Jase, are destined to be Leader of the lightbearers in the battle against darkness. You must unite and help us win Brord before it is too late and Girgum's dream for this city is carried out."

Silence settled between them, but it wasn't peaceful. Lilian could feel it— how his mind wrestled with the idea, how absurd it must have seemed to him. Her heart ached at the confusion clouding his eyes. For a moment, she wanted to take it all back, to let him go on thinking he was just... Jase.

"You don't believe me," she said with a tone of dismay. "But it's true."

Jase let out a breath, staring at the rippling surface of the lake. "I don't know what to say, Lilian."

"You don't have to say anything yet. But you feel it, don't you? Something's been pulling at you— something bigger than either of us. I would not tell you this if El had not told you first." She focused her gaze on him. "Please, trust that I am telling the truth. Which do you think is easier, Jase? Telling the truth or believing it?"

He regarded her, a sense of knowing in his eyes. He lifted his hand off hers, leaving a distinct loss of warmth there. "I just need time to—"

"We don't have time!" Her voice broke, sharp and desperate. "Can't you feel it, Jase? Can't you feel the smoke creeping in, swallowing everything we know?"

Jase's eyes narrowed, tensing as though she forced him to reckon with a reality he was not ready to. "You're asking a lot of me, Lilian."

"Yes, but not too much. And if it is… then you are not the man I thought you were."

"Be fair, Lilian."

"I *am* being fair!" she whined this time, sounding like a moody toddler. Her throat constricted as she fought through the urge to cry. "It *is* fair if you had any idea what I've endured for the past six months." Abandoning all care, she hopped down and walked towards the lakeshore. Her blood coursing furiously as she leaned against the tree.

A sharp silence ensued. Lilian had not expected her divulgence would be well-received. However, she had hoped for a better reaction from him. She believed she'd done rather well in her approach and refused to feel regretful.

Nature filled their silence with a kind, sweeping breeze and shrill chirps. Lilian continued to watch the lake, hoping she had not ruined her friendship with Jase.

It wasn't too long before she heard him hop down and walk towards her. He came close enough to lean behind her against the tree. His tall shadow joining hers. She didn't turn to him, but she listened.

"Lilian," he began softly, "when I first met you, you were just as kind and gentle as you are now. But you were anxious. I could feel that. Now when I look at you, there is a strength inside you that shouts. Those six months you mentioned— you've been through a lot, haven't you?"

Lilian nodded, the thought of her experiences bringing her face to heat and eyes to well.

Jase continued his point, his tone considerate. "If in such a short time, you have become this courageous young woman before me now, I have no excuse." His hand rested on the bark near her neck, the edge of their argument beginning to dull. "I'll be your Leader, Lilian," he murmured. "Whatever that means for me."

Finally, she regarded him, relief flooding through her. But before she could respond, his eyes dimmed with something else. "But what I won't stand by and watch— What I won't see happen… is you marrying a man you don't love."

Lilian's breath hitched, the sudden shift in conversation startling her. "What? What do you mean?" She slid a few inches from him.

Jase leaned about two of those inches closer. His stare, genuine. "Be honest, Lilian. Spencer isn't who you want to spend the rest of your life with."

Lilian shot him a furious look, hoping to fight off his piercing one. "How dare you?" her voice rose. "Who are you to tell me who I should or shouldn't marry when you know nothing about love?" She spoke with a movement of her eyes, looking him up and down.

Jase towered her defensively, his tone adamant. "I know love when I feel it."

"Is that so?" she scoffed, her mind centering on the thought of him and Tess.

"There you go assuming you know what I mean."

"Don't I?"

"No, of course you don't," Jase half-yelled as he stepped closer, disbanding their distance. "How could you? We've been apart from each other for so long…" His eyes drew down to the tip of her nose. "And even now it's like no time has passed," then briefly to her lips, provoking a confused gasp from her. "I know you feel it, Lilian. That warmth, that peace that scares away doubt and fear. I didn't feel it with Tess, I felt it with you."

The pounding in her chest returned as she shared his stare. Suddenly, nothing made sense, or perhaps it did. She wasn't sure anymore. Lilian wanted to scold herself for even entertaining his presence. Yet how would she deny the feelings he had described so well?

Before she could work up a protest, his fingers caressed the line of her jaw. The lids of her eyes lowered, savoring it before glancing back up at his face. His kindred face. Part of her reasoned that she should pull away, but the majority of her said 'stay'.

Jase's breath feathered her face as he drifted near. "Lilian. I love you."

His confession released an overwhelming calm upon her. Allured by the sight of his lips, Lilian felt her heart twang remarkably. With her mouth caught between a smile and a gasp, she tried her best to withstand it. "Jase…"

In the dip of his head, Jase's lips sealed hers, feeling as though they were meant to.

Stunned, Lilian's arms hung in the air, her back pasting further against the tree before lowering them to his chest. Jase's kisses were slow and gentle. There was no trick to it, no suspicion. She felt his love in pulses.

All her worries erased in this moment, allowing her to rest in him. Jase slipped his hands down to her waist, then around to the small of her back. He pulled her up from the tree and against himself.

She melted in his arms. Could it be that Jase was the man her heart had been calling to since she was only a child? Could it be that unlike the other men in her life, Jase was here to stay? She silently prayed so, because suddenly, she could not imagine her life without him.

Jase finally withdrew his lips, kissing her cheeks instead. "Lilian…" his words a sigh. "You are the only woman for me."

She planted her face in his chest, a channel of tears streaming down her face. "Oh, Jase. My love."

After a gentle squeeze from him, he pulled her up to stare at her face. "I know I don't have much right now. But I promise you that soon I will be worthy of you. On my word, Lilian, I will do what it takes to give you a life like what you are used to." He smirked. "I know I can."

She held onto his words, curious as to where he was going with them. Her presumptions were nearly confirmed as he took a knee. She held a patient breath.

Jase turned up his face, staring with tender admiration and humility. "So, I am asking you, Lilian Truit... if you would make me the wisest fool on earth... and marry me."

A little hesitation came, only because she was so overjoyed. Somehow everything was clear, and she was far past denying herself the bliss that awaited her. It didn't matter what her aunt, Miss Cora, or polite society had expected. Lilian knew her answer, and she knew El's hand was in it. "Yes, Jase. Yes."

Jase's eyes lit up. He sighed while hopping to his feet, together laughing. "My heart," he called her, resting his forehead on hers.

"*My* heart," she repeated. Taking a moment to inhale his scent. "But you need not worry about my comfort, Jase."

Jase lifted his head. "Hm? Why?"

"Because the man I marry will gain rights to my uncle's factory. I know I already asked you to be a Leader, but would you mind becoming a factory owner as well?"

An assuring smile preceded his response. "Not at all." He laughed, considering it. "But I wonder how Mr. O'Reilly would feel about that?"

"He would be proud of you," Lilian asserted, knowing how O'Reilly treated Jase as he would a son.

"Would he?!" The sound came from behind them.

Jase turned around to see O'Reilly, Spencer, and two men in fedoras who appeared to be deputies approaching. The sheriff also, right behind them. They positioned themselves to surround Lilian and Jase.

Lilian's joy halted. "What is going on?" she inquired, her voice shaken.

Jase stood protectively in front of her. "Could someone tell me what the issue is?"

"Jase, listen," his director spoke grimly.

"Mr. O'Reilly?"

"I want you to do two things for me, son. First, you need to understand that I'm firing you, and secondly, I'm gonna need you to go peacefully with the law."

Jase stepped back. His head shook fiercely. "What's this all about?"

Lilian spoke over his shoulder. "What is he being charged with?"

Spencer's attention cut to her, sending a look of shame. "Murder."

"Murder?" she echoed, the word striking her heart. She gazed up at Jase, then back at the men. *No, it couldn't be.* "Of who?"

"His landlord, Mister Scott Thomas. The man was found dead not far from the house he'd rented out to Jase."

Lilian refused to believe this, her lips still tingling from the fresh kiss she shared with Jase. Jase wasn't a murderer. She remembered he had expressed an ought against his landlord, but would he do this? "Jase...?" she asked him softly.

He turned to her, earnest in his denial. "I haven't done anything they're saying, Lilian. I don't know who did this. Honest."

Mr. O'Reilly stepped forward. "Don't you play stupid now, son. That man went missing for months. You mean to tell us you didn't know when you never paid your rent?"

Jase's mouth shut, unable to deny it.

Spencer approached with crossed arms. "Mister Thomas's body was found in the forest, bare as a baby and missing an arm. No dignity in that, Jase."

Lilian's gaze fell to the grass beneath her, the story sounded familiar as ever. She never knew of a Mister Thomas, but she did remember a naked man lying dead on the cold forest floor. "It wasn't him."

The men stared with narrowed eyes. Spencer's voice, sharp and testy. "How would you know that?"

"Because it was m—"

"*Mister Foster*, Lilian," he insisted, shutting her down. The look Spencer sent her was a little too telling, as if he knew exactly what she was about to say.

The sheriff then spoke. "Quiet! Now this can go smoothly, Foster, or you can cause a scene in front of your little doxy."

Lilian's mouth hung in shock, a heat of shame masking her face.

"My little what?" Jase charged toward them.

"Jase, don't!"

Unfazed, the men hurriedly caught him at both arms and dropped him against the ground. They cuffed him before pulling him up, his shirt lightly soiled in red dirt.

"Get him up there!" the sheriff instructed as his deputies took Jase to one of the horses.

Lilian ran to him, emboldened. "Wait!" She caught his arm, pulling him down for one last kiss. "I love you, and I promise I will make this right."

Jase's eyes beamed strong. He slowed time with his stare. "Don't worry about me, Lilian. Just use your light, understand?" His detainer jolted him as a sign to keep moving. Jase turned his face ahead. "Use your light."

The men lifted him up to sit backwards on the horse. In seconds, it seemed, they mounted and took him away. Lilian watched, her hopes put to silence.

A sigh came from Mr. O'Reilly as he drew a palm down his face. "I should go." He took his own horse and left them.

Lilian held her arms, her thoughts a wild mess.

Spencer's shadow approached behind her. "So much for only being friends."

She flinched, turning to him. "I'm sorry, Spence—"

"Shut up."

Lilian stared curiously at his annoyed expression. His tone held sheer malice; a tone she had not heard him use in some time, finally befitting of his eyes.

"I knew he'd be a threat to me." Spencer's head shook along with his wry laugh. "Seems he managed to undo what I spent months attempting."

Lilian stepped back, suddenly taken to reservation. "What do you mean by 'attempt'?"

His stare became detached and condescending. "Well, there's no point in keeping up the charade." He inched closer. "I told you I would always be working toward your destruction."

Lilian's eyes widened, a shock of fear zapping her. "You never changed. You— you still hate me. You've *always* hated me."

Tilting his head, he smirked. "You were so easy to fool."

She was silent, somewhat astonished. "Why? Why would you do all this if you hated me?"

"For the factory, of course."

"The factory?"

"Uh, yes," he said like it was obvious. "I came only to secure a marriage with you, and in turn, receive your uncle's greatest asset. It would have been a win for Girgum, giving him the opportunity to really change things in Brord. And all by taking siege of Brord's strongest source of wealth."

Despite his sinister plan, Lilian was more so confused than appalled. "I don't understand. How could you have known about that arrangement unless you read the will?"

Spencer laughed. "Perhaps a little birdie told me. Your, uh, friend, to be frank."

"Paul? No, that's not right. Why would he—?"

"That is the question, isn't it?" Spencer's gaze grew uncanny. "Why would he? Why would he tell me anything? Why would he leave you? Why would he do what he did to your uncle?"

"My uncle?" What was Spencer talking about? "What has he done to my uncle?"

Spencer almost spoke, but just as was like him, he went cruelly quiet. A smile taking him. "Anyway," he murmured in a gravelly cadence. "We aren't going to let you get away so easily. We know what you have been up to, Fisher."

Lilian was stunned beyond words. "We?" Her eyes fell to the strange pin of a morning star. "What have you gotten yourself into, Spencer?" Then the last words Jase had spoken to her echoed through her mind. *Use your light.*

Enough was enough. She had to see things clearly. Lilian closed her eyes and when she opened them again, she saw the number of malellum hovering around his body— too many to count, each one strung to him by a cord of smoke. And they were looking straight at her.

Mildly recoiling in both fear and disgust, she said, "I see you. I see all of you."

They shared glances with each other, staring again at her and snickering.

One said, *Look away, Fisher.*

Another— *He is ours now.*

And another— *You cannot free him.*

"Perhaps. But Shersul can."

The mention of his name provoked squeals out of them.

Spencer cupped his ears as their voices afflicted him. "Enough!" he screamed, his body crouching.

Startled by his outburst, she inched backwards, turning around to run.

"No!"

Her knees locked immediately, and she tripped onto the grass. So many old fears, returning. After sitting up, she waited as he came closer.

Before her eyes, he grew about five inches taller. His skin turned deathly pale, and his eyes bulged. He snarled, fangs protruding from his mouth.

Lilian gasped in horror. "Spencer?"

He stepped closer, convulsing in pain until a mass of sleek, black wings appeared from behind him, ripping through his suit. He made his last step, then bent down.

Lilian screamed, her eyes squeezing shut... nothing happened. She peeled them open to see his open hand before her face. Her chest thrummed still, but she looked up at his inhuman visage.

"Come now. It's time we get better acquainted."

Lilian was too frightened to move, and too frightened not to. She put her hand in his. He yanked her up, his arms wrapping around her and keeping her arms at her sides. She knew what was soon to follow, belting a scream as he took her up through the clouds.

&PILOGUE

"Repeat after me. I— state your name…"

With her hand on her heart, the new convert felt a nervous vigor creep up her body just before she spoke. "I, Tessaline Truit…"

"…vow to remain loyal to the hevel, and to the princes of the earth…"

"…vow to remain loyal to the hevel, and to the princes of the earth…"

"…and to serve Girgum, the one true king. For him you bleed."

Tessaline exhaled slowly. "To serve Girgum, the one true king…" With only a second of reconsideration, the dangerous, binding words fell from her lips. "For him I bleed."

"Arise young bride."

Tessaline rose to stand before the podium. Resting upon it, a slip of paper detailing the fate she was about to accept. Positioned directly under the light of the oculus above her, Tessaline could hardly see everyone through her black lacy veil. The faintly lit pews seated a solemn crowd. The seasoned members watched her expectantly.

Perhaps they were evaluating her commitment: *She won't follow through with it. She doesn't have the zeal. She isn't one of us.*

Tess took no care for whatever they thought. She knew why she was here. And for her own reasons, she would join the hevel.

"Now, Tessaline," the man began. Or at least that is what she thought he was. But she could not see his face under the thick fabric which veiled him down to his feet. The way he drew nearer seemed like he was floating. His presence added no weight to the platform they stood on as if he were only a shadow. "If there is truth in your vow, may you seal it in blood and ink."

As he slipped his arm out from under the velvet robe he wore, Tess was awestruck by the sight of it. His skin shined white, resembling a mother-of-pearl luminescence. He wasn't a man at all.

Slowly, he folded his fingers and snapped. In his hand, appeared a glass dip pen. The end of it was ornamented by the hevel's crest— a morning star. He lowered the pen to her.

Tessaline snatched it from him to prove her readiness. On the line, she signed her name. "There, it's done."

"Done?" The veiled being tilted his head. "*Blood* and ink, Tessaline."

He snapped his finger again. The pen in her hand, now a knife.

Tessaline's breath caught in her throat. The weight of the hilt and glint of the blade in the low light was a command in itself. The pews around her seemed to darken as the realization settled in—there was no turning back now. Her fingers tightened around it, heart racing in time with the thrum of the silence that had fallen over the room. She glanced down at the paper again, her signature bold and final on the parchment. The ink glistened wetly, but it wasn't enough. The vow wasn't sealed, not fully—not until the sacrifice had been made.

She raised the blade to her palm, feeling its cold kiss against her skin. Her pulse thundered in her ears as the reality of it all became sharp and tangible. *For him I bleed.* She repeated the words in her mind until they held her captive.

In a swift motion, she dragged the knife across her palm, the sting immediate. She restrained a squeal by the bite of her tongue. Blood welled up, dark and rich, pooling in her hand and dripping onto the parchment below just after her name. A drop spread into her signature, mixing with the ink.

A murmur rippled through the crowd. The tension that had hung heavy in the air seemed to ease. Tessaline sighed, relieved at the thought that this was the last discomfort she'd have to feel.

The figure extended his ghostly hand once more, motioning for her to step forward. "Come now, bride of Girgum. Your brothers and sisters await you."

Tessaline took a step, her bloodied hand still burning at her side. Sucking in the pain, she raised her hand high. The watchers erupted in an applause so loud compared to their original silence that it half-startled her. Her body became charged with an influx of both pride and strain. She was sure she'd come to understand the feeling soon.

"Go and greet them," her initiator whispered encouragingly. So Tessaline exited the platform, anxious as she came around to be greeted by her new family, so to speak. As they approached her, leaving through each row, it appeared almost like a stampede of people eager to formally meet her. Some of which, she had known for a fact, doubted her. Tessaline made sure to keep *those* members at a fair arms-reach.

It was not long before the crowd began ushering her out of the basilica and through the hall. Amidst the uproar, Tessaline tried to ignore the pain in her hand, twisting her wrist often as a way to cope. She was smiling regardless, happy to be part of something. Something more than the modest town she came from.

They entered the entrance hall of the hevel's castle, a place crafted ornately by the gifted hands of Girgum's architects. Unlike the cool stone walls of the basilica, the home of the complex was crafted entirely of rich, red oak. The floors, a polished herringbone expanse below the imperial staircase which framed a large window of stained glass. Tessaline believed she'd never get used to the luxury displayed in every grain.

Finally, the crowd spread out, leaving her and her bad hand. She held her wrist while examining her palm, aghast since it was easier to see the damage she had done to herself now. While walking off to some corner, a hand snatched her wrist, yanking her to the other side of the wall. Tessaline shrieked just as the person's swift hands began swathing hers in soft cotton.

Realizing who it was, Tessaline kept a mild grimace on her face. "Thanks." Her tone was more dubious than grateful.

Her nurse raised his dark head, his vibrant blue eyes shooting her a furious look. "So, you're one of us now. I hope you're happy."

Tessaline returned a proud smirk. "Actually, yes. After all, shouldn't I be?"

Paul cinched the knot tight enough to make her grunt.

"Ow, careful!" she complained.

"I tried to warn you, Tessaline. You have no idea what you have gotten yourself into."

She pulled her hand from his, a smile gracing her face. "Guess I'll find out soon." She nearly brushed past him before he grabbed her shoulders.

"Well, let me give you the short run." He pressed her against the wall.

"Hey!" Tess roared. "What is wrong with you?"

"You sign in blood, you pay in blood. That is the deal you just made, Tessaline."

The dire gaze that filled his eyes struck her with a sense of omen. For a mere second, her eyes softened with fear. But only for a second. Using her good hand, she forced him back with a blunt hit to the chest.

Paul stumbled back, annoyed but concerned.

"Look," Tess said calmly, "I understand you feel obligated to me because I'm a Truit. But I never asked for your sympathy. Or your help."

"Lil, please— uh…" Paul caught himself in error.

"See," Tess shook her head, chuckling. "You're tryna help the wrong girl. If you think I am *anything* like her, your wrong." She straightened defiantly. "I'm stronger."

"You may be strong, Tess. But you know nothing about what it's like to be me."

"Mm, poor baby," she said while sticking out her bottom lip to mock him. "Well, guess what. I *am* a member of the hevel."

Paul's gaze fell somberly, his sigh ridden with woe. "Yes. And there is nothing either of us can do about it now."

Author's Note

What began as a short fiction idea written by a 10-year-old me quickly evolved into something more intricate than any story I had written before. Its themes deepened as I grew older, wisdom compounding in ways for which I can only thank God. As art imitates life, so has this story become a reflection of my internal, spiritual battle. What Lilian faces in this book are real fears of mine: fear of change, failure, loss, stagnation, and loneliness. Yet through these struggles, this story seeks to remind us of the endurance and hope found by aligning our will with the perfect will of our creator. My hope is this book may encourage readers to have unyielding faith, rebuke spiritual slumber, search the places evil hides, and endure to the end of every trial. As you may have wondered, Lilian Truit's story is far from over. And so, dear reader, the trials of life continue—yours, mine, and Lilian's. But take heart, for the strength and goodness awaiting you are far greater than you can imagine. That is the power of faith.

— O.J.B